SHELDON MAJORS AND THIS QUEER LOVE

Written by

Jason G. Waters

Edited by

Alexzandria Waters

CASTLE
BY THE SEA

TRIGGER WARNINGS:

Sexual Assault
Ableism
Death or Dying
Violence
Homophobia
Torture
Childbirth
Blood

"Being different can be extremely difficult at times, but being true to oneself is worth the struggle."

~~ Jason Waters - January 5, 2016

This book is dedicated to all dreamers. Our imagination is only limited by the limitations of our imagination, so keep dreaming as big as you can.

Chapter One

Taking a Bullet

Laramie woke up with Sheldon's arm draped over him, and he smiled. He pulled Sheldon's arm tighter around him and enjoyed the moment. This moment has been his secret desire for quite some time, but he could never accept having feelings for another guy.

Sheldon stirred awake after Laramie kissed his hand. "Good morning," Laramie said over his shoulder. "How did you sleep?"

"Very well, thank you," Sheldon replied, sitting up, laying his chin on his shoulder, and leaning over to kiss Laramie. "How about you?"

"Like a dream next to you," Laramie replied as he breathed Sheldon in with his eyes. "What would you like to do today?"

"I was thinking…"

Sheldon's mouth continued moving, but all Laramie heard was an annoying alarm sound blaring. "What did you say?" Laramie asked again.

Sheldon spoke again, but all Laramie could hear was an alarm. Laramie woke up and slammed his hand down on his alarm. He moaned as he rubbed his eyes. He kicked back the covers and sighed, disappointed that it was only another dream.

It was a cloudy October afternoon. Laramie had slept in late, and he finally decided to get up and get dressed. He looked at the letter he had written to Sheldon, which was still lying on top of his dresser. He decided today was the day he would find the courage to personally deliver it to Sheldon.

He walked into the living room where his mom was watching her soap opera *One Life to Live*. "Good afternoon. It's nice to see you finally decided to get out of bed," his mom greeted him. "You want to go to Airway Department Store with me later?"

"Sure, but I have to go do something first," he said as he leaned over to kiss her cheek.

"I love you," his mom said as he was walking towards the door.

"I love you too," he mumbled as he walked out the door and headed to Sheldon's place. He sat for several hours at the end of Sheldon's road, working up the courage to talk to him, when he saw Chase's car drive by with Sheldon inside. His heart started to race as they continued to Sheldon's place. He did not want to head to Sheldon's until he was sure Chase was gone. He saw Chase's car pull out of Sheldon's driveway, and as he passed by, he only saw Chase in the car, but before Laramie had a chance to start his truck, someone ran Chase's car off the road.

§

Sheldon was standing in the cemetery next to a headstone. Ruby, Trey, Ninnie, Tommy, and Shawndrea were there. Shawndrea came over and put her arm around Sheldon.

"Hey, you, ok? She asked Sheldon, pulling him closer.

Sheldon looked at her with tears, and hugged him.

"I know… I know…" Shawndrea said heavily. "I'm so sorry. I don't know how, but somehow, everything is going to be ok. Hey, it's not your fault…"

A lady walked up to them. "You must be Sheldon," The mysterious woman said with her hand extended. "You're just like he described."

Sheldon looked at her, confused. "I'm sorry, but who are you?" Sheldon inquired, looking over at Ninnie and Ruby as if they knew more than he did, before reaching out to take her hand.

The lady took Sheldon's hand. "I'm Mrs. Miller," the lady responded. Seeing the confusion still in Sheldon's eyes, she continued. "I'm Laramie's mom."

Sheldon was surprised to run into someone there, as the funeral had been months ago. Her eyes looked sad, tired, and haunted. He could tell she had been crying.

"You're just like I imagined," She said to Sheldon. "He talked about you all the time. I would ask him to bring you by to meet you, but he never did. Oh, here I have something for you, actually," she said, reaching into her purse, pulling out an envelope, and handing it to Sheldon. "This was on the seat of his truck…"

She started to cry as she pulled out a tissue from her purse. Sheldon did not know this lady but could hear Susan say, *hug her* so he stepped forward and put an arm around her. She hugged Sheldon back as she wiped the tears from her eyes and turned to look at Laramie's headstone.

"I don't think I will ever fully understand why he did it," She said, looking back at Sheldon. At the same time, everyone else went to wait by the car to let them talk. "I guess he thought he couldn't talk to me about being gay. I figured one day he would open up. I told myself maybe I should have tried to get him to open up. I know there is no perfect way to approach the subject, and I cannot blame myself. I will take comfort in the fact that one day I will see him again and that whatever he was struggling with, he is not struggling anymore."

Sheldon was awestruck by the level of thought she had put into the whole situation. "I want to thank you for sharing that with me," Sheldon said as he again put his arm around this woman he barely knew but felt an obvious connection with. "You have helped me realize I can't blame myself or be angry with him for the things he has done."

"Yes, I know a lot about anger. Laramie's dad had quite a temper. In fact, I think it's what killed him. No one can walk around with that much anger and not have it affect their heart physically. Was that your boyfriend who was ran off the road?

"Yes," Sheldon replied, unsure of what else to say.

"I'm very sorry that happened to him," she said, shaking her head and looking at the headstone again. "I know there are bad people out there, but you just never think that would happen in a small town."

Sheldon understood what she meant and that you do not think someone can do certain things. Sheldon still had a lot of mixed feelings, one of them being anger for what happened, resentment for the coward that drove Chase off the road, and Laramie for years of torment and then helping save Chase's life and then putting his life in danger.

"Well, we can't blame ourselves for what happened," Sheldon said, knowing the look on her face because it was the same look he saw in the mirror. "We just have to pick up, move on, and make sure we are better people for what has happened or learn from the event."

"No wiser words could have been spoken," Laramie's mom said as she hugged him. "Thank you. I'm planning on opening my doors to any gay teens struggling with the same issues or who do not feel safe at home. I'm going to be taking classes to better educate myself on handling gay teen issues."

"That is a great idea," Sheldon said as he hugged her back. "Let me know if you need any help. It was nice to meet you. I will let you have some time alone here.

Sheldon walked to where his cousins sat in the van, patiently waiting for him. Sheldon looked again to see a mom talking to her son's headstone.

"You ready to go, Cuz," Ninnie asked, opening the door. "We need…."

A beeping sound suddenly pulled Sheldon out of his dream, a dream that seemed so realistic. He sat up as a nurse came in to check on Chase because the machine was sounding an alarm. Sheldon had fallen asleep holding Chase's hand with his head resting next to Chase.

The dream was so vivid. Sheldon could not get the sad look on Laramie's Mom's face out of his head. The dream seemed to be healing and helped him let go of some of the resentment he had towards Laramie.

"Nothing to worry about," the nurse said as she was resetting the machine, and Sheldon rubbed the sleep from his eyes. "Sometimes it does that."

For about two months, Sheldon visited Chase in the hospital. Chase had not regained consciousness but had been stable since the day he flat lined with his parents in the room.

Every time Sheldon visited Chase; he talked to him even though he was not sure if he was even able to hear him. The doctor explained that swelling of the brain was the result of Chase hitting his head during the accident which could be causing the coma. They hoped the swelling would go down soon, and he would wake up.

He told him about Laramie chasing the guy that ran him over and how the guy had shot Laramie.

He shared that he was going to be an uncle. Susan was expecting her first baby.

On this day, Sheldon was talking to Chase like he usually did when Chase squeezes Sheldon's hand. At first, Sheldon thought it was another muscle spasm. The nurse had already explained that someone in a coma occasionally has involuntary muscle movements.

Sheldon's heart leaped when it happened again, and he stood up. Chase's eyelids started to flutter and slowly opened, adjusting to the light. Chase tried to talk, but his throat was dry.

"Let me get you some water," Sheldon said as he went to pour Chase a glass of water and handed it to him. Chase slowly drank all the water.

A nurse walked by, and Sheldon flagged her down as Chase started to speak, "Where am I?" Chase croaked out.

"The hospital," Sheldon responded. "Let me get you some more water. Do you remember the accident?"

"Everything seems kinda hazy," Chase hoarsely replied, taking sips of water as the nurse came in and checked his vitals.

"Last thing I remember, we were sitting in my car talking," Chase continued as the nurse took his blood pressure. "Then I was driving home and was about to drive over the train tracks when I saw lights, a loud crashing sound, and glass shattering everywhere."

"You seem in great shape, young man, considering," the nurse stated as she wrote something in his chart. "But the doctor will be able to tell us more, I'm going to go get the doctor and be right back."

"That's pretty much what happened," Sheldon said with watery eyes.

"Was it Laramie?" Chase asked

"No," Sheldon hesitated, unsure how much to tell him about Laramie being shot while confronting the guy that ran him off the road.

"That's strange 'cause I remember hearing his voice," Chase commented. "The strange thing is his voice was comforting. I felt very cold and drifting to a warm light, but his voice kept bringing me back and seemed to ground me."

Sheldon did not know how to respond. He just let Chase talk and piece it together. He connected the dots Chase missed.

"I remember hearing your voice talking to me, but it was so far away, and you never responded to me," Chase said as he tried to sit up but laid back down. "Okay, maybe that wasn't such a good idea. I remember something about your sister is going to have a baby. Is that true, or a dream?"

"No, that is really happening," Sheldon replied. "I was on the way to see her right after she told us, but I got a call you had moved, and they thought you might be waking up when I got here. But the doctor later explained that the body sometimes has involuntary movements when someone is in a coma."

"I did?" Chase asked as he situated himself in the bed. Sheldon could tell he was already getting antsy, and it wouldn't be long before Chase was going to be out of that bed.

"Yes, but it was a false alarm," Sheldon continued. "So far things are going well with the pregnancy, and she is due in October."

"I guess miracles happen," Chase said thoughtfully and was quiet for a second as he was piecing things together. "How long have I been… asleep?" He was not sure what to call the time he was in a coma.

"About two months," Sheldon replied.

"What? But it seems like just yesterday we were sitting in your driveway," Chase noted as he tried to process this information as the nurse came back into the room."

"I'm sorry, but the patient needs rest," the nurse explained. "The doctor is on his way. He wants to examine you. Your parents will be here shortly. Sheldon can come back tomorrow."

"I will see you tomorrow," Sheldon said as he leaned in and kissed Chase.

"See you tomorrow," Chase said, smiling and kissing Sheldon back.

As Sheldon left, he saw Chase's parents entering the hospital through the other entrance. He smiled at how happy and relieved their faces seemed. He had been avoiding them because he felt guilty about what had happened to Chase. He wanted to let them have their time with their son, so Sheldon quickly turned to head to his vehicle when he ran smack into Laynardia.

"Whoa, where is the fire," Laynardia joked. "Do not injure me on my first day back."

"Hey, it's good to see you," Sheldon greeted her. "Who is watching your baby?"

"My dad is watching her until I can get her into daycare," Laynardia replied. "You should come by and see her."

"I definitely will," Sheldon agreed. "I hope your first day back goes well."

"Thank you. See you soon," Laynardia said as she entered the hospital.

"See you soon," Sheldon resounded.

As Sheldon exited the building, he thought he heard his name being called and turned to see Chase's mom calling after him. His heart was in his throat as she approached. "Chase told us you were here," she said as she walked up and hugged him very tightly, then put her hands on either side of Sheldon's face.

"We have missed you. The house was so quiet without your weekly visits. I have to get back inside, but I wanted to say hello to you quickly. Chase is awake," she said with a smile. Her hands were still on either side of Sheldon's face, and then she put her hand over her mouth, trying not to cry tears of joy as she turned to go back inside.

As Sheldon turned to walk to his car, the sun hit his face, and suddenly, he felt as though he was floating on air, as all the worry and guilt had vanished. He walked to his car with the biggest smile, feeling like he was walking on air because, for the first time in a long time, things seemed right with the world.

§

On the day of Chase's accident, Laramie exited his truck with clenched fists to confront the guy who ran into Chase and took off. He was ready for a fight. But the odds are not always in your favor when you meet a bullet.

It happened extremely fast. Laramie barely got five feet from his truck when it felt like someone punched him in the chest. He smelled sulfur and burning flesh and was unable to catch his breath. It was as if everything started to go dark. He collapsed to the ground, landing on his back on the pavement. He felt like his eyes wanted to close, but they did not. They remained open as he stared at the stars.

As Laramie was staring at the stars, he thought that if he could run to the stars as fast as he could, all his problems would disappear or seem less significant. As he lay there, he felt his life force start to leave his body as the gas station attendant ran out to check on him with a phone in hand, calling 911.

Laramie's mind drifted back to the dream of him and Sheldon in bed together. He wanted to experience that feeling before he died. He heard sirens off in the distance as a pool of blood started to form on the cement around Laramie.

When Laramie first woke up in the hospital, he could not believe that he was still alive and how much pain he was in. He looked over and saw his Mother asleep in the chair.

"Did Sheldon come?" Laramie asked his Mother.

"No, sorry honey, no one has been here but me," She replied.

The doctor explained to Laramie that, somehow, the bullet went straight through his shoulder and missed any vital organs. After a week in the hospital, the doctor released him, and he was never quite the same person.

He became closer to his Mother, explaining how he was bisexual and that he wanted to do something with his life that helped others. His Mother was smiling ear to ear with complete joy, knowing that her son was okay and that he was sharing his feelings with her. It was something she had hoped would happen for an exceptionally long time.

She let him know that somehow, deep down, she had always known he was gay. Also, she wanted to open her home to other children who were not accepted by their parents for whatever reason.

§

After visiting Chase at the hospital, Sheldon arrived home and saw Laramie's truck in his driveway. Laramie had finally worked up the courage to give the letter to Sheldon.

Sheldon's heart started pounding as Laramie walked up to his car.

"Hi, how is Chase doing?" Laramie asked.

"He is doing great; in fact, he woke up and seems like his old self," Sheldon replied.

"That is great news. I just wanted to give you this," Laramie said, handing the letter to Sheldon. Sheldon looked at it, unsure what to make of it. "Open it later."

Sheldon did not know what to say to Laramie. "Thank you for being there for Chase," Sheldon finally said.

"No worries. I'm just glad Chase is okay," Laramie replied. "I will see you around."

"See you," Sheldon said with an awkward smile. "Hey, I'm glad you're okay."

Laramie walked to his truck and looked back at Sheldon one last time before getting to his truck and driving away.

Sheldon went inside the house, walked into his room, and placed the letter onto his dresser, where it sat for a few days.

§

After a long day at work, Sheldon entered his room, and Laramie's unopened envelope caught his eye. He stared at the letter addressed to him. Sheldon hesitated for a moment and then picked it up. He walked over to his bed and sat down. He paused for a moment before opening it up. He had not read it for fear of what it might or might not say. He pulled out the letter and began to read it:

Sheldon,

I'm very sorry for everything I have ever done to you. I was angry at myself and you. I wanted to be as open about myself as you are with yourself. I'm genuinely sorry for all the hurt I have caused you. I was jealous of how you look at Chase, and your love for each other. I don't know if I will ever allow myself to love that openly and honestly with someone like that. You are a far braver person than I ever could be. I hope you have a long and happy life.

Love Always,
Laramie

Sheldon was unsure how he felt about the letter, so he shoved it back in the envelope and put it away. He still had mixed emotions about the "new and improved" Laramie. It was hard for him to forget all the torment Laramie had caused him over the years. Though he was glad, Laramie had not been killed and hoped for the best for him.

Chapter Two

Start of Senior Year

Three months before Chase's car accident...

It was the first day of Senior year and three months before Chase's car accident. Ninnie, Ruby, Trey, Tommy, and Charlotte were seated together for lunch when Sheldon entered the cafeteria. He walked up and sat down. Ninnie and Ruby were already seated, talking about hair and makeup and which foundation they were currently using. They could tell something was wrong.

"What's going on here," Ruby asked with a potato chip in hand, waving it in a circle toward Sheldon before eating it.

"I thought you weren't eating chips anymore," Sheldon replied haphazardly, which was an internal thought he had said out loud.

"Damn," Ruby replied, exaggerating, acting gutted.

"I fell off the no-chip wagon, and you really can't eat just one!" Ruby cried out, holding up a chip before putting it in her mouth.

"Fell off the wagon?" Ninnie questioned as she grabbed a chip out of Ruby's bag. "Hell, girl, you fell off and got dragged behind it." She turned to Sheldon and said, "Now, quit avoiding the topic and spill the beans."

"Sorry, I am stressed because Dr. Leatherland asked me to come to her office during my eighth period instead of going to work at the grocery store," Sheldon explained.

Dr. Julie Leatherland was the high school guidance counselor; before that, she was Sheldon's English teacher. She said his writing reminded her of Stephen King and encouraged him to keep writing.

"Oh, well, I'm sure it's nothing to worry about,' Ruby commented, pulling out and opening another bag of chips as Ninnie was eyeing her new bag of chips.

"Speaking of working for last period I always meant to ask how you got such a cool gig like going to work instead of class for your last period and where I sign up," Ninnie commented, looking at Sheldon. Then, she stole another chip from Ruby's bag.

"Yeah, I always meant to ask that, too," Ruby replied, giving Ninnie a side eye for stealing another chip.

"And I have woodshop for the seventh period. Can this year get any worse," Sheldon groaned, trying to dodge her question, and sitting back in his chair.

"Woodshop?" They both questioned in unison.

"Yeah, I waited too long to pick an elective, so it was woodshop, choir, or mechanics class," Sheldon responded.

"And you chose that over choir class?" Ruby questioned.

"Oh, she doesn't know the history of you and the choir teacher," Ninnie chuckled but stopped when she thought about what it meant.

"Do tell," Ruby sat forward, waiting for the juicy details.

"Well, it's not really that exciting of a story. In fact, it's sad, really," Ninnie responded, seeing Sheldon did not want to share. "Long story short, she thought since he was a man, he should…" She paused before saying the next part because of the subject's sensitivity. "She thought he should sound more like a man, so she encouraged him to practice speaking in a deeper voice to be more manly. She thought he was intentionally making himself sound more feminine."

"What kind of twisted shit is that?" Ruby questioned.

"Exactly, so that's why he dropped out of his favorite class, and now he's just been woodshopped over," Ninnie joked, trying to make light of the situation, but she was the only one laughing.

"It says a lot, and I don't blame you," Ruby said.

"So, woodshop it is," Sheldon sighs. "Yay." They all chuckled.

"Yeah, good luck with that," Ninnie teased.

"I'm off to biology now," Sheldon said grabbing his bag.

"Hold up, wait a minute," Ruby interjected. "You never explained why you were doing this work program for last period."

Sheldon was hoping to escape the conversation around this topic that he did not like to talk about. He would rather go to class early then talk about it. He sighed. "it's a boring story." But Ruby and Ninnie were not going to let this one slide.

"As you know, the guys in this school are always giving me a tough time for being feminine. Calling me names, shoving me around relentlessly," Sheldon explained reluctantly. He did not like to talk about the tough times. "During P.E, the coach was getting sick of it and kept telling them to knock it off and punish them by making them do laps."

"The coach's intervention only made the situation worse because they started getting rougher when the coach was not around. I was showing up late for my next class or looking beat up. The teacher would ask me what was happening, but I refused to tell her because I knew it would only rain down more trouble for me when no one was around."

"The final straw was when they shoved me into a locker and left me there," Sheldon explained. "The teacher had to come looking for me, but the coach said he did not know where I was. They could hear me banging on the locker door. The coach had to let me out. The teacher realized what was happening and talked to the guidance counselor to see what they could do immediately."

"That is when they offered to sign me up for the study-to-work program," Sheldon stated. "Of course, I was like, sign me up, and never looked back or dreaded the idea of ever going back to P.E. class."

"It all started with a semester of classes teaching us how to interview, such as how to dress and answer interview questions," Sheldon explained. "We did mock interviews and how to create a resume. "The last part was to apply to a job we wanted, so I went to GIA, applied, and then eventually interviewed with one of the owners. The next semester, I started going to work there instead of going to a class for my eighth period."

Ninnie and Ruby sat there; mouths open, unsure what to say. "I was thinking of something completely different," Ruby finally said.

"Yeah, me too," Ninnie added.

"I was thinking it was a different reason and not such a sad and infuriating reason," Ruby said. "I'm sorry that you went through that."

"Exactly. I am pissed just hearing about this happening to you, and whose ass do I need to kick," Ninnie said as she looked at the clock. "We better get to class, or our teachers are going to be pissed at us."

§

Sheldon was sitting in Biology class as his fellow students were discussing and guessing who was going to be their teacher since Dr. Spangler retired after having a major heart attack.

Sheldon sat listening to all the students having their own little conversations. Sheldon turned to see Charlize doodling in her notebook. Charlize was a pretty, curly, blond-haired, quiet girl who kept to herself, except when her friends were around, she would open up and come to life with laughter.

"Who do you think is going to be our teacher?" Sheldon asked.

Charlize looked up from her notebook at Sheldon and then around their area. "Who are you talking to?" she asked, looking at Sheldon confused.

"You," Sheldon replied with a chuckle.

"Oh, ummm, I'm not sure," Charlize responded, still surprised Sheldon was talking to her.

"What is going on?" Sheldon asked.

"Sheldon, in all the years we have gone to school together, you have never once talked to me," Charlize casually responded. "You have always acted too good to talk to me."

Sheldon sat there with his mouth open, unsure how to respond, and was utterly shocked.

"In fact, in kindergarten, I tried to play with you and your friends, but you wouldn't let me because I was not cool enough to be in your group."

Sheldon was still sitting there in shock and speechless. He thought he was always nice to everyone.

Also, in kindergarten, you always used to break my crayons," she said before returning to her notebook.

"I'm sorry, but I do not remember any of that happening," Sheldon said, still in shock and embarrassed by this news.

"Well, I remember it very clearly," Charlize replied plainly, returning to her drawing.

"I am so sorry that happened," Sheldon said again, still in shock.

"Don't worry about it. I'm over it now, but I had to share because it stuck with me for a long time," Charlize said as she continued to doodle in her notebook before looking back at Sheldon. "I think we have all done mean stuff to somebody for no good reason."

"Like this one time, a girl got her period in class a few years ago, and I brought it to everyone's attention," Charlize explained. "She was completely mortified and ran out of the classroom in tears. So yeah, not one of my best moments, and I still feel bad about it to this day, but you must forgive yourself and others, move on, and try to be a better person."

Sheldon was even more surprised to hear she had done something like that because she always seemed like the sweetest person in school. Just then, the classroom door opened, and a lady in her mid-forties, wearing glasses and wild, curly, frizzy-looking hair pulled back into a loose ponytail, entered the classroom. She was carrying a handful of books.

"Sorry, I'm late," the teacher said as she set the books on the teacher's lab table. She pushed up her glasses as she surveyed the room.

"Mr. Majors, do you mind helping take a role call while I get set up here?" She requested.

Sheldon was surprised that she knew who he was because he had never seen her before in his life. "Brown-noser," Charlize whispered as Sheldon got up from his stool.

The teacher cleared the chalkboard so she could write on it. "There is the attendance sheet there," she said, pointing to the corner of the table.

Sheldon was not sure if he should read off everyone's name or mark off everyone's name since he knew everyone.

Sheldon read the first name, and the teacher turned to him. "Oh, no. Can you take it back to your desk and mark everyone's name?" The class chuckled, and Sheldon could feel his cheeks flush.

It was unusual for a teacher to request that a student take the roll call. He walked back to his desk but somehow felt empowered and meaningful.

"Okay, class. My name is Dr. Alita Smith," she said as she turned around and wrote her name on the board. "My friends call me Lita, but you can call me Dr. Smith, and I will be your biology teacher this year. I hope to make learning biology fun."

When class ended, and they left, Ms. Smith pulled Sheldon aside. "Is your mom going camping this year?" She asked.

"I'm sure she will because she hardly ever misses it," Sheldon replied, still confused.

She must have sensed his confusion. "I went to school with your mom and used to go horseback riding with her when you boys were little. You probably don't remember me, but I remember you and your brother.

Sheldon was combing through his memories. "Did you used to have short hair?" Sheldon asked.

"Yes! And I had big glasses back then. I have since grown out my hair and look like a hippy now, but I did trade in my big glasses for these smaller ones," she said, smiling that he remembered her.

"I better get to my next class," Sheldon said, heading towards the door.

"Tell your mom that Lita said 'hello,'" she requested with a smile before returning her attention to her desk and preparing it for her next class.

§

Sheldon was sitting in woodshop class when a fellow student, Karen, entered the door and approached the teacher.

"Sheldon Majors?" The teacher called out.

Sheldon's reaction was to shoot his hand in the air, thinking he was calling roll call. Instead, the teacher motioned for Sheldon to approach his desk.

"You are to go with this student to the front office," he gestured to Karen.

Sheldon's heart skipped a beat as he grabbed his stuff and followed Karen out of the room. As they were walking, she turned to him and said, "You were supposed to meet Dr. Leatherman now."

"I thought she said the eighth period," Sheldon said.

Karen turned to Sheldon and said, "No, you were to report to her now." She made it sound so serious that he was in trouble, but he was searching in his mind to see if he had misunderstood the communication.

As they approached the school office, Sheldon saw Dr. Leatherman talking to the secretary. When she spotted Sheldon, she enthusiastically waved him to come inside.

"Hey, there you are," Dr. Leatherman said with a smile. "Follow me."

Her smile put Sheldon at ease. She opened the door to her office and closed it after they entered. "Okay, I have some news about your work program." Sheldon felt his heart start racing because he did not want to return to P.E. instead of working.

"We need to make some changes," she explained, pulling out a folder with his name. She opened it and pulled out two papers.

"So, we are changing your last two periods," she said while writing something on one of the pages. "I have already talked to your boss at GIA, and he has agreed to let you come in after school and work your regular schedule if you still want to continue working for them.

By this point, Sheldon had no clue what was about to happen. She looked up from the paper and noticed Sheldon was as white as a sheet. "Don't worry, this is a good thing, and we are not sending you back to P.E." Sheldon suddenly released the breath he unconsciously held and relaxed his tense shoulders.

We have two first-grade teachers requesting a teacher's aide, and this is a fantastic opportunity for you. For your seventh period, you will go to Mrs. Casey's classroom, and for your eighth period, you will go to Mrs. Hartley's.

"Are you okay with…."

"Absolutely," Sheldon said, interrupting her because he was excited, which caused her to chuckle. "I'm sorry. I'm relieved I do not have to go to the woodshop or P.E."

"Well, I can see you are excited to get started," Dr. Leatherman said with a chuckle. "Since the seventh period is almost over, you will report to Ms. Casey's class starting tomorrow, and today, you can go to Mrs. Hartley's class to introduce yourself and so forth."

"Sorry," Sheldon said.

"No need to be sorry. I love the enthusiasm," Dr. Leatherman said, handing him an updated class schedule. "Do you know where their classrooms are?"

"I believe so," Sheldon responded, looking at the room numbers on his class schedule. Since K-12 was all in one building, it was not too far of a walk to get to the classrooms.

"Well, you know where to find me if you have any questions or concerns."

Sheldon left her office, walking on air, excited about this new opportunity and headed towards the elementary section of the building.

§

Since the seventh period was almost over, Sheldon went to Ms. Hartley's class for his eighth period and peered through the door window. She spotted him and waved him inside. He opened the door, and a room full of first-grade students stared back at him. "Class, this is Mr. Majors, and he will be assisting us for an hour every day, so say hello," she requested.

The class gleefully greeted Sheldon with a big "hello."

"We are just finishing up an art project, and you can sit at the round table in the corner," She instructed, pointing to the corner of the room that resembled a book nook and play area.

Sheldon walked over to the table and pulled out a chair to sit down. The chair was very low to the floor, and he felt very awkward and out of place sitting there.

"Class, you have five minutes to finish gluing the petals onto the flowers," Ms. Hartley instructed. She could see one student getting frustrated with the assembly of his artwork. "Sheldon, do you mind helping Hunter finish gluing on his petals?"

Sheldon was relieved to be doing something. He quickly realized Hunter's problem was that he had put a lot of glue on everything, and it could not stick correctly. Sheldon promptly grabbed some paper towels and tried to wipe off the excess glue. Luckily, someone used a newspaper to cover the top of his desk, or he would have had it all over it too.

"See, with less glue, it's able to hold together," Sheldon said, looking at Hunter, who smiled at him, but Sheldon tried not to laugh because Hunter had glue on his nose and cheeks. Sheldon realized that the boy tried his best.

Sheldon glanced at Hunter's glue bottle. The top looked like someone had cut it, no wonder the glue had been pouring out. Sheldon looked over and saw a brown-haired, blue-eyed girl smirking at Hunter.

"Okay, class, it is time to put away your art supplies in an orderly fashion, one row at a time, please. Place your artwork on the table by the window to dry so we can get ready for reading time," Mrs. Hartley requested. "We will hang them up tomorrow."

The class started one at a time to rush to put back their art supplies, and they were shoving them in their cubby holes haphazardly. "Class, remember to put your stuff away nicely, or we will not have reading time today or start back on calculating our numbers," Mrs. Hartley boomed.

Sheldon immediately noticed that Mrs. Hartley could be intimidating and profoundly serious but in a professional manner. The students hated the numbers, so they did as instructed. One student in a flowered dress raised her hand and said, "I would rather do numbers today, Mrs. Hartley."

"I know Fleur," Ms. Hartley responded and smiled at Sheldon. "But we are reading now. How about I let you pick out the book?"

"While they are reading. I'm going to have you grade some papers," Ms. Hartley instructed Sheldon. She grabbed a stack of papers off her desk and took them to the book nook table. Sheldon thought she might have him sit at her desk, but that seemed off-limits.

Here is the key and my red pen. Mark the wrong ones in red. Here is the grading scale, and you can enter them here in the grade book," she instructed. "Fleur, did you find a book? Once you finish that stack, can you enter this graded stack into the grade book, too? Sound good?" she posed as a question but did not wait for a response before returning to the class.

As Sheldon was grading the papers, he felt it was wrong for him to be grading them. It somehow felt that he was not qualified to be doing it, yet it also felt grown-up. It was nice to have someone believe in his ability to do something meaningful. He felt like an imposter, and they would figure out at any moment that he could not manage this responsibility.

"Fleur, you read the first paragraph and pick the next person to read," Mrs. Hartley boldly said, pulling Sheldon out of his thoughts and back to the task at hand.

Most students performed well on their assignments, missing only one or two answers. Of course, Fleur got a perfect score, but the following paper he started grading was the complete opposite. The first few answers were incorrect, and Sheldon was unsure whether to accept them. Then, it was like the student had just stopped answering the last couple of questions. He looked at the top of the paper for a name and noticed it was Hunter's paper.

Sheldon looked up just as the smirking girl picked Hunter to read next.

He set Hunter's paper aside to ask Mrs. Hartley about it afterward and continued without any other issues. He pulled out the grade book and found the line to mark this assignment's grade. He noticed that all the other entries were small and perfectly done. He panicked momentarily because his handwriting was terrible. He did his best and hoped she would not notice.

"I finished everything except this one paper because the…" Sheldon started to explain when Mrs. Hartley came to check on his progress, and she took the paper from him.

"Ah, yes. Hunter," she whispered. "I'm at a loss with how to help him because I have twenty-seven other students and don't have the time to dedicate to him, which troubles me. Do you mind sitting with him tomorrow and walking through it with him?"

"Sure, I don't mind at all," Sheldon responded.

"Thank you. I genuinely appreciate it and thank you for your help today," Mrs. Hartley said with a slight smile. "See you tomorrow."

On Sheldon's way to work at the grocery store that day, he felt good about Dr. Leatherland's change to his school schedule and thought he could make a difference.

§

The next day at school, it was time for the seventh period, so Sheldon arrived at Mrs. Casey's class. She had the door open because some kids needed to use the bathroom. When she spotted Sheldon, she asked, "Mr. Majors?"

"Yes," Sheldon responded.

"Oh, thank goodness you are here," Mrs. Casey responded. "Come on in. I could use your help."

As Sheldon walked into the classroom, it was a little chaotic. Kids were moving everywhere, and he had no idea what was going on.

"We are about to start our art project, and the kids are getting out their stuff," Mrs. Casey explained. "Do you mind watching the kids using the bathroom to ensure they are not playing in the hall and returning to class?"

"Not a problem," Sheldon responded but pondered for a second. They do not even know who he is, and will they listen to him?

Luckily, they all returned without issue because they were excited about their art project. All except one little girl that made it back into the classroom; this girl was slowly walking down the hall toward her classroom. She seemed to be in her own little world without any awareness of the other people coexisting with her.

Sheldon tried to encourage her to move a little faster, but she stopped and got a drink of water before slowly making her way back to the classroom. When she finally made it back into the classroom, the other kids already had their crayons out and coloring on the paper before them.

Sheldon walked over to Mrs. Casey's desk for further instruction. "They are creating their little garden," Ms. Casey said, looking up from the paper she was grading and pointing to the bulletin board, which was designed to look like a garden without any color. "The kids each pick a portion of the wall they want to color, and I replace the blank ones with the colored ones. After starting it, I thought about what I had gotten myself into, but the kids seem to love it."

"That one keeps me busy," Mrs. Casey whispered, pointing to the little girl who had taken her time returning to the classroom. "Her name is Trianna, but you can call her Tara, and she needs extra help, if you know what I mean. Do you mind seeing if you can help her with her artwork for today?"

Sheldon walked over to her desk to see that she had a purple crayon scribbling way outside the lines in a color that did not go with the design she had chosen, which was a cucumber. Sheldon watched her momentarily, unsure how he could help, but an idea came to him.

"Do we have more of these?" Sheldon asked the girl, who did not respond right away. Finally, she pointed to the corner of the room. Sheldon walked over and found the cucumber paper.

Mrs. Casey looked up from the papers she was grading to notice Sheldon getting up to get another piece of paper before sitting down again with Tara. She smiled because Tara was finally getting the extra attention she needed. Sheldon sat the uncolored piece of paper down on Tara's desk.

Sheldon pulled up a chair and sat down beside her. "Do you mind if I share your desk?" Sheldon asked, but again, she hesitated before moving over, giving him a little space to work with. "Do you mind if I use some of your crayons because I do not have any of my own?"

She looked at her box of crayons and then at Sheldon. "Sure," she responded before going back to her paper and wildly coloring it with brown this time.

Sheldon pulled out a dark green crayon and proceeded to color slowly inside the lines of the cucumber. "Did you choose this particular vegetable for a reason," Sheldon asked, trying to get her to open up and talk, but she did not respond. He noticed her face was dirty, as was her clothes, and her curly light brown hair looked like it had not seen a comb in some time.

"I like cucumbers because they remind me of my grandmother. She always makes a delicious cucumber salad in the summertime." She explained and stopped coloring to look at Sheldon and then at his paper. "How do you get yours to look so nice?" she asked.

"Oh, well, the first step you need to take is pick out a color that would match what a cucumber would look like," he said, opening the crayon box, which a lot of the crayons were broken or missing. "Here, take the one I'm using," Sheldon offered, but she reached for a lighter green and started to make a mark on the page.

"The trick is to go slowly and try to stay inside the line. Think of it as a competition in which you lose if you go outside the line too much." She looked at him curiously as if he had three heads.

Sheldon demonstrated on his paper as she watched. She proceeded to try her best to stay inside the lines.

Mrs. Casey cleared her throat. "Once you have completed coloring your picture, you can put it on the table next to the bulletin board and have some free time," Mrs. Casey shared, putting away the papers she was working on and walking over to Sheldon. "I need to make some copies for our next lesson. I don't know what I did with them. Do you mind watching the classes? Have them put their stuff away in 5 minutes so we are ready for the next lesson."

The kids were starting to get rowdy, and Sheldon wondered if he should try to get them to settle down just as Mrs. Casey came back into the room and started handing out their next lesson.

"Fresh off the press," She called out. "Thank you, Sheldon. I will see you tomorrow."

Sheldon gathered his stuff and headed across the hall to Mrs. Hartley's classroom, which was extremely quiet when he entered the room. Mrs. Hartley motioned with her pointer finger for him to approach her desk, which immediately took him back to elementary school whenever he had done something wrong and was being called to the teacher's desk.

As he approached, he noticed she was wearing some nice-smelling perfume again and always seemed to dress professionally. "Do you mind sitting with Hunter today and helping him with his math problems?" She whispered looking at him square in the eyes profoundly serious like.

"Sure, not at all," Sheldon replied. He liked grading papers, but it felt nice to help the students directly. After Sheldon finished helping Hunter, Mrs. Hartley handed Sheldon a piece of paper.

"I need you to make thirty copies for tomorrow's art project," Mrs. Hartley stated.

Sheldon froze for a second because he had never made copies before. Sheldon already felt like a fraud being there because he knew other students were more qualified to be teacher's aide. Sheldon did not want to disappoint Mrs. Hartley because he did not know what he was doing, so Sheldon decided to pretend to know what to do and hoped to figure it out as he went along.

"The copy machine is down the hall on the right. You cannot miss it," she stated.

When Sheldon entered the copy room, he panicked. He had never used a Mimeograph machine before and was trying to figure out how he could fake his way out of this situation. He struggled to comprehend how to correctly put the paper in the machine when Kent, a classmate, walked by. When he noticed Sheldon inside, he stopped in his tracks.

"Hey, what are you doing here," Kent asked as he popped his head inside.

Sheldon thought, 'This is it. The jig is up.' He will tell someone he is not qualified to be doing this and get someone else to replace him.

"I'm helping Mrs. Hartley make copies," Sheldon responded.

"Cool, I'm helping Mrs. Cash with her fifth-grade students," Kent replied with a smile and seemed happy to see a fellow student. "Do you need help with that machine?"

"No, I'm good," Sheldon responded, but inside, he was screaming, YES!

"Are you sure it can be a bit cantankerous," Kent said. "I really don't mind."

"Sure," Sheldon said, handing the master copy to Kent, holding in his relief. Kent was one of the popular kids in class, and he was always genuinely kind to him. Sheldon watched him very closely so he could learn how to do it the next time.

"You should be all set now," Kent said, heading for the door but watching Sheldon turn the handle. "You got it."

"Thank you so much," Sheldon said, turning the machine's handle and cranking out copies.

"Sure, no problem, anytime," Kent said with a smile. "If you need anything else, you know where to find me."

"Will do," Sheldon said, looking up, but Kent was already gone.

§

Sheldon sat at the cafeteria table and pulled out his lunch as Ruby came to sit down. Ruby gave him a curious look about bringing his lunch because he had always eaten what lunch ladies were serving from the hot bar or what was on the salad bar.

"I thought I'd start bringing my lunch to save money so I can buy some new shoes and new tires for my car," Sheldon said.

"You need new tires already?" Ruby asked

"Yeah, the tires I have on have dry rotted because they are old," Sheldon responded, taking a bite of the sandwich.

"I didn't realize tires got old," Ruby remarked.

"Yeah, they have started cracking, and I could have a blowout driving down the highway," Sheldon explained. "I'm not really feeling this sandwich because we grew up eating ham or bologna sandwiches."

"I get that. I grew up on Chef Boyardee Ravioli, and now I can't stand it," Ruby said as Ninnie sat down beside her, eyeballing Sheldon's sandwich.

"What are you eating?" Ninnie asked.

"Kent saw me yesterday making copies for Mrs. Hartley's class," Sheldon stated, changing the subject.

"Why does that matter," Ruby asked, confused.

"I think he's gonna tell them I don't belong there," Sheldon responded.

"Not this again, Ninnie groaned.

"What?" Ruby questioned, completely confused.

"It's because Sheldon thinks he's not qualified to be a teacher assistant, and that someone's gonna figure it out and that he's gonna have to go back to PE," Ninnie explained.

"But there are no real qualifications to be a teacher assistant," Ruby stated.

"Precisely, that's what I tried to tell him, but he doesn't listen," Ninnie said. "It's like he has imposter syndrome."

"Is that really a thing?" Sheldon asked.

"It definitely is a thing, and I'm sure Chase would tell you the same thing if he was here," Ruby stated. "I'm sure he's experienced it as we all have. You got this, don't worry. Also, no one's gonna send you back to PE."

"I have imposter syndrome all the time," Ninnie explained.

"Thanks," Sheldon said. "I have always been picked last for everything, so I feel like most people do not believe in me."

"I have never experienced that and have always been the popular one," Ruby said, tossing her hair with a serious look and not laughing, which caused them all to laugh.

Chapter Three

Busy Bee

Two weeks before Chase's accident, Sheldon was helping the students with their assignments while Mrs. Casey looked at her book and wrote something on the chalkboard. "Sheldon, were you in a play a few years ago?" she asked, pausing from writing on the chalkboard.

"Yes, my freshman year, I was Funky in the Funky Winkerbean play," Sheldon responded.

My stepdaughter just started working here as an English teacher and is the head of the theater department. She is looking for some actors," Mrs. Casey explained. "I think you should go to the tryouts next week."

Sheldon did enjoy being in the play previously, but his life has been too busy to think about it, and time has just gotten away from him.

"It's something to think about. Besides, I thought you were good in the other play," Mrs. Casey encouraged.

"Thank you," Sheldon said. "I will definitely think about it." He was not sure how he would do it with his after-school job.

The next day, Sheldon shared this opportunity with Chase and the girls. They all agreed he should do it, especially since Mrs. Casey was recommending it, and if anything, it would be fun to try out.

"Do not worry about your job," Ninnie stated. "It will still be there, or you will find another."

"Yeah, this sounds like a fun opportunity," Ruby added. "and if they do not choose you screw 'em."

"I agree," Chased stated. "And, do not be afraid to ask your boss for the time off. Also, there are times I wonder how I am going to do everything. However, I managed to complete all my schoolwork somehow, and you will, too."

It was like they were all reading his mind and all the excuses he had for not doing it. He could not argue with their statements, so he decided to give it a try and went to sign up for tryouts.

The following Tuesday was the day of the tryouts, and Sheldon had requested the day off from work. He went to the tryouts and immediately felt unprepared. The other students were doing vocal warmups, and some ran through lines. He immediately thought about what lines they were rehearsing, where they had gotten their material, and whether he was supposed to have gotten it before the tryouts.

Sheldon vaguely remembered his tryouts during his freshman year. It was a blur now, but he remembered that the tryouts were held in a small room, where people would go around the room, reading from a book that was being passed around.

These tryouts seemed more serious, and he suddenly felt unrehearsed. He thought about leaving when the teacher came out to give them instructions. She immediately spotted Sheldon and waved at him. He knew he could not leave now. He had seen her before a couple of times when she visited Mrs. Casey's class but had never realized she was the stepdaughter of Mrs. Casey. He had just thought she was a fellow teacher because she had a different last name and would only pop in quickly and then leave.

"Hello, everyone; my name is Mrs. Thomas," she greeted them, "and this is Carrie. She will be assisting me and if she asks you to do something. Please listen to her because she is doing what I ask."

Carrie started handing out papers, which Mrs. Thomas called "sides," for them to read quickly, and she would call them up to the stage one at a time. At the same time, Mrs. Thomas and Carrie organized themselves and found a comfortable spot to watch the students' auditions. She gave them a few minutes to prepare.

"Okay, I want to see," she started saying as she scanned the signup sheet. "Can I see Sheldon and then Ashley?"

Sheldon's heart immediately jumped out of his chest because he had barely read through the sides once and was thinking, how can he remember all this in just a few minutes?

Sheldon walked out onto the stage, and Mrs. Thomas and Carrie sat there staring back at him. They both had a clipboard. "I see you were only in one other production a few years ago," Mrs. Thomas stated. "Why do you want to do this now?"

Sheldon did not think he would be asked questions, but immediately, his mind returned to his interview class. "I enjoyed performing the last time and being guided and directed by the director. This play is possibly my last opportunity to do it again."

There was a long pause while Mrs. Thomas made notes. Sheldon was not sure if she appreciated his answer. "You already answered my other questions about taking notes from a director or how you manage instructions. Can you read the sides for me, starting with paragraph three on page two?"

Sheldon turned to page two and found paragraph three. Sheldon paused for a moment to gather his thoughts, and he remembered from his freshman year that he needed to project his voice because he spoke so softly. He started to read and paused when he reached the page's bottom.

"Keep going; I will tell you when to stop," Mrs. Thomas said, looking up from her notes.

Sheldon read another paragraph when she asked him to stop. She continued to make some notes and said something to Carrie. "Thank you, Sheldon. We have what we need. Can I have everyone's attention? Try to memorize most of the material so that you can look up at the audience from the paper. Ashley, you're next, and Peter, will be after Ashley.

Sheldon thought he had blown it because he did not look up from the paper once. He went to sit down and watch. He was somewhat relieved to have it over with, and now he could sit back and watch.

Ashley started strong, but once she looked up from the paper, she would lose her place when she looked back down, and when it was Peter's turn, Mrs. Thomas stopped him.

"We cannot hear you, and we are sitting relatively close to the stage. How do you think people sitting in the back are going to hear you," she said, giving him feedback. "Everyone, please make sure you are projecting your voices like Sheldon and Ashley did. Okay, go again."

Peter started reading again; this time, he was only a little louder and did not look up from the paper. "Okay, thanks," Mrs. Thomas said, writing something down. "Next is Lisa and then Trevor, then Brian and Emilie."

She continued with the rest of the auditions as Sheldon's thoughts drifted in and out until one student came out and was reading without looking at his paper and no one else seemed to notice. Sheldon did not recognize this guy and did not know his name. But Mrs. Thomas barely took her eyes off him. He barely looked down at the paper; when he spoke, it was like he was reading poetry.

"Okay, thank you, Jake." She said, interrupting him. "Is that everyone?"

"Yes," Carrie responded.

"Okay, Everyone, we will be posting the casting list by this Friday."

§

The next day, Chase, Ninnie, and Ruby peppered him with questions about what it was like to audition, and he filled them in on how it went, how unprepared he was, and how well Jake did. "So, I don't think I will get a part, which is okay because I'm too busy as it is anyway," Sheldon stated.

"When will you find out?" Chase asked.

"Didn't you already ask your boss for the time off?" Ninnie asked.

"Did you say a new guy named Jake?" Ruby asked.

There were so many questions flying at him that Sheldon was trying to figure out which one to answer first. "No, I did not ask off from work because I wanted to wait till, I knew for sure," Sheldon responded. "And we should know by Friday. Jake must be some new guy because I had never seen him before."

Ruby started wondering about this new guy with the same name as her ex-boyfriend.

"You are definitely going to get a part, I can feel it," Chase said with a smile and then kissed Sheldon.

On Friday, during lunch, Sheldon heard other students talking about the posted list.

"I heard the list is posted," Ruby said.

"Are you going to go look now?" Ninnie asked.

"No, I'm afraid to look," Sheldon responded.

"I will come with you!" Ruby said it a little louder than she anticipated.

"Dang girl, you are excited for him," Ninnie teased.

"I just want to be there to support you." Ruby tried to recover, but she could not stop thinking about the new guy named Jake. She could not share this with anyone because she felt guilty, as if she were betraying or cheating on Trey.

They walked to the bulletin board outside the gym, and a couple of people were reviewing it when they walked up to read the list. Ruby quickly found Sheldon's name listed, so he got the part of love interest number one. While Sheldon was in shock, Ruby continued to look for Jake's name and found he was playing the lead, but it was not her Jake, and she was somewhat relieved but disappointed at the same time and what were the odds anyway.

That night, during his shift at the grocery store, Sheldon nervously talked to his boss about taking off work a couple of days a week to attend the play rehearsals and he agreed to work Sundays to make up for some of the lost time.

§

The week before Chase's accident, he stopped by to say hello to Sheldon while he was on his way to practice. Mrs. Hartley was at the board writing, and Sheldon was at the round table grading papers when he saw Chase's face appear in the door window. Chase waved at him once he knew he had Sheldon's attention. Sheldon looked at Mrs. Hartley, whose back was still facing him. Sheldon subtly waved back when Mrs. Hartley noticed what was going on. She saw that Chase was waving for Sheldon to come out.

"Mr. Majors, please see that your friend keeps moving along," Mrs. Hartley said as Sheldon sat frozen in the chair. "Go!" she requested. Mrs. Hartley was very intimidating, and Sheldon moved immediately.

"He cannot just stop by interrupting class…no matter how cute he looks in those tight…" She stopped, cleared her throat, and turned back to the classroom, staring at them. "Back to your numbers," she demanded. "Remember, the first one to complete them correctly gets a star on the board."

A few days later, in Mrs. Casey's class, Sheldon was helping Tara with her list of spelling words she had to learn when she turned to Sheldon and said, "My dad said he knows your dad."

"Really?" Sheldon asked. " Barn, is your next word."

"Yeah, he said they used to ride to work together before he became a truck driver," Tara explained. "I wish he still worked there because now I hardly ever see him, and when I do, he is always in a bad mood." She finished writing out the last word and handed the paper to Sheldon.

"His name is Berry Price." She said with a smile.

Sheldon looked at Tara and noticed that even though Tara always looked like she had not combed her hair in a couple of days and her face was always dirty, you could not ask for a kinder kid and felt terrible when the other kids made fun of her.

Sheldon realized he was the adult in the situation and had to put a stop to it, letting them know it was not right. Being a teacher's aide felt like a full-circle moment for Sheldon, being back in elementary school and reliving all the memories that came with it, and it felt grown-up and in charge.

"Okay, now you can go pick your page you want to color today," Sheldon said as he looked up and saw Chase in the door window and panicked because he did not want to get scolded again for Chase showing up. He quickly looked at Mrs. Casey sitting at her desk entering grades into the grade book. She looked up and noticed Chase.

She waved for him to come inside, and Chase gladly entered. "I just wanted to say hello to Sheldon."

"Well, come on in, and you can say hello to all of us," Mrs. Casey offered and flashed an approving smile to Sheldon.

"Hello," Chase said awkwardly to the class, waving his right hand. "I will see you after work?" he asked, looking at Sheldon.

"Yes," Sheldon slyly replied. Chase awkwardly left the classroom, slowly backing out and running to a table along the wall, causing the students to laugh.

After Chase left the classroom, Sheldon quickly put his head down, looking at Tara's paper that she was coloring, trying not to make eye contact with Mrs. Casey out of fear of retribution.

"I can't really see the lines, or which color is which," she said, slowly scribbling with her face as close to the paper as possible, pulling Sheldon's attention back to her. Sheldon looked up to see Mrs. Casey, who looked up from the grade book and gave another approving smile.

As Sheldon watched Tara coloring, it suddenly clicked what might be Tara's issue. "I will be right back," he said to Tara.

He walked up to Mrs. Casey's desk. "Do they still do eye exams during the school year?" Sheldon asked.

"Yeah, they did them last month. Why?" Mrs. Casey asked.

"I think that Tara is having trouble seeing, which is why she seems to be struggling," Sheldon explained. Sheldon could see that Mrs. Casey was thinking about it and processing this new information.

"You know, come to think of it, she missed the day they were here testing everyone. In fact, the day they returned to get the ones that missed the first day, she was absent, too," Mrs. Casey explained. I will call the parents and send a letter to them to have her checked. "Good catch, Sheldon," she said. "And I'm not just talking about Tara." She winked at him.

"You're not upset that he stopped by?" Sheldon asked.

"Not at all," she replied.

"Mrs. Hartley got terribly upset when he stopped by to say hello."

"Why? Has she seen his…" She started to comment but caught herself. "In fact, he can stop by any time he likes, so we, I mean you, can just stare at him." They both laughed.

She looked at the clock. "Speaking of Mrs. Hartley, you had better get out of here and to her class. Yesterday, I kept you too long, and she got upset and let me know about it this morning.

Sheldon had no idea he had been late, so he quickly packed up and headed out.

Sheldon quietly entered Mrs. Hartley's class. The students were taking turns reading out loud when Mrs. Hartley waved Sheldon over. "Can you take Hunter outside and help him redo his math problems?" she whispered. His make-up paper is on the corner of my desk.

As Sheldon was helping Hunter work out his math problems, he realized the stark differences between Tara and Hunter. Tara seemed to come from a family that had very little, and her future was uncertain; however, both students faced similar struggles. However, Hunter appeared to come from a well-off family and was the popular boy in class. Sheldon realized that you could have it all and still struggle. Hunter reminded Sheldon of a future quarterback torturing other students.

Also, both Tara and Hunter were struggling with their math and spelling. Sheldon enjoyed helping them get up to speed with their fellow students, which felt like a vital role. Every class needed someone like him to help those students who were falling behind.

Sheldon observed that when it was just the two of them, Hunter was one of the kindest kids around, so he found it peculiar that when the other kids were around, he had to assert his dominance. After Sheldon got to know him more, he discovered he had two older brothers and must be modeling their behaviors, and they had bullied him his whole life.

When Mrs. Hartley was not having Sheldon helping students with their work, he was grading papers, which he found extremely exciting, but he was sad when someone missed so many of the answers. He also enjoyed it when he got to help prepare the art projects they would be doing for art class. He loved getting to be creative because creativity made him feel fulfilled.

§

The week of Chase's accident Sheldon was helping the students in Mrs. Casey's class with their artwork while she was grading papers. The kids were making ghosts and pumpkins to hang on the board, which said, "Happy Halloween," and they had a haunted house and a scary-looking black tree.

"Mrs. Hartley has me grading her paper if you ever need any help," Sheldon offered.

"She does?" she responded and thought for a moment. "That's okay, I like to see firsthand how my students are doing," Mrs. Casey explained. "Do you mind handing out the Halloween candy for me? I need to run and make some copies before you leave. Do you mind watching them while I am gone? I thought I had enough but must have missed counted somehow."

"I can make copies," Sheldon offered. "I do it all the time for Mrs. Hartley."

"Wow, aren't you a busy bee? She really has you working over there," Mrs. Casey joked. "That would be amazing. I only need five copies."

Sheldon rushed to make the copies, so he was not late again for Mrs. Hartley's class. "There was something nice about the smell of freshly printed papers," Sheldon said, laying the papers on Mrs. Casey's desk.

"Right, it's kind of addicting, huh," she said, picking them up and smelling them. "You better skedaddle before you get us both in trouble." They both laughed as Sheldon grabbed his bag and headed for the door.

§

The weeks following Chase's accident were somewhat of a blur for Sheldon. Dr. Smith's Biology class, Ruby, Ninnie, play rehearsals, being a teacher's aide, and working at the grocery store helped Sheldon get through Chase being in a coma. They all kept him too busy to have much time to think about it when he could not be by Chase's bedside.

In the weeks that followed, Dr. Smith kept her promise, and over the next few months, she would get Sheldon, and the class excited to learn more about topography, human anatomy, and nature. He had always thought science was boring before she made it fun.

One day in Mrs. Casey's class, they were so immersed in what they were doing that Sheldon forgot it was time to go to Mrs. Hartley's class until there was a knock on the door. Mrs. Casey saw Mrs. Hartley peering through the window, immediately at the clock and then Sheldon. "Opps, time just got away from us," Mrs. Casey said with a look of fear at Sheldon.

Mrs. Hartley opened the classroom door. "Can I see the two of you in the hallway for a moment, please," she said and, with her pointer finger, motioned each of them to come with her.

"Its like being called to the Principal's office," Mrs. Casey said under her breath to Sheldon as they made their way to the door.

"Look I do not know what the deal is, and we talked about this, but this is the third time Sheldon has been late to my class, which throws off my whole schedule and we are to share him. So, in the future can you make please make sure he is coming to my classroom on time." Mrs. Hartley said in a sweet but forceful tone. "I need his help too. You know my class is a lot bigger."

Sheldon did not know what she was talking about when she said he was late for a third time. As far as he knew, this was only the second time. However, it did feel nice to be fought over.

"I will definitely ensure Sheldon is headed to your class on time," Mrs. Casey said as politely as she could. "Sorry, I did not know I was hogging him."

"Thank you, I would appreciate that," Mrs. Hartley said with a pursed smile as she turned and headed back to her classroom.

Sheldon went back into Mrs. Casey's classroom to get his stuff to head to Mrs. Hartley's classroom.

"I'm sorry I got us both in trouble," Mrs. Casey said through gritted teeth. "I did not know I had been keeping you here past your time to leave. I thought today was only the second time.

"Me too," Sheldon said, grabbing his bag.

"We will talk later," Mrs. Casey said with a smile. "Have a good one Sheldon and again sorry to have caused you trouble."

"No worries at all, and have a good one," Sheldon said waving goodbye to the classroom.

Sheldon was apprehensive about entering Mrs. Hartley's classroom after what had just happened. But she welcomed him and acted like nothing had happened.

In the following weeks, Mrs. Casey and Sheldon joked that he did not want to be late again when it was getting close to the time for him to go to Mrs. Hartley's class.

The week before Chase woke up, Mrs. Casey was swamped with getting a transfer student adjusted and up to speed with the class's request, so she had Sheldon sit at her desk to grade some papers. He really enjoyed sitting at her desk and he could see himself doing this job.

Chapter Four

Unexpected Plans

Over Christmas break, Charlotte took Levin to show him around her hometown. They had a lot of fun with her friends, who drove them around while getting them drunk and high. Her friends dropped them back off at her mom's car. Since Charlotte was underage, she could not reserve a motel room, so one of her older friends reserved a room at Motel 6 for her. They never made it to the motel because they both had too much to drink to drive, and things got heated up and steamed up. Charlotte had her first sexual experience in the back of her mom's car. The following day, when she woke up, she thought it was all a dream until she woke up in Levin's arms.

When it was time to return to school after the holiday break, they could barely keep their hands off one other. But a few weeks back from break, Charlotte started not feeling well. She thought she had come down with the flu. She was sick every morning, so her mom kept her home from school for the first week. Charlotte did not see Levin for what seemed like forever, and he could not get her on the phone. At first, Levin thought her mom had found out what they had done and that she might be trying to keep them apart, but he soon discovered that was not the case.

Charlotte reached out to Sheldon since she had spent time with Levin at his house and got to know Sheldon. She felt she could confide in him, and since he and Levin were so close, Charlotte knew she could trust him to drive her to get a pregnancy test.

First, she would have to explain to Levin that she needed one, and she went over and over how to tell him. Sheldon was surprised at how calm Levin was when Charlotte told him the news.

While waiting for the pregnancy results, Sheldon thought it would be good to lighten the mood with a few jokes. However, his jokes did not distract Charlotte or Levin. Since jokes were not working, he changed tactics and began to tell stories. He thought about the time Charlotte came out to their house, and they smoked a joint and got high together while they played video games in Sheldon's bedroom. Levin got bored with the game and went off doing something else. Charlotte and Sheldon each had a big glass of Mountain Dew and a bag of Doritos, playing Mario Brothers.

"Hey, Charlotte," Sheldon said. "You remember last year when you came out, and we got high and played video games?"

"Yes," Charlotte replied, smiling. "You were hilarious."

"That was a fun time," Sheldon remarked. "We would get so distracted eating our chips and laughing we would forget who was playing. It was as if time was moving at a slower pace."

"We would stare at the screen, watching the little guy getting killed off because neither of us knew whose turn it was to play. We would die laughing," Charlotte said, chuckling. "We were quite the sight, I'm sure."

"The craziest part about it is I still don't know how we got to the end of the game," he said. "I still can't figure that one out. I can't do it now even if I tried."

"Yeah, that was a fun time, and I still don't know how we did it either," Charlotte said, smiling at Sheldon and then looking at Levin. "By the way, where did you go while we were playing? I always wanted to ask you about that 'cause it seemed like you were gone forever."

Levin hesitated and tried to change the subject, but they were not letting him off the hook. "Well, I went to the fridge and started eating everything I could get my hands on and…" Levin paused, trying to think of a nice way to put his following sentence. "I had to go to the bathroom, and that is where I stayed for a bit, thinking I was going to shit myself to death."

Sheldon and Charlotte stared at him momentarily before busting out in laughter. "Hey, I have a sensitive tummy," Levin defended himself. "Sometimes I have to go really bad."

After he said that, Sheldon and Charlotte were literally on the floor laughing. Levin started laughing at the site of them. "You guys, it's not that funny," Levin pouted, but the more he thought about it, he started to chuckle with them. "Well, I guess it was kind of funny if you were looking at it from an outside perspective, but at the moment, it was not funny."

They all laughed until they realized it was way past time to check the pregnancy test. Sheldon saw that Charlotte and Levin were afraid to look at the test stick. Charlotte looked pasty white, and Levin looked like he was going to be sick. "I can't look," Charlotte said, looking at Levin. "You look."

Levin sat there for a moment. "I can't do it, Sheldon. You look."

Sheldon looked at them both, feeling nervous about their situation. He got up from where he was seated and picked up the box. "Okay, let's make sure we know what we are looking for first," Sheldon said, looking at the box. "If there are two pink lines, you're pregnant; one pink line, you're not pregnant." Sheldon picked up the stick and looked at it. "This thing must be wrong," Sheldon stated, looking at Charlotte and Levin, who were waiting for the news. "There are two pink lines."

Charlotte and Levin just sat there for a moment. "Nuhuh, let me see that," Charlotte insisted, taking the stick from Sheldon. "Oh my god, it does," She said, showing Levin. "Okay, I am going to try another test. That one has to be wrong. I'm going to try the other brand."

Charlotte returned to the bathroom while Levin sat on the couch in shock. "I'm doing two this time," Charlotte yelled from the bathroom. "I want to be doubly sure."

"Wouldn't that be triple sure?" Sheldon said, but no one heard him, or if they did they did not laugh.

Levin got impatient, went to the bathroom door, and knocked. "You okay in there?" Levin asked, knocking on the door again.

"I'm not coming out till I know for sure," Charlottes announced from inside the bathroom.

"Well can I come in then?" he said still standing at the door with his head resting against it as she opened it to let him inside.

Charlotte sat back down on the toilet rubbing her hands together while rocking back and forth. Levin sat down on the floor in front of her. "We are going to be ok," he said as he rubbed her leg trying to relax her. "How much longer to we have to wait?"

"About two minutes left," she said, looking at her watch. "Ooh God," she said, still rocking back and forth while rubbing her hands on her legs. They sat in silence.

"Okay, it's time," she said, looking at the sticks. "This one is a cross," she said as she held up the stick. "Where is the box this came from? Oh, wait. It shows here. If it's a cross, you're pregnant?"

They both just sat there staring at each other, not even needing to look at the next stick.

"Well, say something," Charlotte nudged Levin. "Why are you so quiet?"

"I don't know what to say," Levin said just sitting there looking at the floor. "How did this happen."

"What do you mean how did this happen," Charlotte said sitting up. "You stuck your dick in me is how THIS happened," She said as she motioned around her tummy. "The real question is what are WE going to tell our parents?"

"Do we have to?" Levin asked in complete denial, unable to process the news of becoming a father.

"I think they are going to notice, at some point. We will have to tell them, but I'm in no hurry either," Charlotte said, biting her fingernails.

§

It was late at night, and there was a knock on the front door of the Major's house. Everyone was asleep, so no one heard it, not even Sheldon, whose bedroom was on the first floor, while everyone else was asleep upstairs. There was a tapping at Sheldon's window, which caused him to slowly wake up and raise his head to listen. The tapping had stopped for a moment, so he thought he might have dreamed it, so he laid his head back down on his pillow to fall back asleep.

50

As soon as his head hit the pillow, the tapping started again. This time, Sheldon immediately sat up, fully alert because they lived in the middle of nowhere, and their neighbors lived quite a distance away. Sheldon slowly got out of bed to pull back the curtain to see what was making the sound. He jumped when he saw a face peering back at him. His fears were relieved when he realized the face staring back at him was Chase and his voice asking Sheldon to let him inside because it was freezing outside. Sheldon went to the front door to let Chase inside.

"What are you doing here and how did you get here?" Sheldon asked hugging him tightly and trying to warm him up.

"I got Tommy to drop me off on his way home to drop off Ninnie from their date," Chase replied.

"Here let me take your coat," Sheldon offered.

"I was released today and was going to surprise you tomorrow, but because I missed you so much that it hurt not seeing you one more minute, I had to get here even if it meant walking in the cold," he replied as he grabbed Sheldon and started kissing him so intensely that they were both worked up. Before they knew it, they clumsily removed each other's pants and almost knocked over a plant stand.

"Shhh, we don't want to wake the whole house," Sheldon said, still kissing him and laughing as he tried to take off Chase's shirt. They were both standing there in just their underwear, kissing each other. Chase started kissing Sheldon's neck when Sheldon realized they needed to take this to his bedroom.

"Merry Christmas," Chase whispered, kissing their way to Sheldon's bedroom.

"You're a little late," Sheldon said, closing the bedroom door. "You missed Christmas."

"Oh, yeah," Chase responded as he pushed Sheldon onto the bed. It's never too late for me to give you my gift." He quickly pulled Sheldon's boxers off and started to pull down his own briefs. He climbed onto the bed and shoved them in Sheldon's face. Sheldon's eyes rolled back into his head as he breathed in Chase's musky scent.

§

Sheldon started to wake up unsure of where he was, and as he slowly opened his eyes, he saw a small brown pebble before his eyes had time to focus. At first, he didn't realize what it was he was looking at, and then Sheldon realized he was still lying on Chase's chest, and it was his nipple. They had fallen asleep after a steamy session of lovemaking. His first thought was he wanted to bite it, and before he knew it, his obtrusive thoughts won over, and he lightly bit it, which caused Chase to wake up howling.

"So, that's how it's going to be," Chase cried out flipping Sheldon over and started tickling him. He knew all of Sheldon's sensitive areas.

"Stop!" Sheldon crying with laughter but Chase laughed and kept going.

"Stooooop! Mercy, please," Sheldon pleaded.

Chase dropped down beside Sheldon and they both laughed.

They cuddled each other and enjoyed snuggling together while the world outside was still spinning.

"Should we get up?" Sheldon asked as he started to get up.

"No," Chase said pulling him close. "I wanna feel your naked body against mine a little longer."

He started grinding himself against Sheldon. "You better be careful or you might wake the sleeping dragon," Sheldon said with a chuckle.

"Oooo, really?" Chase questioned with raised eyebrows and then he raised the covers. "I might have to have an intimate conversation with this dragon," he growled as he started to slide down under the covers causing Sheldon to laugh. "Also, I gotta give you your Christmas present," he said popping his head from under the covers before diving back under and causing Sheldon's eyes to roll back into his head as he put his wet warm mouth on Sheldon's raging rock hard cock.

§

Afterward, while still in bed, Chase played with Sheldon's hair and brushed it out of his eyes as they lay there enjoying each other's company.

"I grew up with everyone bashing on gay people, calling them queer and fag so much that I started to believe it was bad to be a gay person," Sheldon shared. "I thought that if I ever told anyone or they found out, that would be my end. I was unsure what would happen to me, but it would not be good."

"I'm sorry that happened to you," Chase said, kissing Sheldon's forehead.

"Guys in this town have called me queer or fag every day so much that I thought I needed to get a girlfriend to convince them. I'm not a bad person."

"So, is that one of the reasons why you thought you had to try to get a girlfriend? Chase asked

"Well, actually, I thought this guy I had a crush on had a girlfriend," Sheldon explained.

"Oh, who is that?" Chase asked, sitting up as he started to get jealous.

"You, you silly boy," Sheldon said, kissing him because a jealous Chase was so adorable.

"Oooo," Chase responded, and they both laughed.

"We better get our clothes before someone wakes up and sees them out there on the floor," Sheldon recommended.

"Let's stay here a little longer under the covers where it's warm," Chase requested. As they snuggled under the covers, the sun was starting to come up. They fell asleep again in each other's warm embrace as the snow started to fall outside.

§

A few of weeks into Charlotte feeling sick, it dawned on her that her mom would start questioning why she was ill so much. She was trying to come up with a game plan by saying it was stress from school but knew that would only buy her a short time because her mom started suggesting that she might need to take her to the hospital, so she finally had to confess to her mom what was going on. At first, her mom flew off the handle, but once she calmed down, she set up an appointment for Charlotte to have her first prenatal doctor visit to confirm she was pregnant and to make sure the baby was okay.

"This is not how I thought you would spend your senior year or the direction I saw your life going," Jeannie huffed as they entered the front door of their home. "This is all very unexpected and I'm feeling overwhelmed."

"You're overwhelmed. How do you think I feel, you think this how I envisioned spending my senior year and you're not making it any easier, Mom." Charlotte said, storming out of the room, slamming the bathroom door, and throwing up again into the toilet.

"I'm sorry, sweetie," Jeannie said, knocking on the bathroom door. "Is there anything I can get you? Maybe some 7UP or crackers?"

Chapter Five

Whispers of you

Mrs. Thomas had been working on the script for her play since high school and through college. She finally finished it and was actively trying to find someone to publish it or a theatre to produce it, but no one was interested in the concept, saying it was too controversial for their audiences.

She based the script on her uncle John, who had been in the army and then came home from the war. When he passed away, she received a box of his belongings, and inside, it included some letters that detailed a love story. She wanted to write a happy ending for his life because, in reality, he struggled with PSTD and who he truly was deep down versus who people wanted him to be and the fact he died alone with only his memories of what once was.

She wanted to call the play *This Queer Love* but was afraid it might be a bit too controversial for the time, so she settled on *The Whispers of You*. When she got the opportunity to be the drama teacher, she decided to see if she could put the play on herself with the high school students. She was surprised when she presented her idea and the script to the Principal and he agreed that she could move forward with putting it on. The only requirement the principal stipulated was to remove the kiss at the end, which she reluctantly agreed to but was grateful to at least finally have her play produced and seen by people.

Sheldon enjoyed being directed by Mrs. Thomas. For him, it was a fantastic feeling like he was clay, and she was molding them into something beautiful and amazing. She would have to remind him to butch it up a bit more.

It was the rehearsals' final week, and Sheldon was excited to have his family, friends, and Chase watch him perform.

"How is the play coming along?" Ruby asked while they were sitting together at lunch.

"Yeah, when is the opening night?" Ninnie asked. "We haven't seen much out of you." Lately, Sheldon had been using lunchtime for rehearsals.

"Tell me about it," Chase said. "Now I know how you felt when I was busy with my sports and playing in the band. I hardly see him."

Sheldon laughed. "It is coming along well. We are in the final week of rehearsals and run-throughs. You're welcome to come to the dress rehearsal next week, which is only open to friends and family," Sheldon offered Chase, Ninnie, and Ruby.

"Can we come to both the rehearsal and opening night?" Chase asked.

"Yes, you can come to both," Sheldon responded, happy they were interested in seeing him in his play.

§

The dress rehearsals went well, and everything went as planned without issues. It was opening night backstage, and Jake came up and whispered something into Sheldon's ear. Sheldon responded, "Are you sure?"

"I'm sure, and I think it's what the play needs," Jake said, but Sheldon was not as sure.

Chase, Ruby, Ninnie, Mandy, and Damian sat in the audience. "Look at this paper. It looks so professional," Mandy said, opening it and showing everyone.

"It's called a playbill," Chase explained.

"Fancy," Damian remarked.

"It's crazy seeing Sheldon's name on here," Mandy remarked, getting excited as the house lights flickered.

"That means the play is about to start," Ninnie explained. "They are called the house lights."

Edwards County Theatre Department

presents

The Whispers of You

By

Robin Thomas

Final Cast List:

James Fowley .... Jake Bower

Micheal [love interest #1] .... Sheldon Majors

Arthur [love interest #2] .... Brian Connor

Carol Fowley .... Lisa Brown

Bobby Fowley .... Daniel Yost

Linda Fowley .... Emilie Nicole

Extras: Earl Baker, Angela Baldwin, Sydney Basinger, Samantha Bernard, Marsha Begs, Willie

"Look at you getting the lingo down," Ruby teased as Mandy and Damian were impressed.

"Sheldon said that Mrs. Thomas had to change the characters' names to protect the people the play was about. She used to visit her Uncle before he passed, and he would share stories about his life that he never shared with anyone else," Chase explained.

The house lights went down, and the curtain opened to the words "The Korean War 1952." A light pans onto James, bent over and working on the jeep's engine, as Michael enters, dressed in a U.S. Army Uniform.

"The Colonel needs his jeep fixed immediately," Michael requested. "We brought the jeep in earlier for repairs and he expected it to be done by now."

"I can let you know when it's done," James said, looking up from the hood of another jeep.

"Unfortunately, that will not work," Michael stated. "My orders are to stay with it and demand it to be made a priority because it's due to take the colonel to a point of interest this afternoon, and my eyes are to be on it at all times."

"Oh well, in that case, let me stop what I'm doing and start working on it," James said, somewhat sarcastically, causing Michael to chuckle but quickly caught himself.

"You have your orders and I expect you to follow them," Michael commanded.

James could tell Michael was a little uptight and made it his goal to get him to loosen up.

As James worked, he tried to make small talk and discovered that they had grown up very close to each other.

As James bent over to get something out of the toolbox, he noticed Michael was checking out his butt. "Something you see that interests you?" James asked with a smirk.

"I don't know what you are talking about," Michael said, staring forward but glancing at James from the corner of his eye.

"You will do well to remember who you are addressing and that this a priority job for Colonel Roberts.

James chuckled as he got on his knees in front of Michael so he could get on the creeper and roll under the jeep.

Out of the corner of his eye, James could see Michael had a slight smile. He felt his mission was accomplished as he slowly melted Michael's heart of ice. The curtain closed, and it was the end of scene one.

When the curtain opens, the spotlight is on James and Michael in line at the mess hall, and they have small talk about it being Christmas, and how they missed their holiday meals. They sat down for lunch together and discussed their favorite holiday dishes. They laughed and enjoyed one another's company. The lights go out, and there is another scene of them over time, developing a close friendship of casual flirting while playing cards

The next scene is at night. Michael is in James's tent talking when Michael notices it is getting late.

"I guess it is getting late and starting to rain, so I better get back to my tent," Michael said, looking out of James' tent.

"You can stay here tonight," James said, putting his hand on Micheal's shoulder. "I guess it can't hurt, at least till the rain lets up a bit," Michael said, looking at James hand on his shoulder. As he turned to face James, he was folded into James' strong arms.

James leaned in to kiss Micheal (just as the stage lights went out). When the stage lights returned, it was dimly lit because it was the middle of the night. Michael reached his hand out of James' tent to check to see if it was still raining. Seeing that the rain had let up, Michael got on his shoes and snuck back to his tent.

Act Two has many fast-paced wardrobe changes. It opens with a scene of James returning home as a civilian, sitting alone in his apartment, and getting invited to a party with some friends. In the next scene, James is at the party where he meets Carol, with scenes of them dating and dancing in 1950s clothing. Next are scenes of them getting married and having two children. James started receiving letters in the mail from Michael, and it left him conflicted.

James contemplates writing back to Micheal as he rereads them when no one is around. Eventually, the letters stop, and he starts fighting with Carol over the most minor things. He does not know why he fights with Carol, but he cannot control his anger.

James becomes distant from his family and does not come home till late. One day, heading home, he stopped at a rest area to use the bathroom. While James was doing his business, someone kept tapping their foot under the stall and then put their hand under, waving him to come closer. He was not sure what exactly was going on. He finished his business, and as he was heading out, he stopped in front of the stall, trying to look inside to see who it was on the other side when the door opened, and someone pulled him inside for the most surprising yet satisfying hook-up in years.

Eventually, Carol asked for a divorce, and James got his own place and started stopping off at the same rest area more and more. Sometimes, the same nice-looking young man was there, but sometimes he was not. The last time James stopped there, the guy James liked to hook up with was sitting in his truck as James pulled up. They talked, and he found out the guy's name was Arthur, a married man of three and a farmer.

Arthur shares that his family had no idea he was out looking for action. They thought he was farming the fields or taking care of the pigs. They started meeting regularly at a local motel. While lying in bed together, James shared that he felt dirty stopping off at the truck stop, so it was nice to be with one person and to be in a hotel instead of at the rest area.

Act three opens, and it is now the end of the '60s. James is in a new apartment and now has a job as a mechanic at a local car dealer. He thinks that moving closer to Arthur would convince him to leave his family, and they would be together. However, Arthur could not leave his family and unexpectedly passed away from a mysterious illness not long after.

In the second-to-last scene, James is at the store picking up groceries when he looks up and sees a familiar face on the other side of the bananas. It was Michael, and they were awkwardly talking over the bananas, trying to figure out where each other was in their lives. There was a pause as someone walked up, squeezing the fruit before moving on. "We should get coffee sometime," Michael recommended.

"Actually, my apartment is around the corner if you ever want to visit," James said. "I have…" There was a pause as another person walked up, grabbed some bananas, and then moved on. "I have missed talking to you."

The final scene opens in James's apartment. James and Micheal are talking about their lives and where they are heading.

"I'm sorry I never responded to the letters you sent," James responded. "I read every letter that came and kept them in a shoebox."

"You read them?" Michael asked. "I wondered if you were even receiving them because I never heard back, and after about a year and a half. I stopped writing. Then, I continued writing for a while, as it was enjoyable to record my thoughts and feelings on paper. I thought that for you, it must have been a one-off and that you had just been lonely at the time, and I was the closest thing at the moment."

"A one-off?" James chuckled. "If my memory serves me, it was definitely more than a one-off. It was several times."

Micheal laughed. "Fair enough. Eventually, I met someone else, and we built a life together until he left me for someone younger, but you were always in my heart. There were whispers of you everywhere, and I thought I was in this queer love alone."

"I know what you mean. Everything I did and everywhere I went, I thought of you. I tried to fill the void you left in my life," James explains and sighs. "It breaks my heart that I never responded to you and lived alone for so long. After a while, it got easier to go on without you, but I was afraid to fall for you again only to have you taken away from me, but you always remained in my heart, too."

"You have always been my everything," Michael says to James as he places his hand on the back of James's neck.

"My life means nothing without you, and I'm in this queer love with you," James said as he stepped forward and kissed Micheal instead of embracing as they did in rehearsals, and the crowd gasped. Many of them had never seen two men kissing before.

Mrs. Thomas gasped with the crowd and put her hand to her mouth. "What the ….I am totally done for," she said. "They will not allow us to continue the full run." Just as the crowd stood and gave an ovation, the curtain came down on the two still kissing. Everyone was standing and applauding except one group of people who, after the shock of what just happened, subsided, got up, and walked out of the theatre. It happened to be a group from the church called the House of Faith.

"Oh my god, oh my god," Mrs. Thomas kept repeating with her hand over her mouth.

"What were you thinking?" she hissed at Jake and Sheldon. "You are going to get us shut down." They started to go out for their final bow when Mrs. Thomas turned to see the principal glaring at her.

"Um, I have to go to take my bow now," Mrs. Thomas said, turning to head through the curtain but having trouble finding the opening through her panic.

"You two are dead," she said through gritted teeth as she took her place between Jake and Sheldon, taking their hand, smiling, and bowing. The crowd stood and applauded for a long time, and afterward, people kept praising the cast for their fantastic job. The local paper gave a stellar review of the play and the acting—something you would expect from a big-time production. The writing was next level.

All this praise made it hard for the Principal to shut it down because people shared that they were coming back to watch it again and asked if they could extend the show times.

A few complaints were lodged with the Principal and the board, but they were from people who did not even have children who went to the school, and several of the complaints came from the House of Faith.

The second night of the play had people outside protesting, saying that it was an abomination against god and that anyone who witnessed such wickedness would burn in hell. The protestors' attention only made it more popular, and people from surrounding towns started showing up to watch.

Eventually, the news got to the mainstream newspapers, and someone from New York came to watch the last night and loved the play so much that they asked Mrs. Thomas if she would come to New York and put the play on for the off-Broadway crowd.

Chapter Six

Aunt Mae

It was early Saturday morning and after weeks of therapy, Chase was itching to leave the house. He was going stir-crazy. He wanted to get out of town, so he decided to go and see his Aunt Mae in Mount Carmel, whom he had not seen in years. Aunt Mae was his dad's sister, whom they had not talked to in years, but Chase stayed in touch through the occasional letter. Sheldon pulled up in front of Chase's house, who was already sitting on the front porch waiting. He always had a smile on his face every time he was about to see Sheldon or spend time with him.

"Aren't you eager to get this party started," Sheldon asked, rolling down the window so he could talk to Chase as he approached the car.

"Do you mind if I drive since I know the way?" Chase asked, walking up to the car.

"You absolutely can," Sheldon responded, climbing into the passenger seat.

"You know I love to drive every chance I get," Chase said, beaming from ear to ear.

"I know, and you don't have to ask me twice," Sheldon said with a chuckle as Chase climbed into the driver's seat.

"Why have you not seen your Aunt in years?" Sheldon asked as they drove out of town.

"My Dad and Aunt Mae had a falling out some years ago. I think it had something to do with her moving to the States from their hometown in France, where my Dad and Aunt Mae grew up, to marry someone he disapproved of, but I have never been able to get a straight answer from anyone," Chase explained. "I asked Mom once, but she said I had to ask my Father."

"Also, we never discussed it in our letters," Chase stated. "Maybe I will find out today."

"A year ago, Aunt Mae shared that she had moved to Mount Carmel from Kentucky and had asked me a couple of times to visit her now that she lived closer, but it never seemed to happen, and time always got away from me," Chase explained. "So, thank you for agreeing to come with me because I don't think I would have done it alone."

"You're welcome," Sheldon responded with a smile.

"So, how is the job as a teacher's aide?" Chase asked as they drove down the highway, and Sheldon smiled before responding.

"I'm not sure how I got this opportunity, but I love it," Sheldon replied, looking out the window. "Every day, it's something new, and time flies by while I'm there. A part of me thinks about becoming a teacher myself."

Chase put his hand on Sheldon's leg. "I love that for you," Chase said, flashing him another smile, and Sheldon placed his hand on his.

Chase pulled Sheldon's hand to his lips and kissed it. He looked over to Sheldon and smiled his dimple smile, which warmed Sheldon's heart and gave him goosebumps. Being in love with the man of your dreams was one of the greatest feelings in the world, and feeling that love in return was indescribable. Sheldon wished he could share this feeling with the world and for everyone to feel this amazing. His body tingled with every kiss of his hand, and he felt like he was flying on top of the world as if nothing could stop them.

"How is school going?" Sheldon asked as they drove.

"I feel so behind, and it's hard not being as active with sports, and I can't wait for the doctor to release me to play again," Chase explained. Unfortunately, Sheldon could not relate to not being able to play sports, but it reminded him every year after winter was over and being able to play outdoors again. "The guidance counselor told me I might have to take summer school to make up for what I missed last semester."

"It seems silly to make you take classes in the summer," Sheldon stated. "Seems like you should be able to test out of it because you only missed a few months. Now that I say it out loud, it feels overwhelming thinking about making up all the work even after just a few months."

"Are you excited about graduating soon?" Chase asked.

"I am, but it's kind of scary at the same time," Sheldon acknowledged. "We spend so much time itching to be out of school, and as it is getting closer, it's a bit nerve-racking, so I'm trying not to think about it." Chase pulled Sheldon's hand to his lips and kissed it again.

They entered the city limits of Mount Carmel. "We used to visit our grandmother when she lived here," Sheldon explained. "My mom grew up here."

"Maybe we can drive by her old place if you like," Chase offered.

"That would be nice," Sheldon said with a smile.

"Maybe we can do it on the way out of town," Chase offered. We are about a block from my Aunt's place, but now I'm second-guessing this idea because I have not seen her in years, so I don't know how welcoming the family will be."

They pulled in front of a faded white two-story corner house across from the Water Department. The house looked to need some new paint and windows, and the roof appeared to be in the middle of a repair or replacement, which his Aunt Mae had shared in one of her letters that his Uncle started months ago but never finished.

Chase knocked on the metal screen door. They noticed the wooden front door was open when someone shouted to enter.

"Come on in, I'm back here," a female voice instructed as she cleared her throat.

As they stepped inside, they saw the living room, which had a dark brown floral couch covered in clothes, papers, and what appeared to be dead flowers. The coffee table was covered in soda cans, dirty coffee cups, and plates. Sheldon and Chase immediately looked at each other with wide eyes. There was a door to their left, which they could see had a hospital bed and clothes piled everywhere.

Chase was unsure what he expected to experience, but this was not it or what he was used to. He felt embarrassed that he brought Sheldon into this situation, but they were already in full swing, and there was no going back because they had already entered the house.

"I'm back here, "the voice called out, this time slightly hoarse and breathy, coming from the back of the house.

They made their way through the living room, and Sheldon immediately whispered, "I'm not taking off my shoes." The carpet was dirty brown and covered in hair as they made their way into the kitchen, which had dirty dishes stacked up to the bottom of the wall cabinets, and the sink was full.

"I would come and greet you, but I'm doing one of my breathing treatments," she explained with a pouty lip from the dining room, which was through a doorway left of the kitchen.

"It's about time you finally came to see your Aunt Mae," she teased. Then she put a clear tube in her mouth, connected to a machine, mak-ing a humming sound as she inhaled deeply. Vapor fumes came out of her mouth as she asked, "And who is this nice-looking gentleman friend you have brought with you?" She chuckled and then coughed.

Sheldon went to sit down, but all the chairs were full of grocery bags containing random items. "Oh, just throw that stuff on the floor," Aunt Mae said, annoyed. "I have told them to put their stuff away so many times." She huffed.

Sheldon reluctantly placed the bags on the floor because there was nowhere else to put them and sat down.

"This is my friend, Sheldon. I wrote to you about it," Chase explained.

"You will have to forgive me, but I was recently diagnosed with emphysema because of years of smoking and working in that damn factory, so I have to do these breathing treatments every day," she explained as she turned the machine off and put the hose on top of the machine and then grabbed a long slender clear tube. "This here is my oxygen, which helps me breathe," she stated as she put it over her ears and then into her nose.

"Ain't I just a lovely site," she asked jokingly. "So, tell me, how is that son of a bitch father of yours doing?"

Chase was taken back at first before responding, "He is doing well."

"He moved this close to me and cannot be bothered to come and see his little sister," she said, taking a sip of something out of a cup with a straw. Sheldon was surprised she said she was younger because, after seeing her, he thought she was much older than Chase's dad.

"He has been busy with getting his business..." Chase started to say but she interrupted him before he could finish.

"Hey, no need to make excuses for him. Remember, I knew him before you were even born," Aunt Mae said, looking around her place. "Sorry about the mess. I asked them to clean up after themselves because I can't do it anymore. They just completely ignore me, so I get to live in this lovely mess that keeps piling up around me."

"Terry, my so-called husband, was supposed to be fixing the roof, but as you can see, he started it but never finished. That was almost a year ago!" she said, completely losing her breath as she pulled out an inhaler and took a puff.

"Sorry, the doctor told me not to get myself worked up, but that bastard moved me from my nice home in Kentucky to this dump, which he promised he was going to fix up, but here we are in this lovely mess," She paused wiping tears from her eyes. "I will tell you something else..." Just then, they heard a noise. It was someone coming down the stairs.

"That's the prick now finally getting up," Aunt Mae grumbled under her breath. He walked into the kitchen and grabbed a six pack of beer out of the fridge. "Where are you off to," she asked as he headed into the living room, ignoring his wife and guests. "Hey, are you going to fix the Cadillac?"

"Yeah, yeah, I will get to it later," he said, heading out the front door.

"That lying son of bitch," she said through tears. "Sorry, I'm crying 'cause I'm pissed, but I don't know who I'm more pissed at, myself or his stupid ass." There was a sound from the front room as if someone had opened and closed the screen door. "Did that son of a bitch come back," she asked.

"No, it's me, Mom," Vanessa said as she entered the dining room. "Mom, why are you crying?"

"Why do you think?" Aunt Mae said, wiping her tears away.

"I don't know why you don't just throw that asshole out," Vanessa said. "Sorry, I'm Vanessa," she said, turning to Sheldon to shake his hand.

"Look who finally came around," Vanessa teased, turning towards Chase. "Mr. California himself."

Chase did not know how to respond. "I'm just giving you shit," she said, bumping his shoulders with her hips. "Soooo, is this a friend or a *friend?*" She asked in air quotes.

"Vanessa!" Aunt Mae shrieked. "I raised you better than that. But inquiring minds would like to know," she said with a chuckle, leaning forward and placing her boobs on top of the table, waiting to hear the juicy details.

"Um, Sheldon and I are…" he looked at Sheldon, who gave an approving nod as Vanessa and Aunt Mae leaned in even more. "He is my boyfriend," Chase replied.

Hearing Chase call him his boyfriend gave Sheldon goosebumps and warmed his heart.

"I knew it!" Vanessa shouted. "Peter owes me fifty bucks." Aunt Mae just shook her head at Vanessa!

"I told him you were gay," Vanessa explained.

"Actually, I'm bi, but I guess it doesn't matter," Chase explained.

"Well, I, for one, think it is a great thing," Aunt Mae said with a huge smile. "Peter is my son," she explained, looking at Sheldon.

"How is Peter?" Chase asked.

"He is doing well," Aunt Mae responded. He just left to go to school in Paris. He is going to study marketing," she proudly explained, her head held high.

"Clean off that chair and sit down," Aunt Mae instructed.

"I can't. I have to go pick up Barb," she explained, walking into the kitchen.

Aunt Mae mouthed *Barb* with a snarl and rolled her eyes. Sheldon and Chase tried to hold in their laughter at the faces Mae was making.

"Mom! You better be nice," Vanessa demanded, knowing her mom was probably making faces because she did not care for Barb.

"What?! I'm a sweet angel," Aunt Mae said with a chuckle. "Right, boys?"

"I'm sure you are," she said as she returned to the dining room carrying a sandwich. "I gotta go, Mom." She started to leave.

"Are you forgetting something?" Aunt Mae called after Vanessa.

"Mom! Seriously?" She huffed as she walked back into the dining room from the living room. She bent over, kissed her mom on the cheek, and rolled her eyes at Sheldon and Chase.

"Be safe out there," Aunt Mae requested as Vanessa walked into the living room. "You can leave that piece of garbage on the curb and don't drag her back here," she half mumbled.

"I heard that!" Vanessa shouted as she went out the front door.

"I'm glad you did cause that was kind of the point," Aunt Mae cackled. "Love ya!"

"I love you, too!" Vanessa shouted through the front door.

"What you must think of us, Sheldon," Aunt Mae chuckled.

"Her girlfriend, if you can call her that, is a little B.I.T.C.H.," Aunt Mae gaffed. "I cannot tell you how many times that sweet girl of mine called me crying to come and get her because of that, "she almost said bitch but refrained. "I call her Barb the butch, and she doesn't scare me. I will kick her little ass if she crosses my path again."

"Sorry, so that woman, if you can even call her a woman, had my baby girl in tears so bad the last time, she was bawling so hard she couldn't even get out the words, let alone breathe. She swore that was the last time, but like a drug addict, she could not quit. I don't know what to do with her."

"So, how does Peter like Paris?" Chase asked.

"He loves it," she replied. "He has a roommate from Maryland or Maine, one of those eastern states, who is studying journalism."

"Journalism? Paris?" Chase questioned more to himself than anyone else.

"Yeah, he has an internship at one of their major newspapers." It was clear by Chase's face that this information intrigued him.

"What are you planning to do after you graduate?" Aunt Mae asked.

"I'm thinking of going into journalism myself," Chase responded.

"Well, if you're interested in something in Paris, let me know, and I can tell Peter to call you the next time I talk to him."

"That would be amazing," Chase responded. "I guess we should head back home."

"Do you have to hurry off now?" Aunt Mae asked.

"Yeah, Sheldon has his closing of the play tonight," Chase explained.

"A play? That sounds fancy," Aunt Mae remarked. "I wish I could come and see it but I hardly ever leave this house."

"We will have to come back again soon and visit," Sheldon offered.

"You better," she said.

"Is there anything we can get you before we leave," Chase offered.

"No, Hun, but you can tell that father of yours to call his sister," Aunt Mae requested as they got up from the table and hugged her.

"Don't be a stranger," she requested as they walked through the livingroom to head out.

"What street did your mom used to live on?" Chase asked as they were getting into the car.

"It was on North Elm Street," Sheldon responded once they were in the car.

As they drove by the house his mother grew up in, it felt so much smaller and lonelier than he remembered it. "I guess we have seen it, and it's not like we can go inside," Sheldon said.

"Yeah, sometimes when we go back to something, it is not always how we remember it to be," Chase stated.

"Thank you for driving me to see it and allowing me to come with you to meet your Aunt," Sheldon said. "Boyfriend, huh." They both smiled as Sheldon grabbed Chase's hand and Sheldon kissed his hand.

On the ride home, Chase and Sheldon were quiet and seemed lost in their thoughts.

The thought of losing Chase panicked Sheldon, who could not imagine his life now without him because he had become accustomed to having him in it.

He decided not to think about it and to cross that bridge when it came. He dropped Chase off at home. On his drive home, Sheldon could not help but feel guilty about not wanting Chase to go away to school, but he knew it was not fair either to want to hold him back.

Chapter Seven

The Bond

The Monday after the play closed, Sheldon arrived at Mrs. Casey's class. "You are famous," Mrs. Casey said, as he entered. The children applauded and cheered. Sheldon turned twelve shades of red. She stood beside him and whispered, "Some of them saw it with their parents, so they might have questions."

They had cookies and Kool-Aid to celebrate the day as they worked on their art projects, which was to draw what they saw for their future jobs or journeys. Sheldon was sitting with Tara, watching her draw what appeared to be a house and a dog.

"Were you not grossed out having to kiss that boy," Tara candidly asked as she drew a stick figure next to the house.

"I did not really think about it," Sheldon said, somewhat caught off guard by the question. "I was acting, pretending to be someone else."

"That kind of sounds like my parents when they think people are watching," Tara said as she drew a big sun in the corner of the paper.

"What is this supposed to be?" Sheldon asked.

"This is me with my dog and we live alone," Tara replied.

"So, no kids or husband?" Sheldon asked.

"No, they are just a liability," Tara responded.

"Where did you hear that word?" Sheldon asked, quite taken aback that she knew the word and used it in the correct context.

"I think I heard it on *Murphy Brown*," Tara responded as she continued to draw.

"So, if you are not going to have a husband or kids, what do you think you will do for a living?" Sheldon asked.

Tara pondered for a bit before responding. "I want to become a veterinarian to take care of people's pets," Tara replied. "Little girls' dads might not have to put them down if more veterinarians charge less money.

"What do you mean?" Sheldon asked, very confused, but quickly regretted asking.

Without looking up from the drawing, she says, "Anytime one of our pets got sick, Daddy would take it out back with a shovel, and it never came back. Sometimes, I think he made up that they were sick because he was always complaining about them being another mouth to feed or he would do things to them, and they would die."

Sheldon had no idea how to respond and was utterly speechless. He was afraid to ask any more questions because he was afraid of what he might hear next and did not want to find out any more information. This explanation provided a clear understanding of why Tara acted the way she did.

Sheldon helped the students put their stuff away and then he grabbed his bag to head Mrs. Hartley's classroom. He stopped by Mrs. Casey's desk.

"Do you ever feel like a complete mess and struggle to hold it together so no one can see?" Sheldon asked.

"Every day," she replied, putting her head on her desk and raising it. "Why? Is it that obvious?"

"No, I was thinking about myself," Sheldon said with a chuckle.

"You are too young to be worried about that, but I get it," She responded. "What has got you feeling like this?"

"I don't know… It's just that I'm about to graduate, and I have no idea what I want to do with my life," Sheldon replied.

"Trust me. Most people your age have no clue, and they are just going along with whatever someone has told them to be in their lives or an idea of who they think they should be. One day, it will all change, or they will wake up and realize it's not what they wanted for their lives and then change it, and if they can't, they learn to live with it."

She lowers her voice. "And, in some cases, people turn to drinking or other things, if you know what I mean. You'll be just fine.

Just keep putting one foot in front of the other and strive to improve yourself. Don't be too hard on yourself if you think progress is happening too slowly. Trust me, you keep trying, and somehow, it will come together someday."

"Thank you, I needed that," Sheldon responded.

"And remember, if you ever need to talk, you know where to find me. Unless I win the lottery and take off to some deserted island," She joked. "You better get out of here before that is the least of your concerns." They both laughed.

When he arrived at Mrs. Hartley's class, it was unusually busy, and the kids were working on an art project.

Has anything exciting been happening lately?" Mrs. Hartley casually asked, barely looking up from a paper she was grading. "Do you mind making a couple of copies for me?" she asked, handing him a paper.

"Umm, okay," Sheldon said, turning to walk towards the door, confused about why everyone was acting weird. He looked at the paper just before he opened the door, as there was some shuffling going on behind him, but he was too distracted reading what the paper said to take notice. The paper read, "Congratulations on your successful performance of *Whispers of You*."

He started to get a bit emotional as he turned to see the children lined up across the room, each holding a letter they had colored that said, "Congratulations, Sheldon Majors." Mrs. Hartley said, "Wait a minute." She rushed over to the end with a big exclamation point that she had personally colored herself. Sheldon could not contain himself and got emotional.

"Boys don't cry," Hunter said.

"That's not true," Mrs. Hartley commented.

"Okay, everyone, return to your seats and take out your math books," Mrs. Hartley requested. "Seriously, though, congratulations," said turning towards Sheldon.

"Thank you," Sheldon said. "What do you need done today?"

"There are some papers on the corner of my desk that need to be graded," she responded before turning her attention to the students.

§

It was finals week and Sheldon had liked Mrs. Smith's Biology class so much that he had decided to take her geology class for his last semester. He found learning about the tectonic plates and the Earth's movements throughout history fascinating. He especially liked studying fossils, the history of life on Earth, and where it all came from.

However, he was not looking forward to the final exam. Part of it involved identifying rock samples she had setup around the room and identifying and explaining different erosions, which he found easier than the fifteen multiple-choice questions.

"If only my other finals were this easy," Sheldon said on their way out of class.

"Tell me about it," Charlize said. "See you at graduation."

"See you there," Sheldon responded. He was glad he had connected with Charlize and ended things with her on a good note.

They bonded over the things they had each gone through and were able to laugh about how their journey began together and how they came full circle and ended their school journey together.

§

On Sheldon's last day as a teacher's aide, he entered Mrs. Casey's class, and they had prepared a party for him. Each student had made a drawing for him. He was emotional as the students went around the room, sharing what their drawings meant and what they learned from Sheldon.

"You can tell the kids have really bonded with you," Mrs. Casey stated. You have made an impact that will stick with them for some time.

"Also, I got you a little something, too," Mrs. Casey said, handing Sheldon a colorful and beautifully wrapped gift. "Go ahead and open it."

Sheldon slowly started to unwrap the gift not wanting to rip the paper. "Go ahead and rip into the paper," Mrs. Casey requested. "The suspense is killing me, and I know what's inside!" They both laughed.

It was a slender box, and Sheldon started removing the lid. "Now, you can return it if you don't like it. I saw it and thought of you," Mrs. Casey explained, anxiously awaiting his reaction.

It was a beautiful navy-blue sweater with a gold stripe across the chest. "Did you see it's a turtleneck? It has a zipper for when you don't want it to be, and you can fold it over the neck," Mrs. Casey showed him.

"It's beautiful!" Sheldon said, hugging her and getting a little emotional.

There is also a tie in there," Mrs. Casey said. "I'm told it is very hip with the younger people." They both chuckle.

"Wow, it is very niiiiice," Sheldon said, as he pulled it out of the box. "I have never had a tie this nice."

"You better get next door. We cannot have you be late on your last day,' She joked as she hugged him goodbye.

Before Sheldon walked out of the door, he turned to take one more look at the students. Some looked up to say goodbye and waved as he walked out the door.

When Sheldon entered Mrs. Hartley's class for the last time, it was strangely busy.

"Hey, Sheldon, come on in," she said, unusually cheerful. "We are just celebrating our last day together because a couple of students are not here on Friday, so we thought we could all celebrate our last day together."

The room had a few banners put up that the students worked on in groups and signed their names on. "Sheldon, will you do the honor of signing each of the banners?" Mrs. Hartley requested. Who knows, your signature might be worth something one day when you become famous."

As Sheldon signed the banners, they started going around the room, stating what they learned from Sheldon and from each other. After they finished, it was time for cupcakes and homemade punch. "Also, everyone has made their own hand-made card for you, too," Mrs. Hartley explained, as Hunter handed him a stack of papers.

"Here is just a little something for you from me," Mrs. Hartley said, handing Sheldon a big envelope. "Something for your future."

Sheldon opened the envelope, which included a thank you card and something he had never seen before. "It's a savings bond," Mrs. Hartley explained. "It matures over time; eventually, you can cash it in or continue to let it grow interest."

"I don't know what to say," Sheldon said.

"It's nothing, really," she said.

"Thank you," Sheldon said, wanting to hug her, but she did not seem to be the hugging type.

"Come here," she said, giving him a big hug. "Now get out of here early before you make me emotional, and do not forget us," she requested, pointing her finger at him.

"I can never forget you and what this has meant to me, too," Sheldon said, grabbing his bag and waving to the class as he walked out the door for the last time.

Chapter Eight

Jerni James

Chase and Sheldon were getting back into town. They had gone to buy outfits to wear to Sheldon's graduation. "I have my last physical therapy appointment tomorrow afternoon," Chase stated. I've tried to reschedule, but I've had no luck. I'm determined to get back in time to attend your graduation."

"Do not worry about it," Sheldon said. "Do what you go to do."

"We can do our own celebration afterwards," Chase said, biting his lip.

"Now that sounds like a graduation gift I could use," Sheldon responded as he pulled into the grocery store parking lot to pick up some things for his Mom.

Mandy was planning to have a cookout to celebrate the day after his graduation but needed a couple of items. "You want to come in with me?" Sheldon asked, putting the car into park. "I only have to get a few items."

"I think I will wait here," Chase responded, deep in thought.

"You want me to grab you anything?" Sheldon offered.

"No, I think I'm good, thanks," Chase replied, half-smiling.

Sheldon was going to grab a shopping cart but opted for a basket instead because he was not getting that much stuff. Plus, it would help him avoid getting more than he needed. He turned the corner of the aisle, almost running into someone's cart.

"I'm so sorry," Sheldon said as he continued down the aisle.

"Sheldon, is that you," the lady pushing the cart asked. She had a fussy toddler in the shopping cart seat.

Sheldon turned to look, and it took him a minute to recognize his neighbor, Jerni. Their parents used to hang out together and play card games when they were young.

"I have not seen you in so long," she said, playing with her toddler's hair and trying to soothe her.

"Where have you been keeping yourself?"

"I'm still living with Mom; she works at Pathmasters now," Sheldon responded. "I will probably start to work there, too."

"Oh nice, so you have a girlfriend now, or are you married," Jerni asked, now rubbing her toddler's back.

"Umm, I well…Haven't even graduated yet," Sheldon stammered, trying to think of an appropriate response because, in most circles, he was out, but her family was very religious. Sheldon was quickly saved by Chase, who walked up next to him.

"Hey babe, I decided to get a couple of things as well," Chase said, putting his hand on Sheldon's shoulder and continuing down the aisle.

Sheldon suddenly turned red hot, unsure why it mattered, but for some reason, it did, as he glanced back at Jerni.

"Oh. Ooh," Jerni said, unsure what to say because she was slightly embarrassed, uncertain of how to act around gay people, but also somewhat intrigued.

"Remember when I was your first kiss? Because I do," Jerni coyly said with a smile.

Sheldon was caught entirely off guard by her statement and was trying to scan his memory of what she was eluding to, and it hit him. She was confusing the history.

"No, that was not me, remember…

§

Sheldon and Levin's Dad, Vernon, drove their blue and white Surban up their neighbor's long driveway. "Now boys, I want you to be on your best behavior and play nice with their son," their mother commanded from the passenger seat, turning to see if they acknowledged her request.

"I need to use the bathroom," Levin said because he always had stomach issues anytime, they went anywhere and could not use other people's bathrooms.

"Too bad because we are not turning around and going home. You will have to use the neighbor's bathroom," their mom demanded.

Levin moaned and put his head to the window. Mrs. Jenny Fisher greeted them before they had a chance to get out of their vehicle.

"Boys, Chad is out back playing with his friend. If you wanna join him, "Jenny told Sheldon and Levin.

"Here are the baked beans," Mandy said, handing Jenny a crockpot.

"Oh, great! Thank you," she said. "You can put it over... On that counter, which has an electrical outlet."

"Denis is in the backyard grilling up the steaks if you want to join him, Vernon," Jenny said, turning her attention to Vernon and then back to Mandy.

Sheldon sat in a swing in the backyard and watched Levin walk over to where Chad and Logan were playing. Sheldon knew to steer clear of Chad when he had a friend around because he would treat Sheldon and Levin like subordinates to show off in front of his friend, so Sheldon opted out and let Levin forge ahead onto the battlefield.

Ironically, it appeared they were about to play army or something similar that typical eleven-year-old boys would play, which never made sense to Sheldon. They were in Levin's grade, so he didn't know Logan, but Chad rode the school bus with them and was usually quiet. But in true Chad fashion, today, Chad was being very bossy, showing off in front of Logan.

Sheldon heard some giggles and turned to see Jerni and some girl looking out the window and laughing.

Sheldon looked back to where the boys were playing some army game, they had on camouflage jackets, and were putting some camouflage paint on their faces. Levin did not seem to want to play along. Suddenly, Sheldon heard tapping and turned to see the girls waving him to come inside.

"Forget it, Chad. I'm not going to play your stupid game anyway," Levin shouted as Sheldon turned to see Levin walking towards where Sheldon was sitting in the swing.

As Levin plopped down in the swing next to Sheldon, they could hear Chad yelling, "We don't need you anyway, Majors.

Come on, Logan." The two boys took off, heading for the barn with sticks for guns.

There was tapping and giggling again. Jerni opened the window, "Come inside. You don't want to play with Chad anyways."

Sheldon looked at Levin, whose face went pale. Neither of them was used to talking with older girls, or girls in general, except for their older sister. Sheldon could not remember if she was 13 or 14.

When Sheldon and Levin entered through the patio door, it was clear that the girls had been painting each other's nails. "I want to do Shelby's toenails, but my hair keeps getting in the way," Jerni said, glancing back and forth between Sheldon and Levin. Sheldon looked at Levin, exploring his face to see if he knew what they should do with this information. Levin only looked at Sheldon and shrugged his shoulders because he was just as confused.

Seeing the confused looks on their faces, Jerni decided to explain further. "Can you put my hair up so I can paint her nails? If you could do a French braid, that would be amazing." Sheldon looked at Levin, who had a horrified look on his face as Jerni got into position to have her hair done.

Sheldon remembered that Ninnie had shown him how to do it years ago, but he had forgotten how to do it. "Sure," Sheldon responded, but he felt betrayed by his own mouth, as he had agreed to do something he had no real experience with. However, something about Jerni's confidence in them felt pretty good, and hanging out with older kids felt cool.

He felt like this was his opportunity to fit in for once. He looked at Levin, and his face was still pale, and he was frozen in place.

Sheldon started by dividing her hair like Ninnie had shown him. "Don't be afraid to pull it really tight," Jerni said. "I like a tight braid."

"You know what," Shelby finally spoke. "How about if Levin paints my toes?" She stuck her feet out at Levin in a flirty way.

At this point, Sheldon could no longer hold in his laughter because he thought Levin was about to pass out.

"Don't worry, you two, we won't tell anyone," Jerni said, sensing their concern. "Besides, Chad does this for us when no one is around. But don't tell anybody because he would kill me."

This news immediately calmed Levin's fears enough to pick up the nail polish bottle.

"Wait," Shelby said, causing Levin to jump. "Instead of that purple, do this pink one." She handed him the bottle.

"Okay, so where were we… oh yes, you were about to kiss Josh, but your dad walked into your room," Jerni said as Sheldon struggled to get her braid straight and tight.

"Oh yeah," Shelby picked back up their conversation as if nothing had just happened. "My dad was pissed. You should have seen Josh climb out that window, practically jumping out of the tree as he climbed down. My dad did tell Josh previously that if he caught him anywhere near me, he would cut his dick off and shove it down his throat," Shelby said candidly, looking at Levin's work.

"Have you kissed anyone," Jerni asked over her shoulder to Sheldon and then looked at Levin.

"No," Levin quickly responded as Sheldon remained quiet.

"Shelby here can show you how it's done," Jerni teased as she looked directly at Levin, whose eyes were the size of saucers.

"All done," Sheldon said, finishing the last piece and putting on the hair band. He was impressed how it started out great but went sideways, and some pieces stuck out. Hopefully, she won't look at it that closely.

"I don't want to get anyone pregnant," Levin blurted out as Shelby was pretending to lean in and kiss him.

"You what," Shelby asked in a very southern accent. Sheldon had already told Levin you cannot get a girl pregnant by simply kissing her. Levin shared this thought with Sheldon while riding bikes to their grandmother's house last summer. Sheldon initially thought he was joking and died laughing when he discovered he was not kidding.

"I have to use the bathroom," Sheldon suddenly said, standing up and heading to Chad's bedroom, which had its own bathroom. He had to escape the embarrassment Levin was about to face. Sheldon jumped when he saw Logan sitting in the dark on Chad's bed, looking upset. It was so dark that he barely noticed him at first.

"You, okay?" Sheldon asked.

"Yeah," Logan responded, lying back in bed. "Chad went to a dark place and I couldn't follow, thinking about calling my mom to pick me up."

"Sorry to hear that," Sheldon responded, sitting on the bed. "When you say dark place."

"He climbed up a tree and into some rocks that looked like a cave," Logan responded as Sheldon put his hand on Logan's leg.

"Oh, sorry that happened," Sheldon said, surprised he was so bold to put his hand on Logan, who he thought did not seem to take notice, but he did and moved closer to Sheldon as if he was about to kiss Sheldon.

Suddenly, the bedroom door handle started turning, and Sheldon panicked and ran to the bathroom. He was unsure why he did that; maybe it was because Sheldon did not want Chad to catch him sitting on his bed or because of how close he was to Logan.

Sheldon was not sure what was happening because the room became quiet, so he quietly opened the door to peek out to see if the coast was clear. The room was dimly lit, but he could make out Jerni sitting on the bed and leaning down to kiss Logan, who, in this light, looked very similar to Sheldon. He was surprised by how deep they were kissing and using tongues.

Suddenly, there was a slight commotion as they both suddenly realized who they were kissing. Jerni jumped off the bed, and Logan scooted away from her. Sheldon was so shocked by what he witnessed that he opened the door quite a bit.

"I thought you were…." Logan started to say to Jerni but stopped before saying a name and looked at Sheldon with wide eyes and confusion. They were both looking at Sheldon, whose mouth was half open. He was jealous that it was not his lips touching Logan's.

"I thought I could be your first kiss," Jerni shrieked at Sheldon. "I didn't know Logan was in here." She said, whipping her mouth. "I can't believe I kissed my brother's friend. You can't tell anyone," she said, pointing at both of them and then fleeing the room as if that would make what just happened never to have existed.

Sheldon did not know what to do at this point. He felt he should comfort Logan, but what if Chad came in and saw him in his room with Logan, which could set Chad off. Should he go check on Jerni? He was afraid to do that, too. Sheldon left Chad's bedroom and acted as if nothing had happened.

When he walked back into the den where the girls and Levin were talking about how nice Shelby's nails turned out. "What do you think, Sheldon?" Jerni asked when she had noticed he had come back into the room.

"Looks…" Sheldon was searching for the correct answer, but his mind was blank, and he felt the blood leaving his face.

"Well, I think it looks gorgeous," Levin said, saving Sheldon from whatever was going on with him.

Jerni gave Sheldon a sharp look before turning her attention back to Shelby as Chad entered through the patio door.

"Have you seen Logan?" Chad asked.

"Why would we know where your friend is?" Jerni asked, giving Sheldon the side eye, which told him to remain quiet because his mouth was open as if he was about to say something.

Chad grunted as he headed to his bedroom. Just then, Mrs. Fisher called them all to come and eat.

§

Monday morning, Sheldon was sitting in his usual spot on the bus. The older kids sat in the back, and the younger kids sat in the front, so Sheldon liked to sit in the middle of the bus. The bus stopped to let on the Fishers, and Chad rushed on first and sat two rows behind Sheldon, not even noticing him until his sister Jerni unexpectedly sat down next to Sheldon.

As the bus took off, Jerni looked over at Sheldon. "I wanted to apologize," Jerni whispered, staring straight forward. "I was upset by what happened and took it out on you." She continued, still staring forward.

"No worries," Sheldon responded, unsure what to say.

"I can't stop thinking about it and cannot talk to anyone about it," she confessed, looking at Sheldon as if he was going to provide some sage wisdom.

"If you like him, why not tell him," Sheldon offered.

"Ew! Are you crazy? He is my brother's best friend," she hissed. "I guess I could go to one of his soccer games and watch him. No, that is just crazy." She started talking more to herself. "My brother is on the same team. I could pretend I'm there to watch him play. No, I don't think he would believe that after all this time, I suddenly take an interest in watching him play."

"Okay, I have a game plan you will go with me. Yeah, that's a brilliant idea. Thanks, Sheldon," she said, getting up and heading to the back of the bus, leaving Sheldon confused as to what just happened and what he agreed to.

§

Jerni's kid was getting restless in the shopping cart. "Oh, that is right. I had forgotten about that," Jerni acknowledged, trying to settle her toddler. "We even went to a couple of games. Why did we stop going to them?"

"Remember, he moved away," Sheldon explained.

"Oh yeah," She said kind of dreamily. "I always hoped I would run into Logan again one day." Her daydream was interrupted by her kid pulling on her shirt. "I better get going this one is getting restless. It was great seeing you. We have to catch up more later." She started to walk away and stopped and was rummaging through her purse. "Here is my business card in case you know of anyone needing my services."

Sheldon looked at the business card, which read Jerni James Detective Agency, and thought about how much detective work there could be in this small town.

"You would be surprised how busy people keep me," she said as if she read his mind. "I also, do work in the surrounding counties as well. Actually, it was something you had said years ago that inspired me, but that's another story for another time, gotta go." At this point her kid was screaming they wanted something they saw on one of the shelves. "Don't be a stranger," she said as she disappeared around the corner.

Sheldon grabbed what they needed from the store, and as he headed to the car, he racked his brain about what he had said to

Jerni to inspire her to become a detective. "Who was that?" Chase asked as Sheldon got into the car.

"One of our neighbors growing up. Our parents used to hang out," Sheldon replied.

"Well, if we don't get going, you're going to be late for your graduation rehearsal," Chase stated. "We must drop the refrigerated stuff at my house first because you don't have time to run it to your house."

Sheldon looked at the clock and didn't realize how long he had been in the store talking to Jerni. "You better put the metal to the pedal," Chased recommended.

"I think you meant to say, put the pedal to the metal," Sheldon corrected him, and they both laughed.

§

As the months went on and Charlotte's pregnancy progressed, she was home sick so much that she started doing her schoolwork from home for the last couple of months of her senior year. No one at school knew the real reason, only that she had been sick.

At the beginning of April, she and Levin renovated her Mom's guest house, which she had been using to store gardening supplies so that they could move in together. That way, Levin could help take care of her through her morning sickness and would bring her schoolwork home for her to complete.

As May drew near, Charlotte was reluctant to attend her graduation because she had started to show. Her Mom convinced her that the graduation gown would hide her baby bump, so she ordered her cap and gown.

"You cannot miss your high school graduation," her Mom said. "I want to see you walk across the stage to receive your diploma.

"It's not like the diploma is even in what they give you," Charlotte countered. "They mail it to you later."

Her Mom had her arms crossed was not having any of it. "Also, I'm not sure how I feel about the two of you living together, and you're not married," her Mom said. Charlotte gave her an immediate glare, which halted the conversation, and she did not mention it again.

Mandy glared at Levin while he and their Dad loaded his stuff into their dad's truck. His Mom was not happy about him moving out, and it put a strain on their relationship. "I don't understand why the two of you can't move in here. We have plenty of room.

"I told you, Mom, there we have a place of our own so we can have privacy," Levin exasperatedly explained.

When Sheldon got home from work, Mandy met him at the door. "Did you know he was going to move out?" Mandy asked, but with the look on Sheldon's face, she knew immediately he had no idea.

"Who are you talking about?" Sheldon asked. His first thought was that she was talking about Damian moving out.

"Levin showed up here with his dad, took some of his stuff, and said he would be back for the rest," Mandy explained.

"Honestly, I had no idea," Sheldon said. "Since he has been with Charlotte, I never see or hear from him."

Mandy fumed for days, and Sheldon tried to avoid her till she calmed down.

§

Shawndrea was driving home to visit her parents a few weeks earlier than planned for Ninnie's graduation. Earlier that day, she was bored and sitting on the couch with the coffee table covered in bridal magazines. Jack was on deployment, and she was tired of being home alone. Her little car flew down the highway with the wind in her hair, singing Alabama's *I'm In A Hurry* at the top of her lungs.

She still had a key to the house. Walking in, she was stunned to find boxes filling every room. Some were sealed and labeled with their original room, while others sat half-filled, their contents spilling over.

"What the…" Shawndrea said out loud as she walked through the empty house. A thought occurred to her as she turned to run to her room. When she opened the door, she just stood there in disbelief.

Everything was in boxes. Several boxes were labeled donate, a couple were labeled for sale, and one was labeled Shawndrea storage.

The mattress was up against the wall, and a few of her posters were ripped and barely hanging on the wall.

"Seriously," She said, stepping into what used to be her bedroom. She started to open one of the boxes when she heard the garage door open.

Her bedroom, tucked next to the garage with its own private entrance, had been her escape route for countless late-night adventures. She slipped out to meet whichever guy had caught her eye that week. To her, boys and men were challenges to conquer once she had them, or boredom set in, and she moved on without a second thought.

She heard brakes squealing as a vehicle pulled into the garage. She went to confront whoever it was. She was a bear ready for a fight. No one messes with her stuff.

"Oh hell," Letty said as she put the van in park, spotting Shawndrea standing in the doorway of her bedroom with her arms crossed and a stern look on her face.

"Ha!" Jimmy cried out. He knew shit was about to hit the fan.

Letty and Jimmy got out of the van. Letty hadn't even closed the door when Shawndrea started in. "Who the hell touched my shit" Shawndrea demanded. "I told you I was gonna do it."

"What the HELL did you expect?" Letty asked as she slammed the van door. "This SHIT isn't gonna pack itself. I told you several times to pack your shit. We are selling the house." Letty snapped back as she walked towards the door, but Shawndrea stepped before her.

"Selling the house?! Since when?" Shawndrea asked, looking surprised. "I thought you were just talking about it."

"Little lady, you better take a step back if you know what is good for you," Letty sternly requested, and Shawndrea did.

"Did the for-sale sign that's been in the front yard for the last two and a half months give you any clue that I wasn't just talking about it?" Letty asked, still standing in the garage, purse over her shoulder as she reached in and pulled out another cigarette. "Now get back in the damn house, or get out of my way!"

"I packed up your shit," Jimmy confessed with a giggle as he ran past her just out of her reach.

"Uuuuugggh, I can't stand you, people!" Shawndrea shouted as she returned to her room, slamming the door one last time.

Chapter Nine

Kidnapped

A loud noise pulled Shawndrea out of a deep sleep. She staggered to her bedroom door and cracked it open. She was half awake and did not recognize the hallway she was looking out to. She stepped into the hallway and was still confused by where she was. She saw a figure at the end of the hallway. She called out, but the figure moved away and turned into the living room. The figure appeared to be holding a long, slender object.

Shawndrea walked closer to the living room. Her mom was sleeping in a chair, and she suddenly realized they were in their old house in Louisiana.

The figure stood in the shadows and quickly turned the long, slender object towards Shawndrea's mom. Suddenly, gunfire rang out in the quick recession. Shawndrea realized the figure was holding a semi-automatic.

For a split second, she froze. Then, panic propelled her to spin around, and she sprinted down the hall in search of Ninnie or their father. As she ran, loud explosions erupted outside the house, each one shaking the walls and her resolve.

She made it to Ninnie's bedroom, and as she opened the door, she saw a gruesome scene of blood splattered on the walls, floor to ceiling. She could not wrap her mind around what or why this was happening. As she continued back down the hall, she heard a loud bang and turned to see a large cannonball approaching her.

She reached her parents' bedroom door and opened the double doors. Just as she closed the doors behind her, the cannonball ripped through the door and continued through the room, busting through the house's outer wall. Now, she could see outside through the hole, and bombs were exploding everywhere. She rushed to her parents' bed and found her father sound asleep. Desperately, she shook him, but he would not wake up. Each time she tried, it felt like the shaking was mirrored as if she were being shaken along with him.

Shawndrea opened her eyes to find Ninnie hovering over her. "You're moaning so loud I cannot sleep," Ninnie growled as she collapsed back into bed.

Shawndrea looked around, realizing she was in Ninnie's bedroom and had only been dreaming. She was sleeping in Ninnie's room because her bedroom was empty and had no bed because the person her mom sold it to came and picked it up that day. She rolled over to see that the TV was still on and playing some black-and-white war movie. Suddenly, she felt nauseous. She got up and ran to the bathroom, barely reaching the toilet before she started retching into the bowl.

She dragged herself into the kitchen for a glass of water the following day. Ninnie was pouring Mini Wheats into a bowl and quickly glanced up to see Shawndrea slowly shuffling into the kitchen and looking back down. "Don't forget graduation is at 1 pm. I made this toast but decided I wanted cereal," Ninnie shared, shoving her plate towards Shawndrea.

Shawndrea filled her glass with water and took a sip. She turned around and leaned against the counter, taking a breath. She was relieved that the water had stayed down. She saw Ninnie take a bite of her cereal, and her stomach turned a little.

Ninnie looked back up at Shawndrea, who was still awaiting a response. "What?" Shawndrea asked, feeling her mouth watering and that feeling in your throat just before you're about to throw up. She was more focused on not throwing up and not on what Ninnie had said.

"Shit, you look like hell," Ninnie remarked, taking another bite. "I didn't know you went out drinking last night. Here, eat my toast," Ninnie offered, pushing her toast towards Shawndrea.

Shawndrea took one look at the toast and ran towards the bathroom. Ninnie half chuckled. She was trying to be nice to her sister, but it sent her running out of the room. "Life is wonderful," Ninnie said to the now-empty room.

"What's so stinking wonderful about life?" Letty asked as she walked into the kitchen with a cigarette hanging out her mouth. "Don't just leave that bowl dirty in the sink," Letty demanded as Ninnie placed her cereal bowl into the sink before she even had a chance to turn on the water.

"Who do you think washes your dirty dishes," Ninnie mumbled through the sound of running water.

"What did you say?" Letty snapped.

"I love you, Mommy," Ninnie replied.

"You better not try and get smart with me," Letty stated, smacking Ninnie on the ass as she walked past her to get something out of the fridge. "You know you're not too big for me to still take you over my knee. Love you too!" Letty shouted as she left the kitchen with a Diet Coke in hand.

Shawndrea, retching in the hall bathroom, brought Letty back into the kitchen. "What the hell did she get into last night," Letty asked, taking a drag of her cigarette.

"I have no idea," Ninnie responded, drying her hands. "She woke me up around ten-thirty when she came stumbling into my bedroom."

"Huh, oh well, not my problem," Letty said with a smoker's chuckle, turning and leaving the room.

§

Sheldon felt like this day would never come now that he stood before the entrance to his school on Graduation Day. A wave of nervousness washed over him. He had no clear idea of what he wanted to do with his life, but Sheldon was confident of one thing: he didn't want to follow in his parents' footsteps as a farmer or factory worker. In their small town, opportunities felt scarce unless your family owned a business or a farm or you managed to make it to college.

He knew he liked to entertain people, but nothing in that direction came into his life. Sheldon knew he could not continue working at the grocery store because it would not lead him to the future he wanted, even though he was unsure what that future was or even what it looked like.

Sheldon was feeling very anxious and fidgeting with his gown, but as soon as Lyssa Mallozzi came and stood beside him, he calmed down some.

Lyssa and Sheldon have known each other since kindergarten. Since their last names started with Ma, they were always seated next to or adjacent to each other. In high school, their lockers were side by side, so it was fitting that they walked in together. They basically grew up together even though they never ran in the same circles.

"What are you doing after we graduate?" Lyssa asked as they stood side by side dressed in their cap and gown, anxiously waiting to go inside. "Are you still planning to go to Illinois State?"

"I have had a change of plans and not going away to school just yet. I have decided to stick close to home to be near Chase," Sheldon explained.

"Not you, too," Lyssa scoffed, rolling her eyes. "You cannot put your life on hold for someone else. So, what are you planning to do if you're not attending college?"

"In a week or two, I plan to start applying for a fulltime job at a few factories like Campion or Pathmasters, where my parents work," Sheldon responded as Lyssa tried to hide her horrified expression. "What about you?"

"I have gotten a creative writing scholarship to go to Northwestern," Lyssa responded matter-of-factly. "with the scholarship and the money, I saved from selling my hogs during the 4H fairs, I shouldn't have to bug my parents for too much money."

Sheldon was shocked by this, but not totally because Lyssa had always been very practical and seemed always to have her life together. As the line started moving a little toward the entrance, he began to think about where all his money went from selling his pigs at all the fairs they had attended over the years.

"Are you ready for what comes next?" Lyssa asked Sheldon as they started to make their way closer to the entrance to the gym and collect their diplomas.

"Yes… No… I cannot believe it's really happening," Sheldon stammered a bit as he answered. "Are you ready for this?"

"No!" She exclaimed. "I thought I was, but I'm scared shitless now that it's really happening."

Sheldon was surprised by her answer. He thought Lyssa had always seemed so grounded and ready for anything. Also, he was relieved to know he was not the only one scared shitless with the uncertainty of it all.

She looked at him and noticed his tie was crooked. "Let me fix your tie," Lyssa stated. "This is nice. Where did you get it?"

"Mrs. Casey gave it to me," Sheldon replied. Sheldon could hear Pomp and Circumstances playing as they got closer, making his heart pound. Students began to march into the gym.

"This is all happening too fast," Lyssa moaned as she started to fidget under her gown, and they began to move through the gym entrance.

Sheldon could not help but feel she had read his mind then. Sheldon could not even form a word, let alone a sentence, in the moment. Just before they stepped into the gym, Sheldon looked pale. "Here we go," Sheldon finally got out as Lyssa released a breath, she had been holding in.

§

As usual, Shawndrea was running a little late when she pulled into the high school parking lot. She had a tough time finding a parking spot and had to park near the city park. She thought she would be the last one to show up for graduation. As she walked toward the school, she spotted Chase walking across the parking lot.

"Hey, stranger!" Shawndrea shouted across the parking lot.

"Hey, here I thought I was the only one running late," Chase called back with a big smile. "I'm glad I don't have to walk in alone."

"Welcome to my life," Shawndrea joked as she looked around for his car. "Where did you park?"

"I have not had time to get a new car yet because replacing that one is hard. Plus, the walk here helps with my recovery," Chase replied. "I hope to play football again in the fall, so I must get back in shape. I hoped to play baseball or tennis this summer. I was not sure I could make it today because I had my final physical therapy session, but I made it, and I am excited to see Sheldon graduate."

"That's right, I forgot it was totaled in the accident, and you seem to be doing quite well considering. It looks like the seniors are lined up to go inside. Let's go in after they are done marching," Shawndrea recommended.

§

Sheldon felt like his body was moving on its own. He looked towards the bleachers, searching for his family. Deep down, Sheldon wanted to see Chase in the stands, cheering him on. Sheldon did not see Chase yet, but he spotted his mother and brother waving at him. He smiled a half smile as Mandy snapped a photo.

As Sheldon sat, he saw Ruby smiling back at him. She was at the other end of the row, and her smile relaxed him.

Sheldon felt a pull to turn around and look back at his family. He immediately spotted Chase taking a seat in the bleachers. They made eye contact, and Chase smiled and waved. Sheldon turned around with the biggest smile on his face.

They sat through a series of speeches destined to fade from memory, memorable only to the speakers themselves. Sheldon, however, was caught between conflicting emotions. Part of him reveled in the moment, savoring the idea of graduating, while another longed for it to be over.

Before he knew it, his name was called. He stepped onto the stage, resisting the urge to dance his way across. He was focused on shaking the principal's hand, smiling for the photo, and not tripping. A few classmates stole the spotlight, yelling or leaping across the stage with playful antics, but Sheldon stayed grounded, determined to keep it simple.

However, he was impressed that few students had the ability to make a scene by yelling or jumping up and kicking their heels together. Sheldon was more focused on holding it together and getting everything correct than celebrating in front of everyone.

When Sheldon sat down after receiving his diploma, a wave of relief swept over him, and he relaxed. Sitting there, he tried to remember if people cheered when they called his name. It did not matter because he was done with school.

"We did it," Lyssa said, bumping her shoulder into Sheldon. "Are you going to throw your hat even though we were ordered not to?"

"I don't think so," Sheldon replied as he looked at everyone and then at her. "It seems dangerous."

"That's the Sheldon I know," Lyssa said with a laugh, her familiar smirk tugging at the corners of her mouth. As always, Sheldon could not tell if she was joking with him or at him. "I'm with you because it's too dangerous."

At that moment, he had no way of knowing this would be one of their last conversations for years. Life had a way of unraveling like that—quietly and without warning. The ceremony was over and it was time to exit the gym.

Sheldon could not wait to get outside and get some fresh air. A sea of bodies slowly exited the building. So many people were talking all at once, so it was hard to focus on finding his family. He made his way through the crowd when he saw his family congregating together.

He first saw Grammy, "I'm so proud of you," she cooed, giving him the tightest hug.

"Here you go," Uncle Tom said with a huge smile, handing him a card as he patted Sheldon on the shoulder. "We sure are proud of you."

"I see you're still puffing on those fags," Uncle Bob cackled to Aunt Letty as he walked up, pulling Sheldon's attention away from Grammy and Uncle Tom. "Hey, sis," he said, smiling as he hugged Mandy and kissed her forehead. "Congratulations, Sheldon," he said, shaking Sheldon's hand.

"Yeah, and I see you're still FAT!" Letty said, smacking his belly as she exhaled smoke. She started to chuckle at herself so hard that she began to cough her smoker's cough as smoke continued to be exhaled. "What?" She asked because everyone just glared at her.

"What about me!" Ninnie exclaimed as she pushed through crowds. "I graduated too," She said, hugging Grammy.

"We are proud of you too, sweetheart," Grammy said, giving her a big hug.

"You came, Dad!" Ninnie said as she hugged her father and gave her sister an unexpected dirty look.

"You all better straighten up before I jerk a knot in all your tails," Grammy demanded.

"What?! He started it," Letty justified, taking another long drag of her cigarette.

"I don't even want to know what happened," Ninnie commented.

As the crowd parted, Chase stepped through, and Sheldon grabbed him and pulled him into his arms. As their lips touched, he felt at home. "You made it," Sheldon cheered, smiling a big smile that would not stop, and hugged him so tight.

"I could not miss this big day," Chase replied, kissing. "I love you so much,"

"Gag me with a spoon," Jimmy shouted.

"Oh, grow up," Ninnie said. "Here, let me give you some kisses." This caused Jimmy to run away screaming.

Sheldon requested a group picture with Chase, Ruby, Trey, Ninnie, and Tommy. They were trying hard not to laugh as they took the photo, but one or the other would say something funny.

They were a joyful group of friends that day. "Give me that camera," Shawndrea demanded, taking the camera from Levin, who was having difficulty taking the picture. "You have never been good at taking photos. Now you and Charlotte get in there."

They took a few more photos and chatted for a bit before going their separate ways agreeing to meet up at Mandy's the next day for lunch.

"I thought you said Charlotte was around four months pregnant," Letty whispered to Ninnie as they returned to the van.

"Yeah, that's what they told me," Ninnie replied curiously.

"Well, she is either further along than she thinks, or she is having twins," Letty explained. Ninnie did not know how to reply but was relieved that her mom had not said anything in front of Charlotte.

§

Shawndrea had driven separately to the graduation because she could not stand to look at her mom. She still blamed her mom for their parent's divorce, and on top of that, she was selling the one house they had lived in the longest. She wanted a place she could come back to. A place she could call home, but all of that was being taken away from her.

Her emotions were running a little high already. She had not shared with anyone that she might be two months pregnant. The worst part is she could not tell her husband because he was sterile and not able to have children. She did not know who the father was either, though she had her suspicions.

Shawndrea was lost in thought when she went to get into her car. She had a long walk back to where she had parked the car. She got into the car, and as she started to put the key in the ignition, a hand covered her face with something soft. Not again was her final thought as she took a deep breath to scream and got a mouthful of something chemical and sweet tasting but strangely familiar.

She started to fight, but it was like her limbs would not work, and then she was fighting to stay awake. The person holding her seemed to have surprising strength. As she drifted off, she heard a voice whisper into her ear.

"I'm gonna teach you a lesson about fucking with someone else's man," the mysterious voice whispered into her ear.

Chapter Ten

Summer School

As Chase slowly walked to school, he was literally kicking rocks and did not want to go. When he opened the school doors and stepped inside, it was eerily quiet, with hardly anyone else in the halls. He had been in the school before when it was empty, but now it felt even emptier, maybe because it was summertime, maybe because he did not want to be there, or maybe because he knew he would not be seeing Sheldon.

Being in school during the summer was odd, and only four students were in the class. He was sitting there trying to listen to the teacher with the sound of lawnmowers mowing outside the window, and the smell of freshly cut grass wafting in through the open windows made it hard to concentrate. The teacher recognized this, walked over to close one of the windows, and asked Chase to close the window near him, but Chase was staring out the window, longing to be free because he should be out enjoying the summer break like everyone else.

Chase was wondering what Trey and Tommy were up to now. They were probably still in bed before going to the park to play basketball, play video games, or just vegging on the couch. He was pulled out of his daydream when the teacher cleared his throat before closing the window.

"Well so much for trying to enjoy the early morning summer breeze," the teacher sighed. "My name is Mr. Stonecipher, and as you have guessed, I will be one of your summer schoolteachers."

"Look, I'm sure you all are as excited to be stuck inside on a nice summer day as I am, but if we work hard, finish all the required material, and return promptly from your other class, I will let you out early, but only on the days we finish early, and I'm not sure if that can happen every day." He turned back to the chalkboard and started finishing the algebraic equation.

During Chase's lunch break, he would get a can of Sprite and cheese peanut butter crackers, and they both seemed to taste better, maybe because it was the highlight of his day. Afterward, it was time for shop class before returning to Mr. Stonecipher's classroom to finish the day.

In shop class, the teacher had each student rebuild an engine, which he figured would keep them busy while he could sit back and read the Wayne County Press newspaper. He knew they would never finish but did not count on the fact that Chase had grown up rebuilding engines and was finished with that day's assignment in no time and asked for the next assignment or if he could work on the next part.

"I'm impressed," the teacher said, looking it over, thinking he would find many mistakes, but he was even more surprised that everything looked in order. "Look, this was supposed to take you all summer to complete," the teacher whispered. "Let's make a deal; when you finish each day's assignment, you can keep yourself busy, so I don't have to find you something else to do. Let's stretch this out."

"I'm sure I can do that," Chase replied.

Since Chase had some extra time, he found some extra metal scraps. He started molding the piece of metal into an infinity symbol. At first, he was just playing around to see what he could make of it, but once he saw it coming together beautifully, it reminded him of his love for Sheldon, so he thought, why not try and make it into a necklace for Sheldon? If it did not work, no one would be the wiser, and he would get something else for Sheldon.

After the workshop class, he returned to Mr. Stonecipher's class, where they had to finish a couple of things and then he was released 30 minutes early.

§

The following week Sheldon worked a morning shift at the grocery store and decided to visit Chase at lunch and brought him some goulash and mashed potatoes from the grocery store's hot bar and a Dr. Pepper.

"This is so delicious," Chase said.

"It's one of my favorite things to eat," Sheldon explained taking a sip of his Mountain Dew.

"I'm afraid, though, it's going to make me sleepy for my next class," Chase stated, rubbing his stomach. "It's so filling." They both laughed.

"Maybe these will help keep you awake," Sheldon said, handing him a packet of peanut M&Ms.

"Thank you. These are my favorite. Actually, I like the green ones for some reason," Chase said.

"I love the orange ones even though technically they are all the same flavor," Sheldon said.

"Right, but something about the color makes it taste better," Chase added. They both laughed again.

"Hey, my doctor said I can start doing light sports again," Chase said as he threw his garbage away. "I'm going try and start lifeguarding again on the weekends."

"That is great news," Sheldon said.

"Also, I was hoping to get to play baseball, but the season is almost over, so it's too late," Chase said kind of somberly.

"If you get out early today, maybe we can go play some tennis or go to the batting cages," Sheldon recommended.

"Tennis is a great idea," Chase replied. "I'm going stir-crazy sitting in these classes all day and need to work off some of this extra energy. Maybe next week or this Saturday, we can go to the batting cages." Chase paused, thinking about whether he wanted to share his concerns, as he felt somewhat embarrassed to do so. "I think starting with tennis first before swinging a bat might be a good idea."

"Thank you for sharing your fears, and we can take it easy at first," Sheldon shared.

"That is a great idea and I cannot wait," Chase said as he kissed him goodbye.

"Awesome, I will run home and get my racket and some extra balls," Sheldon stated kind of excited. "I better let you get back to class and I will be back here at 3pm."

Sheldon returned at 3pm but Chase did not get out till 3:30 pm that day, which he did not mind because it gave him time to read a book.

Sheldon watched Chase approaching the car shaking his head. "Sorry to make you wait," Chase said getting into the car. "The teacher decided today was the day for a pop quiz."

"No, worries." Sheldon said as he gave him a kiss hello. "I'm just happy to get to spend as much time with you as I can before I start working full time somewhere.

"At least we can still do stuff on Saturdays or Sundays," Chase stated.

"Now, it's been sometime since I have played," Sheldon confessed. "So, don't expect too much."

"Don't worry, I will take it easy on you," Chase teased, and they both laughed.

§

Saturday morning, Sheldon and Chase were going to meet Ninnie, Ruby, and Jimmy at the pool. Ruby was preparing to head to Rhode Island to find a place to live while attending Brown University in the fall, and Ninnie was planning to move to Fairview Heights, just outside of St. Louis, at the end of the month so she could attend the University of Edwardsville in the fall. So, it was perfect timing one last time at the pool before everyone went their separate ways.

"You can't tell he was ever in an accident," Ruby said looking at Chase and laying a towel down on a lounge chair "He seems so happy, too."

"And he still looks amazing, too," Ninnie said licking her lips and almost tripping over her chair. "Look at those abs and how does he already have a nice skin tone too."

"Down girl, doesn't Tommy give you enough?" Ruby teased.

"What is enough?" Ninnie joked.

"He does have a nice suntan," Ruby commented.

"I don't know, because all he has to do is have his shirt off out-doors one day and bam perfect brown skin," Sheldon said pulling up a chair between Ruby and Ninnie. "Me I have to burn a few times before I turn brown."

"Speaking of which let me get out the sunscreen," Ninnie said putting some on and handing to Sheldon.

Jimmy was already splashing in the pool playing by himself. Because Chase was the lifeguard, he let them in early before every-one else showed up.

"It's nice having this place to ourselves," Sheldon remarked.

"Yeah, and it feels less dramatic then the other times we were here," Ninnie said laying back in the chair. "Hummm, I wonder why." She chuckled soaking up the sunshine

"Speaking of which, where is Shawndrea?" Ruby asked.

"Mom thinks she went home after they got into it," Ninnie stated. "Personally, I think she has run off to Florida somewhere, living it up with some new man, and when she has used him up, she will be back home. However, if she is gone much longer, Dad will be the only one left living in the area."

"What is Jimmy going to do if your Mom moves away?" Sheldon asked.

"I'm sure he will go with Mom because Dad does not let him get away with half the stuff Mom lets him get away with," Ninnie explained.

"I'm going to miss this when you go away and this freedom be-fore I start working full-time somewhere," Sheldon shared laying back putting on his sunglasses.

"Aren't you going to do some laps, Majors?" Chase teased. "or have you forgotten everything I taught you."

"I'm relaxing," Sheldon called back, still relaxing in his chair. They enjoyed having the place to themselves for a little while, but the peace and quiet did not last long as kids started showing up at the pool screaming, hollering, and jumping into the pool.

"I think I have had enough pool time," Ninnie said getting up from her chair.

"Same," Ruby said. "I need to get home and pack for our flight on Monday. My Mom is so excited to get to visit the school she attended and that I'm going to be going there. She wants to show me all her old stomping grounds. Lord, help me," Ruby chuckled.

They all got dressed and met out by their vehicles. Ninnie gave Ruby a huge hug. "Don't worry girl, I will be back before classes start and maybe you can come and visit me. I will get the lay of the land and show you around when you come out."

"I hope you have a wonderful trip and good luck finding a nice place to live," Sheldon said giving her a hug. "We will definitely have to come and visit. I heard the east coast is beautiful."

Ruby got into her car and headed out. "What are you doing now," Ninnie asked.

"I'm going to wait for Chase to get done life guarding and the going to the batting cages," Sheldon said. "I was supposed to work today but asked for it off so I could spend time with Chase."

"How butch of you," Ninnie teased causing him to chuckle.

"Right? What are your plans," Sheldon asked.

"Ugh, I need to finish packing up some of my stuff because we are moving temporarily to mom's new apartment before I move to Fairview Heights. She almost put the sale of the house on pause because Shawndrea is missing, but she got too good of an offer to pass it up."

"What about Tommy?" Sheldon asked. "Everything good with the two of you?"

"We are doing great. Also, he will be moving with me and attending the same school. He is planning to get a degree so he can become a teacher. Tonight, he is picking me up to take me out to the movies. You're welcome to come if you want."

"I would love to, but I have to be up early for work," Sheldon stated. "After the batting cages we are going to have a quiet night at home. I'm wondering if he will be up for that because he is still getting back to his old self."

"Well don't be a stranger," Ninnie requested giving him a big hug before getting into her car. "Also, you can come a visit me and Tommy in our new place if we ever find one."

Sheldon watched her leave before going back to the pool area. Luckily, he found a chair with an umbrella to lounge in while he watched Chase doing his job scanning the pool before pulling out a book to read. Later, Chase woke him that his shift was over, and they could leave. Sheldon had fallen asleep reading his book.

§

A few weeks later, Sheldon and Chase were having lunch at the high school.

"I got a call to come in for an interview at Pathmasters," Sheldon shared. "So, I won't get to come by for lunch because the interview is in the afternoon."

"That is okay, I can go play basketball with Tommy and Trey," Chase said. "Since they graduated, and we are no longer in the band together I hardly see them. They are planning their future lives, and I do not fit in it anymore. They get together once a week to shoot hoops, but that won't happen for much longer as they are both going off to school."

"That is sad," Sheldon said. "It's like life keeps moving on and sometimes we feel left behind. I'm curious to see how Ruby and Trey are going to do since they are going to go to different schools."

"Yeah, I hadn't thought about that," Chase pondered. "Long distant relationships are hard, but not impossible, right?"

"Do you miss being in the band?" Sheldon asked, trying to change the subject because he did not want to think about the future because it was so uncertain for the two of them.

"I miss being creative and being as active as I once was, but it's just a matter of time," Chase stated. "It was inevitable that we wouldn't get to play together forever, but glad I got to experience the time I had doing it and who knows down the road I might find some others looking to join a band and play together."

"Just curious, are you going to get a new car?" Sheldon asked, thinking it would be nice to have Chase meet him at his place once he starts working at the factory.

"Funny you ask that because my dad asked the same question," Chase responded. "He was wondering if I was going to get something to fix up again or something ready to go. I decided to get something ready to go but still red. He has offered to help pay for it too."

"Nice," Sheldon responded. "You better take him up on it before he changes his mind." They both chuckled.

"We might go in a couple of weeks," Chase stated. "I'm in no hurry but that way maybe I can visit you on your lunch break, but I definitely need one before schools starts back up in the fall. This walking to school is okay in the summer but when it gets cold outside again, no thank you."

§

Shawndrea's captor pulled the gag tighter to keep it from being pulled off again, which was pulled so tightly Shawndrea thought the sides of her mouth were going to split open. A single tear from the pain ran down her face, and this only pissed her off even more. Shawndrea was so angry she started struggling against the bondages that kept her hands behind her back and tied to the wooden chair where she was seated. Her struggle to get free was futile. She looked at her captor with a deathly glare.

She suddenly realized that her captor was a female, which made no sense. As her captor turned to leave, Shawndrea kicked out, trying to trip her captor, but it was too late. The captor walked out the door, leaving her in darkness. Shawndrea heard the click of the padlock snapping shut.

Another tear began to run down Shawndrea's face as she struggled against her bondages. She looked around and tried to figure out where she was being held captive. It reminded her of the old metal corn crib she and Sheldon used to play in at their grandmother's place. However, someone crafted this one from wood instead of metal. Plus, you could not see out of it either. It was primarily dark except where light would enter through small cracks in the broken boards. As her eyes adjusted to the light, she looked around the space. She could make out a ladder going up to what appeared to be a hatch on the roof.

She commanded herself to stop crying when a snot bubble formed in her nose from her inability to wipe it away. Her rage only grew. She stood up quickly and ran backward into the wall. She heard the cracking and splintering of wood just before falling face forward onto the floor, knocking herself out.

Chapter Eleven

Goodbye to GIA

It was the afternoon of Sheldon's interview at the bicycle factory called Pathmasters, and he pulled into the packed parking lot. He circled until he found an open spot way in the back. He walked up to the entrance of the building and checked in with the security officer for his interview. The security guard told him to wait and that someone would be out to get him.

A man with a mullet opened the door to the factory and called out his name. The man introduced himself and shook Sheldon's hand but tried to crush it. Sheldon was so nervous that he could not remember what he said and felt he was only going through the motions. As Sheldon followed the guy up a set of stairs, he thought, *What did he say his name was?* and "What kind of questions were they going to ask him, and where are we headed for this interview?"

"Hey, Terry," someone said, greeting them as he came out the door, which turned out to be the cafeteria. Sheldon quickly made a mental note of his name.

"Did you get the parts you needed," Terry asked.

"Yes, we did. Thank you," the guy responded as he went down the stairs and out of sight.

"In here," Terry motioned inside as he held the door open for Sheldon, and he noticed Terry had some papers in his hand. "Their break is over, so it should start to quiet down here as people return to the line, at least enough so we can talk. Have a seat over there." He pointed to a row of bench-style cafeteria tables.

Sheldon did as he was instructed, but he could not help but wonder what he was getting himself into because this was not what he imagined and was so different from the world he was used to. Terry sat across from him and started looking through the papers before him. He seemed very unprepared, and Sheldon got the impression he did not know what he was doing. Sheldon could not believe this was the guy who would be interviewing him.

"So, tell me, why do you want to work here?" Terry asked right off the bat.

"Both my parents work here, and I think it will be a great opportunity for me," Sheldon responded as Terry wrote something down.

"Are you able to stand on your feet for hours at a time?" Terry asked.

"That is definitely not a problem," Sheldon answered as Terry wrote something.

"Are you able to lift items that are over 25 pounds?" Terry asked.

"I believe so," Sheldon replied. Terry chuckled as he wrote something down again.

"I see here you worked as a teacher's aide and at a grocery store, and then before that, you bailed hay. What does a teacher's aide even entail? It couldn't have been that strenuous," Terry commented.

"No, you're right. It was a pretty easy job compared to bailing hay," Sheldon remarked as Terry looked him up and down. "But I would need to go to college if I want to become a teacher, and maybe that is something I will do down the road," Sheldon explained.

"I'm still curious why you want to go from a teacher's aide to working in a factory," Terry commented.

Sheldon started to answer, but Terry said, "No, that was not a question." He made some more notes, and Sheldon sat awkwardly, waiting for more questions. "I don't have any more questions for you. Do you have any for me?"

Sheldon asked, "What shift would I be working?"

"Does it matter?" Terry countered as he made another note.

"No," Sheldon responded, caught off guard, and thought he should stop asking questions.

"Okay, I think we have what we need, and we will be in touch," Terry said standing up. "Let me show you out."

Sheldon stood up and followed Terry out the door and down the stairs. Terry opened the door and said, "Thanks for coming." And turned and walked away as the door closed.

As Sheldon walked to his car, he thought about what had just happened. He had not really asked him any of the interview questions they practiced in his class a few years ago. Based on Terry's reactions to his answers, he was sure he did not get the job.

Also, Terry did not ask him many questions, which made it seem that he did not take Sheldon's desire to work there seriously.

However, Sheldon was shocked when he received a call on Friday stating that he would start work in two weeks and report for orientation at 3 p.m. on the following Monday.

Part of Sheldon was excited and thought he should have been jumping for joy that he had gotten the job, while another part was apprehensive about the change.

"You're going to do well," Mandy said. "We can ride together. I don't mind going earlier, either. I can just wait in the car."

"I feel like I'm not going to get to see Chase anymore," Sheldon confessed.

"Well, soon he is going to be busy with school and sports, and you cannot just sit around and wait for him to be available," Mandy explained. "You must move forward with your life. Unless you want to stay working at the grocery store." Sheldon was quiet for a beat.

"No, you are right," Sheldon acknowledged. "I will share the news with Chase on Sunday when I see him. I'm going with him and his dad to look for a new car for him."

"It's about time," Mandy joked. "I cannot imagine my life without my vehicle because it's always been my symbol of freedom."

§

It was Saturday morning and Sheldon's last day working at Grocery International Association (GIA). He starts his new job at Pathmasters in a week. He parked across the street from the grocery store for the last time. As he got out of his car, he could smell the freshly made donuts from the bakery.

The smell immediately took him back to the first Saturday morning he worked at GIA. That first day when he entered the store, it was hectic and overwhelming because it was the day the trucks made their deliveries and they would drop off pallets full of supplies, which had to be taken out onto the floor and the shelves restocked. As he headed to the backroom to clock in, there were people buzzing about everywhere. After he clocked in, he put on his apron, and it felt a bit overwhelming because he wasn't sure what he should be doing. His boss James told him to clock in and wait there he would be back with a name tag for him.

"What are you doing?" the owner, Ted, asked Sheldon, who did not know what he should be doing because he had been told to wait there.

"This is my first day," Sheldon responded as he nervously fiddled with his apron.

"Come with me," Ted ordered. Sheldon nervously started to follow him, and Sheldon's boss, James, came to the back.

"Where are you going?" James asked.

"He is coming with me," Ted snapped. "I need help in the meat department."

"No, he is helping me," James explained. "Come on, Sheldon."

Sheldon felt very conflicted about whether to follow his boss or the owner. As James said, "Dad, you know he was hired for the front of the store, plus he is under 18 and cannot run the meat slicer."

"Okay," Ted said and turned to walk away. Sheldon was shocked because he did not know Ted was James's dad until that day. From that day on, Ted always gave Sheldon a blank, emotionless look that he did not know how to react to.

Sheldon was suddenly snapped back to reality when he heard Krissy come on the intercom asking for a bagger. As Sheldon headed to the front of the store, he still could not believe it was his last day working at GIA and that he would start working at Pathmasters, the same factory where his parents worked.

He did not want to work at a factory, but he had yet to pick a University and was not ready to move away from Chase and his mom. So, he decided to take some time to think about what he wanted to do next before going to college.

In the meantime, he would work to make money to pay for his expenses and take a couple of classes at a local community college.

He bagged his last bag of groceries and turned in his apron. He reflected on when he was fifteen and just started working at GIA. At first, he was under the impression that he would only be stocking shelves. He did not know he would be dealing directly with customers, so when they took him to the front of the store and started showing him how to bag groceries, he was scared to death of making a mistake. Before he knew it, he had become one of the best baggers they had and received tips from some of their customers. However, secretly, he had always wished he could run the cash register instead.

Krissy walked up to Sheldon. "Remember when I asked you why Chase kept coming around? I will never forget when you told me you two were seeing each other, and I called you a liar and that you always liked telling stories," she laughed. "Boy, was I surprised when you two danced together at prom. But seriously, you should consider writing for a living. You are good at telling interesting stories that are so believable and relatable."

"Thank you," Sheldon responded.

"Don't forget us here," Cherry said, bumping his shoulder. Sheldon was glad he got to work with her one more time. She was the one who showed him the ropes of bagging groceries. He did not get to work with her that often because she primarily worked the day shift.

"Well, you will see me around a lot because we are here every week shopping," Sheldon responded.

Sheldon was surprised that Linda was even there because she only worked weekdays. He rarely worked with her and typically ended her shift as he was getting there. She usually scared him because she was always so serious, but Linda had helped him a few times when something went wrong, and she never made him feel judged or like he was in trouble. She would tell him sometimes things happen.

He said goodbye to everyone, but it did not feel like goodbye. It was different from saying goodbye to Mrs. Casey and Mrs. Hartley because he regularly saw his grocery store family.

Mandy stopped by Letty's to check on her because she had not heard from her in a bit. Jimmy answered the door. "Oh hey, Aunty Mandy," Jimmy said as he opened the door further and stepped back to let her inside. "Come on inside. Mom is in the den." Jimmy took off back to the living room, where he was playing video games.

"Letty," Mandy called out from the foyer.

"In here, right where they left me," Letty chuckled as Mandy entered the den. "What brings you by." She put down her romance book to light a cigarette.

"I just wanted to see how you're doing," Mandy said, looking for a place to sit down and saw boxes everywhere.

"Jimmy come and clean off this sofa," Letty demanded, as they could hear Jimmy huffing and puffing from the living room.

"I better not have to ask you again," Letty boomed. Causing Jimmy to rush in, throwing the stuff on the floor, and taking off. "Get your little ass back in here and pick that up off the floor. Actually, could you take it to your room? In fact, you need to start bringing your boxes down."

"What boxes?" Jimmy questioned.

"Have you even started packing?" Letty asked as Jimmy looked around, thinking of a response. "So, help me, God, if you tell me, you have not even started, I will end you."

"Okay, then I won't tell you," Jimmy said, grabbing some empty boxes and taking off up the stairs.

"How's the move going?" Mandy asked as she sat down.

"Well, we were supposed to be out of here last week, but my new place isn't available till next week," Letty explained. "The new owners are not happy, but what can I do? I can't very well live on the streets."

"You are always welcome to stay at our place," Mandy offered.

"I'm glad you offered because I was about to ask if we could store some of our stuff in one of your barns because my new place is too small to hold it all," Letty explained. "At least till I move to California, and I can take it all with me then."

"I don't see why not," Mandy said. "I will have the boys clean out a spot for you. Speaking of boys. How's your boy toy Trevor doing?"

"Trevor, who?" Letty joked as she lit another cigarette from the current cigarette she just finished.

"Do I sense some trouble in paradise?" Mandy asked.

"Where are my manners? I did not offer you anything to drink," Letty said as she was about to holler for Jimmy, but Mandy interrupted her.

"I'm good, and don't avoid the subject," Mandy demanded, which caused Letty to moan.

"He just needs more attention than I can give him right now," Letty explained, trying to act like it was no big deal, but Mandy knew otherwise. "With moving and Shawndrea missing, I just don't have time for him."

"Well, I guess no one can argue with that," Mandy said.

"Exactly, he cannot, so case closed," Letty said. "I don't need another kid to worry about or another mouth to feed. Plus, I will be moving out of state soon, and his job and family are all here."

§

It was Sunday morning, and Sheldon pulled up in front of Chase's house. He was going with Chase and his dad, Louis, to get Chase a new car. Louis decided to drive, so they climbed into his big Ford F-350 crew cab long-bed truck. Sheldon was reminded of his time working on the farm and his dad's big truck, but he tried to imagine how he parked this huge vehicle in parking spots.

At the dealership, the Salesman tried to convince them to buy a brand new 1993 Ford Mustang Cobra or Mustang GT, but Chase did not like the new body style and wanted a convertible again. No matter how much Chase's dad insisted, the Salesman was not listening.

Finally, Louis said, "We are walking."

They were heading for the door when suddenly the Salesman said, "Look, we just got in an old 1970 cherry red Mustang convertible. The old man who had it before rarely drove it and kept it in his shed under a tarp. It might need a little TLC, but it would make a great car."

"Great, we will look at that one," Louis said.

Chase tried to contain his excitement as they looked at it because it was exactly the car he was looking for. "How much is it?" Chase tried to casually ask. Sheldon did not know much about cars, but he did like this particular shade of red.

"For you, we can do $11,999.00," the Salesman said.

"Come on, man, I'm not some chump off the street here," Louis demanded.

"Okay, let me talk to my manager. If you can follow me," the Salesman said as they followed him inside, where he took them to his office and got an extra chair for Sheldon.

He returned approximately 30 minutes later and said, "My manager says we can take $10,999.00."

"That's it. I'm done with you jokers jerking me around. We are out of here," Louis said as they got up to walk out. "You are completely wasting our valuable time."

"Wait, wait, what will you give for it?" the Salesman asked, almost pleading.

"We will not pay any more than $8,000 for it," Louis said.

"Okay, let me see what I can do," the Salesman said. "Please wait here."

Another 30 minutes passed, and Louis was getting impatient. The Salesman finally returned looking a bit disheveled and unhappy.

"My manager says the lowest we can go is $8,999.00," the Salesman explained as he braced for impact while Louis stared at him momentarily.

"Deal, but I want that to include sales tax and title transfer," Louis demanded.

"Let me see what I can do," the Salesman said, quickly leaving his office.

He was gone for about 15 minutes this time, and when he returned, an older gentleman followed him.

"I wanted to meet the man who is as good a negotiator as me," the Sales Manager said, reaching out his hand. "We have made you a very good deal here, and we hope you don't forget us in the future."

As they pulled out of the dealer, Chase was on cloud nine and driving his new car home.

§

When Jack got home from deployment, Shawndrea was nowhere to be found. He knew she had gone to attend her sister's graduation a couple of weeks ago, but she should have been home by now. He had come home early from deployment and wanted to surprise her on the anniversary of the day she almost ran him off the road and stole his heart.

He picked up the phone and called her mom's house, but it only rang. The answering machine did not pick up. After a few days of no word or contact from Shawndrea, this time, when he called, it said the number was no longer in service, so he grew even more concerned. Jack decided to drive to her mom's house to check on her.

"Jack?!" Ninnie asked, curiously opening the door and looking past him. She was not expecting to see him standing at their door. "Where is my sister?" Ninnie asked, looking past him again for her sister.

"What do you mean where is she?" Jack asked. "Isn't she here?"

"No, we have not seen her since the graduation. We thought she went home," Ninnie replied. He just stared at her.

"We had assumed Shawndrea went home or to a friend's house after the confrontation she had with mom about selling the house," Ninnie stated. Ninnie still could not understand why she had such an issue about selling a place she was in such a hurry to escape.

"She hasn't been home, and I have been calling here looking for her, but no one answered," Jack explained. "Where could she be?"

"I have no idea, and honestly, it's not a priority for me to try and figure out," Ninnie replied as she started to close the door, but Jack stopped her and walked inside.

"Where is your mom?"

"Right here!" Letty called from the den. Jack walked into where she was seated. Letty put down her book and put out her cigarette. "What's up," she said, exhaling a cloud of smoke. "Where is my daughter?"

"That's why I'm here," Jack replied.

"Well, she is not here," Letty said. "We assumed she returned home after the little scene she caused here." Letty stood up and reached for the phone before remembering she had it turned off. Now, she realized she might have shut it off prematurely. "We need to go to Mandy's and use her phone to call Shawndrea's friends to see where her ass has been for the last couple of weeks." They got in the vehicle and headed to Mandy's place.

They made several phone calls, but no one had seen her. Letty had to finally make the dreaded call to the police and explain that her daughter had been missing for some time. She hung up the phone and looked at Mandy. "They say we have to come down and file an official report," Letty explained to Mandy.

"I will drive you," Mandy offered, grabbing her purse. They got into Mandy's vehicle.

"What the fuck Mandy. What kind of mother does not know their child has been missing for about a month?" Letty questioned from the passenger seat.

"First off, she is no longer a child. Secondly, she has been known to disappear or go without contacting you for several weeks at a time. Thirdly, you have been busy trying to sell a house and move," Mandy replied.

Letty moaned, putting her head back against the headrest. "I think I'm gonna be sick. Pull over!" Letty demanded as she barely got the door open and leaned out, throwing up on the gravel road.

"Okay, I'm good," Letty said, closing the door, whipping her mouth, and taking another cigarette from the pack.

§

The next day, the phone rang at the Major's house, and Mandy ran around to find where she had left the cordless phone. They had just bought their first cordless phone and were still getting used to it. They were used to the phone being attached to the wall attached to a cord. She finally found it, hit answer, and out of breath, she said, "Hello."

"Mandy, it's John. Susan is having contractions, and we are headed to the hospital," he said from the other end of the call.

"Okay, I'm heading to the hospital," Mandy said as she hung up. "Now, don't panic, Mandy. Keep a level head. First, let everyone know and get your to-go bag."

Sheldon was the only one at home, so they jumped in Mandy's truck and headed to Bloomington. "Oh my god, what about work," Mandy said as they drove down the highway.

"We will call them when we get there and let them know you won't be in," Sheldon calmly said. "I'm glad I gave myself some time before starting at the factory, so it works well for me."

"You are right," Mandy breathed. "It's not like I haven't been telling them for weeks about this was coming, and I will need off work to be there for the arrival of my first grandbaby."

"You mean months?" Sheldon corrected her.

"Oh, you be quiet," She said as Sheldon smirked. "It's not every day you become a grandmother for the first time."

They arrived just in time for Susan to deliver a baby boy, whom they named George. They could only stay for a few days because Mandy had to return to work, and Sheldon was starting his job at the factory in a few days.

Chapter Twelve

Jerni James Detective Agency

Sheldon was grocery shopping with his Mom and Damian when they heard someone calling out to them. They turned to see Jerni James coming down the aisle. "Hey, Mandy and Sheldon, and who is this?" Jerni asked, looking Damian up and down. "This must be your new *man* everyone is talking about."

'Everyone is talking about?" Mandy questioned.

"It's good to see you both," Jerni said. She was alone this time and seemed excited to talk to someone. "We need to catch up sometime. How have you been?"

"We have been good," Mandy responded. "How are you doing?

"Good, busy with my detective work and being a mom," Jerni said. "Mattie is at mom's house. It's nice being out of the house without a kid to worry about, but Freddy now wants to have another. I think one is enough for now, but don't get me wrong, I love my daughter. It's just nice to talk to other adults once in a while."

"How is your mom?" Mandy asked.

"She is doing well, and she loves being a grandmother. She loves it when I bring Mattie over to see her," Jerni explained. "I heard you're about to be a grandmother."

"She IS a grandmother," Sheldon teased as Mandy gave him a sharp look. "Susan just had her baby."

"Congratulations," Jerni said cheerfully.

"When people say grandmother, I think they are talking about my mom," Mandy explained. "I still cannot wrap my mind around the fact that I'm a grandmother even when I'm holding Susan's baby. We just got back from visiting them."

"Sheldon, remember the last time I was going to tell you about how you gave me the idea to be a detective? It was when our parents were out searching for the older man missing in the snowstorm that you said something that inspired my dream of becoming a detective, so I wanted to thank you." Sheldon was trying to remember what he had said or done.

§

When Sheldon was nine and Levin was eight, they were dropped off at Jerni's parents' house while their parents went to search for the missing man. The Majors were asked to participate because they had horses that could help search the woods faster than on foot. Additionally, the day before, a significant snowstorm had occurred, bringing over a foot of snow, which made it difficult for the search party to trek through the woods. The temperatures were dropping, so time was of the essence.

Jerni was upset because her parents refused to let her go help search for the missing older man. "He is probably out there stuck in the snow and slowly freezing to death," Jerni said, staring out the window. "I hope they can find his tracks and they are not snowed over by now."

"I'm sure they will find him alive and well," Mercedes said as Jerni gave her a sharp look. "And don't look at me like that."

"But…" Jerni started to say. Mercedes interrupted her,

"No, but s. Now, stop being so morbid and sit down. It's your turn," Mercedes demanded of her little sister. They were playing Uno to take their minds off what was happening. Sheldon felt cozy with the fireplace and the hot chocolate that Mercedes had just made them.

"While we are sitting here, where it's nice and warm. He is out there cold and alone," Jerni said, refusing to sit down. "I can't just sit here and do nothing. I hope they are looking along the creek because when people get lost, they will follow a creek or river to find their way home."

"How do you know this?" Mercedes asked her sister.

"I watch 48 hours. I know what happens when people go missing, and if they don't find him soon, it could become a cold case, literally," Jerni explained.

"Does Mom and Dad know you watch that show?" Mercedes asked, collecting the cards. "I will shuffle and redeal without her because when she gets like this, she is a dog with a bone and won't let up till she figures it out or something else distracts her."

"Maybe you should be a detective when you grow up," Sheldon commented to Jerni while he was looking at his cards. She finally looked away from the window and directly at him. He was unsure if he had upset her by the serious look on her face.

"No, she wants to be a housewife when she grows up," Mercedes said as she picked up her cards, and Jerni gave her a nasty look. "Besides, girls are not detectives."

"That's not true," Jerni snapped. "There is Cagney and Lacey, oh and…. that new one with the older lady, Jessica Fletcher."

"You mean Murder She Wrote," Sheldon responded.

"Yes, that is the one!" Jerni said excitedly. "I love a good detective show."

"When and how are you watching these shows?" Mercedes asked.

"Don't worry about it," Jerni said, looking out the window and daydreaming of becoming a female detective one day.

"She does have a point," Sheldon said, looking at Mercedes.

§

"So, did they ever find the old man," Damian asked, interrupting the story.

"Sadly, yes. I found the old man leaning against a tree, frozen to death," Mandy commented. "His beard was like a frozen popsicles."

"Oh, that is sad," Damian remarked.

"Yes, it was a sad sight that has haunted me for years. The old man, in fact, was near a creek, too." Mandy explained, looking at Jerni.

"See, I was right!" Jerni said excitedly again.

"Sounds like you are in the right line of business then," Sheldon commented.

"Here is my business card," Jerni said, handing it to Mandy. "I better get going. It was great running into you."

"It was great seeing you, Jerni," Mandy remarked as they waved goodbye to her.

"Do you two run into someone you know and talk every time you go to the grocery store?" Damian teased them as they put the groceries into the truck. "I have gone to the grocery store with both of you, and every time we run into someone, and it's like a thirty-to-forty-minute reunion."

"I can't help it if I'm popular," Mandy joked, tossing her hair just before getting into the truck. They all laughed at the sight of her being dramatic and the way she got into the truck.

§

Just after Jerni married her husband and bought their first house together, there was a knock at their front door. When she opened it, her neighbor Rita was frantically talking so fast that Jerni could not understand her, and her child was crying.

"Okay, slow down. You said something is missing?" Jerni asked, opening the door wider. "Come inside."

Rita and her daughter came inside. Rita took a deep breath and exclaimed, "Midnight is missing, and we cannot find her anywhere!"

"What is a Midnight," Jerni asked.

Rita explained Midnight was their dog and had been missing for three days. Jerni immediately leaped into action and started planning how she could help.

Jerni printed out flyers and went door to door to ask if anyone had seen Midnight. Jerni walked up to one house that looked like no one was home but thought she would try to see if anyone was home anyway. She first knocked on the front door, and there was no answer, so she decided to try and see if she could knock on the back door, but it was fenced in.

She heard a dog barking and thought their dog was warning her to leave when the neighbor came out.

"Can I help you?" She asked.

"My neighbor's dog, Midnight, has gone missing, "Jerni explained as the dog started barking again.

"That is strange because they do not have a dog," the neighbor said. I was over there just the other day watering their plants because they are out of town." She opened the gate and outran a black dog, which ran up to them cheerfully.

"That's my neighbor's dog," Jerni said.

"She must have got in when I was not looking," the neighbor said.

"Thank you," Jerni said as she led the dog down the driveway to her car. "My neighbor's kid is going to be so happy."

Jerni was the talk of the neighborhood for weeks. She would solve small cases here and there.

The summer Sheldon and Chase started dating, Jerni received a knock on her door. When she opened it, her neighbor Patty was standing there.

"I need your help with an issue," Patty stated, somewhat distressed.

"Sure, come on inside," Jerni said, opening the door and ushering her into her sitting room. "Have a seat."

"Thank you," Patty said, sitting down, standing up, and finally sitting down again. Jerni gave her a sideways look.

"Can I get you anything to drink, water or tea?"

"I'm good, thanks," Patty said.

Based on Patty's tone, Jerni thought this must be a serious issue and decided to get straight to the point. "What can I help you with?" Jerni asked.

"It's quite embarrassing, really," Patty started off saying.

"That is okay, out with it," Jerni requested.

"Well, you see, the liquor from our liquor cabinet has started to go missing, and when I asked my husband and son, they acted like they had no idea what I'm talking about," Patty explained. Jerni started to wonder how this could be embarrassing because stuff like that always happens, especially when you have teenagers in the house.

"Are you sure it was not your son drinking it?" Jerni asked.

"No, he said it wasn't him, and I believe him," Patty said. "I fear it's far worse than that."

Jerni could not imagine anything worse than her teenager drinking all the liquor in the house. "What do you think is happening to the missing liquor?" Jerni asked, curious to hear Patty's wicked thoughts.

"I think my husband is having an affair," Patty blurted out.

"How does missing liquor equate to a cheating husband?" Jerni asked. "Could it be your cleaning lady?"

"No, the only alcohol that Magda drinks is the holy communion wine during Sunday mass," Patty said, getting herself even more worked up.

"It's obvious that he is taking it to meet up with the hussy he is banging," Patty huffed and pulled out a tissue as she began to cry. "I bet it's that tramp Becky from his office."

"Well, before we jump to conclusions, how about I come over Thursday and discuss what I can do to solve this mystery or bring you hard proof."

They agreed to meet while everyone was out of the house. As Patty left, Jerni realized she might not be as prepared for this case and might need a camera to provide proof her husband is or is not cheating. She saw enough detective shows in the 1980s and 90s to have an idea of what she needed to do to investigate a cheating husband.

Jerni went to the electronics store in Evansville to get a good camera at a reasonable price. The salesperson explained how to load and unload the film, but that was about it. While there, she decided to get an extra few rolls of film because she did not know when she would be back to buy more. When Jerni got home, she had to read the manual that came with it to understand what all its buttons did.

On Thursday, she went over to Patty's house as instructed. When she knocked on the door, Patty quickly opened it and pulled Jerni inside. "I don't want anyone to see you here," Patty explained, acting paranoid, which made Jerni think Patty was just delusional and had made this whole thing up in her head. "Let me show you the liquor cabinet. All this liquor was gone but is now replaced with new bottles, thinking I would not notice."

Jerni examined the bottles, unsure what she was looking for, but she went along with it, thinking how Patty could tell if someone had replaced them. Jerni did notice that the liquor cabinet had no lock, so anyone could have taken the bottles, but to replace them was a bit odd.

Jerni got out her notepad to ask questions. "So, tell me where your husband works and what hours he works."

Patty explained her husband's comings and goings. "Harold is such a routine person, which is why it made me suspicious he was cheating when he started coming home late," she said.

Jerni looked around the living room at the pictures on the wall and the fireplace mantel. Even though they were her neighbors from a few blocks over, she did not even know what her husband looked like. "Which of these photos of your husband is the most current?"

"I keep the most current on the mantel," Patty explained as she started to cry. "I fear my marriage might be over."

Jerni walked over and saw one family photo in the middle and several pictures of their son in different athletic uniforms: one in a basketball Jersey and then baseball and football. "Do you just have the one boy because that first photo shows two babies?" Jerni asked.

"We had twin boys, but the one disappeared when he was eight years old," Patty said, wiping more tears away with the tissue she pulled from her apron pocket.

"I'm so sorry," Jerni expressed, now wishing she had not asked, but thought she would like to come back to that at some point. She turned her attention back to the mantel to look at the family photo again, studying the husband's face so she would remember it. "What does your husband do again?"

"The same as yours," Patty said, surprised Jerni did not know that already. "I know what you're thinking. He is not the kind of attorney who keeps long hours, probably like your husband might. He leaves the house around 7:20 a.m. and is at the office by 7:30 a.m. He is there before his partners to get ready for the day. He is very regimented about his time. Also, if he will be late, he calls but has not been doing that lately."

Jerni wrote down his work address and agreed to report what she discovered or uncovered in the next couple of days as she showed herself out the door.

She was thinking about how she would explain to her husband what she was leaving before him for the next few days. Since Harold goes to work much earlier than her husband, she will have to make something up, and she does not like hiding things from her husband. Still, she had already bought the camera and not told him about it, but she had felt more productive than she had in a very long time.

She told her husband she had to do something for her parents. The lie made it hard to sleep that night, but it could also have been the excitement of investigating her first big case. Additionally, Patty gave her $500 upfront and an additional $ 2,000 if she solved the case. She liked having her own money instead of relying on her husband's monthly deposit into her account. She realized she needed to set up a separate account. Still, everyone in that town knew them, so she would have to go to Grayville or Mount Carmel to establish a business account, which was inconvenient but necessary, as she did not want people in her town to know about her business. account.

The following day, she got up early, drove, and parked in front of Harold's office, an old house turned into a law office. Ironically enough, it was down the street from Chase's house.

§

After sitting outside Harold's office for three days, she began to think she was wasting her time when suddenly, there was a knock on the window, causing her to scream.

She looked to see an older woman at her passenger-side window waving at her. Jerni cracked the window. "Yes, can I help you?" Jerni asked.

"I was about to ask you that because I have seen you sitting here for a few days."

"I'm good and just working," Jerni said, hoping the older lady would just leave. Instead, the lady opened the door and got inside.

"Whatever it is, I want in," she stated. "I'm Mrs. Franny Clem-ens, but you can call me Franny."

"I'm just sitting here observing," Jerni said as she noticed someone entering Harold's office.

"Bullshit, you are watching that law office for some reason," Franny said. Jerni quickly looked at her, wondering who this woman was and how she knew what she was doing.

"You are!" She said gleefully.
"You're not the first person to be sitting out here, but at least you're not stalking someone, I don't think," Franny said. "I have a sense for these things. The last person was watching that house on the corner down there."

Jerni furrowed her brows as she listened. "How do you know it wasn't a detective doing surveillance?"

"Ha!! You are surveilling that place," Franny said joyfully. "Tell me, are they dealing drugs, prostitution, money laundering, or something even darker than I can imagine?"

"Nothing like that," Jerni laughed. "Did you find out who it was watching that house and why?"

"No, because he would take off when I came out to ask," Franny said. "Though one time I got a good look at him and made eye contact, it was like I was looking straight into pure evil, and it gave me such a chill all the way to the bone as if someone had walked across my grave."

"Interesting," Jerni said, returning her attention to the law office.

"Oh, wait, here. I did get his license plate number," Franny said, getting out of the car. She disappeared as Jerni watched someone come out of the office and quickly snapped some photos.

Suddenly, the passenger car door opened again, causing Jerni to scream when Franny entered. Jerni noticed Harold coming out of the office and getting in his car.

"I'm sorry, but I have to go," Jerni said, staring at Harold as he got into his car and then looking at Franny.

"I told you whatever it was, I'm in," Franny said, putting on her seatbelt.

Jerni huffed because this was finally her chance, and she feared losing Harold.

"Okay, but I'm not responsible for what might happen to you," she said as she pulled away from the curb and followed Harold. They drove out of town, heading towards Fairfield.

"Okay, so what is it that this guy has supposedly done?" Franny asked.

Jerni was uncomfortable sharing someone else's personal information, but that ship was already leaving the harbor. "His wife thinks he is cheating, and she hired me to find out," Jerni explained.

"I knew it," Franny smiled from ear to ear. "Here is the license plate number of the guy stalking that house." She placed the price of paper into the cup holder.

"I just can't figure out why he is going towards Fairfield," Jerni said, shaking her head. "I thought for sure Patty was wrong about him cheating."

"Well, you don't know that yet," Franny said. "So, his wife's name is Patty."

Jerni put her hand to her head because she had let the cat out of the bag again and was out there telling all of Patty's business. "Don't worry, Hun. I'm not gonna tell anyone. Well, except maybe my cat Sunny, but Sunny on General Hospital now he could get me to confess all my sins and dirty little secrets."

Jerni laughed, while trying hard not to get too close to Harold's car.

"If we make it to Fairfield, can we stop at Rax because they have the best-baked potatoes? Jerni gave her a "Are you serious look." "Of course, after we find out he is completely innocent."

"Seriously?" Jerni questioned.

"Sorry, I don't get out much, so this is extremely exciting for me," Franny said. "You better step on it, or you're going to lose him, Shortbread."

"Shortbread?" Jerni questioned as she punched the gas pedal to pass the vehicle before them.

"Sorry, that is what I used to call my granddaughter, who was just as feisty as you," Franny said. "Unfortunately, she passed away." There was silence in the car as Jerni focused on getting around the car and back over before the oncoming semi hit them head-on.

Franny chuckled. "She used to call me Old Woman," Franny said as she put her hand to her mouth and looked out the window. "I sure do miss her. You know, she reminded me of myself when I was younger. I would not let any man, or anyone for that matter, try to tell me what to do."

Jerni did not know how to respond to such a sad story but thought she probably did not want sympathy. Without thinking she said, "Is there a point to this story, Old Woman?" Jerni was shocked at what came out of her mouth and waited for Franny to be upset.

"Awe, you just reminded me of her because that is definitely something she would have said," Franny said, smiling at Jerni, who was relieved by Franny's reaction.

They started to enter Fairfield, driving through town and getting close to leaving it. "I hope he isn't going to Wayne City," Jerni said. "He wouldn't have time to have an affair and not be home very late."

"You never know; I had one boyfriend before my husband, of course, who was like a rabbit. It was over with before I knew we had begun," Franny remarked as Jerni gave her another sideways look. "He is putting on his turn signal."

"Thank goodness, because I was starting to think of excuses, I was going to have to tell my husband why I was late coming home," Jerni said.

"Looks like he is pulling into that assisted living facility," Franny commented.

"Quick, grab my camera," Jerni requested as she pulled into the business next door to get an angle of the entrance to the assisted living facility. She snapped a few photos of Harold entering the facility and, 15 minutes later, came out with an older woman on his arm.

"Oh, dear lord, do you think he is doing her?" Franny questioned.

"Nooooo," Jerni said, snapping photos of them exiting the building and him helping the older woman into the car. "They can't be. Can they?"

"Well, I have heard of crazier things," Franny said as Jerni put away her camera in order to follow them. "Are we still going to follow them? Don't you have the evidence you need?"

"Why is it past your curfew, old woman?" Jerni asked again, trying to keep a straight face.

"Touche," Franny stated. "Drive on shortbread."

"Let's just see where they are going first," Jerni commented as she followed them. Harold drove barely a block when he pulled into Rax's parking lot, ironically enough.

"Oh my, can we go inside? Please…." Franny pleaded.

"Only if they go inside," Jerni stated.

They parked at the other end of the parking lot, watched Harold get out and go around to help the elderly woman out of the car, and then they walked inside.

Jenri looked over at Franny, who was smiling ear to ear. "Okay, old woman, let's go get your baked potato, and maybe we can sit close enough to hear what they are saying."

"That sounds like a great plan to me," Franny said, getting out of the car.

"Wait!" Jerni said, stopping Franny from getting out.

"What?" Franny snapped. "You scared the crap out of me."

"You can't use my real name in there," Jerni stated.

"What do you want me to call you?" Franny asked, looking at her sideways. "I know! I will call you Rachel."

"Rachel?" Jerni questions as she thought about it. "Not bad."

"Let's go, shortbread; there is a baked potato in there with my name on it," Franny said, getting out of the car.

They went inside, and Jerni spotted the older woman sitting at a table. Harold was nowhere in sight but suddenly reemerged from the bathroom just as they called his order. "I will get us a seat. Can you get me a Diet Coke? Here is twenty. Knock yourself out," Jerni said, handing her a twenty-dollar bill.

Jerni sat down two booths behind Harold and she strained to hear what they were saying. Harold mentioned something about bills and maybe living together, but she was straining to hear them over the noise in the restaurant.

"What is happening?" Franny whispered. She sat down with her tray of food and gave Jerni her diet coke.

Jerni looked at all the food on Franny's tray. "I said, knock yourself out with the baked potato, not everything on their menu," Jerni said, trying to keep her voice down so as not to draw attention to them.

"Here is your change," Franny coyly said, pushing seventy-five cents towards Jerni as Jerni's mouth fell open.

"Hey, I have to eat, and you don't want me to report you for elderly abuse, do you?" Franny said, taking the top off her baked potato and pouring the sour cream onto the baked potato.

"Old Woman, I'm gonna lock you up in that assisted living facility," Jerni remarked. "I believe he called her Carolyn, so it's obviously not his mother, but he did say something about wanting her to live with him or them. I could not hear because of the ice machine. I should have sat right behind him.

"I really don't think she should be eating that roast beef sandwich," Franny commented as she took a big bite of a roast beef sandwich herself.

"Seriously?" Jerni said, looking at the sandwich Franny was shoving in her mouth.

"Hey, I'm old, but not that old. I can still eat this kind of food," Franny scoffed and then looked down at the food she had bought. "I may get a bag to take the rest of this home."

While Franny was getting her bag, Jerni heard Harold saying, "Patty does not have to know, but maybe we should tell her. I think she might understand."

When Franny returned to the table, Jerni was just as confused and lost in thought. "You realized they just left?" Franny asked.

"I don't feel like I have help to solve this case at all," Jerni said, disappointed.

"Look, you have the photos right. You can explain what you do know and leave it in Patty's court at this point," Franny said.

"True, but that doesn't explain the missing liquor," Jerni explained.

"What liquor? I thought this was about infidelity," Franny stated. Jerni explained what started the investigation to bring her up to speed.

"Well, if it were me, I would be looking closer at the son," Franny said.

"I think you're right," Jerni said. "Maybe I'm investigating the wrong person." Franny threw her garbage away, and they headed to Jerni's car.

"You never even called me by my name," Jerni chuckled as they entered her car.

"What?" Franny asked, confused as she put on her seatbelt.

"We made up the name Rachel, and you never had to call me by it," Jerni said, laughing again.

"Oooh, I thought you were talking about the song, *You Never Even Call Me by My Name*, by David Allan Coe," Franny explained.

Jerni pulled out onto the highway, and they headed home. They both laughed, and the car grew silent as they drove through town. Jerni was lost in thought, thinking about how to explain her lateness to her husband and explain to Patty the situation with her husband and this older woman. Franny was thinking about all the people she had lost in her life.

"It's too quiet in here," Franny said, turning on the radio. A commercial was playing, so she started scanning the stations, looking for music. When she came across the song she just mentioned was playing on the radio.

"Oh, that is freaky," Jerni said. "I haven't heard this song in years. I have goosebumps."

"It's serendipitous," Franny said as they cruised down the highway and headed home, singing along to the song.

§

Jerni had the photos she took developed so she could show Patty who her husband was meeting up with and what they were doing. She was still unsure exactly what was happening with Harold or the missing liquor.

She knocked on Patty's door, and Patty answered, covered in flour and holding a whisk. "Come in. I'm baking my cakes for the neighborhood bake sale," Patty explained. "Please follow me into the kitchen. I was about to whisk some eggs for the next cake. Please help yourself to anything we have in the fridge to drink."

Jerni placed the package of photos on the counter, and Patty spotted them. "Oh, god, you have proof," Patty said, looking like she was going to pass out or throw up. She paused for a moment and regained her poise.

"Honestly, I'm not sure what I have proof of," Jerni said.

"I don't have time to stop because they have to be ready by 3 pm," Patty exasperatedly said as she started to whisk the eggs. "Can you please show me the photos?" Patty requested.

Jerni pulled out the photos, and Patty took a deep breath before looking at them. "What is he doing with my mother?!" Patty exclaimed. "He knows I cannot stand her and that she killed Daddy."

As Jerni was holding the photos, she got another view of the tree house in the backyard. Something in her gut kept tugging at her the first time she saw it. She was so lost in thought that she totally missed Patty's rant about her mother.

"Can I take a look at the tree house?" Jerni asked, putting down the photos and walking to the back door. Patty did not notice because she was whisking the eggs and ranting about her mother.

Jerni climbed up the ladder to the treehouse and looked around at some of the sports equipment, action figures, comic books, and a

132

blanket. She noticed something sticking out from under the blanket. She pulled out a bottle still half full, which happened to be one of the same missing liquor bottles. Suddenly, she heard her name. Patty finally realized she was gone and was standing in the backyard. Jerni looked out the window at Patty and showed her the liquor bottle.

"Case solved," Jerni said with a smile, but she quickly felt bad because Patty's world seemed turned upside down. Jern placed the liquor bottle on the countertop while Patty folded the eggs into the cake batter and talked to herself. Jerni did not know how to help her, so she stared at the door looking to escape.

"I will be back in a few days for my fee," Jerni said, letting herself out and glad to be out of the drama happening in that house.

§

Letty took the movers to Mandy's house to drop off some of their extra boxes that she did not have room to store at her apartment. These boxes filled up the entire section of Mandy's barn. Letty stayed around afterward to escape the mess of her new apartment while Ninnie and Jimmy unpacked a few items. She needed a break from unpacking and to take her mind off Shawndrea's disappearance.

"So, what is new with you?" Letty asked while sitting at the kitchen table.

"Nothing much, really," Mandy responded. "Damian is busy with his job, and Sheldon is enjoying his last day of freedom before starting to work at the factory. We just got back from seeing Susan's baby George."

"Oh my god, that's right, you're a grandmother now," Letty cheered as she lit a cigarette.

"Sshh, don't say that too loud," Mandy joked. "How is everyone doing on your end?"

"Ninnie is about to head off to college," Letty said. "I can't believe she is already grown and planning to leave the nest. That will just leave Jimmy and me moving to California once Shawndrea comes home. Ninnie said they might move out there after she and Tommy finish college, but that might depend on where she or Tommy find a job."

While sipping her coffee, Letty found Jerni's business card as Mandy refilled her coffee cup. "Who is this?" she asks, showing Mandy the business card.

"Oh, that is our neighbor's daughter. I guess she has opened her own private investigation company," Mandy explained while Letty was staring at it.

"Can I take this card," Letty asked.

"Sure, you can have it," Mandy said.

"I hate to run, but I think I want to get home so I can call her," Letty said.

"Why not call her from here," Mandy offered.

Mandy hands her the phone, and Letty calls Jerni to see if she can help with the investigation. Letty felt the police had not been helpful or taken the situation seriously.

Jerni agreed to meet with Letty so Letty could explain what was going on and if she could help her investigate what happened to her daughter.

Chapter Thirteen

Jerni Into the Unknown

Letty met with Jerni and explained everything that had happened with Shawndrea up to that point. She gave Jack's address to Jerni so she could go to talk to him. Jerni agrees to investigate it for Letty and will keep you updated.

Jerni knocked on Jack's door and a blonde girl opened the door. "I'm here to see Jack," Jerni requested

"Can I ask what this is about?" the blonde asked.

"Ummm," Jerni started to say when Jack showed up at the door.

"Letty has asked me to investigate Shawndrea's disappearance," Jerni explained, looking at Jack and then at blonde, somewhat confused because she thought Jack was Shawndrea's fiancé. However, now he has this girl hanging on him, marking her territory.

"She still thinks she is missing?" Jack asked. "Come inside. This here is my girlfriend, Tiffany."

Jerni stepped inside the apartment, which seemed relatively new and nicely decorated.

"Fiancée," Tiffany corrected him.

"Do you have any idea what might have happened to Shawndrea?" Jerni asked.

"Yeah, I think she took off with some guy and will try to pop back up in our lives when she gets bored with him," Jack remarked, as he was going through some stuff on the counter.

"Is there any particular place you think she might have gone?" Jerni asked. "Or someone you think she might've run off with?"

"Look, I can't tell you more than that," Jack said. "In fact, I have moved on and am so much happier now."

"Well, if you think of anything or hear from her, would you call me?" Jerni asked, handing him her business card.

"Actually, I'm glad you are here," Jack said. "You can take some of Shawndrea's stuff and give it to her mom."

He left the room and returned shortly, carrying a cardboard box. "Here is a box of Shawndrea's stuff. The rest we have already thrown out," Jack said plainly. "Wait, here is her mail, too." He placed it on top of the box.

"Can you have her Mom update her address, too," Jack requested. "Seeing her mail coming here upsets Tiffany."

"We would not want that," Jerni said as she headed for the door.

Jerni was glad to be out of there and headed back home.

As Jerni got out of her car, she felt like she had accomplished nothing and had no new information to share with Letty. She felt like she was in uncharted territory, in unknown waters, and in over her head. As she was getting Shawndrea's stuff out of her car, some pieces of mail fell on the ground, and she started picking it up when she realized some of the envelopes looked like a bank statements.

Jerni wondered if anyone had thought to check her banking statements. If she had run off, she would most likely be using her debit card, and that would explain where she was located.

Jerni knocked on Letty's apartment door and started ringing the doorbell, getting excited.

"Okay, I heard you," Letty said, opening the door. "Oh, it's you. That was fast. I was not expecting to see you back so soon."

"Can I come inside because this box is getting heavy?" Jerni requested.

"Oh, of course," Letty said, opening the door and stepping aside.

Jerni walked straight to the kitchen and placed the box on the counter. "Jack said this is Shawndrea's stuff."

"That little prick can't wait to be rid of her," Letty huffed.

"Oh yes, and it's stressing Tiffany out," Jerni said in a bubbly voice.

"Who is Tiffany," Letty asked.

"She is his new girlfriend," Jerni explained. "Correction fiancée."

"Fiancé! Wow, that bastard moved on rather quickly from saying he could not live without her to now erasing her existence and getting a new one," Letty said.

"A thought just occurred to me," Jerni said. "Has anyone checked Shawndrea's bank statements?"

Letty paused thoughtfully before responding, "I don't think so. Why would we check that?"

"Because it might tell us where she is," Jerni said, holding up a few bank envelopes. "If these envelopes do not have the statements, we need then we could request more."

"Give me that," Letty requested as she took it from Jerni, tore it open, and started scanning it. "This statement makes no sense because it indicates that the last transaction was for gas, the day she came home to attend Ninnie's graduation. And why is there a transaction for an adult sex shop on here?"

"Let me see it," Jerni requested.

"Obviously, there is nothing on there that will help us," Letty said as she lit a cigarette.

"Wait, this other statement has a charge to a local bar," Jerni pointed out. "Is it something you all frequent regularly?"

"I don't recognize this bar," Letty remarked, looking at the statement.

"Maybe she met up with someone there, and they might have a clue where she could be now," Jerni suggested.

"Hmm," Letty replied, taking a drag from her cigarette. "I doubt it."

"It can't hurt to check out. Do you want to go with me to check it out?" Jerni asked.

"I mean, I guess it can't hurt to check it out," Letty said, putting out her cigarette. "I will drive."

"Do you have a photo we can take with us?" Jerni asked.

Letty grabbed a photo, and they went to the bar together. "I can't believe she would have come here," Letty said as they exited Jerni's vehicle and looked at the building.

"Maybe it's nicer inside," Jerni said as they approached the entrance and walked inside. "Or maybe not."

They approached the bar, and Letty pulled out the photograph to show the Bartender. "Hey, have you seen this person," Letty asked as the Bartender approached.

He takes a quick look with a flicker of recognition and says, "No," because he is unsure why someone is asking.

"Can you please take a closer look," Letty requested. "She is my daughter, and she has been missing for some time now."

"We know she was here a few months ago because it shows a charge to this bar," Jerni said, holding up the bank statement.

The Bartender was quiet for a moment before responding. "Yeah, I know her. She has been coming here for several years and always leaves with a different man," the Bartender said.

"No, that can't be her because she only turned 21 not long ago," Letty remarked.

"Maybe take a closer look," Jerni requested, taking the picture from Letty and stepping closer to the Bartender.

"I don't need to look at it again to know who that is," the Bartender stated. "Because I know that is Shawndrea, and she drives a big green van and has been coming here for a few years. I mean, I haven't seen her much lately."

This news caught Letty off guard, and she needed to sit down. "Can you please get her some water," Jerni requested.

"No, I'm fine," Letty stated. "I just need a moment to process all of this news."

"I can tell you that the last time she was here, she was being harassed by a man called Berry Price," he explained. "I was trying to keep an eye out for her, but I turned help someone, and when I looked up, they were both gone. I have not seen her back in here since."

"Would that have been about three or four months ago?" Jerni asked, looking at the statement.

The Bartender thought about it and nodded yes.

"Thank you," Jerni said, holding the statement for Letty. "That is about the time of this charge."

They were both lost in thought as they walked out of the bar. "Who is Berry…what did he say the last name one?" Letty asked.

"Berry Price," Jerni responded. "I don't know who that is, but that name is familiar. I'm going to start researching to find out where he lives so I can question him myself."

"I want to be there," Letty requested as they entered Jerni's vehicle.

"I will definitely keep you posted, and we can go together," Jenri remarked, but in the back of her mind, the name gave her cold chills up her spine, and she was relieved at the idea of not going alone.

Jerni went home and rummaged through her files and notes because the name Berry Price was gnawing at her, and she had to find out where she knew the name. Suddenly, the light bulb went off, and she remembered Franny had given her the license plate number.

§

Weeks ago, Jerni reached out to her friend at the police station who ran the plate number, which was registered to a PJ Ferguson.

Jerni wanted to talk to PJ, but she did not have his address. As she sat there, she began to think, how are these two things tied together, and how can I get someone's address when all you know is their name?

She started yawning and couldn't focus. She realized it was getting late, and it was going to take her full brain power to think this one through. She would need to figure out how to get Berry's address, but first, she was going to have to get some sleep. Her husband was reading a bedtime story to their daughter, who, for some reason, started preferring her daddy read her the bedtime story, so Jerni was trying not to feel hurt about it.

Jerni woke up in the middle of the night, realizing she could look up PJ in the phone book to see if he was listed. She slipped out of bed and made her way downstairs, trying not to wake anyone. She went to the kitchen, found the phone book, and started searching through it. She found it, and he lived in Ellery. Suddenly, there was a noise, and her heart jumped as her husband came down the stairs.

"Your little hobby has you working more hours than me, and I'm an attorney who is supposed to be working long hours," her husband said as he sleepily went to grab a glass and some water out of the kitchen sink while Jerni was writing down PJ's address.

"Is there anything I can help with?" he asked as he finished his water and headed back upstairs without waiting for a response.

Jerni was relieved he did not give her a hard time. She slipped the address into her purse and returned to bed. It took her some time to go back to sleep because she was anxious about getting up and talking to PJ, but what could she ask him about his truck being parked down the street from Chase's house? Franny kept insisting she check it out. She thought about making Franny go with her into the unknown to have some backup in case things went south, and maybe she should take up that self-defense class her husband kept recommending.

As she pulled up to PJ's house, he was in the yard with his dog and came to greet her. She explained why she was there, but PJ told her his uncle Berry Price had been driving the truck until he wrecked it. He was supposed to be fixing it up, but it never happened. He had no idea why his uncle would be parking in the neighborhood but gave her his address. Just being in PJ's driveway gave her goosebumps, and she did not know why, but she saw someone looking at them from a window in PJ's house.

She filed away Berry's address, completely forgot about it, and ignored Franny when she asked about him. Franny refused to go with her, so she never dared to talk to him because she had no reason to pursue it further.

She called Letty to let her know she had Berry's information, and they agreed to meet and talk to him. Franny would be so happy to hear they will finally track Berry down.

Chapter Fourteen

Factory Life

The phone rang at Sheldon's house, and Sheldon ran to answer it, thinking it might be Chase or an update that they had found Shawndrea. It had been several weeks, and there had been no word on her whereabouts.

"Hello," he said into the phone.

"How are you doing?" Grammy asked.

"I'm doing well, thanks. How are you doing?"

"I'm good," she replied. "You told me to let you know when I got some more sweet corn. When do you want to come by and pick it up, let me know."

"Grammy, it's Sheldon."

"Oh, wow, you two sound so much alike these days," Grammy chuckled. "How are you doing, Sheldon? I'm sorry. I guess I asked that already."

"It's okay. I'm doing well," Sheldon replied with a chuckle. "Mom is off somewhere with Damian."

"Have her call me when she gets home and tell her that is not an option," Grammy said sternly and was about to hang up.

"Wait, how are you doing?" Sheldon asked because he had not talked to her lately and felt guilty for not seeing her more since his graduation.

"I have my good days and my bad days," she replied with a chuckle and half-sad sigh. "I just can't do the things I used to be able to these days, but today is a good day."

Sheldon was not sure how to respond and felt terrible for her.

"Yesterday, I went to repaper my shelves and fell off the stepstool trying to get something off the top shelf. Fortunately, Tiger broke my fall." Tiger is her little black and white dog, which she has had for years and goes everywhere with her. "I thought for sure I broke my hip and killed my dog at the same time. Luckily, they are both alive and well. Best believe I got an earful from your uncle when he got home. He had told me we would do it together on Saturday, but I thought, why wait when I'm doing nothing but sitting here anyway."

"I have to go see what Tiger is barking at outside," Grammy said. "Don't forget to have your mother call me and come and see your grandmother soon."

"Yes, Grammy, I will tell her to call you, but it does not mean it will happen," Sheldon said.

"Boy, she better; you tell her she is not too old for her mother to take her over my knee still," Grammy growled.

"Oh, I'm sure I'm gonna tell her that, Grammy," Sheldon said with a chuckle.

"You better, or I will skin both your hides," Grammy stated with a slight laugh. "Bye, Sheldon."

"Bye, Grammy."

§

It was Monday afternoon and Sheldon's first day at the factory. Sheldon and his mom decided it made sense to ride together to work because their commute to work was 45 minutes, which made him anxious. Because, he was supposed to arrive early, but Mandy seemed to be taking her sweet time. He was worried about being late on his first day and had no idea what his job would be. When they called to tell Sheldon he got the job, they did not tell him exactly what he would be doing, only when to be there, and it did not occur to him to ask.

Mandy had started working at the factory a few years ago after her divorce. She was excited to have Sheldon working at the same factory. Now, he would keep her company on the drive to and from work.

Ironically, they instructed Sheldon to head to the cafeteria for orientation with the other new hires, which was the same place he had interviewed. The plant manager welcomed them and talked about the company's mission. Then, they showed a video of the company's history and workplace safety. Sheldon was so nervous that he was only half paying attention.

They filled out several new hire documents, and because Sheldon was so nervous, it all became a blur. Before he knew it, it was time to head down to the plant. Sheldon looked over at the door and noticed Terry, the guy who had interviewed him, standing there. Terry took them down into the plant. Sheldon thought they were going to get a tour of the plant. Instead, Terry started leaving behind some of the people in the department where they would work.

Sheldon was excited to see where his mom worked on the assembly line. He was unsure exactly what she did because his mind drifted to something else when she talked about work. He wished he had paid more attention when she spoke about her job and department.

As they continued, they walked along a yellow-lined path through the plant. The floor was so dirty that the yellow was barely visible. Loud presses were banging away, and machines with sparks were flying out of them. Now, Sheldon understood why they were made to put in earplugs and safety glasses before leaving the cafeteria.

The first department they walked up to was called the Welding department. They told six people this was the department they would be working and introduced them to their foreman. Terry joked awkwardly with the foreman of that department.

Sheldon was getting more eager to see where his mom worked and hoped he would be working close to her. They had to be getting close.

As Terry walked them through the factory, Sheldon was surprised at how dirty and scary it was. Terry acted arrogantly, waving at people in other departments along the way, but it was clear they did not know who he was or did not want to wave back. Sheldon could not help but stare at his cartoon-like wild hair, which was light brown and stuck straight up.

Terry acted overly confident and thought he was better looking than he was. Sheldon chuckled at this character.

They continued to the following department. Terry was talking with someone from another department, and, at first, this department seemed calmer until the presses started. The presses were so loud Sheldon could hardly hear what Terry was telling them. Plus, he became distracted by the sparks behind the curtains on what appeared to be an assembly line. As sparks were flying everywhere, presses pounding loudly, Sheldon could have sworn Terry just called his name to work in this department, which he called Bike Fab.

Terry smirked at Sheldon, watching panic flicker across his face as the rest of the new hires were led to their assigned departments, leaving Terry behind with Sheldon and a few others. Sheldon watched as the foreman of the following department, who had been speaking with Terry, guided the others away to their departments.

Sheldon looked around in disbelief that this was where he would work, and that Terry would be his boss. How could this be? This department was even dirtier than the last department. The floor was black and greasy, the air was full of smoke, and his mom was nowhere in sight.

Sheldon stood there looking around, taking it all in and waiting for someone to tell him what to do next. A short blond-haired guy in his mid-thirties walked up to the group.

"Everyone, this here is Strand. He will show you what you will be doing," Terry smirked as Strand eyeballed the group, then looked Sheldon up and down, shaking his head at Terry. "He is your line maintenance man. If there is anything, you need to be fixed. He is your guy." Strand gave a side-eye snarled look to Terry, who took notice.

"Come on, this way," Strand said as he turned and walked over to show them how to clock in and out every day.

"First, find your timecard with your name on it," Strand said, pointing to a large metal frame that hung on the wall. It had slots that held paper cards. Strand grabbed his card as an example and held it up.

"Most importantly, you want to make sure you arrive here at the factory in enough time to clock in before your shifts start," Strand said, looking around at them to make sure they were listening. If you are late clocking in or forget to clock in, you might not get paid for that time. If you are late for work, the first time is a warning, the second time you will be written up, and the third time you could be fired."

"Please find your card, and let's get this show on the road," Strand requested, and the new hires hesitated for a moment. "Come on, it's not going to bite. You go first," Strand said, pointing at Sheldon.

Sheldon scanned the wall for his name, found his card, and shoved it in the machine.

"Good job, except for one thing," Strand said. "You stamped yours backwards, buddy. Try again. Please make sure you put the card in with the information facing upwards."

Sheldon felt his face turn red. He quickly shoved the card into the machine and put it back into a slot on the wall. His fellow new hires followed his lead.

"Now follow me and I will show you what you will be doing today. Make sure you are always wearing your safety glasses," Strand said looking at one of the new hires who had put them on the top of his head. Then he continued to walk them towards the back of one of the assembly lines. "Why do I always get...?" Sheldon could hear Strand mumbling something to himself.

Strand quickly showed Sheldon the tedious job of grinding off weld plater from welded joints on bike frames. Strand called it Dyno Filing. "You are also responsible for checking for holes and the quality of the welds," Strand explained. "This is a two-person job, and this here is Ben, who can give you tips on working faster," Strand stated before walking away.

Sheldon quietly worked and tried to keep up with the amount of work that was piling up on their table. Sheldon tried to stay focused on his job but could not help but look around to see what others near here him were doing. Their workstation was the second from the end of the line.

At the end of the line was an older lady using a press to put end caps on the tube where the handlebars would go down to the wheel and then strategically stack them on a metal palette on rollers so that she could easily roll it onto the rollers that go to the paint department when it is full of frames. She would look over at Sheldon and smile while chewing gum. She patiently waited for Ben and Sheldon to complete their work so she could do hers.

Suddenly, she stood beside Sheldon, grabbing a hand file and cleaning a frame to help. "These welds are terrible tonight," she remarked. "I'm Stella, and that's Moe," She said, pointing to an older man banging on a bike frame. "That machine he is using is called a straightener. His job is to ensure the frame is straight and aligned."

The line started to get backed up when a tall, blond, blue-eyed guy flung back the curtain that he was welding behind to see what the holdup was.

"That is Cary," She whispered to Sheldon as she grabbed another frame.

"What the fuck is going on?" Cary yelled, not to anyone in particular. Sheldon tried not to look up and kept grinding the weld splatter off the bike frame. "Who the fuck is this?" Cary asked, pointing at Sheldon and looking at Moe, who worked between the welder and the dyno filers straightening the bike frames on a machine.

Cary walked away, shaking his head and cussing some more, throwing his welding glove onto the ground as he walked to the foreman's office.

"Don't worry about him. He is just a prick," Ben stated, continuing to work as a cigarette hung from his mouth and was furiously working to smooth out a huge weld.

Sheldon nodded. He could not help but wonder why he got put in the seventh realm of hell, that this must be a joke or a bad dream, and he would wake up soon.

"So, where are you from, and what brought you here?" Ben asked as he was banging a large piece of weld splatter off. Sheldon gave him a little background as they continued working. Sheldon did not know him well enough to share too much, so Sheldon explained that he was from a small town and grew up on a farm, and now both his parents work there. Cary came back and continued working.

"God damn, this is messy shit," Ben said loudly and then laughed as he picked up his dyno file and started grinding away. "I guess I shouldn't say that too loudly. Little princess might get mad and start sending us a lot of shit to grind off." He laughed a nerdy laugh this time.

Sheldon noticed that Ben had an easy demeanor and did not seem to get excited about too much. However, that night Ben seemed to be losing his patience with Cary's crappy work. It somehow gave Sheldon comfort in knowing it was just as challenging for Ben and that this was not a normal amount of clean-up that was typically required.

By the end of his shift, Sheldon was tired, dirty, and covered in metal shavings. He even had bits of metal shavings in his hair. The one thing he had to look forward to was getting to see Chase that weekend. Chase had been busy with his schoolwork and life guarding when he could and playing basketball with Trey and Tommy.

§

Chase pulled into the grocery store parking lot and parked. He hesitated a moment, debating on putting the top up on his new car, but he was only running into the store for a quick moment. Chase ran into the grocery store and grabbed a Coke and something to snack on. He was hungry after a long day of summer school.

While deciding which candy bar he wanted, people had started clamoring near the front of the store, looking out the windows. Lost in thought, Chase did not hear someone come in and shouted to call 911 that someone's car in the parking lot was on fire.

He got in line to check out when he heard an older lady in front of him telling the cashier that someone's car was on fire and that the fire department was on its way.

By now, many people were at the windows looking out at the scene. Chase walked by the window to check out the commotion. Through the cracks of people, he could see that it was his car that was on fire. He ran out to check on his car, but it was too late and engulfed in flames. His head was reeling, wondering how it could have happened. He could hear more sirens as another fire truck grew closer. It took him back to the night of the accident.

The sound of the sirens gave him flashbacks to that awful night. He remembered hearing sirens and Laramie's voice talking to him. He thought about how Laramie's voice had soothed him. It was even stranger that it ended up being Laramie who was there for him. A second fire truck pulled up as firefighters from the first truck worked to extinguish the blaze.

Sheriff Bolden walked up to Chase to get his statement. He told the Sheriff he had no idea what happened. It seemed like something Laramie would have done in his mind, but that did not make sense. He had not even seen Laramie or had a chance to thank him for being there for him that night. The Sheriff continued talking to Chase, but Chase was lost in thought, thinking back to the night of the accident.

"Mr. De Longpre, did you hear me," The Sheriff asked again. Chase turned to look at him. "Do you usually leave the top down?"

"No, I was only going in to grab something quickly," Chase replied.

"The city fire inspector will be in touch with you," Sheriff Bolden said, handing him a piece of paper. "Here is the report to give to your insurance company, and this is where we are towing your car."

Chase was half listening; he was surprised by the memory of the night of the accident and that his new car was just totaled. "Are you sure you're okay," Sheriff Bolden asked. "Do you need a ride home?"

"Thanks, but I live close and I can walk," Chase said as he turned to head home. The Sheriff watched him with concern before he turned and climbed into his police cruiser.

§

Chase had barely said two words since Sheldon had picked him up. As Sheldon drove silently, he debated what to say to Chase. "You, okay?" Sheldon asked, glancing over at a brooding Chase.

There was a long pause before Chase cleared his throat to speak. "I'm just upset about my car," Chase responded.

"I'm sorry," Sheldon said, placing his hand on top of Chase's hand.

"I'm upset because I was supposed to pick you up in my car. I wanted tonight to be special," Chase explained.

"Tonight is special because I get to spend it with you," Sheldon stated.

"Thank you for being so sweet," Chase said as he took Sheldon's hand to his lips and gently kissed it.

Despite Chase's concern about what had happened to his car, he could forget it for the moment as they shared a nice dinner. It was one of their best nights since Chase's accident. They laughed and kissed the whole night, lost in each other; it was like the last six months had not happened. When Sheldon pulled up in front of Chase's house to drop him off, they sat in the car for another hour, kissing and saying goodbye.

"I have to go. I have an early morning of exercising. I have to get back in shape for football this fall," Chase said while kissing Sheldon. "Grrr, I just can't stop kissing you."

Sheldon laughed as he started the car, still kissing Chase. "Go, get some rest," Sheldon insisted, even though he did not want to leave Chase. They smiled big smiles at each other as Chase got out of the car. Sheldon waited so he could watch Chase walk away. "Man, he still has a nice ass," Sheldon said to himself as he drove off.

§

Sheldon's time at the factory was flying by. One day, when Sheldon clocked in for work, a bubbly, petite brunette bounced up to Sheldon. "Howdy, I'm Teana," She said with a big smile and extended hand. "Today, you will be working with me on one of the presses since my partner is late."

Sheldon struggled to work fast on the presses because his mind would wander and daydream, and he would slow down. Teana would have to come over and quickly knock out what she had built up. Luckily for Sheldon, Teana's partner, Torrie, showed up and relieved him.

When Sheldon returned to his regular job, Ben was relieved to see him because the table was piled up with bike frames that needed cleaning. "Where have you been?" Ben asked. "Thank goodness you're here."

Sheldon explained where he had been. After weeks of working together, Ben and Sheldon began to open up about each other's life.

Ben explained that he had been laid off from an oil rig and was working at the factory until the rig started back up. Working at the factory was a piece of cake compared to working on an oil rig. Ben was a very tall and skinny young man in his late twenties. He explained that he and his dog, Bo, lived alone.

His girlfriend wanted to move in with him, but he was not ready to live with someone. He liked living the life of a bachelor. He had to answer to only himself. There was no one else to clean up after or to fight with. Ben seemed like a very mellow guy.

"How do you stay so mellow all the time?" Sheldon finally asked Ben.

Ben looked around to see if anyone was listening. "My little secret helper," Ben whispered. Sheldon just looked at him, not sure what he meant by that. He figured he did not want to tell him. "If you come with me at break, I will show you."

"Okay," Sheldon replied.

Sheldon had no idea what he was agreeing to, but at break, Sheldon followed Ben towards the bathrooms. The men's room was on the second floor, so he followed Ben up the stairs. He wondered why they were going to the bathroom.

Instead of entering the bathroom, Ben turned and continued up the stairs. Sheldon had not noticed before that the stairs continued up. They came to the top of the stairs, and Ben opened the door that led out onto the roof. They stepped outside, and the night air hit Sheldon in the face.

"Quick, close the door and follow me," Ben requested. Sheldon followed Ben around to the other side of the stairwell. "Just in case someone was to come up, we want to have enough time to stop what we are about to do." Sheldon had no idea what "what we were about to do" meant.

"Now you have to promise not to tell anyone about this. You promise?" Ben asked.

"I promise," Sheldon replied nodding in agreement.

Ben pulled out a small, white, slender object and lit it. Sheldon recognized it immediately from the time he smoked one with Charlotte and once with Chase. Ben took a huge drag and then passed it to Sheldon.

Sheldon, forgetting about his previous promise to himself to never smoke again at work, took a hit from it and started to cough profusely, which caused Ben to bust out laughing. Sheldon had smoked only a couple of times before, but something was different about this stuff. After Sheldon stopped coughing, he started to laugh, too.

Sheldon took just a couple of hits, and the effects were already buzzing through him. He felt fantastic, and the view from the rooftop was breathtaking. The city lights stretched before him, sparking a strange sense of freedom. They both laughed like school kids for a while before heading back inside.

Sheldon felt pretty good until he returned to the break area and saw his co-workers. He grew concerned that they knew he was high. He started to feel like everyone was staring at him. Sheldon returned to his workstation and started working before it was time to. He was working with his head down because he did not want to make eye contact with anyone.

Moe was watching Sheldon and noticed he was acting differently. He tried to ask Sheldon what was wrong, but Sheldon could not understand Moe's words. To him, Moe looked like a clown laughing at him. It was freaking Sheldon out even more. He started hallucinating and was seeing things that were not there.

Ben watched Sheldon work furiously to get every little spot. He was dyno-filing so much that he made the frames shine more than usual.

After a couple of hours, Sheldon's head started to clear, and he began to feel normal again. "How you are feeling," Ben asked Sheldon during their last break.

"Better now, I was seeing things that were not really happening," Sheldon replied.

"Yeah, sometimes that happens," Ben chuckled.

"I don't think I want to do that again," Sheldon said, and they both laughed.

"Fair enough," Ben said, sipping water from his glass. "It's not for everyone."

As Sheldon returned to his workstation, his eyes landed on the pallet of bike frames they'd finished that night. The frames gleamed, their edges smoothed and shining more than usual. Sheldon couldn't help but chuckle.

Chapter Fifteen

Train Wreck

Shawndrea had been missing for a couple of months when Letty received a call from Sheriff Bolden saying that a farmer was checking his crops when he discovered Shawndrea's car. "What are the Bottoms," Letty asked Mandy as they drove to see Shawndrea's car.

"The Bottoms are down in the lower-lying area near the river where it tends to flood in the spring," Mandy replied. "Some people might call it the back roads or backwoods."

When Letty called Mandy to share the news, Mandy immediately told Letty she would be right over to pick her up and take her to see Shawndrea's car. Letty was beside herself and was highly anxious about finding Shawndrea's car and what it meant.

"I figured Shawndrea would have shown up by now, that she was just pulling one of her stunts of running off with a friend and not telling anyone," Letty confessed. "But finding her car abandoned sort of throws a wrench in that idea." There was a pause, and silence filled the car.

"Oh god, Mandy, I'm afraid of what we are going to find," Letty stated, biting her lip and looking out the passenger side window. "God damn that girl. I'm gonna kick her ass."

Mandy did not know how to respond, as Letty stared out the window as the trees and fields passed.

"I'm sure we are going to find her soon, and you're probably right that she has run off with a friend," Mandy finally said, reassuring Letty.

They pulled down a tiny dirt road barely wide enough for one car to drive down. Corn stalks were on both sides of the road. Letty started to look white as the road became grassier due to the lack of traffic.

"Jesus, we are literally miles from anyone's house. I'm thinking we went the wrong way," Letty said exasperated as they turned a corner and saw the Sheriff's car. Letty's heart started pounding as she spotted Shawndrea's car abandoned in the middle of nowhere.

Mandy parked behind Sheriff Bolden's car and got out. As they walked up, they saw that Deputy O'Grady was taking pictures as Sheriff Bolden was completing a report.

"Morning, Ladies," Sheriff Bolden greeted them. "We have called in all available officers to help search the area for your daughter, or any clues to where she went. There does not appear to be any foul play. It seems to have just been left here with the keys still inside."

The Deputy climbed inside the car and dusted for fingerprints before starting it up. "It seems to be running just fine, and half a tank of gas still in it," the Deputy yelled from inside the car.

"It's just protocol in situations like this," Sheriff Bolden offered after he saw how big Letty's eyes were and that she looked pale.

A flatbed tow truck pulled up, and the Deputy went over to tell him they were ready for him to take the car into town. There was not enough room for the tow truck to go around the other vehicles, so he had to drive over some of the corn to get in front of Shawndrea's car. Even though the car was drivable, they decided to have it hauled out to preserve any evidence.

"We are going to start searching the area here shortly. We didn't find any tracks to indicate which direction Shawndrea might have headed, so we will sweep the entire area, working our way outwards," Sheriff Bolden explained. "I recommend you go home, and we will keep you posted," He suggested to Letty.

"I don't think so," Letty said, offended by the suggestion. "Mandy, do you mind dropping me off at home so I can change into different clothes and put on more suitable shoes?"

Mandy did not even have a chance to respond. "I will be back shortly to help with the search," Letty stated as she returned to Mandy's car and opened the door to get inside.

§

Meanwhile, Sheldon was in town visiting Chase on his lunch break, and today, Sheldon brought Chase a chicken sandwich for lunch.

"I really look forward to the days you can bring me lunch. It is far better than sitting in the empty cafeteria eating whatever is in the vending machines. Even though it's only for forty-five minutes, I appreciate this time together," Chase explained, taking a drink from his Dr. Pepper. "How is the new job going?"

"I hate it," Sheldon stated. "I don't feel like I'm doing anything with my life. Though I do like the paychecks."

"Well, don't stay too long, or it will be harder to get back into school," Chase stated.

"I know, and I should be enrolled in school for this fall, but it was too late, and I missed the deadline. Also, I don't know where I would go or what I would do."

"This is a great opportunity to think about what you want to do," Chase said, taking a bite of his chicken sandwich. "But don't wait too long, though, because it will be time to register for Spring Classes."

"You are right," Sheldon said while Chase finished his sandwich.

"I will be glad when summer school ends," Chase mentioned. "Even though I only get two weeks off before school starts again for the fall. I will go with you to register for classes if you like."

"That would be nice," Sheldon said, giving him a big smile and a kiss. "I better get home."

"Yeah, I better get to my next class," Chase said, getting up to throw his garbage away. He then gave Sheldon a long, tight hug and a kiss on the lips.

"The boys are planning to play basketball later so I might join them," Chase stated as he walked Sheldon to the exit and held the door for him. "Don't work too hard."

"I won't," Sheldon said smiling and turning to wave goodbye and headed to get in his car.

§

Sheldon had just arrived home from seeing Chase on his lunch break as Mandy pulled in behind him, returning home from dropping Letty off at her home. They were both making lunch before they had to go to work. Sheldon was making mac and cheese to go with the chicken and salad Mandy was making.

"Have you heard from Levin since he moved out?" Sheldon asked as he stirred the cheese into the pasta, trying to see what his mother was in a mood about. He could tell something was happening, and she had barely said a word to him.

"Nope, and I'm not reaching out to him," she responded, turning off the stove, taking the chicken out of the frying pan, and putting one on each of their plates. Sheldon shook his head because they were both as stubborn as the other. He was at a loss as to what could be going on.

"Chase is about to finish with summer school," Sheldon commented as they sat down to eat.

"They found Shawndrea's car," Mandy finally stated as she pulled out her chair to sit at the table and eat lunch.

"What?" Sheldon asked, not entirely sure he heard her correctly. Mandy explained that her morning was spent taking Letty to see Shawndrea's car and she left her to go back alone to assist in the search.

"I feel bad we are going on with our lives and heading to work instead of searching for Shawndrea," Mandy stated.

"That is understandable," Sheldon acknowledged. "Unfortunately, we cannot put our lives on hold, right? I hope she shows up soon and she is okay."

"I don't think I can even eat this," Mandy said, pushing her plate away as she began to explain. "They found Shawndrea's car in the cornfields, down in the bottoms. My stomach's in knots. I should stay home from work and help with the search, but…"

The sudden, piercing screech of the train brakes cut off her words. The sound echoed ominously, followed by a heavy silence as the train ground to a halt.

Sheldon and Mandy looked at each other. Trains suddenly stopping on the tracks near their house happened many times before, but something this time felt different. They both looked out the windows but saw nothing out of the ordinary.

"I will go out to the road and see if I can see anything," Sheldon offered as he took off for the door and ran out to the road.

At first, Sheldon could not see anything. "I see a vehicle sitting sideways off the road," Sheldon said to Mandy as he turned towards the house and saw Mandy standing with the cordless phone. Somehow, she knew something was wrong. "Here, call 911, and I will drive up and see if I can help. She handed the phone to Sheldon and ran to get her keys.

As Mandy backed out of the driveway, the phone rang. "911, what's your emergency?" the Operator asked.

"Yes, there has been a train accident, and a vehicle has been hit," Sheldon quickly explained.

"You said a train hit a vehicle?" The Operator asked.

"Yes."

"Where are you located?" The Operator asked.

"We live at RR7 Box 214 near Ellery. It's the tracks just west of our house," Sheldon stated, trying to remain calm. He walked up the road but was afraid to get too far from the cordless phone base. "The ambulance must take Orange Hill Road because both crossings are blocked."

The Operator repeated what Sheldon shared. "Can you see if anyone is injured?" the Operator asked.

"No, because I'm on a cordless phone and cannot move that far from the base so I cannot get close enough to see."

"Okay, we have help on the way," the Operator said. "Please call us back if they are not there within about 20 minutes."

Sheldon hung up the phone, his mind racing about what had happened and who was involved. He ran up the road with the phone still in hand.

On the right side of the road, he could see a van facing towards him and noticed the smashed-in driver's side of the van where the train clipped it, causing it to spin around. The van was halfway off the road and covered in dust. He saw deep skid marks in the road where the train flung the van around. As he got closer, he saw the license plate that read Snape.

He recognized the van, and the name on the plate was familiar. His mind raced as he tried to piece it together. At first, he did not make the connection of who the person was sitting in the driver's seat and that they were not moving. Her head rested against the headrest, and her mouth was slightly open. He noticed dust covered everything, including the driver. It looked like she was peacefully sleeping.

The passenger-side double doors were open, and Mandy was inside the van, talking to the lady and trying to feel for a pulse.

"Help is on the way," Sheldon said, slightly in shock as he surveyed the scene.

"I can't get a pulse," Mandy said frantically, turning to look at Sheldon with great emotion in her eyes. "I saw someone walking on the other side of the train towards her parent's house."

At that moment, it dawned on Sheldon who this woman was: Mary Snape, his old bus driver. "Can you go look for the other person and tell them to come back that help is on the way?" Mandy requested.

Sheldon turned towards the tracks as Mr. Thompson pulled up. He jumped out of his truck and climbed into the van to help Mandy.

Sheldon sprinted toward the train, craning his neck to peer to the other side. Despite his efforts, there was no sign of anyone. He wondered how someone could have made it to the other side of the train so quickly because they would have had to crawl under it to get to the other side. Still, on the off chance they were out of his line of sight, he called out desperately, "Come back!"

It would take a lot of work for someone to get to the other side. Sheldon looked down the tracks and saw someone walking way off in the distance, but he could not tell which direction they were walking in. He only knew that whoever it was too far away to be the other person his mother was referring to. There would not have been enough time for the person to get that far. He headed back to the van.

"We decided not to move her in case there are internal injuries," Mandy stated, frazzled and unsure what to do. "We will let the professionals remove her and see if they can revive her. Did you find the other person?"

"No, I didn't see anyone on the other side of the train, up the road, or in the field," Sheldon responded, trying not to look at Mrs. Snape.

It was such an eerie scene. "I saw someone up the tracks. I think it is someone from the train. Maybe they are walking this way."

"Where is the damn ambulance," Mandy bemoaned through tears of frustration because she could not help this woman.

Sheldon could only stand there. He was in shock. Sheldon had never seen a dead body before. Of course, he had seen them in the funeral home, but this was somehow different.

"I have said for years this track is dangerous because of the angle," Mandy said in a shaky voice, pulling Sheldon back to reality. "She was probably looking to her right and rolled up to the tracks, not seeing the train coming around the bend on her left."

"Yeah, I think you're right, Mandy. If she had been a little further on the tracks, it would have drug her along with it," Mr. Thompson said, seeming to try to hold it together and kept rattling on and on. "I bet there is hardly a scratch on the train either. The train's front end is steel and designed to remove things from the tracks to avoid derailment." Finally, they could hear sirens off in the distance.

Sheriff Bolden arrived first, followed by the ambulance and fire trucks. Sheriff Bolden was talking to Mandy to get a recount of what happened from what she knew.

The paramedics were not able to revive her at the scene and loaded her into the ambulance. As they drove off the train conductor appeared on the scene. The Sheriff pulled the conductor aside to get his statement.

"It happened very fast," The conductor stated. "She flew up to the tracks, and I could see she was looking to her right as we approached from her left. She never stopped; by the time she looked to her left, she was on the tracks, and that's when we collided. It's like she never heard the horn blowing."

Sheldon and Mandy had to rush or be late for work. That night, on the way home, they were both exhausted. As Mandy drove down the highway, they were silent, each lost in their thoughts. Both were still in shock over Mary Snape's death and finding Shawndrea's car, but no Shawndrea.

"How's Chase doing?" Mandy asked, breaking the silence. "With so much happening and thinking about Shawndrea, I didn't get to ask when you came home."

"He is doing well," Sheldon responded. "He is almost done with summer school. This job is getting in the way of me seeing him like I used to be able to. It feels like we are not quite as close as we once were."

"That is kind of what happens in most relationships. Welcome to adulthood," Mandy joked.

"Well, I don't like it," Sheldon countered.

"Well, you got to make money, and laying around isn't going to cut it," Mandy stated. "Besides, boys come and go. If he cares, he will still be there for you and you for him." The truck was quiet for a moment, except for the sound of the tires on the pavement.

"I did hear from Levin," Mandy confessed, breaking the silence. Sheldon looked over at her, confused. "He left a message on the machine, but I deleted it." Sheldon had no energy to deal with her and Levin's drama. They were both quiet again. Sheldon was thinking about how the guys at work had teased him that night and how he felt out of place.

Sheldon returned from break and started working. Moe and Stella were chatting when Moe asked Sheldon if he had a girlfriend again, which Sheldon typically tried to play off because he's heard them making disparaging comments towards gay people, so Sheldon chooses to stay in the closet with them as Ben looked up from where he was seated waiting for Sheldon's answer too. Sheldon just said no and continued working, feeling even more alone. It's very isolating being the only possible gay person and surrounded by straight people. Sheldon put his head down and focused on his work while Stella and Moe returned to their workstations.

Sheldon had gotten good at grinding weld splatter off the bike frames and checking for holes in the welds. Tonight, he found a lot of holes in Cary's welds and stacked them up next to his station. Cary saw this, stopped welding, and started cussing loudly. Sheldon pulled back the curtain to see what was going on.

"What the fuck are you looking at, you queer?" Cary shouted as he threw his helmet and walked out of his station. His partner Marcus just stood there watching Cary have another outburst.

"You don't want to mess with him tonight," Old man Moe said as he put chewing tobacco in his mouth. "He and his girlfriend got into a fight at lunch, and he has not been welding worth shit since."

Marcus came out from behind the curtain. Tonight, he had on a pair of tight black jeans, which showed off his bubble butt and had quite a bulge to boot. "See what you did, little fagot," Marcus was mocking what Cary had called him. Everyone laughed, and Sheldon was embarrassed.

Marcus grabbed Sheldon and put Sheldon in a headlock. It was Marcus's way of making the situation not as awkward. He let Sheldon go, then he hugged Sheldon and smacked him on the ass. Sheldon felt uncomfortable with how Marcus was treating him, but the attention from another guy felt nice.

The assembly line that worked beside them broke down, and their welder offered to repair some bike frames with bad welds. The welder asked Sheldon and Ben to bring some frames to his station. When Sheldon bent over to pick up some of the frames, Marcus ran up behind him and started bumping his crouch up against Sheldon's ass and crying out in pleasure.

"Get off me!" Sheldon yelled as he tried to get his hands around the bike frames, but Marcus was making it difficult to get his arms around them. Sheldon was highly embarrassed because, by that time, several people were standing around and laughing at the sight. However, Sheldon was somewhat turned on at the same time because he was not used to that much male attention.

"What the fuck are you doing?" Cary came back and was yelling at Marcus. "Get your ass over here and get to work."

Suddenly, Sheldon was pulled out of his thoughts when his mom swerved to miss an animal running across the road. "I think that was a turkey," Mandy stated as she pulled off the highway and down the gravel road to their home.

Chapter Sixteen

Bar Fly, Lonely Eyes and Cherry Popped

A few years ago, when Shawndrea was in high school, she would sneak out as often as possible. In the previous house they lived in, her bedroom was on the second floor, so she would have to climb out the window and shimmy down the pipe to sneak out. When they moved into the new house, she requested that the bedroom be on the ground floor. Her bedroom was separate from the main house, running along the length of the garage, which made it easy for her to sneak out at night.

Her parents did not seem to notice or did not care about the extra miles she would put on their vehicles. She did not realize that at the time, but she was so sexually active because when she was younger, her uncle had done things to her.

Shawndrea would spend hours driving around, looking for someone, anyone, to hook up with. She became increasingly addicted to the thrill of being with different men, seeking out new encounters as a way to escape routine. Though she avoided vaginal sex, most of the men did not seem to mind as long as their desires were satisfied. Repetition bored her; being with the same man more than once rarely held her interest.

Eventually, she found a local bar that would let her in without showing her ID. There were times she had been so drunk she was unsure how she made it home without getting caught or into an accident.

One night, she was playing pool alone while waiting for a hot guy to walk through the door. She was bent over, lining her sites up to make a difficult combo shot. She tried remembering Aunt Mandy's tips about positioning the cue ball. Shawndrea was about to take the shot when she looked up and saw a young man sitting at the bar.

"Damn, how did he sneak in here without me noticing?" she muttered to herself.

She walked over and sat down beside him. She tossed her hair and flashed a smile in no particular direction. She asked the bartender for a Jack and Coke and acted nonchalant. Pretending, she had not noticed how cute he was.

"Hi," he said with a sideways smile as she caught his eye.

"Well, hi there," She responded with a flirty smile as she played shy, innocent, and coy. The bartender sat a drink in front of her.

"Would you like some nuts?" the cute offered, pushing the bowl towards her.

"Those are not the kind of nuts I want in my mouth," she implied as she put the straw in her mouth, taking a drink suggestively as if she was going down on a guy, which caused him to choke on the nuts that were in his mouth.

They both laughed loudly. Something in this guy's laugh reminded her of someone, but she could not put her finger on it.

"I'm Shawndrea," she said with her hand extended.

"Hi, I'm PJ," he replied, taking her hand. She laughed at everything he said and took every chance to touch his hand casually. The more he talked about himself, the more she realized she did know him.

He was a bit thinner now, but she recognized those lonely eyes and his unkempt blond hair. She used to have a massive crush on him.

"You dated my sister briefly in high school, didn't you?" she probed. He smiled a big smile and looked at her out of the corner of his eye. They had only met a few times, but she remembered him well. However, she never acted on her desire to have sex with him because he was dating her sister.

When they broke up, her sister only said that he was a creep and refused to mention him again. However, these days, neither of those red flags would stop Shawndra from pursuing him. In fact, it only motivated her to conquer him.

"That's right, you're Laynardia's little sister," he acknowledged, looking at her with a sinister crooked smile. Something inside her said to get out of there before she did something she would regret, but something in his eyes held her in place, listening to him talk about his life.

She decided to finish her drink and go home before getting in over her head. "Have a good night," she said just before she downed her drink and stood up to leave.

"Why are you leaving so soon?" PJ asked, flashing a sexy smile at her.

"I have to be up early for sch… I have to be at work early," Shawndrea corrected herself. She did not want anyone to know she was still in high school, or they might not let her come back.

She was digging out the keys as she walked up to the van. She glanced up to put the key in the door when she saw the reflection of a figure standing behind her. Her heart jumped as a hand wrapped around her mouth, and his other hand quickly spun her around. Before she knew what was happening, PJ had her pressed up against the van and kissing her. Heat flushed throughout her body as she felt his body against her, and her nipples suddenly rippled, too. She was extremely turned on and kissed him back.

He opened the door, and they climbed inside. "This opens into a bed," Shawndrea said, but they were so engrossed in each other that there was no time to make a bed as they found themselves on the van floor. As they were kissing, he slipped his hand down her pants. "Wow, you are already wet," PJ commented. "I like it."

With his thumb, he started working her clit in a circle, getting her even more wet and causing her to moan as she had never moaned before. She had trouble catching her breath because it felt so good, and no one had ever done that. Suddenly, she wanted him deep inside her. She took over her pants, and he followed suit. He climbed back on top of her and started kissing her neck. She could feel his hard cock inches from her opening.

For a moment, she flashed back to her uncle on top of her, but she pushed those thoughts away. She quickly noticed the way PJ was doing it felt completely different as he slowly started to slide inside her. He looked deep into her eyes. As he slid further inside, there was an instant sharp pain that made her scream out as she saw stars. He started passionately kissing her as he moved slowly in and out of her.

The pain slowly subsided as he began to thrust inside of her, and she slowly started to enjoy it and became close to orgasm, which surprised her because that only happened when she was masturbating. The boys she had messed around with were never able to bring her to orgasm. Before she knew it, she had the most intense orgasm. Her whole body was jerking. It was so fierce as she was screaming out in ecstasy. Before she knew it, PJ was coming, too, as she felt him exploding inside her. She could feel his cock throbbing inside her with each ejaculation. PJ collapsed on top of her as they both lay there, breathing heavily.

"Thank you," he said, kissing. "That was the best sex I have had in a very long time."

She did not know how to respond to that statement. "You're welcome," she finally said.

They briefly fell asleep in each other's arms before PJ left. As Shawndrea drove home, she wondered if this was what it felt like to be in love. She had not seen PJ again for a long time and had been chasing the feeling of that night ever since with other guys but never had any luck.

§

It was months before the sale of their house or Ninnie's graduation. Shawndrea struggled to be in a monogamous relationship with Jack, and she felt the itch with him being gone all the time. While she was at her mom's house, she was bored and horny, so she snuck out in the van for old time's sake because the van had more room than her little car for having a good time. She was proud of herself for getting back out there alone. She had previously made Ninnie go with her because of an incident, but she felt confident she could do it alone; this way, there would be no one else to judge her.

She walked into the bar where she first time saw PJ after he had broken up with her sister and he had taken her virginity. She had been chasing the feeling ever since it, but nothing lived up to that night. She had hoped to see him in there as she looked around. There were only a couple of people in the bar. Two guys were playing pool, and an older man was sitting at the end of the bar. "What can I get you," the bartender asked as she sat at the other end of the bar from the older man.

"Can I get a Jack and Coke?" Shawndrea asked, wondering if he would ask for her ID.

"Sure thing," the bartender responded as she started making her drink. He sat it in front of her, and she started taking a sip. She was going to drink it slowly, but it tasted so good she drank it faster than anticipated. The entrance door opened, and she turned, hoping it would be PJ, but a man and woman entered.

"I couldn't help but notice you from the moment you walked in," a voice from behind startled her, and she turned to see the old man had approached her and sat down next to her. "I'm Berry, and you are?"

"I'm Laynardia," she responded, shaking his outstretched hand. For some reason, she did not want to give this man her real name, so she automatically said her sister's name.

"You okay over here," the bartender asked, walking up after noticing Berry was creeping her out.

"I'm fine, thanks. But can I get another one of these?" Shawndrea asked.

"What are you drinking," Berry asked.

"Jack and Coke," Shawndrea responded.

"Wow, that is pretty strong for a young lady," Berry responded.

"Well, I gotta put hair on my chest somehow," Shawndrea joked, and Berry laughed louder than she expected.

Something about this guy's laugh and appearance reminded her of someone, but she could not put her finger on it. He was creeping her out, so she decided she should probably head home because PJ was not coming.

"Laynardia," he said thoughtfully. "That's not a name you forget."

Shawndrea immediately thought, *Oh no, the jig is up and is on to me, but also, how does he know my sister?*

"Didn't you used to date my nephew PJ?" Berry asked.

"Briefly," Shawndrea casually responded, playing along.

"I used to have the biggest crush on you then," Berry stated, putting his hand on her leg. "You look even prettier now that you have slimmed down.

"Thanks," Shawndrea responded, unsure what to say but was ready to run.

"I used to drive around looking for you and hoping to bump into you," Berry explained. "Then, for a while, I thought you were dating the high school football player. But it turns out he was one of them there queers. Sorry about that."

Shawndrea had no clue what or who he was talking about, but she was getting clear stalker vibes from this guy and needed an out.

"I will be right back," Shawndrea said as she got up and headed to the bathroom. If she still felt creeped out by this guy and there were no other attractive guys in the bar after she used the bathroom, she would head home.

The bartender was at the other end of the bar, attending to some patrons who had just come into the bar. Berry kept an eye on the bartender as he stirred something into Shawndrea's drink.

Shawndrea exited the bathroom and decided to finish her drink, calling it a night. She thought the first sip of her drink tasted funny, but she downed it anyway. She told Berry and the bartender good night and proceeded out the front door. She was frustrated she did not get any dick that night as she crossed the parking lot towards the van.

She walked up to the van and reached for the door handle. She started seeing double and felt woozy. She thought about going back inside as she saw her blurred reflection in the driver's door window. Suddenly, she saw someone else's reflection standing just behind her. At first, she thought it was PJ, but before she could confirm, someone put a piece of cloth over her face. The sharp, chemical scent filled her senses, and within moments, everything went black.

"This is going to be even better than the truck," the attacker said, eyeballing the van. He dragged her around the van and popped open the passenger sliding door. He pulled her inside and laid her on the floor.

He got out of the van and walked over to his truck. He reached into the back of his truck and pulled out his toolbox. When he climbed back into the van, Shawndrea was still unconscious.

"Ohhh. Yes, this gonna be fun," the attacker said with a spine-chilling smile as he pulled down her pants, then his pants as he climbed on top of her.

Halfway through, Shawndrea woke up with his sweaty face in hers. He quickly put the rag back over her face as she drifted back into unconsciousness, she wondered if this was a dream.

When he finished, he started fumbling through his toolbox. The sound caused Shawndrea to wake up. She saw him pull a hammer and a pipe wrench through the haze. He noticed she was starting to wake up again. He sprayed something into a rag and held it over her face again. She tried fighting back but was too weak and fell unconscious again.

When she woke, the van was eerily silent. Her mouth was parched, and a relentless pounding throbbed in her head. As her senses sharpened, a new dread settled over her—her lower body felt numb, as if it were no longer part of her. Panic bubbled up as she tried to move, but her legs remained unresponsive.

She realized she was in shock, and the absence of pain was only temporary. It would come soon enough. Determined not to wait for it to take over, she resolved to move. She needed to get up—needed to get home. Summoning every ounce of strength, she braced herself to try.

She rolled onto her side and looked around for any sight of PJ or whoever attacked her. She could not be sure it was PJ, even though it looked like him. Shawndrea had just started to pull up her pants when she noticed she was covered in blood. She had no idea what time it was but knew it had to be late. She did not have time to clean this up now. She went to the van's bathroom to grab the rug when she noticed the mess left in the sink. She grabbed the rug and threw it over the spot on the floor.

The next day, Shawndrea stayed in her room and only came out for a snack or something to drink. She ensured no one was downstairs to see her hobble into the kitchen. It never occurred to her to report what had happened or to go to the hospital. She was too embarrassed, felt it was her fault, and wanted to put it all behind her as quickly as possible.

She made her way back to her bedroom and just closed the door when she heard the garage door opening. She thought about how to get the spot out of the carpet. Somehow, cleaning the spot would make the whole incident disappear. She heard the van door slam shut.

"Shawndrea, Ninnie, and Jimmy get your asses out here!" Letty yelled.

Shawndrea's stomach dropped. She immediately thought her mom discovered the spot.

With her heart pounding, she opened her bedroom door that led to the garage.

"Will you get your asses out here and carry these damn groceries into the house," Letty demanded just before she walked into the house carrying only her purse.

The others flew past her, and each grabbed an armful of bags. Shawndrea ambled over to the van and looked inside. She saw a corner of the rug flipped over, revealing part of the spot. She quickly flattened it back out just as Jimmy came running up to grab two more bags and left one for her to carry.

Shawndrea carried the bag into the house, trying to walk as normally as possible. Her mom was already seated in her favorite spot in the Den, with a romance novel in hand and a cigarette hanging out of her mouth, and Shawndrea hurried past the doorway.

Shawndrea sat the groceries on the counter and hobbled back towards her bedroom. Ninnie turned and noticed that she was trying to get out of helping put the groceries away.

"Stop right there. Do you think these groceries are gonna put themselves away?" Ninnie asked, halting Shawndrea in her tracks.

"Shawn, will you get me another pack of cigarettes out of the freezer?" Letty asked with a cigarette still hanging out of her mouth.

Shawndrea did as she was requested. While leaving the Den, her mom noticed she was walking funny.

"Why the hell are you walking like that?" Her mom queried over the top of her reading glasses.

"I - I stubbed my toe earlier."

"Huh, well, hurry up and get that ice cream put away before it melts," Letty demanded.

"Already done! No thanks to anyone else," Ninnie replied with a snarl to the back of Shawndrea's head as she hobbled back to her room. "Aliens should have abducted her at birth," Ninnie grumbled and then giggled at the idea of Aliens torturing her sister.

"I heard that young lady!" Letty called out. Ninnie quietly mimicked her mom, mouthing the words I heard that young lady. "Do not get sassy with me!" her mom yelled.

Ninnie looked around, wondering how her mom could have seen that through the wall, but her mom had always been intuitive like that. Except when it came to Shawndrea, who somehow got away with everything, and Ninnie could never figure out how or why.

§

One rainy Saturday afternoon, Chase and Sheldon were lying in bed. They had Sheldon's house all to themselves. Sheldon decided to get up and take off his clothes. After stripping for Chase, he climbed back into bed.

"Aren't you the naughty one," Chase said, biting his lip while looking Sheldon up and down. He stood up in the bed, nearly getting caught in the ceiling fan. "Ey," Chase said, ducking as he proceeded to get undressed.

Chase went in for a deep kiss as they breathed each other in. Chase started kissing his way down Sheldon's chin, neck, and bare chest. Sheldon sucked in a breath when Chase reached his nipples. Chase looked up, smiling, pleased that he was making Sheldon moan.

"Have you ever been rimmed?" Chase asked

"Uhh, I. Don't. Know," Sheldon stammered, unsure what it meant.

"Here, roll over," Chase instructed. Sheldon flipped over onto his stomach. Chase straddled Sheldon's thighs and leaned in to kiss the back of Sheldon's neck. With their naked bodies pressed against each other, Sheldon could feel Chase's hardness pressing between his cheeks. Chase reached around to kiss Sheldon, and this aroused them even more. Sheldon thought is this it, as Chase began to run his tongue down to the small of Sheldon's back.

Sheldon panicked when Chase spread his cheeks because no one had ever come this close to it before, and before Sheldon had time to think about it further. Chase buried his face between Sheldon's cheeks as he flicked his tongue across Sheldon's hole, which caused him to moan even louder this time. Sheldon had no idea that it would feel this good as Chase's tongue targeted Sheldon's hole like a torpedo, causing another moan to come out from deep within Sheldon. He had no idea where this was going, but it felt good and scary. He felt vulnerable and exposed, but it turned him on at the same time.

Sheldon could not believe there was this much pleasure in the world. He grabbed Chase's hand as he thrust his hips into Chase's tongue, begging for more. Chase knew Sheldon was ready for more. Chase spit on his hand and proceeded to lube his cock.

With Sheldon still on his stomach, Chase pressed his body against Sheldon's and held onto both of Sheldon's hands. As Chase entered him, Sheldon saw stars and cried out in pain. Chase paused and held it there. "Now relax and take a deep breath and let it out as push out just a little to let me inside you," Chase whispered in his ear and then kissed his neck. "I wanna be the one to pop your cherry."

Sheldon wanted nothing more than to feel Chase inside him at that moment. He listened to Chase's suggestions and took a deep breath, and as he let it out, he pushed out a little, allowing Chase to enter him a little at a time.

Chase paused again, letting Sheldon get used to it and relax. Then he pushed gently past the first ring of muscle, taking it slowly. Sheldon's first reaction was to tense up, but he did as Chase suggested and relaxed. Sheldon grunted, squeezing Chase's hands as Chase slipped past the second ring. After a beat, Sheldon began to moan with pleasure as he pushed himself against Chase, begging for more.

They became two bodies entangled in one another as they tried different positions. They were both covered in sweat as they both cried out in pleasure. Chase released his load deep inside Sheldon as Sheldon's load flew over their heads and onto the headboard. Chase collapsed onto the bed next to Sheldon, panting and laughing. "Man, do you always shoot that far?" Chase asked, laying on his back and taking a deep breath.

"Yes, especially when I'm worked up," Sheldon answered while still breathing heavily, laying his head onto Chase's chest. They lay there in the afterglow.

"I had no idea," Sheldon said with a laugh as he laid his head back onto Chase's chest. "Thank goodness no one was home, or they would've gotten an earful and we would never heard the end of it."

As Sheldon got out of bed, he looked out the window. "It has stopped raining," he commented. They had been too busy to notice. Sheldon opened the door to his bedroom and ran naked to the bathroom as Chase strolled behind him. They heard a noise from the kitchen. They turned to look, and Mandy, Damian, and Susan sat at the kitchen table.

Mandy had a look of horror while Damian and Susan were both holding in their laughter. Sheldon freaked out as he covered himself and ran into the bathroom while Chase casually entered the bathroom confident and proud with what he had swinging between his legs.

"Don't worry, boys, we only arrived in time for the climax," Susan said while stifling her laughter. "We weren't here for the whole show."

After they finished washing up, Sheldon was too embarrassed to leave the bathroom. He popped his head out of the bathroom and, with a towel wrapped around him, ran to his bedroom. Chase walked out wrapped in a towel, smiled, and waved as he casually strolled to the bedroom. He did not seem worried about Mandy being upset about them having sex in her house. Chase had to convince Sheldon to come out of the bedroom after they got dressed.

"Damn it, boys, you have set the bar high now!" Damian exclaimed.

"Bar? By the sounds of it, they went places I have yet to venture to," Susan teased. They all laughed except Sheldon, who had turned twelve shades of red.

"Oh god, you two stop," Mandy demanded, trying not to laugh clearly over her shock.

"Gotta go," Damian said, getting up from the table and kissing Mandy goodbye. "I will be back later to make more sparks fly in this house."

Mandy just shook her head as Damian left. "I hope he is joking. We had sex last month," Mandy stated casually. "Though I'm afraid Damian is going to get tired of me and run off with some younger woman,"

"Why do you think that?" Susan curiously asked, giving Sheldon a sideways glance that told him, "Here it comes, the real story."

"Well, he likes to do, you know what, a lot, and I'm okay with just once a month," Mandy confessed to Susan and Sheldon's horrified faces. "Well, is he not making you cum?" Sheldon blurted out, shocking Mandy and Susan, whose faces swung to meet his as Chase chuckled.

"He does have a point," Susan said, looking back at Mandy. "Does he make you have an orgasm?" Mandy just sat there with a blank look on her face.

"Have you ever even had an orgasm?" Sheldon queried cautiously, afraid of hearing any actual details.

"That is none of your damn business!" Mandy blurted out.

"Fine, but you should not have started the DAMN conversation," Susan retorted with a chuckle.

"Maybe that is true, but I'm your mother, and I'm ending it," Mandy snapped, pushing her chair back from the table as she got up and left the room. Sheldon and Susan both busted out laughing.

"Did that just happen," Susan said, still laughing.

"I think we hit a nerve," Sheldon whispered. "I don't think she has ever had an orgasm."

"I don't think she has been in the neighborhood of an orgasm," Chase whispered.

"That makes sense and would explain why she is always on edge and grumpy," Susan added.

"I wish I could be as open with my family about this stuff," Chase stated with a huge smile. "That was quite entertaining."

"Did she say last month!?" Susan questioned quietly, and they all laughed again. "She makes it sound like it is something you have to do, like doing laundry or the dishes."

"It is as necessary as laundry, if not more so," Chase added with a giggle as he stood up from the table. "I hate to run, but I have homework calling my name and early morning practice." He kissed Sheldon goodbye before leaving.

§

Shawndrea was losing track of time and was not sure how long she had been held captive, whether it had been weeks or months. She could tell it had to be closer to August because the nights were becoming slightly cooler. She did know she was getting tired of being tied to a chair.

When Shawndrea managed to break free of the ropes that bound her, her captor would find her untied and punish her with a few slaps and kicks, and each time, the ropes were tied even tighter. She no longer felt as strong as she once had, and her captor, despite being small, was unusually strong. The only time Shawndrea was untied and allowed out of the chair was to use the bathroom.

Over the last few hours, Shawndrea dragged herself and the chair to the wall. Every movement was a battle, her muscles screaming in protest, but she persisted. She'd tried to break the chair quietly, hoping to free herself, but she only managed to snap one of its legs. The damage was useless for escape, leaving her drained.

She slumped against the wall, exhaustion overtook her, and she drifted into a restless sleep.

The sharp clinking of a padlock opening jolted her awake. Her heart raced as she realized her captor was returning. Panicked but resolute, she knew she had to return to the center of the room before they noticed she had moved. Summoning the last of her strength, she began maneuvering the chair again.

A few days ago, Shawndrea had been leaning against the wall, her body heavy with exhaustion, trying to catch even a moment of sleep when the sharp click of a padlock opening snapped her awake, sending a jolt of fear coursing through her veins.

When her captor discovered she had moved the chair, she slapped Shawndrea until she had blood running down her face and left her alone for almost two days without food or water.

Remembering the last time caused the adrenaline to kick in, and she quickly straightened up as her head pounded. Her curly hair covered most of her bloody face and swollen lips. She quickly moved to where her chair had been and sat down just as the door opened. She felt the chair start to fall backward.

She would make every effort to make sure her captor would not notice the broken chair for fear of being punished again. What if she were to break the chair now and free herself? Could she overpower her captor with her hands still tied behind her back, and where would she go? She does not even know where she is being held.

She concentrated on keeping the chair steady, her breath shallow, and her movements deliberate. The door suddenly swung open, and her captor strode in, slamming it shut with a force that echoed through the room. Shawndrea froze, her pulse quickening, praying her efforts to conceal her struggle had gone unnoticed.

Shawndrea screamed into the gag, her muffled cries full of rage and terror.

"Now, now, you don't want to make me angry again," her captor said with a cold edge to their voice. "You remember what happened the last time."

In their hands was something grotesque, a flattened, mangled creature resembling a squirrel, its lifeless form reminiscent of roadkill. Shawndrea recoiled as her captor stepped closer, holding the limp, broken body up to her face, the rancid smell hitting her like a wave. Her stomach churned, but she forced herself to stay still, knowing any sudden reaction might provoke them further.

Shawndrea lunged backward in her chair. It was a dead squirrel. She felt the chair give more and was afraid of going backward. In the captor's other hand was a knife, which she brought up to Shawndrea's face. Her captor laughed an evil laugh through the handkerchief that covered her face. All Shawndrea could see were these sad, lonely eyes. She still did not recognize the captor or why she was holding her against her will.

Shawndrea had no idea what her captor was about to do with the knife she was waving in front of her face. As she leaned back, balancing her weight on the chair, she suddenly heard a voice yelling from outside. Shawndrea recognized the voice but could not place it, which frustrated her.

Her captor turned towards the direction the voice came from. The yelling was too far away for Shawndrea to make out the name he was calling. She looked back at Shawndrea as she dropped the squirrel on her lap.

"Eat bitch," she said with another sinister laugh as she ran the knife down Shawndrea's arm, penetrating the uppermost layer of skin and bringing forth a slight pool of blood. Shawndrea screamed through the gag, flaying her head back and forth. Her captor brought the bloody knife to Shawndrea's lips and shushed her. "Since you ate all my leftovers and junk food, I thought you could use a little fresh meat." She laughed as she headed for the door. "You can't seem to get enough food, huh, little piggy."

For the last several weeks, her captor had fed her stale chips, leftovers that appeared to have mold and flat Mountain Dew. She would shove the food into Shawndrea's mouth, sometimes almost choking her. The cans of Mountain Dew looked so old that the label was faded, but she knew the label well enough to know what it was even though it tasted nothing like Mountain Dew anymore.

For a split second, when her captor opened the door to leave, Shawndrea thought, "This is it." I could finish breaking the chair and charge at the open door, but the problem would be the ties that bound her hands. She would not be able to thwart the attacker's knife in time. The opportunity passed as the door closed and the padlock snapped shut.

She flung the dead squirrel off her as soon as the door closed. She felt like she was going to vomit from the thought of it and the smell. She had to suppress the urge because she might choke on her vomit due to the gag in her mouth.

After a while, she thought her stomach was rumbling because she was hungry, but she quickly realized that was not the case. She started to get emotional as she felt her stomach moving from the now apparent movement of the life that was inside her.

Tears streamed down her face as she rocked herself back and forth, a motion that mimicked cradling a baby, offering a sliver of comfort in her despair. Suddenly, a small but distinct flutter caught her attention—a kick.

Her heart leaped with a mixture of relief and joy. She had not felt movement in what seemed like forever, and this was the first real sign of life from her baby in weeks. Then it hit her. She had to be about five months along if she felt strong kicks now. The horrifying realization followed: she had been held captive for at least three months.

The thought made her stomach churn, but the tiny kick gave her hope—a reason to keep fighting.

She hoped her captor would return quickly because the kicks made her realize she needed to pee. She was hungry but did not want her to return and feed the dead squirrel to her.

Chapter Seventeen

Harriet Castor

Mandy was rearranging things in her pantry when the phone rang.

"Hello," Mandy said into the receiver.

"Woman, what are you up to?!" The voice on the other end shouted into the phone. "Want to go to an auction with me?"

"Harriet, is that you?" Mandy asked shocked that she was receiving a call from her.

"It's meeee!" Harriet replied in a singsong voice. "You have something better to do?"

"No. How have you been?" Mandy inquired still in shock. They both had gone through divorces around the same time and helped each other through the tough times. She had not heard from Harriet since she started dating a new guy over three years ago and then married him.

"Eh, I will fill you in on the ride to the auction place," Harriet replied, inhaling a drag from her cigarette.

"Still smoking, I see," Mandy chortled.

"Hell yes, they will have to pry these damn things from my cold dead hands. Besides I have to have something to do with my hands." Harriet stated and laughed a smoker's laugh, which made Mandy bust out laughing. "Now get your ass ready. I will be by in about an hour to pick you up."

A large grey double-cab truck pulled into Mandy's driveway. "You like my new ride?!" Harriet asked as she looked over the top of her sunglasses at Mandy, who walked up admiring her new truck. Harriet's new truck was set high off the ground, and Mandy grunted as she climbed into it. "Good lands. I know you're about to be a grandmother, but could you hurry it up?"

"Look here, lady. I may be a grandmother but I can still get my foot high enough to kick your ass," Mandy joked. They both laughed.

During the ride to the auction, they spent it catching up. Harriet told her that her second divorce was still ongoing and nastier than the first. "This guy was a total freeloader, always looking to grab whatever he could from anyone he could," Harriet said, shaking her head.

"Would you believe this man had the audacity to start selling my stuff behind my back and stash the money for himself? When I asked where my stuff was, he tried blaming my boys." She said, fuming as she lit a cigarette. "Boy, did that get my blood boiling. And when that did not work, he tried saying that someone must have taken it when we were not at home."

"After I kicked him out, I changed the locks, got a dog, and put locks on all the buildings outside so he could not steal anything else. You better believe I changed those locks the same day," She chuckled as she flicked the ashes out the window from her cigarette and took another puff. "I showed his ass," she said as she exhaled smoke.

They arrived at the auction site and immediately started walking around to see if there was anything they wanted to bid on.

"Oh my God, Mandy, we are surrounded by a bunch of old pervs," Harriet remarked, puffing on her cigarette. "Boy, just look at 'em ogling us like a bunch of horny teenagers, ready to pounce on the last available Happy Meal." Mandy just laughed as they continued looking through the stuff to be auctioned off.

One old man kept following them, and it started to make Harriet angry. Finally, she stopped and looked him square in the eyes. "Look, I don't know what you think you're after here, BUDDY, but this Happy Meal does NOT have a toy inside," Harriet blurted out and turned back to see what Mandy was showing her.

"Aren't you Dennis's old lady?" The old man asked

"Let's get one thing straight here, BUDDY. I ain't no one's OLD lady, least of all his," Harriet snapped back. "I kicked his sorry ass to the curb!"

The old man moved in and cupped Harriet's ass as he did. She swung around and punched him square in the eye.

"That's what you get for putting your HANDS on me asshole," Harriet snapped. He turned to walk away, and as he did, he looked at her like she was crazy. "Try explaining that to your wife!" She turned and grabbed Mandy's arm. "Let's get out of here before he calls the cops. Besides, there is nothing but junk here anyway."

They were parked a couple of blocks down the street from the auction. As they walked to the truck, they looked back to ensure no one was following them, and laughing at what had just happened.

"You clocked him so fast I did not see that coming," Mandy snickered. "By the look on his face, he did not either."

"Damn straight, and I bet he won't be doing that again anytime soon," Harriet said, climbing up into her truck. Something caught Harriet's eye as pulled into the alley to turn around and head home.

"My word, would you look at that? Is someone throwing that stuff away?" Harriet called out as she pulled her truck into the alley, put it in the park, and got out.

There were a lot of boxes stacked next to trash cans behind what appeared to be an empty house. Upon closer inspection, it was boxes of books, appliances, and nice dining wear. "Forget the auction lets load this stuff up," Harriet requested.

"Are you sure we can?" Mandy asked, looking around.

"It's next to the garbage. I do not see why not," Harriet said matter-of-factly as they stared at each other momentarily.

"Okay, if we are going to do this, let's be quick about it," Mandy demanded.

"I say we load it all up now and go through it later to see what's not worth anything to save time," Harriet suggested.

"Good idea!"

They both grabbed a box and started loading them into the truck. Under the piles of boxes was a dresser.

"Well, I be damn, this looks like an antique," Harriet declared. "We have to take this too."

They both looked at the dresser and then at the truck's bed, which was full of boxes. "How about we put some of these boxes inside the cab since you have the whole back section of the cab still empty?" Mandy recommended.

"Excellent idea," Harriet cooed.

They made room in the back of the truck and started carrying the huge dresser over to the truck. It was a long dresser, and despite their strength, it was too much for the two of them to get it up and into the truck.

They were standing in the middle of an alley, trying to think of a way to get the dresser into the truck.

"Give me a minute, and we can try it again," Mandy requested.

"What the hell are you doing," a deep voice said from behind them. The two startled women slowly turned around to see a tall, lanky, middle-aged man standing behind them.

Both women were silent for a moment. "Uuuuuuh, we are picking up my friend's stuff," Harriet replied.

"Oh, well, in that case, would you like some help then?" The man asked.

"Suuuure," Mandy said coy like.

The two ladies got on one end, and the man got on the other and loaded the dresser quickly into the truck.

"I'm Ricardo," the man said, extending his hand.

"I'm Harriet, and this here is Mandy," Harriet said, shaking his hand, and then Mandy shook his hand.

"Good. Now I have names to provide to the cops when I report you stole my mom's stuff," Ricardo smirked. Both women looked at each other like the jig was up. It seems they were determined to go to jail that day.

"Oh my god," Harriet said. "Are you serious?"

"No, I'm just kidding," Ricardo chortled.

"So, this isn't your mom's stuff," Mandy asked.

"Well, technically, it is my mother's stuff, but she passed, and we are clearing out the house to sell it."

"Oh, I'm so sorry for your loss," Harriet said, touching his arm. "I wish there were something we could do but we really must be going now." Harriet looked at Mandy to get into the truck and get the hell out of there before he changed his mind.

"Well, there is sooomething you could do for me," He said, looking at Harriet.

"Oh, and what's that," she replied, looking at him and then Mandy.

"How about you have dinner with me next weekend," Ricardo requested.

"Sure, we can do that," Harriet said, climbing into her truck and shutting the door. She started the engine when there was a knock on her window. "Oh, shit, we are not going to get out of here, are we," Harriet said through gritted teeth to Mandy.

She rolled down the window, and Ricardo handed her a piece of paper. "Call me," he said with a wink.

"Sure thang," Harriet said as she placed the piece of paper on the dash then put the truck in gear and they drove off. She looked into the rear-view mirror to see him standing in the alley watching them drive away. Something about that image stuck with her.

"Let's get home before anything else happens," Mandy suggested and then she half laughed as Harriet was quiet and lost in thought.

"Yes, let's get home," Harriet agreed. "Somehow, when we are together, we always have interesting encounters. I do things with you that I would never do with anyone else."

"Same here!" Mandy laughed. "Another great escape."

Harriet was quiet again. "Though, it looks like you may have left something back there with Ricardo," Mandy teased.

"What are you talking about?" Harriet hissed.

"I saw how you were looking at Ricardo," Mandy replied. "I think he got your Mona purring for some attention."

"For heaven's sake, Mandy, you have lost your damn mind," Harriet scoffed, inhaling a drag from the cigarette she had just lit. "Plus, how do you know what I call my lady business anyway?"

"Secret," Mandy laughed loudly.

"Well, that is okay because I heard you made out with a woman last year," Harriet smirked.

"How did you hear about that," Mandy gasped.

"Seeeecret," Harriet drawled out tauntingly. "See, two can play that game." They both chuckled and were quiet for a moment except for the occasional chuckle.

"Remember when the boys were little, and we were out scavenging for aluminum cans and ran into those crazy people?" Harriet asked, breaking the silence.

"Oh yeah, I had forgotten about that!"

"They were trying to say that we were on their territory like they had a claim on it," Harriet recounted. "They tried stealing all our cans out of the back of your truck."

"I swear she was drunk and did not have one tooth in her head," Mandy added. "The look on her face when you told her off was priceless. Remember how dirty her kids looked, too? They were such a damn sad sight."

"My lands, yes, it was terrible, those poor children didn't stand a chance," Harriet acknowledged. "Say, do you mind if we store this stuff at your place? I do not want my soon-to-be ex-husband to get his dirty little hands on it."

"Yea, that's not a problem," Mandy replied. "Let's just unload it and call it a day. We can go through it tomorrow or next weekend."

"Sounds like a solid plan to me," Harriet said as she pulled down the road that led to Mandy's home. "So, does this mean you're a lesbian now?"

Mandy busted out laughing again, "That's a secret between me and my loooover." They both laughed as they drove down Mandy's road.

They spotted Damian's car as they pulled into the driveway. He had just gotten home himself. "Oooo, I finally get to meet this new man of yours. My word Mandy, you said he was young, but hot damn, he is young." She remarked as she spotted him in the yard.

Damian had wasted no time taking off his work shirt. He was about to jump on the riding lawnmower when he saw them. He walked over to greet them. Mandy introduced the two of them.

"Are those abs," Harriet queried, biting her lip and reaching out to touch them. "I have never actually seen any up close, but I have always wanted a set of my own." She made Damian blush.

"Let's put these young muscles to work unloading this stuff," Mandy requested.

"You got all this stuff at the auction," Damian asked, picking up a couple of boxes like it was nothing.

"Yeah, sure," Harriet said, smirking at Mandy.

§

When Sheldon returned from break, he put on his work gloves while Moe was at his workstation rolling a cigarette. "Do you have any plans for the weekend?" Moe asked.

"Just hanging with…," Sheldon paused because he was about to say Chase but caught himself because he did not want to explain to Moe who Chase was. "Just hanging with friends. What about you?"

"Mmmm," Moe said, licking his lips as he licked the cigarette paper and finished rolling it. He watched two girls approach them and watched them walk past them. "The things I would do to her if I were twenty years younger," He remarked as he put the cigarette in his mouth and lit it.

"You mean, if you were 30 years younger," Stella said, laughing as she startled them. They had not seen she had walked up from behind.

"I'm going to mow the yard?" Moe replied, changing the subject.

"Did you finally get that old mower running again?" Stella asked.

Sheldon was glad for the change of subject because it's always awkward when straight men start ogling women around him and expect him to reciprocate the same reaction.

"Yeah, my son-in-law changed the carburetor, and it's running like new," Moe said, putting on his work gloves and starting to work.

§

Sheldon and Chase were lying in Sheldon's bed, discussing what to do for the day. "How's the new job going?" Chase asked, snuggling up next to him. "You don't really talk about it."

"It's not what I thought it was going to be," Sheldon responded.

"Why is that?" Chase asked.

"It's just that I'm not sure why they stuck me in the dirtiest and smokiest department," Sheldon finally replied, looking out the window. "I thought I would be working with Mom in her department."

Chase put his hand on Sheldon's leg. "Somehow, it will all be okay," Chase reassured him as he flashed him another smile, and Sheldon placed his hand on his. "Just think before we didn't have this time together because you were working that grocery store."

"You're right," Sheldon said, kissing his lips.

"I have an idea," Chase said, sitting up. "Let's get a book and go down, lay by the river, and read. Just enjoy the peace of the day."

"What about your homework?" Sheldon asked.

"Oh, it can wait," Chase said. "I want to enjoy what summer we have left." They jumped out of bed, grabbed bookbags and their books, and headed out.

They arrived at the river, made their way to the riverbank, and found a place to throw the blanket down and get comfortable.

"Remember the last time we were here? We got high, and you had to go to work?" Chase chuckled, lying back and looking up at the sky.

"Yeah," Sheldon responded as he lay down beside Chase. "It's nice not having to be anywhere, and we can just be here and listen to birds, the breeze blowing, and the water flowing."

Sheldon picked up his book to start reading and looked over to see Chase had already drifted off to sleep. Sheldon breathed in the fresh air's scent and soaked in the sounds as he drifted into the story he was reading. He loved relaxing in the summer haze, becoming immersed in a story, and even better, he was lying next to Chase, whose hairy legs just brushed his, sending a warm sensation throughout his body.

Sheldon used to be afraid to be this close to the water because his parents always scared him and Levin that the snakes would get them, but next to Chase, he felt safe enough to let his guard down and get lost in his book. He could not ask for more, and all his stress melted away, forgotten for the time being.

Chapter Eighteen

Do You Really Want to Know

It was Chase's last day of summer school, and he was excited for it to be over so he could enjoy what summer was left before his fall classes started. He made his way to his last day of shop class and wondered how Sheldon was doing. As he crossed the parking lot, he stared out at the highway just before opening the door to shop class, wishing he was going for a drive with Sheldon instead of being stuck in school.

"As I explained last week for your final exam in this class, you will explain the step you took to rebuild the engine, and then we will see if it runs," Mr. Paul explained to the class and saw a panicked look on some of the students' faces. "Don't worry if you do not finish; just tell me how you got to where you are in the process of rebuilding their engine. Your grade is not dependent on whether you finished but on how well you did with what you were able to accomplish. Though there will be bonus points for those you have finished," he explained, looking at Chase.

Chase was ready to give his presentation and get it over with, but he kept waiting for the teacher to call him, and he had everyone else go before him.

He finally called Chase's name to present. Chase got up and faced the class to explain the steps he took to rebuild his engine.

"First, I disassembled the engine to inspect it, checked the condition of each part, and replaced those that were damaged, such as some of the bearings, gaskets, piston rings, and seals," Chase explained. "Then, I cleaned the camshaft and crankshaft and cylinder head."

"Next, I reassembled the engine, and lastly, I checked to see if it would turn over. I discovered something was wrong with the camshaft, and the replacement seal was faulty, so I swapped it out, and now it should be running like a new motor," Chase finished explaining and looked at the teacher.

The teacher was excited to see if the engine would turn over because he rarely had a student who could rebuild an engine on their own and get it to work properly. He walked over and hit the switch, and it did turn over. The teacher was the only one impressed enough to applaud.

§

It was Sunday morning, and Letty parked in front of Jerni's house to go to Berry's place. Franny was trying to convince Jerni to let her go with them.

"What's going on?" Letty asked as she walked up to them.

"Letty, this is Franny, and Franny, this is Letty, the mother of the girl we are searching for," Jerni explained. "Franny wants to tag along with us today."

"Come on, I want to come along because I need some excitement in my life," Franny pleaded as Letty gave a serious look. "I promise I will sit in the car and not get in the way."

"I mean, I don't see how this is going to be exciting, but more the merrier," Letty stated.

"Okay, old woman, like the last time, I'm not responsible for you if something goes sideways," Jerni said, pointing her finger at Franny as Letty gave her a look of "Oh damn, she means business." "You got it, Short Bread," Franny said gleefully.

Until now, Letty had felt like no one cared about her missing daughter, so it felt nice to be doing something, even if she did not know what it would lead to.

Since Jerni had some difficulty tracking down Berry, she felt somewhat accomplished as they drove down the road towards Berry's place. However, the closer they got, the bigger the knot in her stomach got.

"How are you feeling?" Jerni asked as they pulled into the driveway and glanced over at Letty.

"My stomach is doing flips and mixed emotions," Letty explained, her leg bouncing up and down. "I also need a smoke really bad, and your fucking no smoking policy is not helping."

"And, don't forget the no cursing policy, too," Franny said popping her head between them.

"Ugh! You are killing me bread," Letty said.

"Its Short Bread," Franny corrected her.

"Be quiet Old Woman," Letty snapped. "Sorry, I'm a little on edge here."

"Hey, you got that right," Franny said chuckling as she sat back in her sit.

"Sorry, I'm just a good Christian woman," Jerni said, putting the car in park, and they got out of the car. "Do you want to ring the doorbell, or should I?"

"I will do it," Franny said from behind as they both looked at her.

"You know it's not a bad idea," Letty said, looking at Jerni and then at Franny.

"He might be more willing to talk to an old woman," Jerni said, as Franny looked hopeful. "We could stay back and observe the property."

Suddenly, there was a knock-on Letty's window, causing them all to scream. They looked to see a young girl with a dirty face and curly hair smiling at them. "Hello, there," Letty said, rolling down her window. "What is your name?"

"I'm Tara," the little girl said as she picked her nose and wiped it onto Jerni's car, which caused Jerni to gasp. They got out of the car, and Franny walked up to the front door to see if Berry was home.

"Are your parents at home?" Jerni asked as she went around and wiped the burger from her car with a tissue.

"My mom is home, but our daddy is out driving a truck and is never at home," Tara explained.

Jerni and Letty watch Franny talking to someone from the front door, look at them, and look back at the person talking, but they cannot hear what she is saying.

"I want to show you my kittens," Tara said, taking Letty's hand

and pulling her towards the barn. Letty looked at Jerni, who only shrugged, "Why not?" while Franny was still talking to Mrs. Price.

Letty followed Tara into the barn, which smelled funky inside, and Tara noticed her reaction. "Sorry about the smell; Daddy buried some of our previous pets that passed away." Tara stood beside a wooden box with some straw when she reached down and picked up a calico kitten.

"They are adorable," Letty said, looking at the fluffy, long-haired calico kittens. "These are very rare."

"Shh, don't let my mom know they are here because she will tell Daddy, and he will make them disappear," Tara requested.

"Okay, sweety, it will be our little secret," Letty said, picking up a light-colored calico kitten. "You are just too precious."

Back outside, Jerni was watching Franny chatting with the wife and looking back to see where Letty was when she observed some trash cans. She looked around, but no one could see if she were to go over and peek at them just as she looked back at Franny, who suddenly disappeared into the house. Jerni gasped, and she was conflicted. Should she go after Franny or check out the trash cans while everyone was distracted? She made up her mind. "Old woman, I hope you're okay because I have some trash to look through."

Meanwhile, back inside the barn, Letty was still petting the kitten. "The smell in here is terrible. How do you stand it?" Letty asked, thinking she could not take the smell much longer.

"You get used to it," Tara said, as her mother was calling her name. She put down the kitten. "We better get back out there."

"Okay," Letty said, putting down the kitten and taking one last look around. There were large mounds of dirt in the back, about six or seven, she counted. They seemed too big for a pet.

Franny and Jerni were waiting by the car. "Let's get out of here," Jerni requested. "This place gives me the creeps."

"I second that," Letty said, looking at Tara going into the house and back to the barn before getting into the car.

"What is that smell?" Jerni asked as she pulled out of the driveway and onto the highway.

"Yeah, it smells like a rotting corpse," Franny said as they looked at her strangely, wondering how she knew what a corpse smelled like.

"I think it's me," Letty confessed. "That barn smelled like something was dead, and Tara said it was the pets her dad had buried. However, by the size of the mounds in there, they had to be some big pets."

"What was she showing you?" Franny asked. "Whatever it was, the mother didn't like you there. And lord did their place smell like dirty animals, but nothing as bad as that smell."

"She was showing me these beautiful long-haired calico kittens," Letty shared.

"Long-haired calico, that is rare," Franny said.

"That's what I said!" Letty explained. "I wanted to take it with me. I might just have to go back sometime and get them."

"More importantly, what did you find out about Berry," Jerni asked.

"Yeah, what did you learn?" Letty asked.

"She said she hardly sees her husband now that he is a truck driver," Franny started to explain. She said that he would use PJ's truck anytime he was on vacation because he sold his truck to buy the rig and had nothing else to drive. According to her, he used the truck for a while, too. She said he should be home on Wednesday if we want to come back and talk to him. "Did you get a sense if she knows what he is up to in his spare time?" Jerni asked.

"I did ask her if he ever went to that bar, and she said he had better not go without me," Franny stated. "Actually, her exact words were that bastard better not go without me. I got the sense she didn't know much of what anyone around her was doing because she was pretty lit herself, and I saw a lot of empty vodka bottles on the floor and the counter."

"Yeah, I saw some in the trash can, too," Jerni stated, and they looked at her. "I had to do something while the two of you were distracting them. I got a look at some of their mail. There were a few things in the name of Kelli, but the wife's name was Mable. Maybe it's one of his kids."

Letty let out an audible sigh. "But what does any of this get us?" she asked.

"Oh, I did ask her why he would be parking on my street," Franny explained. "She did slip up and say he used to be obsessed with one of the Meyers girls and asked me if they lived on that street because he promised her that was over."

"One of my girls?" Letty asked.

"Oh, sorry, is your last name Meyers?" Franny asked.

"Should we stop and go back?" Jerni asked.

"Do you think we would get a straight answer from her?" Letty asked, looking at Franny.

"I don't think so, but if I had known she was talking about one of your girls, I would have asked more about it," Franny said.

Letty thought about it as they drove down the road, wondering whether she wanted to go back and ask what she meant. "Let's go talk to my oldest daughter; something tells me she knows something," Letty requested. "Otherwise, we can ask Berry himself on Wednesday."

"Sure, just tell me where to go," Jerni replied.

They pulled up outside Bob's house, and Letty went to see if Laynardia was home. She met Letty at the door and stepped outside so that Letty did not have to go inside.

"Everything, okay?" Laynardia asked.

"Yeah, I'm just doing some investigative work searching for Shawndrea, and a name has come up that you might know, so I wanted to come and ask you," Letty explained. "I know things have been awkward between us since my separation from you father, but I need your help."

"Sure, anything I can do to help," Laynardia said, pushing her hair behind her ears.

"Do you know someone by the name of Berry Price?"

"Boy, that name is a blast from the past, and not in a good way. He is the foster father of my friend Kelli," Laynardia explained. "Well, I should say we used to be friends until she started sleeping with my boyfriend PJ. Though, if you ask me, Berry and Kelli have always had a weird, creepy relationship, and I was always surprised Mable let it go on, but then again, she was always either drunk or high on something."

"So, that is the only way you know Berry and PJ?" Letty asked, feeling she was not getting the whole story from her daughter.

"Do you really want to know everything?"

"Yes. I do if it helps with the investigation," Letty replied, hoping she did not regret asking.

"Well, I spent the night at their house a couple of times. Her creepy foster father would sneak into where I was sleeping and wake me up with him fingering my pussy," Laynardia said.

"Oh, Jesus," Letty gasped.

"A couple of times, I let him stick it in me to see what it felt like, and one night, Kelli found out and got upset. I later found out he had been doing the same thing to her, and she got jealous, which is why she stole PJ from me because I stole her daddy from her."

"Why did you not tell anyone," Letty said.

"Because I thought no one would believe me, and a part of me felt like it was my fault that I let it happen," Laynardia explained. "Wait, he is not the father of this baby, is he?"

"Nooo," Laynardia responded. "I have not seen him in a few years. And if you want to talk to Kelli, I believe she is still a CNA in the maternity ward at the hospital and last I heard she was living with PJ."

"I'm sorry that happened to you," Letty said, hugging her tighter than she had in years.

"Thanks, Mama," Laynardia said, hugging her back.

"Come and see me soon," Letty requested. "After Shawndrea comes home, I will be moving to California to be closer to your grandmother because she is not doing well."

"I will," Laynardia said, turning to go back inside.

As Letty walked back to the car, she was hesitant about how much of this information she felt comfortable sharing with Jerni and Franny.

Chapter Nineteen

Cheers to Old Friends

Recently, Sheldon's department shut down a few hours early because it ran out of different parts to make the bicycle frames. They would go down the line, asking each person if they wanted to stay and do clean up or help the other line that had enough parts to keep running. Otherwise, they could go to another department to work or go home early unpaid.

Since Sheldon rode with his mom, he would stay and clean up or work in her department when that was an option. When he would work in Mandy's department, they would have him doing odd jobs such as breaking down parts that were not working correctly, cleaning up scraps, or sweeping the floor.

The last couple of times Sheldon went to the department where his mom worked, they would put him on the line helping, when someone would have to leave early, or they were shorthanded. One day, they needed help lacing the spokes on the rims, which was very tedious and hard on the fingers.

"Hi, I'm Dani. I'm friends with your mom, and you must be the famous Sheldon she always talks about. I have seen you talking to her and doing odd jobs on the line. I can show you how to lace the spokes. Follow me."

"I'm not very good under pressure and not always fast with my hands," Sheldon explained.

"Don't worry; when we see you struggling, we will tell you to move to the next one so that you don't slow down the line,"

Dani said, grabbing the bicycle rim. "First, you put a rim in the jig on the carousel, and then grab a hub and put it here in the center."

Sheldon grabbed a couple of rims, put them on the carousel, and then grabbed some hubs.

"To start, we will have you remove completed rims and replace them just like you did."

Sheldon was struggling to keep up, and it did not help that his mom was waiting on the finished rims so that she could put the tire onto the rim.

Dani and Mandy would tell jokes to lighten the mood and sometimes sing a song to boost morale and keep the team moving faster.

Another day, Sheldon was sweeping the floors in Mandy's department when he suddenly felt that things were about to change. He did not know what it meant, but he knew something was about to change.

§

The following week, Sheldon and Mandy were heading home, and they were both tired. "How was your day?" Mandy asked Sheldon as they drove down the highway. She was making conversation to stay awake.

"It was okay," Sheldon responded. "It's weird how we went from working six days a week to running out of parts."

"That is what happens now that they relay more and more on parts and supplies coming from Mexico," Mandy explained. "Sometimes it's super busy and then slow periods."

"How was your day?" Sheldon asked.

"It was okay," Mandy replied. Sheldon thought it was strange because she usually had stories about someone doing something funny or messing up the line, but she did not that night. Instead, they drove in silence for a little while.

"I just heard that Mary's visitation has been moved from Friday to Saturday just before the funeral itself, so we will be able to attend if you want," Mandy said, breaking the silence. Mary was Sheldon and Levin's bus driver when they were growing up. "We can at least go to the visitation, but we don't have to go to the funeral. Do you want to go with me?"

Sheldon did not want to go, but he knew he should because she was a big part of his childhood. Because he would see her every morning before school and after school until his first year of high school. "Yes. I will go with you," Sheldon responded. They were quiet again.

"Also, I was offered a job at Felgen Industries by my old boss," Mandy said, breaking the silence. She had not given it much thought until she thought about Mary getting run over by the train and passing away. Felgen is the German word for rims and is a German-owned company. They manufactured bicycle rims for various companies.

"He started working for Felgen nine months ago and has asked me several times to come and work for him. He said that he could offer me better pay," Mandy explained, but there was a long pause. "I was thinking about just how short life is and that sometimes change is good. Also, I could use the extra money."

Sheldon did not know how to respond. He was utterly shocked by this announcement. His first thought was that he would have to drive to work alone. Then, he realized that he was being selfish.

"I'm excited for you," Sheldon finally replied. "You would be foolish to turn down more money."

"We can still ride to work together," Mandy pointed out, sensing his initial hesitation. She knew her son well enough because they were so much alike. "With the new job, I start work at three-thirty, so you could drop me off first since you do not start till four and then pick me up after you get off work."

"Sounds like a plan," Sheldon acknowledged.

§

It was Saturday, the day of Mary's visitation and funeral. As they walked into the funeral home, Sheldon followed Mandy, unsure of the protocol or what to expect, as it had been a while since he had attended a funeral. When he was younger, he went to his Aunt Pearl's funeral, but it was different because Sheldon and Levin were kept in the back of the room and did not see the body until the end. It felt so long ago that he could barely remember.

Sheldon continued to follow Mandy to the front of the funeral home and got in line to shake the family's hand as they passed by on their way to view Mary in her casket. He looked at her daughter, who was devastated as he shook her hand; he could not find the right words to say to her even though they, in some form, grew up together but were not close.

"Sorry for your loss," Sheldon said as he shook each family members hand.

Seeing Mary lying there in the coffin and the look on her face took him back to the day of the train wreck and how it felt in some way that it happened to someone else. It all felt surreal, and he could not believe it had happened.

He could not imagine what her children must be going through as he sat there listening to the preacher talk about Mary's life and all the children, she touched over the years.

"Wanna get some ice cream after this?" Mandy asked as quietly as she could. "I could use a pick me up."

"That sounds great to me, and it's on the way to Chase's, so that works for me," Sheldon said.

They said goodbye to the family and headed towards Mandy's truck. "I can't believe Levin didn't want to come," Mandy stated as they got into her truck.

"It's probably a good thing because he would have had comments when the preacher talked about all the children she touched," Sheldon stated as he got inside, and Mandy gave him a curious look. "You will have to ask Levin, as it's not my story to tell. But I think he had to work today."

"Knowing him, I can only imagine," Mandy stated as they pulled out of the funeral home parking lot. "Did he ever tell you about the time he got suspended for a week but told you he was sick?" Mandy asked.

"No, I just thought he had the flu and never questioned it," Sheldon responded.

"Next time you talk to him, ask him about it," Mandy stated. "I still don't know if I believe the whole story because it is kind of crazy."

"Now I'm intrigued, and I will have to ask him next time I see him," Sheldon said as they pulled into Dairy King. "Though, I never see him anymore since I'm not in high school, and he works nights."

"Do you see his car?" Mandy asked, looking at the cars in the parking lot for Levin's car. They placed their order and pulled up to the drive-thru window.

"Is Levin working today?" Mandy asked.

"He transferred to Fairfield," the worker said, taking Mandy's money and handing her their order.

"I guess you did not know either?" Mandy asked Sheldon as she started licking her ice cream.

"This is news to me," Sheldon responded as he motioned for Mandy to take her change from the worker.

"Thank you," Mandy said before driving off. "I guess we have something else to ask him about."

After Mandy dropped Sheldon off at Chase's house, she stopped by Letty's to see how she was doing.

Mandy was about to ring the doorbell when the front door opened, and Jimmy flew past her with his skateboard in hand. "Sorry, I can't talk right now, Aunt Mandy. My friends are waiting," Jimmy said as he jumped on his skateboard and rode away.

"Hello," Mandy said, walking into Letty's apartment.

"I'm here in the kitchen," Letty said.

Mandy entered the kitchen, where Letty sat at the table with a book in one hand and a cigarette in the other.

"What brings you by?" Letty asked, putting out her cigarette in the ashtray. "Have a seat. Do you want anything to drink?"

"We were just at Mary's funeral and thought I would stop by and see how you're doing." Mandy stated.

"Didn't she pass away like a month ago?" Letty asked.

"Yeah, but they were waiting for her brother to arrive before having the services," Mandy explained.

"Oh wow, how was the body," Letty hesitantly asked.

"You know, I was thinking the same thing when I walked up to view her body, and surprisingly, you couldn't tell it had been that long," Mandy explained. "Granted, the last time I saw her, she was covered in dust, but she looked like she was sleeping."

"Hmm, how bizarre," Letty remarked, lighting another cigarette.

"You want to go camping with me," Mandy asked. "It might do you some good."

"Unfortunately, I can't get off work long enough to go camping, and it doesn't feel right to go while Shawndrea, is still missing," Letty explained, taking a drag of her cigarette. "Have you talked to Bob lately?"

"No, every time I stop by, Laynardia says he is in bed and never comes out of his bedroom to visit," Mandy explained.

"The grandbaby is probably keeping him up aaaaand I heard he has been seeing someone," Letty said.

"Oh, I had no idea," Mandy remarked. "Do you see much of your grandbaby?" Mandy asked.

"No, and I have invited her to come and visit me, but she always says she is too busy,'" Letty growled.

"Yeah, Bob's my brother and he never comes to see me either," Mandy remarked. "Well, I will hear from him when he needs something. Speaking of relationships, how are you and Trevor doing?"

"Ha!" Letty said, coughing as she exhaled a cloud of smoke.

"Oh, do tell," Mandy said.

"There is nothing to tell. That ship has sailed," Letty stated. "I just stopped returning his calls, and he came by a couple of times, but I do not have time for him right now, and he got the hint and stopped calling or coming by."

"Oh," Mandy responded with a sigh, unsure of what else to say. "Has Jerni been able to help at all with the search?"

"We are going tomorrow to follow up on a lead," Letty stated.

"A lead? It sounds so professional," Mandy responded.

"I hope it leads us to something because we are at a loss right now," Letty explained.

"Well, let me know if there is anything I can do and how tomorrow goes," Mandy requested.

"I better get home and make something for dinner for Damian," Mandy said, getting up from the table. "He had to work today."

"Well, don't be a stranger," Letty said, getting up from the table to see Mandy out.

"If you change your mind about camping, let me know," Mandy requested as she walked outside and turned to look at Letty.

"Will do," Letty said, waving goodbye before closing her front door.

§

Mandy heard a vehicle coming down the road and saw Harriet pulling into her driveway. Mandy went out the back door to greet Harriet, who got out and grabbed a box of something.

"Hey, Lady," Mandy said, greeting Harriet.

"We had some extra sweet corn and wanted to bring some to you," Harriet said as she greeted Mandy. "Also, I wanted to share some gossip with you," Harriet confessed, laughing so hard that she started coughing. "You're not going to believe this. We have so much to catch up on."

They made their way to the kitchen. Mandy walked over to the coffee pot and opened the cupboard to grab another coffee cup while Harriet placed the box of sweet corn onto the counter. "We might have gone a little overboard when we planted our sweet corn this year. It was dip-shit's idea. He thought we could sell it to our neighbors and make a lot of money. What the idiot didn't think through was the fact that most of our neighbors grow their own damn corn," Harriet explained, shaking her head and taking the cup of coffee from Mandy and sitting down at the kitchen table.

"So, what is new with you, lady?" Harriet asked, taking a sip of coffee, and continued before Mandy could respond. "How is your man doing? Don't you have a family member still missing? And how is Sheldon doing working at the factory?"

Mandy didn't know where to start. "What was your question," Mandy joked, and they both laughed.

"I told you we have a lot to catch up on," Harriet cackled taking a sip of her coffee.

"Where do I begin," Mandy stated. "Let me start with the simplest. Damian is doing well. He keeps busy with work and makes good money, so I cannot complain. Sheldon is adjusting to working in the factory, and I am very proud of him because he is really trying to make it work and becoming his own person." Mandy paused to take a sip of her coffee.

"Oh! Before I forget, do you want to go camping with me?" Mandy asked.

"Oh, hell no, are you crazy?" Harriet asked. "You won't catch me anywhere without running water, a flushable toilet, or my nice comfy warm bed. I never travel too far that I can't make it back to sleep in my own bed."

"Come on. You're my last hope," Mandy pleaded.

"What about your man?" Harriet asked, taking a sip of her coffee.

"He is working on a huge construction project, and they are behind schedule, so he can't get the time off," Mandy explained.

"What about Sheldon or Levin?" Harriet asked as she lit a cigarette and exhaled a cloud of smoke.

"Sheldon is going to Rhode Island with his friends, and Levin is too busy preparing for the arrival of their baby, school and working at Dairy King."

"Ah, I get it. What about Letty?" Harriet asks.

"I asked her, and she does not really leave the house because she is waiting for Shawndrea to come home and would feel too guilty to have a good time."

"Oh, that's right," Harriet acknowledged. "Poor thing. I can't imagine having a child go missing like that, and they still haven't any clue?"

"I feel bad because I don't know how to help," Mandy shared. "Most of the family still thinks she has run off with a friend, and they will find her in Florida living it up. It's a bizarre situation, and I'm on the fence. Part of me believes she is missing after finding her car abandoned in a remote place, but another part thinks she just ran off because of her parent's divorce and maybe running away from her fiancé because she is afraid of getting married."

"A lot of what ifs, huh," Harriet stated lighting a cigarette.

"I guess and they are trying to track down some guy named Berry Price," Mandy explained.

"I don't know who that is and I know most everyone," Harriet remarked. "I will ask around."

"Thanks," Mandy responded.

"Oh, did I tell you I start my new job on Monday?" Harriet asked.

"No, you did not," Mandy responded. "I thought you didn't have to work because of grandma's retirement money and your rental property income?"

Harriet gave her a look that told Mandy she was about to hear it all. "I guess I have not told you the latest to come out of my divorce from the son of bitch. He threatened to come after my home, all my possessions, and all my properties if I did not agree to give him seventy thousand dollars. My divorce attorney got him down to fifty thousand, stipulating that he could not return later for anything else. I wanted to go down to thirty-five thousand, but my attorney advised me not to push it. Cut my losses and run."

"You know what the dumb son of a bitch forgot when he moved out?" Harriet asked, but Mandy had no clue.

"He forgot his granddaddy's gun collection in the gun safe."

"So, the joke is on him because I sold those sons of bitches, and there is nothing he can say because he signed that paper."

"They were actually worth something?" Mandy questioned.

"You know, I figured they were just junk and worthless, but come to find out, three of them were worth some coin. Two were 1899 pistols—I forget the names of them—and I got two thousand for each of those. I also got eighteen hundred for a Colt 1911 and a couple of 1903 rifles, for which I got three hundred a piece."

"He is going to have a heart attack when he discovers they are gone. He left several other items, which I had to discard or dispose of. I think he truly believes he will be able to come back and get it all. I'm laughing all the way to the bank."

"I should have listened to Grandmother when she said I should get a prenup, but noooo, I was in loooove, and he would never try to screw me over. If I could go back in time, I would like to smack some sense into myself."

"What is your new job?" Mandy asked.

"I'm going to be assisting older people with simple stuff around the house and taking them grocery shopping," Harriet explained. "It's a very easy job, and it will keep me busy too now that the boys are older; they are doing their own things and probably moving out after they graduate."

§

The phone rang at Mandy's house, but no one was there to answer it, so the answering machine picked up.

"Um, Mandy, it's Lita," there was an awkward pause. "Call me when you get a chance," Lita said. She always felt weird leaving a message on anyone's machine.

When Sheldon and Mandy got home from shopping at the supermarket in Fairfield, Sheldon saw the answering machine flashing and hit the play button.

When Mandy heard Lita's familiar voice, she walked into the living room to listen to the message again. "I have not heard that voice in many years," Mandy said after listening to the message. "I'm going to call her back. Do you mind putting the groceries away?"

While putting stuff away, Sheldon could hear Mandy laughing while she was talking to Lita, which caused Sheldon to smile.

"I was just thinking about you, too," Mandy said. "I would love to go camping with you. I was trying to find someone to go with me, but everyone is busy."

It was as if no time had passed since they last talked. They had a long conversation, and Mandy was full of cheer after she hung up with Lita.

§

Mandy and Sheldon had just entered Mandy's truck and headed to work. Mandy was in an unusually good mood. Things were going well for her: she had started a new job, which she liked, her two best friends, Harriet and Lita, were back in her life, and things with Damian were going well, too.

Sheldon's thoughts drifted away as they drove by the high school and saw all the cars parked in the school parking lot. Sheldon thought it was strange that there were students there where he used to learn and sit in classes all day and sometimes get to see Chase in the hall. He started to miss it and then thought about all the homework and the stress of passing his exams. He had been in such a hurry to escape it as if it were a prison, but it was not that much better on the outside.

"I'm just worried the other shoe is going to drop," Mandy said out of the blue as the got into the vehicle to head to work. "Things are going well. So much has changed, yet some things are still the same."

"I guess I can relate," Sheldon remarked as they drove through town and past GIA. "I'm happy things are going well for you."

Sheldon thought about how much his life had changed. Working with people he had only met recently made him feel grown up and accomplished, but he did not always feel like it because he was not where he wanted to be yet.

Chapter Twenty

Dani

It was Friday and Mandy's last day at Pathmasters. Her coworkers threw her a little going-away party. After seeing so many people come and go, it was finally her turn to leave the factory for the last time. She had learned a great deal working there and made many new friends.

When Sheldon dropped Mandy off at her new job on Monday, he had not seen her this nervous in a long time. "You're going to do well, and they are gonna love you in no time," Sheldon stated.

"Thanks," Mandy said, getting out of the vehicle and grabbing her stuff.

Dani and Mandy had worked together for a couple of years at Pathmaster, and Mandy had taken Dani under her wing, much like a little sister Mandy never had. Dani worked on the carousel, lacing the spokes onto bicycle rims. When Dani completed a rim, she would send it down the line to Mandy, who would then put the tire onto the rim. They would crack jokes to make each other laugh, helping to pass the time. Dani was so beside herself when Mandy announced she was leaving.

Mandy taught Dani how to speak up for herself. While everyone else was afraid of their boss, Mandy had no trouble calling him out or putting him in his place.

After Mandy left Pathmaster to work for another company, Dani told Sheldon they had to continue hanging out. They became close friends. They would have lunch together and talk about what they wanted to do with their lives.

"Life flies by, so don't lay down roots working here at this factory," Dani suggested to Sheldon. "You think you will only work at this place for a year or two, but before you know it, it's been six years and two kids later. Also, get out of that small town you're living in because you never were a small-town boy."

"I know, and you're right. That is why I'm planning to take classes at the community college," Sheldon explained. "I want to make sure I get my associate's degree and transfer to a university close to where my sister lives." Sheldon got up to throw his garbage away. "I guess I better get back to my department. We are behind on our quota. We have to kick it into high gear."

"Ugh, don't talk to me about quotas," Dani grumbled as she began to put her work gloves back on and started to work before anyone else was even back from lunch. "Since your mom left, we have been behind. No one can do that job as fast as she was able to."

"You better make sure you get those nipples screwed on straight!" Sheldon teased over his shoulder.

"Get your ass back to your department, Majors," Dani retorted, throwing a nipple at Sheldon, just missing him and landing in her foreman's coffee, who had just walked up. He glared at her, and she quickly looked away. She went back to screwing nipples onto the spokes acting like she had no idea what was going on. Sheldon turned and promptly returned to his department, trying hard not to laugh.

"If you weren't such a hard worker, I would write you up, so let this be a verbal warning," Her foreman said, snarling at her. "Make sure you get your nipples on straight. I do not want this line stopping to correct any mistakes." Dani chuckled when he said get your nipples on straight, and he glared at her again before heading to his office.

§

Monday at work, Dani and Sheldon were having dinner together, laughing and talking. "What are you eating?" Sheldon asked Dani as he eyed her food inquisitively.

"It's something that Dennis was trying to make us for dinner last night. It was supposed to be a lasagna casserole, but it turned into a mishmash. It's definitely better than it looks," She smirked.

"I can't believe my department has to work again this Saturday. I need the money, but it's exhausting. I'm going to have to ask my mom to watch the kids."

"Yeah, we have to work Saturday, too," Sheldon stated. "I kind of like working dayshift, though."

"You know I do too," Dani concurred. "My request to transfer to the day shift just went through, so I will start working days at the end of the month."

"That is funny because most of my department is thinking of transferring to the day shift, too," Sheldon stated. "A lot of people have retired or quit. I'm not sure how I feel about working with day shift people, though; they always seemed like I don't know."

"Stuck-up?" Dani finished his sentence.

"Yeah, like they look at us like we are dirt," Sheldon explained. "Possibly, after the first of the year, I might see about getting transferred to days as well."

"Then it won't be long, and we will act that way too," Dani joked taking a bite of her food.

"We will become one of them," Sheldon said in a trance-like state, and they both laughed. "Thank goodness Labor Day Weekend is coming soon. Do you have any plans?"

"We are thinking of going to the Wisconsin Dells," Dani replied. "The kids will be at their dad's house, and we need some alone time, if you know what I mean. Are you planning to do something fun?"

"Yes, Rhode Island. Actually, I will be taking the whole week off. This weekend, I need to start to pack," Sheldon replied.

"Rhode Island?" Dani inquired as she snatched one of Sheldon's potato chips and shoved it in her mouth.

"Yeah, my friend Ruby, my cousin Ninnie, and I are driving to Rhode Island next Friday," Sheldon explained joyfully. "She has been in school there for a few weeks with only a suitcase full of clothes. We are helping her move some of her stuff into the dorms there," Sheldon answered, gathering up his garbage. "We are supposed to stop in New York first, which I'm very excited about. I hope we get to see the Statue of Liberty."

"How exciting!" Dani exclaimed. "I have never been further east than Indiana."

"Me too," Sheldon said. "Well, we went to the Ohio border once when I was young to pick up my uncle. "

"I hope to visit the northern observation point just north of Canada one day. I have been reading about it on the library computer. There are no roads, so you have to fly to get there and then camp."

"No roads? That sounds insane but interesting." Sheldon remarked.

"Right! It sounds wild, but I have been thinking about it a lot lately. I will ask Dennis about planning it for next year," Dani explained.

"That does sound like fun," Sheldon said. He could see the excitement in her eyes as she explained the details. "You should definitely do it. Would you take the kids?"

"Oh no, it will be too rugged for them," She replied. "I will have my mom watch them. You have to take pictures of your trip to Rhode Island, and I will want to hear all about it when you get back. Well, I better get back to work."

"Me too. See you later." Sheldon said, turning to head back to his department.

§

It was Friday night, and Dani and Sheldon were at the end of a long work week. The assembly line Dani worked on had been down for half the night, so they had already cleaned up their workstation and were ready to head home.

When a line went down again thirty minutes before the end of the shift, the maintenance guy threw his hands in the air and said, "Fuck it, leave it for the day shift." Dani quickly grabbed her stuff and walked over to Sheldon's area.

"Do you have any plans this weekend?" Dani inquired while Sheldon cleaned up his area.

"Chase comes home this weekend from looking at colleges. He said he wants to talk to me about something." Sheldon answered as he swept a pile of metal bits into a dustpan. "I have a feeling it's about changing his college plans. Also, I need to pack for next week's trip. What about you? Do you have any big plans with your young hot boy toy?"

210

"Ha! No, not really. His younger brother Billy wants to come over and stay the weekend again." Dani scowled with a snarled lip. "When he comes, he never seems to leave and..." She lowered her voice as she continued. "He gives me the creeps. I have tried subtly telling Dennis, but it's his baby brother. What can I do?"

"Hmm, that is a tough one," Sheldon replied, trying to think of something to say or recommend doing, but nothing came to mind. They walked over to the break area and sat at the table, waiting to clock out. "What is he doing that creeps you out?"

She took a breath before answering. "Billy doesn't seem to respect personal space like a normal person would and..." She paused, looking around before continuing. "He continuously brushes up against me. I blew it off as coincidental, but it is happening more frequently, and I noticed him doing it with my eight-year-old daughter, too. I have to do something because I don't feel comfortable with him there, especially not alone with my kids."

"Yikes! Yeah, that is unacceptable. How old is he?" Sheldon asked as they got up to get in line to clock out.

"He is fourteen," Dani responded, grabbing her purse off the table.

"Do you think he is just being a curious teenager?" Sheldon quarried as they clocked out and headed for the front doors to exit the building. She did not answer and was quiet as they left the building and walked to their cars.

"I don't know... Maybe you're right," Dani replied as she opened her car door. "Maybe I am overreacting."

"I would definitely talk to Dennis about it," Sheldon recommended.

They said bye to each other as they got in their cars and headed home.

§

Franny watched from her front porch as the City Fire Inspector and Sheriff Bolden knocked on Chase's front door. Chase had just returned home from visiting college campuses with his dad. He was hoping it was Sheldon knocking, but he knew he was still at work, so it could not be him.

Chase was surprised when he opened the door and saw the Sheriff standing there. They handed him a report and were there to talk to Chase about his car. They explained that it appeared to have been set on fire by someone matching PJ Ferguson or his Uncle Berry Price's description. Someone saw one of them throw a lit cigarette in Chase's convertible.

"Do you know any reason why either of them might have done this?" Sheriff Bolden asked.

"No, I don't even know who either of these people are," Chase replied.

"I'm about to go out to his place and question him, but wanted to talk with you first," Sheriff Bolden explained. "Thank you for your time. We will be in touch." The two gentlemen left, but Chase was more confused than ever.

When Franny walked up, Chase sat on his front porch reading the report he would take to his insurance company.

"Did they find out what happened to your car?" Franny asked.

"Yeah, but I do not know the people they suspect or why they would do that to my car," Chase responded.

"Who was it?" Franny asked, and Chase handed her the report. After she read it, she quickly returned it to him, saying, "I gotta go." Chase gave her a curious look as he watched her walk back towards her house.

§

Saturday afternoon, Dani was exhausted from all the overtime. Typically, they worked the second shift on Saturday, but their bosses had them work the day shift. She had just gotten off work and pulled into her driveway. She sat in the car for a moment. When she got out of her car, she could hear that the TV was already on, which was odd because her mom would not be dropping the kids off for at least another 45 minutes.

Walking into the living room, she found Billy sitting on the couch. She said hi and went into the bedroom to change out of her work clothes. Dani was a little annoyed that Dennis gave his brother a key to their house. She decided taking a shower might help her relax. Plus, she wanted to wash off all the work grime, so she grabbed a fresh pair of clothes and went to jump into the shower.

Dani was lost in thought as the warm water from the shower hit her body. She was thinking about what to make the kids for dinner that night. Dani was trying to think of something simple to make. She was too tired to cook. She could order a pizza…

Her thoughts were interrupted when she saw someone outside the shower watching her. She immediately jumped, screamed, and covered herself with her arms. She did not expect anyone to be standing there.

"Billy, what are you doing?!" She asked louder than she intended.

"The TV stopped working," Billy said, looking her up and down.

"Get out!" She demanded. He just stood there for another beat before turning to leave.

How he looked at her gave her goosebumps from head to toe. She got out of the shower and dressed in a huff. She decided to have a serious talk with Dennis as soon as he got home.

When her mother dropped the children off, she sent the children to their room to play. She didn't want them near Billy. She was making mini pizzas and french fries per the kids' request when Dennis walked into the house and greeted her with a kiss.

Immediately, Dani could sense that something was wrong with Dennis. "What's wrong, babe," she asked, kissing him back.

"Next month, we are getting laid off, and this time for a whole month, not the usual two weeks for the plant shutdown," he replied, putting his lunchbox on top of the fridge. "Dinner smells good."

"Don't worry, babe. We will make it through," she said as she tried to reassure him. She pulled the first batch of mini pizzas out of the oven and put more in to cook.

"Thanks, sexy," he teased, smacking her on the ass. "I'm going to continue taking all the overtime available. I was thinking with all these Saturdays, we are both working. I had hoped we could buy some nice Christmas gifts for the kids."

"Awe, that is sweet of you, babe," Dani cooed as she hugged him tightly.

"Well, thank you for convincing me to make extra payments on my truck this summer. At least, that will be one less thing to worry about," Dennis stated. "Are the kids in the living room?"

No, that's your brother," Dani replied with annoyance.

"Billy?" He questioned with his head cocked to the side. "When did he get here?"

"I have no idea," Dani replied as she tried to decide whether to talk to him about Billy walking in on her in shower. "Did you give him a key?"

"No, I didn't give him a key."

"Then how did he get in?" Dani asked, trying to read if Dennis was telling the truth but She believed him.

"I have no idea," Dennis replied with wide eyes as he turned and entered the living room to confront his brother. "Billy, how did you get in here today?"

Billy only sat there staring at the TV and laughing at Scooby and Shaggy. Dennis reached and turned off the TV. "Hey!" Billy screamed. When he caught his brother's line of sight, Billy's attitude became more docile.

"How did you get in here today?" Dennis asked again, wondering if he would get a response from his brother.

"Through the front door," Billy unemotionally replied, giving Dani a cold chill as he reached and turned the TV back on.

Dani stared at Dennis, unsure how to respond, as the kitchen timer went off. She went to the kitchen to get the food out of the oven. She was leaning against the counter when Dennis walked in and wrapped his arms around Dani.

"I will talk to him later," Dennis remarked, trying to reassure her. "I'm going to shower up for dinner."

He kissed her and left the kitchen, but she did not feel anything was resolved and grew concerned that this was how their family handled issues with Billy. They seemed to let him have his way.

She did not want to mention the shower incident because it might cause Dennis to fly off the handle with her kids in the house. She decided she would need to have a serious talk with Dennis when the kids were at their dad's in a couple of weeks. She could not let this stand.

"Come on, kids, and eat!" Dani called out to her kids. Billy was the first at the table; he and Dani stared at each other. Their gaze broke only when the children burst into the kitchen, scrambling into their chairs with excited energy.

§

Dani and Dennis were lying in bed. She was going over things in her head. Dani was thinking about so many things, bills, and holidays coming up, but mostly Billy. She wanted to talk to Dennis about her feelings regarding Billy. The room was dark and quiet. She was not sure if Dennis was asleep.

"You asleep?" Dani broke the silence.

"Not yet, what's up?" Dennis asked. Dani was quiet momentarily, thinking about addressing her issues with Billy.

"So, I was thinking," Dani said, cutting the silence that hung in the room.

"Yeah, what's that?"

"How about next year, you and I go on a trip together? " Dani said, determined to keep things on a happy note.

"I would love that," he said. "What do you have in mind?" he asked excitedly, turning on his side and resting his head on his hand.

"I was thinking we should go to Aulavik National Park in Canada. We would have to fly there, and it's very rural," Dani explained, getting excited and forgetting her worries about Billy. "Where we would be going, there are no roads, electricity, running water, or beds, and you get around on snowmobiles. I'm not sure how I feel about no running water, but something inside me is saying we should do it now. Escape this place and run far away."

"Wow, I had no idea you wanted to get out of here so badly," Dennis stated, slightly concerned and sitting up. "Why this sudden urge to have a great escape?"

"I don't know," she replied thoughtfully. The room became quiet again for a moment. Dennis lay back down. Dani was lost in her thoughts, searching for the reason for her sudden urge to escape, when Dennis cleared his throat to speak.

"I would go with you anywhere," Dennis remarked as he pulled her closer. They both fell asleep, lost in their thoughts.

§

Sheriff Bolden pulled into the PJ's driveway. Walking across the lawn, he noticed the quietness of the PJ's place, which is very isolated. His nearest neighbors were miles away. He walked up and knocked on the door. There was no answer. He knocked again and was about to leave when he heard something from inside the house.

The Sheriff saw that someone had pulled back curtains to see who was knocking. "It's the Sheriff; open up!" he demanded as he struck again, only with more authority this time.

Kelli PJ's girlfriend was inside, and when she looked out and saw it was the Sheriff, she panicked. "Fuck! Fuck! Fuck!" She quietly mouthed as she leaned against the wall as if he could see her through the door. She ran, grabbed her shotgun, and laid it on the wall next to the front door.

"Sheriff!?" She said in a sing-song voice as she cracked open the door and stuck her head out. "What brings you all the way out here?"

"I'm looking for PJ. Is he home?" Sheriff Bolden asked.

"Nope, he is not here." She answered and started to close the door, but the Sheriff stopped her by putting his foot in the door.

"Do you know when he will be home?" He asked, looking at her with increasing curiosity. He knew she was odd, but this was even strange for her.

"He should be home next week, I think," Kelli replied, and this time, she did not try to close the door.

"You mind if I have a look around?" He asked.

"Uh, well, do you have to? I think you should wait till PJ comes home for that," She quickly answered.

"Okay, I will do that," He said as he turned to leave. He did not have genuine cause to search the property besides his gut instinct. As he walked back to the police cruiser, he turned around and surveyed the property again.

He got into his car, and instead of heading back to town, he headed down the dead-end road past PJ's house, surveying the barns and outbuildings. He turned around as he drove back past. He scoped the place out one more time. He did not see anything unusual, so he left feeling uneasy for some unexplainable reason.

§

Chase was waiting on his porch for Sheldon when he gets home from work. They greet one another and went inside the house. "It's good to see you. How were the college campuses?" Sheldon asks, taking off his work clothes to go shower.

"They were okay, but nothing truly felt right about them. It's kind of hard to describe. A couple had a great writing program and beautiful campuses, but nothing felt quite right," Chase explained.

"I think I know what you mean," Sheldon acknowledged. "It's like when you just know something is the right fit."

"Exactly," Chase said. "I thought maybe it was because I was distracted by what was going on, which is why I wanted to talk to you but couldn't talk about it because my dad was always around."

"What happened?" Sheldon asked.

"My dad was acting weird this whole trip," Chase explained. "He has this cell phone now, and he kept getting calls and would step outside to talk to whomever it was, and it was odd."

"What do you think he is doing?" Sheldon asked.

"I'm worried he is having an affair because there were a few times he left for a work thing, but it didn't make sense," Chase explained. "I was observing them together, and nothing seemed out of the ordinary, and my mom seemed okay and did not seem to suspect anything. I didn't want to say anything to her that could cause her unnecessary stress. I have wanted to discuss my concerns with you, but it never seemed like the right time. I thought I was imagining it all when it was happening, but now I'm concerned."

"What are you going to do?" Sheldon asked. "You don't have any hard proof of anything, do you?"

"I don't know. That is why I wanted to talk to you," Chase said.

"I mean, where there is smoke, there is fire, right?" Sheldon commented. "I mean, it sounds like something is happening, but what exactly?"

"Ugggghh," Chase said in frustration, laying back on the bed.

"Sorry, I'm not much help," Sheldon said, as he slipped off his underwear when Chase sat back up to say something else but stopped when he saw Sheldon naked.

"I have been dreaming of seeing you naked all week," Chase said, standing up. "Do you know how hard it is to share a hotel room with your dad, and you can't jack off but in the shower?"

"Talking about your dad is not making this scene any sexier," Sheldon commented, grabbing Chase's crotch and kissing him.

"Sorry," Chase said, kissing him back. "I'm going to miss you like crazy when you're gone to Rhode Island."

"I will miss you too," Sheldon said as he removed Chase's shirt.

Chapter Twenty-One

Labor Day Weekend

As they loaded up Ruby's car, Sheldon could not help but feel guilty. "What's with the long face?" Ninnie asked Sheldon as she put her bag in the back of Ruby's car. "You should be excited." He just gave her a look. "Oh, do not start with that. I'm NOT going to feel guilty about my sister being missing while I drive across the country."

Ruby and Sheldon just looked at Ninnie. "No, No, and No," Ninnie said, pointing her finger at Ruby and Sheldon and then waving it at them both. "She is probably on a beach somewhere in Florida living it up. It's what she does and has done my whole life. The poor Shawndrea card is not being played on my last break of freedom! Now let's get IN this car and roll out of here."

Ruby and Sheldon both laughed as they got into the car. Ruby offered to drive the first leg of the trip. They all sang along to the radio till about halfway across Ohio. They were quiet until they crossed the Ohio border.

"Yay! I have officially been further than I have ever been," Sheldon cheered.

"Amateur," Ninnie teased, and they all laughed.

The car was quiet again for quite some time. "Oh my god. I never knew Pennsylvania had so many cows," Ninnie shouted, causing everyone to jump. Sheldon pressed his face to the window to see cows on a plateau high above the freeway.

"Wow, there are cows," Sheldon remarked. "Guess that's where Philadelphia Cream Cheese comes from."

"Huh, never thought about it before," Ninnie added. "I guess when I think of Pennsylvania, I do not think of cows."

"I'm going to pull over at the next exit for gas and to stretch our legs," Ruby stated.

Sheldon took the driver's seat after filling the car with gas, using the restroom, and stretching their legs. "There was not much to see in Ohio or Indiana, but Pennsylvania is beautiful," Sheldon commented.

"We are about to go through a tunnel!" Sheldon exclaimed. He was amazed at how the road went right through the mountains. As they drove through the tunnel, they lost the radio signal.

The girls fell asleep shortly after Philadelphia, and Sheldon fought to stay awake. When he saw the lights of the city, he became wide awake. He thought about waking the girls but decided to let them sleep.

Since it was so late, there was hardly any traffic, and an idea occurred to him. He followed the signs that said the Statue of Liberty.

Sheldon pulled into the parking lot, put the car in park, shut the lights off, and then the car. He stared out at the lights of the city dancing on the water. Sheldon spotted the Twin Towers. He smiled as he continued to look out at the water. Sheldon was excited to have finally made it to New York. He laid his head back, and his eyes slowly closed. He was exhausted from the drive.

He awoke to the sounds of Seagulls and Ninnie and Ruby laughing. As he stretched, he wondered how long he had been asleep. The sun was up, and people were already lining up to take the ferry to the statue. Ninnie and Ruby sat on a park bench as Ruby pointed out places of interest throughout the city.

"Well, good morning," Ninnie greeted Sheldon as he approached them. "We were just talking about getting breakfast with her friend Jeremy."

The path along the waterfront started to fill with people exercising and tourists sightseeing. A small group were trying to take pictures of the Statue of Liberty.

One of the tourists said, "I can't focus the camera on her face." Ruby quietly chuckled.

"What are you laughing about?" Ninnie queried.

"They are trying to take a picture of the statue's face," Ruby said as Ninnie and Sheldon squinted, which reminded Sheldon to get his camera.

"And?" Ninnie asked

"We are at the back of the statue, which faces the entrance to the harbor," Ruby explained.

"Ooooooohhh, that explains why her face looked so deformed," Ninnie chuckled. They all laughed, and Sheldon went to get his camera.

"I want to take you two over to see the statue, but we do not have enough time," Ruby stated.

They took a few pictures before meeting Ruby's friend Jeremy for breakfast. Ruby offered to drive since she knew where they were going. She drove them past her old brownstone home in a quaint neighborhood. A few blocks away, she took them to the dinner where she and her dad used to have Sunday breakfast when she was a little girl.

When they arrived at the diner, Jeremy was already waiting for them. He was standing in front of the diner, smoking a cigarette. Jeremy had long hair shaved on one side. He was wearing ripped jeans and a black leather jacket. He looked like a bad boy.

Ruby and Jeremy greeted each other with squeals and a big hug. Ruby introduced Jeremy to Ninnie and Sheldon.

"He isn't as backward as you said," Jeremy remarked to Ruby as they entered the diner. Sheldon looked back at them as Ruby slapped Jeremy's arm.

"You're full of shit," Ruby scolded Jeremy. "I never said that."

"He is much better looking than I imagined, and Mmmm, look at that ass," Jeremy said, licking his lips as a waitress walked them to their booth.

"Okay, calm down, horn dog," Ruby demanded.

"Whoa, look at you," Jeremy said, surprised at how firm Ruby was with him. "Looks like you have gotten hard living in the cornfields."

"Damn right!" Ruby said, and they all laughed.

Ruby and Jeremy did some catching up over breakfast, and they hugged each other tightly as they said their goodbyes.

"I'm going to come to Rhode Island to visit you!" Jeremy shouted as he walked down the street towards his home.

"You better," Ruby retorted as she got in the car.

"Rhode Island, here we come," she cheered as she started the car. They got on the freeway. Sheldon and Ninnie were amazed at how many apartment buildings there were in the city.

"Where do all these people work?" Sheldon remarked as they passed many apartment buildings, one after another.

"That is the Bronx. I think a lot of those particular buildings are government assistant housing," Ruby explained. "But most of the buildings are apartments, and they probably work in the city."

Their energy was high as they drove through Connecticut, which looked much like Southern Illinois. Sheldon felt it was taking forever to get to Providence, probably because he was running on only a few hours of sleep. "Did I just see a cornfield," Sheldon asked as they entered Rhode Island.

"You sure did," Ninnie replied from the passenger seat. "I did not expect to see that here."

"Me either," Sheldon said. They enjoyed the rest of the drive to Providence, which reminded them much of Illinois.

They tried to find parking near her building, Olney House. Unfortunately, there was no parking near her building, so they had to park a few blocks away and walk. Luckily, they did not have much of Ruby's stuff to carry because they had hike up a steep hill to get to her building. A hint of fall was in the air, and the leaves had already started to change there, which was weird considering it was the first of September.

"It's quite a beautiful campus," Sheldon remarked as they walked through the campus grounds. Seeing the students walking around made him wish he was going to a university like this one.

"Class isn't until ten a.m. on Tuesday, so we have a whole day and a half to check the campus out," Ruby said, looking sad. "I wish you two were going to school with me here."

"Awe, do not start getting sappy on me now," Ninnie demanded, acting like she was rubbing dirt from her eyes. "I think something just flew in my eye."

"Okay, let me show you the bookstore first. If you want souvenirs, you can get them now before we forget or run out of time," Ruby stated. "Then I can show you where my classes will be before getting dinner down by the river."

Ruby shared a dorm room with two other people, and neither were home. One of the bedroom doors was closed, and a keep-out sign was on it. The other bedroom door was open, and clothes were everywhere. The floor was about knee-deep in clothes and garbage.

"The messy room is Bianca's, and she is a senior. Thank god she has a private bathroom," Ruby explained, giving them a tour of her apartment. "The other one is Amelia, and she is a sophomore, and we share a bathroom. Thankfully, she is very clean but very weird," Ruby whispered.

Before they knew it, their time in Providence was over, and it was time for Sheldon and Ninnie to make their way home.

"You know, if we flew, we could have stayed longer," Sheldon commented, getting into Ruby's car.

"And I told you this chick does not fly and prefers the comfort of a car or train," Ninnie retorted.

Ruby pulled the car into the train station parking lot. As they said their goodbyes, Ruby could not stop hugging them. "Thank you two so much for coming with me," Ruby said as she started to tear up.

"No! Do not start the waterworks again," Ninnie demanded. "This is not the end. We will see you again very soon."

"You're right," Ruby agreed.

"The grey skies are gonna clear up, so put on a happy face," Sheldon sang as he danced around his suitcase. "So spread sunshine all over the place."

"You are crazy," Ruby said to Sheldon as they laughed at Sheldon being a goof. "I will miss that the most."

After their tearful hugs, they waved goodbye from the train and headed home.

Ninnie and Sheldon found their seats on the train and got settled in for the ride.

"This has been a nice little adventure," Ninnie remarked as the train swayed slightly back and forth as the scenery flew by the window. "Thank you for convincing me to come."

"Seeing where Ruby is going to school makes me wish I could go here too," Sheldon said as he watched a field of trees fly past the window.

"Oh my god, thank you for saying so. I thought I was the only one thinking about that," Ninnie said. "But we were not blessed to have a doctor for a father." They both chuckled.

"Are they going to come by with food or something?" Sheldon questioned, looking down at the train car and trying to investigate the connecting train car. "Food? Already?" Ninnie teased. "I guess I could use a snack too." They were both craning their necks, looking for an attendant.

An older lady overheard them and giggled at their innocence as she watched them. "You have to go to the café car for food. There is not anyone here to serve us," the older lady explained.

"Don't they know who I am?" Ninnie joked as she stood up. "And don't say that if we were on a plane, the flight attendants would be serving us?"

"Who me?" Sheldon joked.

"Okay, come, let's get you some food," Ninnie said, standing up.

When they returned from the café car, Sheldon placed his food and drink onto the table and climbed into the booth. Ninnie sat down her box of food, but before she sat down, she started pulling food out of her pockets and a second soda. Sheldon just looked at her with shock. He did not know she had bought so much food.

"What? My box was full," Ninnie stated after seeing the look on Sheldon's face. "Don't judge."

"I thought you said you could use a snack?" Sheldon explained.

"I couldn't decide, so I just got it all. Besides, it's a long trip back," Ninnie professed.

Ninnie sat down and surveyed all the food she had bought. "Okay, maybe I went a little overboard, " she confessed, and then they both chuckled.

After eating his ham sandwich and chips, Sheldon pulled out a book while Ninnie curled up in the other booth to nap.

Ninnie burped loudly. "I'm so sorry, excuse me!" Ninnie exclaimed, and then she started moaning, "I should not have eaten that last hotdog. I'm soooo stuffed."

"How many did you eat?" Sheldon asked over the top of his book.

"Four," Ninnie replied with her hand raised, holding up four fingers. She belched even louder this time, and the older lady looked at her in surprise.

Sheldon tried not to laugh at the older lady's expression regarding Ninnie's bodily noise. "I'm so sorry, guys," Ninnie apologized again, hand in the air.

"You realize if we were on a plane, you would be home in your bed sooner," Sheldon commented, but there was no response from Ninnie and none of her usually witty repartee. He was secretly hoping she did not start farting because he might lose it. Instead, she fell asleep and started snoring, which made it hard for him to concentrate on what he was reading.

§

Mandy loaded her riding equipment, camping supplies, groceries, and cooler into the Suburban and then loaded her horse into the stock trailer. It was weird for her to do this alone just for herself. Before the boys came along, she used to do it all the time alone because Susan was never interested in camping, so Mandy was used to only looking out for herself, but when the boys got older and would tag along, she would have to make sure not only did she have her stuff and horse ready but for the boys as well until they got old enough to take care of themselves.

Though it was odd pulling out of their driveway alone, it was nice and freeing at the same time. When Mandy rolled into the campsite, she was looking for Lita's old green truck and matching stock trailer, but she was nowhere in sight. She pulled up next to a huge RV and rolled her eyes. It was parked where Lita had said to meet, which was the old spot they used to camp. "Some people call that camping," Mandy mumbled to herself and snarled at the monstrous camper as she got out of her suburban.

Mandy looked inside the trailer to see if her horse, Lady, was okay. "I can only imagine what Lita is going to think of this monstrosity when she gets here," she said, petting Lady through the slats of the trailer.

"Mandy is that you?" someone said from behind, and Mandy instantly recognized Lita's voice. She turned to see Lita coming out of the RV.

"What the…" Mandy started to say

"Right, isn't she a beaut?" Lita said, closing the door and stroking the side of the RV.

"What happened to people who camp in RVs are not really camping?" Mandy asked.

"That went away just like my 20s and 30s, and after camping in one of these, you never want to camp any other way again," Lita said. "Besides, sleeping on the cold, hard ground is for kids, so this is how adults camp.

"I guess," Mandy responded.

"Once you get unloaded, come, and I will show you around," Lita said. "Let me know if you need any help."

"Okay," Mandy said, still in shock, as she turned to get Lady out of the trailer and tied her up. Mandy was brushing her when Lita walked up.

"Is this Lady?" Lita asked.

"Yes," Mandy responded.

"I can't believe you still have her," Lita said as she petted Lady. "How old is she now?"

"She will be 20 in January," Mandy responded.

"Wow, I have never had a horse live that long," Lita said. "Come and let me show you around the RV."

They make their way inside. "You have a stove and a fridge?" Mandy asked as she stepped inside.

"Heck yeah, and a coffee pot!" Lita responded, and Mandy gave an approving look. "I get to enjoy nature but still have some of the comforts of home." Lita started making some coffee.

Mandy opened cabinet doors and a door to the pantry, then opened another door. "And you have a bathroom!" Mandy shrieked. "Okay, maybe I can see that being better than using the outhouse or behind the bushes."

Mandy started to warm up to the idea of RV camping when Lita handed her a warm cup of coffee. "Let's sit outside and soak up the nature," Lita said. "I have two folding chairs already set up."

They sat outside sipping coffee and listening to the birds. "I'm glad we got here before everyone else," Mandy remarked.

"Yeah, it's always nicer when no one else is here making noise,"

Lita responded. "I got this, so when I retire in a few years, I can come down here anytime and enjoy it without all the other people. Wade and I even plan to drive across the country and see America. One of the places at the top of my list is the Arches National Park in Moab, Utah. Then I want to make our way to Yellow Stone and then up to Bozeman, Montana. I want to visit some horse ranches too. But it will be hard leaving all our babies behind."

"That sounds like an amazing trip," Mandy said. "Where is Wade? Why didn't he come?"

"He is taking care of his mother," Lita said, sipping her coffee. "She is not doing well."

"I was just thinking earlier how weird it was to be here without the boys or even Damian," Mandy said, sipping her coffee and then sitting back and taking a deep breath. "It's kind of nice, though, not having them around."

"It's kind of like old times," Lita sighed. "Oh, remember the second time we came here when I thought it was a good idea to bring that horse Pepper, who we were just breaking to ride?"

"Oh my gosh, yes," Mandy responded. "How many times did she throw you before you decided you had enough? Was it three times?"

"It was four, and I hit that log so hard it knocked the wind out of me," Lita said. "I thought for sure I had broken a rib. To be twenty-something again, you think you can do anything. I would not do that again even if you paid me."

"What time do you want to get up and ride tomorrow?" Mandy asked.

"I way we head out around 8 am if that works for you," Lita said.

"Works for me," Mandy responded. "I guess I better finish unpacking so I can be ready to sleep in the suburban." Mandy got up, looked at the suburban, and then back to the RV.

"The couch folds out into a bed," Lita said. "You can always sleep in here." She patted the side of the RV.

"Oh, no, I'm good," Mandy said, heading to the Suburban. Since the boys did not come with her, she had a lot less to unpack.

"You can put that cold stuff in my fridge," Lita said, causing Mandy to jump and scream. She was lost in thought and had not heard Lita walk up.

"You're as bad as Sheldon. He always scares me like that," Mandy laughed.

"Here, give me the lunch meat and the hot dogs," Lita requested. "Oh, and the sodas. I guess I should have told you not to worry about bringing a cooler and ice, but next time, you know."

Lita gathered all the items and headed back to her camper. Mandy thought it felt nice having someone take care of her. Damian does in his own way, but this feels different.

The two ladies had a wonderful man-free weekend and looked forward to continuing this tradition next year. She knew they would have many adventures together in the future.

Chapter Twenty-Two

Bitch, Where Do You Think You Are Going?

One time, while still in high school, Shawndrea was attacked and almost sexually assaulted while out looking for some action, and she started having difficulty sleeping, so she started making excuses for sleeping in Ninnie's room and then started making Ninnie sleep in her room. Then she began to drag Ninnie out with her to places after she started seeing her attacker's face in other people almost everywhere she went.

At first, Ninnie thought it was exciting to sneak out on a school night and go to bars. That was until she had to listen to her sister having sex in the van with strangers.

After being attacked, Shawndrea became sex-obsessed, and having her sister along made her feel safe. Then, Shawndrea started bringing some of them back to the house and sneaking them into her room, making Ninnie endure the moans and groans. Ninnie was disturbed that she was having sex with some very young guys and some older married men, too. Shawndrea didn't seem to have any limitations as to whom she would have sex with.

"Hey, a stiff dick is a stiff dick." She would tell Ninnie.

When Ninnie started dating Tommy, she refused to hang out with Shawndrea as much. That is when Shawndrea started seeing Jack. He started taking her to other towns on dates. Over time, she saw her attacker's face in other people less and less. She had begun to forget about him. She even started to think less of PJ, too.

However, PJ always remembered Shawndrea, even when he started dating Kelli, who slightly resembled Shawndrea.

Kelli was the kind of person who got crazy jealous. She would burn him with a cigarette, set his clothes on fire, and even threaten to cut his dick off if she ever caught him cheating.

Once, when they were having sex, she was riding him, and he called out Shawndrea's name. She flipped off him extremely fast and pulled her knife out of the dresser where she had previously stuck it into the wood. She grabbed his penis and was going to hack it off.

Seeing what she was about to do to him, he quickly raised his right leg, which caught her square in the nose, sending her backward. When she stood up, blood streamed down her face, covering her mouth. She spit the blood at him before leaving the room.

§

"You eat more than our pigs," the captor said as she pulled Shawndrea's hair. She proceeded to cut off a considerable chunk of Shawndrea's hair with a pair of scissors. Shawndrea's hands were still tied behind her back, and she could not fight back. "You kinda smell like them too." She spat at her. "You're disgusting. I have to do everything for you, and you do not appreciate it." She slapped Shawndrea so hard her ears rang.

"You know I always wanted a sister," the captor sweetly spoke as she brushed Shawn's hair nicely. "But then I realized I would have to share my daddy with her, which would just not do." She started hacking again at Shawndrea's hair with the scissors. Her hair was becoming very short on one side and looked utterly lopsided.

"When a little sister did come along I would try to leave her places like the woods, stores or with older men, but she always seemed to turn back up like a bad penny."

"Hold still," she demanded as she pulled Shawndrea's head back by her hair and pointed the scissors at her. "You do not want me to cut off one of your ears! It can get quite messy. Once I cut off one of our pig's ears, there was blood everywhere. He just squealed and squealed. There's nothing like the time I cut off our dog's balls.

He kept sticking it in the neighbor's dog, and they would get stuck together for hours."

"I blame that whore of a dog from next door. She was such a filthy little bitch. You know, she had three litters of puppies from our dog before I cut off his balls. The funny thing is, later that day, he found them lying on the ground, and he ate his own balls," She laughed a creepy laugh. "There, your hair looks much better." Shawndrea's hair was extremely short on one side with random strands hanging down, and the other was now jagged.

"You know my daddy always said I should have gone to school and learnt to do hair. He thinks I'm wasting my time working at the hospital."

Her crazy captor stepped out of the cage, put down the scissors, and picked up something else. The next thing Shawndrea knew, she was being sprayed with water.

"Time to hose down the hogs!" Shawndrea screamed as the cold water hit her.

§

Shawndrea was daydreaming of eating a greasy, cheesy hamburger with lettuce, tomato, ketchup, and mayo. As the ketchup dripped down her chin, the realization that she had to pee pulled her out of her daydream, which was so real she thought for a split-second there was ketchup on her chin only to discover it was drool as she wiped it away.

Her captor had not come to untie her since the day before. She tried not to focus on how badly she had to pee. She tried to free her hands, but it was too late. The movement released her bladder. She knew she had to get free before she was to shit herself too.

"Enough is enough!" She shouted as she stood up. The left rear chair leg finally came loose and fell to the floor. She knew she had to break the back of the chair where her hands were bound, which her captor tightened every day, but they felt like they were starting to fray a bit.

In a previous attempt to break the chair, she knocked herself out and woke up with her captor standing over her and torturing her.

She needed to do it without knocking herself out this time. Suddenly, she thought she could use the leg that came off the chair to pry the wood backing off the chair. She had to get onto her knees and lie on her side. As she attempted to do so, she fell over.

She tried to grasp the chair leg, which had come loose, but it kept sliding just out of reach. She heard a dog barking, and her heart jumped. The thought of her captor finding her in the position scared her. Who knows what she might do next to her or try to force-feed her this time?

With adrenaline pounding through her body and her hand grasped around the leg of the chair, she started prying at the back of the chair. She felt it was hopeless because she could not get the right angle to pry hard enough to break it. Suddenly, something snagged the side of her hand. It was a screw sticking out where it once had been attached to the chair. "You idiot, why didn't you think of this earlier," Shawndrea said out loud to herself. She proceeded to turn the leg around and aligned the screw with the rope, and started to saw at the ropes.

She missed the rope and nicked her wrist. Suddenly, she thought she heard the door. She paused momentarily and realized it was just birds coming to roost. She feverishly started trying to cut the rope and not herself.

As the rope started to give, she heard a dog barking again and what sounded like a car on a gravel road. She knew she had to get out of there. She had not eaten for a few days and knew she would not have the strength to fight her captor on another day. Also, her captor was coming less and less, which meant she might stop coming altogether and leave her and her baby there to die.

The rope finally broke free, her arm felt foreign as she brought them around. Something in her stomach lurched, and she knew she needed to relieve herself soon, and this time, it was not to go pee. She paused for a second and realized this could not wait until she climbed out.

After using the bathroom, she walked to the entrance her captor used to enter and exit, but she found the door locked. Then she walked over to the wooden ladder leading to the roof hatch. She had no choice but to check the roof hatch for an exit. As she put her weight on the second rung of the ladder, it snapped, and she started to fall, but adrenaline kicked in, heightened her reflexes, and kept her from falling.

When she reached the top, she pushed on the hatch, but it did not open. She had done pretty well keeping her shit together, given the circumstances, but she started to panic and started pounding on the hatch. Something caught her eye. She saw a lever, and through her frustration, she chuckled as she called herself an idiot again.

She had to rock the rusted lever back and forth as rust fell onto her face. She looked away as she continued to rock it back and forth until it became loose enough to slide over.

As she popped her head out, she noticed how great it was to have the setting sun on her face. A light breeze brought coolness and fresh air, which somehow comforted her. She noticed that her prison was attached to a barn, and the back of the barn faced a small, wooded area and a cornfield. The section she was in was slightly shorter than the top of the second-story part of the barn.

There appeared to be a road to her right, just past the brush and a line of trees. She climbed onto the roof and looked to the other side of the barn but could not see what was beyond a giant oak tree. She realized she had no idea where she was.

She leaned over the edge, searching for the ladder to climb down. Her stomach lunged as she realized how high she was—and no ladder was in sight. Only bolts jutted out where the ladder had once been.

There was no way down on the other side either. The other section of the barn was too high to climb up, and there was no way around it. With her back against the wall, she slid down and put her head in her hands. She needed a moment to think. She was tired, hungry, and angry. She finally began to cry, which made her even more furious.

She knew she had to get out of there, and going back down inside was NOT an option. She had to do something because her captor would be back soon. She thought that she could try tying her clothes together and climbing down.

She took off her pants and then her flannel shirt. She tied them together and then realized it was still not long enough.

Next, she removed her undershirt and socks, but they did not add much, so she took her bra off and tied it to the end.

She tied the pant leg to the lever on the lid and closed it for added security. She threw the clothing rope over the side of the barn and her shoes on the ground.

She saw it did not even go halfway down, but she had no choice. She worked up the courage to climb over the side of the barn, trying not to look down and lose the courage to continue. She started to make her way down the rope made of her clothes. As she reached the flannel shirt section, the crotch of her pants began to rip. She knew she had to hurry, but not too quickly, because she had to avoid the bolts sticking out.

The crotch ripped a little more, and she lost her balance, slamming against the side of the barn. The back of her head hit the barn just inches from a protruding bolt. She got herself back on track and continued to climb down the wall. She reached the t-shirt section as the flannel shirt began to rip in the armpit. Shawndrea reached the section where her bra was tied, which was the end. She was still far off the ground, about ten feet. I could jump and roll.

Just as she was about to jump, the pants ripped a little more, which caused her to lose balance. She slammed into the side of the barn as a bolt ripped through the skin on her leg. She screamed out in pain just as the plastic clasp of her bra snapped, sending her hurdling towards the ground.

She landed on her back, knocking the wind completely out of her. As she started to catch her breath again, she noticed the sound of locusts, which was extremely loud. Also, it was getting dark. She had lost some blood from the gash in her leg. She got to her feet, and as she did, she heard a twig snap.

Around the corner came her captor. "Bitch where do you think you are going?"

Shawndrea started to run, but her captor was faster, grabbing her by the back of her head with a handful of hair. She yanked her backward, pulling her off her feet. Kicking and screaming, she fought wildly against her captor as she was drug back toward the cage. Her captor could not drag her while she was flailing around, so her captor took a big stick and knocked her out.

Chapter Twenty-Three

Haunted

The start of Chase's senior year was tough, and the first few weeks back to school were the hardest he had faced in a while. Some of the fellow students did not know how to act around him. To them, he was the boy who had been in an accident and then a coma. People treated him like he was fragile, and it started angering him. He even noticed the coach going easy on him.

On top of it, he felt the pressure of being the oldest kid in school and the weight of everyone's stares. He could not help but feel alone and left behind. Usually, he would spend time with Trey, Tommy, or Sheldon, but they had graduated. The halls seemed empty without them, and he longed to see Sheldon's smiling face. The incoming freshman girls swooned when Chase walked by. The senior girls would laugh and say, "Good luck!"

Chase looked for Laramie for the first couple of weeks, but he was nowhere to be found. He still had not had a chance to thank him. He overheard someone saying that Laramie had gone to Evansville and joined a gang. Another rumor was that Laramie was sent to military school over the summer and might not return this semester. Yet another was that he chose to go back to military school this time instead of being forced to go. But Chase was too busy focusing on his goals and did not give much thought to the rumors.

Part of him wished he had skipped school and went to Rhode Island with Sheldon and the girls. But Sheldon would be back soon, and they would celebrate his nineteenth birthday together in a few weeks. He missed Sheldon more than he knew and kept expecting him to turn the corner to greet him.

§

When Shawndrea woke, she saw her captor standing near her holding a lighter to a knife. "You thought you were going to get away from me, didn't ya, stupid bitch," her captor spat at her. "I should cut this bastard of a baby out of its whore of a mother!" her captor shouted.

Her captor moved towards her with the knife in hand. Shawndrea thought she was really going to cut the baby out of her, but instead, she stuck the hot knife to the gash on her leg, which appeared to be bleeding again. Shawndrea let out a scream just before passing out from the pain and lack of food. It had been a few days since she had eaten or drank anything.

When she woke up, she was alone, naked, in pain, and hungry. She reached for her belly and was relieved to feel she was still pregnant and that the crazy bitch did not cut the baby out of her. She panicked for a moment when she did not feel any movement from the baby. She grew concerned that the fall could have hurt the baby. She had unconsciously held her breath till she felt the slightest movement and released it in relief.

She had lost track of time months, perhaps even longer, since her captivity began. The thought haunted her more than the dim, suffocating walls around her. Was anyone searching for her? Or had the world moved on without her? She pushed herself upright, the motion sending a wave of dizziness crashing over her. Her breath hitched as pain flared in her leg, her fingers instinctively clutching at the swollen and bruised flesh.

Shawndrea rubbed her wrists. The faint sting from the rope burns was a sharp reminder of her narrow escape. The chair that once restrained her now lay splintered in the corner, a symbol of her defiance. She froze as her eyes landed on a can of government-issued peanut butter nearby, its lid pried off. It sat there, ominous and out of place, as if it had been waiting for her all along.

She shoved her fingers into the peanut butter, scooped some out, and ate it. She had always hated peanut butter, but it tasted like heaven at that moment. As she tried to swallow, she looked closer at the can and noticed it had expired two years ago, but she did not care. She shoved another scoop into her mouth.

She ate several more scoops before lying down and staring at the ceiling, thinking this all had to be a bad dream, and she was going to wake up just like the dream of her family being shot and killed. Her eyes closed even though she fought to keep them open.

She woke to a throbbing pain in her leg. For a split second, she forgot where she was. As she lay there in pain, she began to think she was going to die, but getting to sleep lying down was amazing. She drifted back to sleep. She awoke again to the sounds of birds singing. She sat up, rubbing her face. As she touched the wound on her leg, she winced in pain. She saw something by the door that she had not noticed before. It was a black rubber bucket like the ones she used to water and feed her horse out of.

She hobbled over to the bucket and stuck her hand inside. It was water. She smelled it before putting it to her lips. It tasted okay. She scooped handfuls of water into her mouth and then washed her face.

Shawndrea was left alone for several days. She slept off and on. A few times, she woke, and it was sweltering. She decided she needed to ration the water and peanut butter because Shawndrea did not know if she would get any more. After all, her captor was coming even less. After several days, she could put weight on her leg. Thankfully, there did not appear to be any infection.

Suddenly, she felt a wave of tightening sensation go across her abdomen, which caught her off guard, and she could not breathe. She had a couple more cramping sensations, which took her breath away again, and she eventually passed out from exhaustion. When she woke up, her captor was standing over her.

"It looks like you're water has broken, and you are gonna need to push," her captor demanded, as she cut off her underwear to deliver the baby.

"I can't," Shawndrea said.

"I said push you dumb bitch!!" the captor said, spreading her legs apart.

Shawndrea did as she was instructed and pushed with all the energy she had left and was fighting to keep from passing out just as she saw the captor cradling the baby and said, "He is dead, and you killed him," the captor spouted.

"No!" Shawndrea cried out just before she passed out.

She woke up briefly in a haze of exhaustion to see her captor cutting the umbilical cord, and she could not hear the baby crying.

"Thanks to all your attempts to escape, your baby is dead," The captor shouted at her as she exited the enclosure carrying what appeared to be a lifeless baby in a gunny sack just as she passed out again.

§

Growing up, Mandy's coworker Dani had a desire to go away to school and become a paralegal. Being a mother was not one of her plans, but she would not trade her kids for the world and loved them more than anything. Dani would go to the library down the street from her house to use their computers. While surfing the internet, Dani researched schools that offered paralegal courses.

Dani daydreamed of sitting in class one day, which Sheldon and she had in common. She also dreamed of having her own computer one day, which they talked about often, and this gave Sheldon the idea that, at some point, he would need to get a computer, too.

Recently, she had a lot of dreams of losing her kids. In one dream, her kids were on a boat caught in a raging river, and she could not get to them fast enough before they went down the river and disappeared.

In another dream, she was reaching for something on the shelf at the grocery store, and when she turned around, her children were gone. She ran frantically around the store, looking for her children as she screamed their names. She ran into her mother, who looked at her with concern.

"Dani, what are you talking about? You do not have any children," her mom told her. Dani woke up covered in sweat and holding her chest.

In her most recent dream, Dennis's brother Billy shoved the kids into her bedroom closet and laughed an evil laugh. Dani tried calling out for Dennis, but nothing came out. Dani felt as if her vocal cords were no longer connected or working. Dani looked towards her bedroom door, Dennis's feet sticking out from the hallway. Billy was still laughing his evil laugh as she tried calling out again.

When nothing came out, she reached for her neck to feel her throat, and she felt something wet. Dani pulled her trembling hand back to examine it. Warm, sticky blood coated her fingertips, seeping into the lines of her palm. Her breath hitched as she scanned the room, searching for its source. She started screaming with her eyes, and she turned to get away from Billy and get help. Her first thought was to find her mom. She was trying to run, but her feet would not move.

She awoke with her feet tangled in the sheets. She bolted up, sitting in bed, realizing it was a dream. She looked over to Dennis's side of the bed, and it was empty. As she put her foot on the floor, she thought she heard a noise from the hallway. Something ran across the floor and jumped onto the bed, causing her to let out a little scream. It was only her cat.

"Taffy, you scared the shit out of me," She said, petting her cat.

She walked out into the hallway. The rest of the house was still. She walked down the hall to check on her babies. It dawned on her that Dennis had already left for work. She found her kids were sound asleep, safe in their beds.

She walked into the living room half expecting to see Billy, but she knew she should not see him since Dennis had a conversation with him about coming over less, and he was not allowed to enter their home without Dennis there.

She still could not get the look on Billy's face out of her head when Dennis explained it to him. His face had remained emotionalist and cold. Dani got a chill thinking about it. She had braced herself for some reaction from Billy. Instead, he just got up and walked out of the house. They had not heard or seen him since.

She walked back to her children's bedroom and stood in the doorway momentarily. She walked over and climbed into bed with her youngest child. After the nightmares, she held her kids even closer.

§

The shrill ring of the phone shattered the quiet of the Major's house, echoing like an alarm in the stillness of the night. Mandy stirred, her heart pounding as she reached for the handset on the bedside table. Calls at this hour were never good news.

"Hello?" she mumbled, her voice thick with sleep and worry. For a moment, all she heard was static on the other end, and then, faint but unmistakable, came a voice she had not expected to hear.

"Mom?" Levin said, his tone laced with something she couldn't quite place—urgency, fear, or both.

"What's going on?" Mandy asked immediately, sitting up in bed and looking at the clock.

"Mom, we are headed to the hospital. The baby is coming," Levin explained.

"I will meet you there," Mandy said, throwing back the covers. "Drive safe, and I will see you soon." She woke Damian and Sheldon, and she insisted on driving.

Charlotte's screams echoed from the delivery room, reaching the waiting area. Sheldon, Mandy and Damian sat patiently, waiting for Levin to come and tell them everything was okay. The screams made Mandy more anxious.

"Things seem to have quieted down in there. Someone should be out soon," Mandy stated as she nervously rubbed her hands back and forth on her pants. She got up, investigated the room, but could not see anything, and sat back down. "Why is it taking so long?"

They heard a baby crying. Then, there was more silence, and suddenly, the screaming started again. "What the fuck is going on?!" Mandy cursed, getting up from her chair again. Sheldon was shocked that his Mom said fuck and thought for sure she was going to bolt into the room.

"I'm sure everything is fine, and they will be out to let us know soon," Sheldon explained, trying to calm his mother, but it was useless.

Damian worked to get Mandy calm and to breath. Sheldon called him the Mandy whisper and Mandy was not amused.

§

When they rolled Charlotte into the delivery room, Levin's stomach dropped. He thought he was prepared for this moment, but no amount of preparation can truly prepare a non-medical person for bringing a life into the world. He was concerned about Charlotte because he did not know how to help her. She was in so much pain.

At one point, she screamed for him to leave the room. Roberta got her to calm down and breathe while wiping the sweat from her forehead. Then Charlotte begged him to come back. When the baby was delivered, and it was not crying, he began to panic that something was wrong but was relieved when the baby started whaling. He looked back at Charlotte, who was smiling, crying, and covered in sweat from the effort it took to push a human being into the world. "It's a girl," Levin said with a big smile.

There was a moment of completeness, then suddenly Charlotte started having more pain, and the Doctor became quickly concerned. The Doctor looked to see what the problem was, and when he looked back up, he had a shocked look on his face.

"There is another head crowning," the Doctor stated.

"What!" Charlotte said, breathless. "Oh my God! I don't think I have the strength to push anymore."

"Yes, you do," Roberta commanded. She was rocking her new grandchild. "You're going to push because I said so." She walked over to her daughter and put her hand on her shoulder. "Now push!"

Charlotte started screaming as she pushed down. The second baby came much faster. They placed the baby on the other side of Charlotte after they cleaned it up.

"What are you thinking of naming them?" Roberta asked, cooing at the baby in her arms.

"We had decided on Ashildr Maebh Majors," Charlotte replied to her mother and then looked at Levin. "But we also really liked Kaylynn Jo Majors."

"So that settles it. The firstborn is Ashildr, and the youngest is Kaylynn," Roberta cooed again while holding Ashildr and smiling at Kaylynn.

§

When Chase walked into Sheldon's house, he thought it was strange that Sheldon did not greet him, and the house seemed unusually quiet. When he closed the door, everyone jumped out, screaming, "Surprise," causing Chase to jump backward against the door. He was not expecting to see so many people.

"Happy birthday," Sheldon said, greeting Chase with a kiss. "You had no idea, huh?"

"No, and I think my heart just jumped out of my chest," he said, smiling as everyone greeted him. "I kind of thought you had forgotten because of everything that has been going on over the past few weeks," he whispered with a smile.

"Lunch should be ready soon. I'm making your favorite, lasagna," Mandy stated. "Go in the living room and catch up with your friends."

Sheldon led Chase into the living room, where everyone else sat and talked.

"Do you still think Shawndrea has simply run off?" Sheldon asked Ninnie as everyone sat perched, waiting for a response. Everyone was thinking about it, but no one else felt comfortable asking. "I mean, it has been months and not one word."

"Honestly, nothing, and I mean nothing, would surprise me with her," Ninnie replied, but everyone was waiting for more. "I do know, but it has taken a toll on Mom, and now Grandma is not doing well. I do not know how much more mom can handle."

"You think she would do that to your family?" Chase asked.

"You all realize that Shawndrea never graduated, right?" Ninnie asked.

Everyone was looking confused. "But Shawndrea told us she graduated?" Sheldon said, "We even celebrated it at the roller rink."

"Come to think, we never were invited to her graduation," Tommy remarked. "I did think it strange at the time."

"Also, did you notice how there never was this big wedding she kept talking about having?" Ninnie pointed out. She went on to explain, "Shawndrea used to make me listen to her having sex with all these random guys in her bedroom in the van. It did not matter to her." Everyone's mouth was hanging open.

"She doesn't seem to form real connections with people," Ninnie explained. "She's gotten good at feigning concern, but it's usually tied to how it benefits her."

"Oh, wow, I had no idea," Sheldon said while everyone else sat there speechless.

"Happy birthday, Chase!" Ninnie shouted, breaking the silence. "Today is about Chase and not her," Ninnie demanded as she side-hugged him.

"So, how are the babies?" Chase asked Charlotte and Levin, trying to take the spotlight off him.

"They are good," Charlotte responded, looking as tired as expected. "I was worried everyone yelling surprise might wake them. I just fed them and put them down for a nap, but that will only be short-lived. Currently, they have not been sleeping for very long. So, I'm sure we will hear them very soon. At least now, they are both sleeping at the same time. That was a nightmare when one would be asleep, and the other would be up because I never had time to nap, shower, or anything."

"With Levin in school during the day and going to work at Dairy King in the evening, I rarely see him. Luckily, when Mom comes home from her night shift at the hospital, she watches them for a bit so I can shower or take a quick nap. Between crying, bottles, and diapers, I'm about to lose my mind. So, this is a nice change of pace. DIAPERS, did you remember to bring the diapers," Charlotte frantically asked Levin.

"Yes, I even brought the backup diaper bag just in case we have another incident like last weekend at your grandmother's," Levin reassured her.

"I cannot begin to imagine having twins," Ninnie stated. "I'm intrigued by the previous event that required so many diapers, but I'm also afraid to find out."

They all laughed. "Trust me, you don't want to know. I still have nightmares about it," Charlotte chuckled. "Excuse me, but I must go pump now."

§

"Hey, lady," Harriet greeted Mandy as she entered the kitchen. "Is there anything I can help out with?"

"I think I have it all under control," Mandy replied. "You can make us some coffee if you like," Mandy said as she turned around, but Harriet was already filling the coffee carafe with water. It was like old times, like Harriet had not been missing from her life for the last few years.

"Soooo, have you heard that Walter Snape already has a new woman?" Harriet asked as she scooped coffee grounds into the coffee pot.

"Nooo?!" Mandy questioned loudly, turning around and looking at Harriet to see if she was joking. "But his wife just died four months ago."

"It's only been about three months, and the word is they are set to get married next month," Harriet explained as Mandy looked at her, speechless. "My source told me that they met at church. If you ask me, it sounds fishy, like maaaaaybe something was already going on prior to Mary's death, but what do I know."

"You think," Mandy stated sarcastically, and they both laughed. "Something about it seems fishy to me, too. Also, he seemed too calm at the funeral, too."

"You went to the funeral?" Harriet asked, and Mandy nodded yes. "You cannot make this stuff up; if you did, people would not believe us."

"I still can't believe he found someone else to take care of him so fast," Mandy said sipping her coffee.

"You're telling me," Harriet chortled. "I can't even find a man, and the ones I do are complete looooosers, HA!"

"What about *Ricardo?*" Mandy asked.

"Wow, is it getting hot in here," Harriet said, getting up and opening a window.

"Nice change of subject," Mandy smirked. "Speaking of Mary Snape," Mandy spoke in a lower voice and looked around. Harriet came closer to hear what Mandy had to say. "I really haven't talked with anyone else about this, but at the time I saw Mary dying, I swear to God I saw someone walking on the other side of the tracks."

"You have got to be kidding me," Harriet stated, even more intrigued. "Really?"

"Yes, I saw the person walking away before I saw Mary in the van. The person was walking towards Mary's parents' house. I yelled that help was coming, but whoever it was kept on walking. Sheldon even went to search for them but saw no one."

"I just got a chill up my back," Harriet said, quivering.

"When I saw Mary in the van, I figured it must have been her daughter because they looked alike, and she did not hear me. But..." Mandy paused in suspense as Harriet was on the edge of her seat. "It wasn't her daughter; her parents said she was alone."

"Oh My God, who could it have been then? You don't think," Harriet paused before saying the following line as if the possibility of what she was about to say was utterly crazy. "It was her spirit, do you?"

"I don't know... What else could it have been," Mandy replied, shrugging. "For a while, I tried to convince myself that it didn't happen, but the more I think about it, the other person I saw was as clear as you or I right here, right now."

"Oh, hell, Mandy, you're starting to freak me out," She shivered as if she just got goosebumps. "Has she visited you here? Is she here now?" Harriet whispered, looking around. Mandy busted out laughing. "I'm serious here," Harriet snapped.

Mandy continued laughing. "No, I have not seen her again," Mandy finally pulled herself together to answer. "However, I do think this house is haunted. I mean, think about it: this house was built over a hundred years ago and has seen many people come and go."

"You're joking, right?" Harriet said, looking at her with wide eyes.

"No, I'm serious," Mandy responded. "We will come home, and someone or something has moved stuff from one room to another or around the house. There have been times we would come home to find doors open that always remain closed. Other times, I have come home to the TV being on, and I know I turned it off. Also, you will hear someone walking upstairs when you're home alone."

"Shut up!" Harriet demanded. "Why the hell do you still live here? I'm starting to rethink my whole coming over to hang out with you. You need to have someone come and bless this house. Is there such a thing as a home exorcism?"

"The spirits are not evil. They are harmless," Mandy reassured her as they heard Damian pull into the driveway. "Please, do not mention this to Damian," Mandy requested as Damian was about to walk inside the house.

"Well, now I cannot make any promises," Harriet chuckled as Damian walked into the house. "Well, aren't you a sight for sore eyes," Harriet greeted Damian, who walked into the kitchen, causing him to blush. He gave Mandy a big kiss on the lips. "Oh shit, I think I just orgasmed watching you two."

"Stop!" Mandy requested as she was belly laughing, and turning red.

§

After everyone left the party, Mandy and Damian decided to go shopping, leaving Sheldon and Chase home alone. Sheldon started making out with Chase, which got them both sexually aroused. "I have your real birthday present right here." Sheldon took Chase's hand and placed it on his crouch. Chase could feel he was already extremely excited.

Sheldon led Chase to the bedroom, and he undressed Chase and himself. They continued to make out as Sheldon straddled Chase. He raised Chase's legs over his shoulder and started kissing him passionately as his cock was pressing up against the entrance of Chase's hole. "I have never done this," Chase whispered.

"I know," Sheldon responded, kissing him again. "There is a first time for everything. Don't worry, I will be gentle. Now remember to relax and take a deep breath and let it out as you push out just a little to let me inside you," He requested with a smirk and a chuckle. He began kissing Chase's neck. "I wanna be the one to pop your cherry." Chase breathed in and then let out a moan of pain and pleasure as Sheldon slowly entered him.

Chapter Twenty-Four

The Escape

Franny shared with Letty and Jerni what she saw on the police report for Chase's burned-out car, and they had been trying to meet up with Berry, but every time they went to his place, he was never there, and the last time they were there, they got the sense he was hiding in the house and refused to talk to them.

They made one last ditch effort to talk to Berry, but he had told his wife they were stalking him, and she believed him. She told them not to come around anymore. Since Letty felt this was the last time they would be at Berry's place, she made sure to get her long-haired calico kitten to help keep her company when no one was home. However, Franny fell in love with them, especially the one that Letty wanted.

"Look, old woman, you're not getting my cat," Letty said, and the three laughed.

"Your cat is cute, too," Jerni said. Franny had gotten a darker one that Tara called Midnight.

Letty and Jerni decided to take all the information they had collected to Sheriff Bolden in a last-ditch effort to get him to investigate Berry and PJ's homes. They kept bugging him until he agreed to see what he could do but would not make any promises.

§

The phone at Letty's apartment rang, startled her because she had forgotten she had just paid part of the bill and convinced the phone company to turn it on temporarily. She got up to answer it.

"Hello," Letty says, unsure who could be calling because no one had their new number.

"Mrs. Myer?" a voice on the other end asked.

"Yes, that is me," Letty responded.

"This is Nurse Janis from Kit Carson Nursing and Rehabilitation Center, and I'm calling to let you know that your mom has had a serious fall and is currently in our care. She arrived here unconscious and has yet to regain consciousness."

"What? Is she okay?" Letty asked in complete shock.

"The doctor does not believe anything is seriously wrong with her and believes she should wake up any day. We thought a family member would want to be here with her when she wakes up, but I have not been able to get a hold of any other family members."

"Thank you for letting me know," Letty said. "I'm going to make some arrangements and get a flight out there."

Letty called her work and Ninnie to tell them she must go to California to be with her Mom.

"Oh, and don't forget to feed the cat," Letty told Ninnie.

"What cat?" Ninnie asked. "You don't have a cat."

Just feed the cat," Letty said and hung up.

"Okay," Ninnie said, but her Mom was already gone, and she was confused because her Mom didn't have a cat.

After arriving in California, Letty went to the assisted living facility, where she learned it was not just a fall. Her mother had also suffered a heart attack.

She called to let Ninnie know what was going on, that she would probably be there longer than expected, and to take the cat with her. Ninnie did not have the space for a cat, so she dropped it off at her Aunt Mandy's house because they had space for animals.

§

Shawndra woke up the next day and felt like the day before had to have been a bad dream, but she quickly realized it was not when she moved and felt that her baby was gone. Her captor must have known what she was doing because she did not bleed out. Her captor could have left her there to die, but she did not. She lay there crying and moaning at the loss of her baby.

She slept off and on for the next day when she finally woke and was dying of thirst. Shawndrea was drinking water when she looked up at the hatch in the roof. She noticed that it looked like part of her pants was still attached to the hatch. She thought about it and decided she would try climbing up to investigate. How could she afford not to? She did not know how much longer she would be held captive, or what her captor might do to her next, or if her captor would come back.

She climbed up and pushed to open the hatch. She laughed because her clothes were still attached to the hatch. She was sure her captor would have removed her ability to escape.

"Who's the dumb bitch now," Shawndrea said with a laugh.

As she climbed out onto the roof, she looked down at the ground where she had fallen the last time and then back down at her prison. She could stay there, and the next time her captor came back, she could use something to knock her out, but who knows how long that could be. Or she could try to climb down the building. She was hesitant since that did not go so well the first time.

She had not seen her captor since she lost her baby, and the captor left with her baby's body. She decided she could not stay there any longer. She knew she had to take a chance, so Shawndrea climbed down the side of the building as far as she could and then hung for a second before letting go. As she hit the ground, something snapped in her ankle, and she fell over, curled up, screaming in pain from an old volleyball injury. She was afraid she had pulled something but knew she had to get up and run for help.

She grabbed her shoes, which were still lying on the ground from her first attempt to escape. She headed towards the road, limping, and slipped her shoes on. She was relieved that nothing seemed broken, but she may have sprained her ankle. She jumped through the brush as the sticker bushes scratched her bare legs.

As she walked down the road, she felt something moist between her legs. She looked down and saw blood running down her legs, and her panties were soaked in blood. She had no idea she was bleeding that much.

Then it dawned on her they were not even her panties, and she had no idea where they came from because the crazy bitch cut hers off. Also, if she gave her panties, why didn't she give her more clothes? She realized she did not have time to dwell on the whys of a mad woman.

The road became grassy and looked like it had not been driven on in a while. Shawndrea grew concerned that she had gone the wrong way but was not about to turn around and go back, so she pushed on. The sun was almost set, and lightning bugs were beginning to take flight all around her. She could hear crickets chirping. She started to hear the sound of frogs growing closer. She came to a wooden bridge that had rotted away and was no longer crossable.

She went down the steep bank and walked over to the creek's edge. She hesitated to climb in the water for fear of what was in it, she could continue walking along the bank to find an easier way across. However, that would mean wading through more brush, and as she looked down at her bare legs, which were scratched up, she couldn't take more climbing through the brush.

Looking down at her legs, it suddenly occurred to her that her captor must have taken off her own panties and put them on her. The thought grossed her out so much that she jumped in the water, which was so cold it took her breath away and took her mind off the fact she was wearing another woman's dirty panties.

She waded deeper into the water, which came up to her neck. She did not realize it was going to be so deep. She started to swim quickly to the other side. As she started to climb out, she slipped on a rock and rolled down the bank in the mud. She muttered to herself as she began to get up.

She climbed back up to the road, which was completely overgrown with weeds, and in some places, trees had started to grow. She made her way through the overgrown road. As the sun set, it became harder and harder to see the path. Luckily, a full moon lit the pathway.

She grew cold from the dampness of the night and her muddy wet hair. She came to a point in the road that seemed to be the end, but she noticed that to her left, it appeared to be a similar overgrown road. So, she turned left and continued walking through the weeds when she noticed something on her right. She thought she saw a light through the woods, which motivated her to keep moving even though she wanted to stop and rest.

She finally came to a place in the road that became less grassy and then back to gravel. She found what appeared to be a driveway leading to the light. As she walked up the lane, she thought maybe it was not such a good idea, but she was exhausted, and this seemed to be the best option.

What if these people are just as crazy as the person who held her captive? At this point, she did not care. She saw two vehicles in the driveway and a house with no lights on. She hesitated just a moment before knocking. There was no answer, so she knocked louder. She almost gave up when a light came on in the window right of the front door.

Her heart started pounding. She was scared and relieved at the same time. When the porch light came on, she squinted at its brightness. The couple that lived there looked out at a naked, wild-haired woman covered in dirt, mud, and blood. They hesitated before opening the door.

§

On Saturday morning, Sheldon stopped by to watch Chase practice, and afterwards, Chase came over and sat on the grass with Sheldon.

Chase was wearing a practice jersey and black shorts. Sheldon could not help but stare at his lips when he talked or his legs with his arms wrapped around them. Then, he stretched one leg out and wrapped his arms around the other as he told a story.

However, Sheldon could not help but notice his sexy, muscular, hairy legs, which became smooth the further you went up. His shorts had road up, which highlighted his huge bulge as he spread his legs, and Sheldon caught himself licking his lips.

I'm so glad you can stop by and surprise me with your beautiful smile.

Chase stands up to head home and change, but Sheldon is still on the ground. "Let's go," Chase requested.

"I can't," Sheldon said, looking down.

"Here," Chase said, extending his hand. Sheldon looked at him and showed that he was excited.

"Oh, nice," Chase said, smirking at Sheldon. "Let's go take care of that," he said, extending his hand. Sheldon reached out and was pulled into Chase's arms as he breathed in his musky, sweaty body. Chase ground himself into Sheldon.

"That is only going to make it worse," Sheldon said, laughing and looking down. "Now we both have a problem."

"Who cares," Chase said, grabbing Sheldon's hand and leading him towards home, where Sheldon made Chase sweat even more. They finish lying there out of breath, staring at the ceiling.

"I'm going to get in the shower so we can head out," Sheldon said, getting up from the bed.

"Not if I beat you to it," Chase slapped him on his bare butt and ran to the shower.

"Hey," Sheldon said, chasing after him. He got into the shower with Chase, and they both could not stop laughing.

"Here, wash my back," Sheldon said, turning around. "Whoops, I dropped the soap," Sheldon said, bending over.

"Don't tease me unless you're ready to take another load," Chase said, grinding up on Sheldon as Sheldon put his hands against the wall to brace himself.

"If you two don't hurry up, we are going to leave you," Chase's mother, Maya, called out to them, cracking open the door. "Are you two in the shower together?"

They both laughed. "I guess we're going to have to pick this up later," Chase said.

"You promise?" Sheldon asked, biting his lip.

Chase leaned over and whispered in Sheldon's ear, "I'm gonna fuck you all night."

"Here, turn around. Let me wash your back," Sheldon requested and whispered into Chase's ear. "Not if I fuck you first."

"I'm surprised your parents invited us out to dinner," Sheldon said as he got out of the shower. "They never seem to eat out."

"Well, Dad said he has some news he wants to share and celebrate," Chase said, drying off.

At dinner, Chase's dad ordered for everyone at the table. Sheldon was not used to a man taking charge, so it was odd but nice. "Why don't we shower together anymore?" Maya suddenly asked her husband.

"Because we would need a much bigger shower," he said as she slapped his arm. "Hey, I don't mean you. Have you looked at me? I'm not as thin as I used to be." They both laughed.

Sheldon was always surprised at how open they spoke in front of them but was always impressed by how affectionate they were to each other after being together for so many years. Sheldon was not accustomed to a family that was so affectionate with each other and always hugged one another.

The wine he ordered arrived, and the waiter poured some for everyone, even Chase and Sheldon.

Louis cleared his throat, "As you know after my business partner took off with all the money, I gave up and escaped or ran off here to the Midwest. Growing up, I always thought I would do something creative with my life, and I loved creating new things. I found a lot of joy in building sets for movies and TV shows. Then, I thought I would enjoy owning my own business even more, but owning your own business is a lot of work and not that creative."

Chase looked at his dad, confused about where this story was going. He knew most of it, but he thought his dad enjoyed being his own boss.

"Bear with me," his dad said, sensing Chase's confusion. Chase looked at his mom, who smiled at him.

"I thought coming to Illinois and starting new would fulfill me, but it's not as fulfilling as I thought. You will be graduating soon and going to college, so I think this will be a perfect time to take my old boss up on an offer he made me."

"What is the offer?" Chase asked.

"My friend in Los Angeles has this new show he is going to be producing at Warner Bros. Studio, and he wants me to help build the stages and sets. It's about this group of friends that live in New York, but it's filmed in Los Angeles, so he wants my expertise."

"It means good, steady money, and your mom can be close to her mother again," Louis explained.

Chase sat there in shock. He wanted to say congratulations, but all that came into his mind was, "When?"

"Well, we would need to be there by next summer to start building the stages and sets for filming for the fall pilot season, and I hope it gets lit for a full season. So that means right after you graduate," Louis explained. "These next few months will allow me the time to wrap up the construction projects we have started and sell the house."

"Congratulations, Dad," Chase said, getting up to hug his dad and his mom, who was full of emotion.

They raised their wine glasses to toast to new beginnings and celebrate. They had an excellent meal filled with laughter and joy.

§

Sheldon and Chase were lying on Chase's bed after getting home from dinner with Chase's parents. Chase was staring at the ceiling while Sheldon was lying beside him.

"What are you thinking?" Sheldon asked.

"I have a lot of mixed emotions," Chase replied. "At least now we know what was going on with my dad. I'm relieved that he was only looking to move back to Los Angeles and is not cheating on Mom."

They were quiet for a bit. " I remember when we first moved here, I couldn't wait to go back to California, but I have built my life here. But my Dad is right. I'm going to go away to college eventually," Chase explained as they fell asleep in each other's arms.

Chapter Twenty-Five

Common Courtesy

After several weeks of badgering and hounding Judge Bradbury, the Sheriff finally convinced him to issue a search warrant for PJ's property. The day he got the warrant, he was going to search the property, but there was a major accident east of town, and he was tied up most of the day.

This gave him time to consider the situation, and he realized that going out there alone might not be the best idea.

Two cop cars pulled into PJ's driveway. As they got out of their cruisers, they saw only one car parked in the driveway. The Deputy approached the Sheriff, who stood beside his cruiser and surveyed the property.

"Go around and watch the back door," the Sheriff instructed his Deputy. The Sheriff proceeded to the front door.

There was a loud commotion from the back of the house before the Sheriff even had a chance to knock on the front door. He ran to the backyard to find the Deputy holding PJ to the ground.

"He was trying to run, boss," the Deputy explained, slightly out of breath.

"Why are you trying to run PJ?" the Sheriff asked while the Deputy was putting handcuffs on him. "Where is Kelli? Is she in the house?"

"She left me," PJ explained. "She didn't even leave a note. She just took some cloths and was gone when I got home."

"Did she now?" The Sheriff asked, not entirely convinced. "Put him in the car while I search the house."

The Sheriff announced himself before entering the home, but Kelli was nowhere to be found, and by the looks of the place, she left in a hurry. Drawers were still open with women's clothing half hanging out of them.

He saw a pink T-shirt lying on the floor with what appeared to be blood on it. The Deputy entered the house and called out for the Sheriff.

"In here," The Sheriff replied. "We are going to need to bag this up," he said, putting on some rubber gloves and pointing to the bloody shirt. "And anything else that looks suspicious. It appears that PJ was telling the truth about Kelli taking off, and it seems she left in a hurry. I will start checking the buildings outside, just in case."

The Sheriff started searching the smaller buildings nearest to the house. The first building was divided into two sections. The first section was a tool shed with a small bench and tools hanging on the wall. The following section had lawnmowers, shovels, pitchforks, and pruning shears. Nothing seemed out of the ordinary.

He walked over to one of the other larger barns. He climbed a couple of steps up to the door, opened it, and stepped inside. The area he entered would have been where farmers would feed their animals on either side, but now it was where junk was stored.

Something caught his eye. It looked like a vehicle covered with a tarp, but it was too dark to be certain. He went back outside and tried to open the large double doors where the truck was located, but the weeds had grown into them, making it hard to open. Suddenly, the Deputy was there, helping him to pull the doors open, and together, they succeeded.

"What is it, boss?" The Deputy asked. "What's special about this truck?"

"I'm not sure, but my gut tells me it's something," the Sheriff replied as he pulled back the tarp.

"Isn't this PJ's old truck?" The Deputy queried.

"It sure is," the Sheriff acknowledged as he stepped back to get a good look at it. "The real question is why the driver's side is damaged."

"Are you thinking what I'm thinking?" the Deputy asked, holding his hand to his chin and staring at the front driver's side of the truck.

"Well, gauging from the damages and the description Laramie gave. I believe we are looking at the truck that ran Chase's car off the road, which means PJ is the person who shot Laramie," Sheriff Bolden explained. "What's even worse is that we didn't piece this together sooner."

"I will get the camera out of the car and call Perry to come and tow it into town," the Deputy stated as he headed to his police cruiser.

"Son of a Bitch," the Sheriff swore under his breath, upset with himself.

He walked over to one of the other barns to check it out but found nothing. There was one last barn behind a large oak tree. However, he would have to wade through tall brush to get to it. He walked the perimeter, debating whether it was worth checking out, when he saw a path that led back to the barn.

As he walked along the path, he realized someone had recently been walking back there quite frequently, which piqued his curiosity and alerted his senses. The path led up to the barn's corn crib, and the door was padlocked shut.

"Deputy O'Grady, I'm going to need you to bring me a pair of bolt cutters," the Sheriff said over his walkie-talkie. Then, he explained where he was located.

He continued to the back of the barn wading through the tall brush. When he reached the back of the barn, he saw vehicle tracks. The tracks looked like they were from a rather large vehicle, but he was unsure what vehicle it would have been.

The tracks led back to an old silo. As the Sheriff made his way to the silo, the Deputy called out for him. "I'm back here," he yelled back as he grabbed the handle on the silo door. When he opened the door, a strange burnt smell hit his nostrils and slightly burned his nose.

"What the fuck?" he said as he covered his face with his arm and pulled out his flashlight. He flicked on the light and took a moment for his eyes to adjust. The light beam went from one side to the other as he examined the inside. At first, nothing seemed unusual, but the smell was strange. It seemed to him that someone had been burning garbage in there, which was an odd place to burn garbage.

Something white and round caught his eye as he scanned the space again. He brought the beam of light back and studied it for a second.

"Hey," the Deputy said, startling the Sheriff, who did not hear him approach.

"Shit!" He yelled, turning around and inadvertently shining the flashlight in the Deputy's face, causing him to flinch from the beam's brightness.

"Sorry," the Deputy apologized.

"What the hell…" the Sheriff said as he stared past the Deputy and back to the barn.

The Deputy turned around to see clothes hanging from the roof. The Sheriff had been too busy following the tire tracks to notice the clothes hanging from the building.

"We have got to open the door to that barn," the Sheriff demanded, and the Deputy looked at him, completely lost.

They moved quickly to the front of the building. The Deputy cut the lock off, and the Sheriff opened the door. The smell about knocked them over.

"Oh damn!" the Deputy gasped, covering his face with his hands. This smell was different than the silo. It smelled more like an outhouse.

The Sheriff shined his flashlight into the room. The first thing they noticed was the blood on the floor. The Deputy let the Sheriff go in first.

The Sheriff saw something lying on the corner. It looked like bloody skin or intestines. "Come and tell me what you think this is," the Sheriff requested, pointing towards the corner. The Deputy was still standing just outside the door and did not want to go inside.

Reluctantly, the Deputy stepped into the building, still covering his face. He briefly examined the blob in the corner and then stepped back. "I'm not an expert, but that looks like afterbirth."

"Afterbirth?" the Sherriff repeated with an inquisitive look.

They both stood there examining the scene, not touching anything yet. They were both in a bit of shock at the scene and very confused.

"Come and look at something else," the Sheriff requested as she stepped out of the corn crib and walked back to the back of the barn. The Deputy could not get out of there fast enough. He was about to throw up. He felt it in the back of his throat but did not want to seem weak in front of the Sheriff, so he forced it back down as they made their way to the back.

"Take a look a look inside the silo," the Sheriff said, pointing towards the opening. The Deputy walked over, pulled out his flashlight, and turned it on. "To the left and towards the back," the Sheriff instructed.

The Deputy started looking intently at the object and then stepped back, turning off his flashlight. He looked the Sheriff square in the eyes. "Is that…?"

"A skull?" the Sheriff finished his sentence. I think we are going to have to call the State Boys in on this one," the Sheriff said. "This has turned out to be a bigger crime scene than we are equipped to handle. I'm wondering if whoever was in that barned was burned in the silo."

"I guess we shouldn't touch anything else," the Deputy said, kind of relieved. Secretly, he was excited that there was finally a big case, but disappointed he wouldn't be handling it. "I will start taping off the property."

This was the strangest scene he had ever seen in all his years as a Sheriff. As he followed the Deputy back along the path, his CB squelched.

"Dispatch to the Sheriff," a female voice called out.

"Sheriff here."

The dispatcher stated, "Shawndrea Meyers has been found, and she is at Wabash General Hospital. "

There was a pause as the Sheriff stopped, and the Deputy looked back at him.

"Did I hear her correctly," the Deputy asked.

"Sheriff, did you copy?" the dispatcher's voice came over the CB again

"Copy that," the Sheriff replied. "Deputy O'Grady is headed there now. We need you to request that the State Police come and investigate a possible homicide out here at PJ's place."

"I'm going to wait here for them."

"Copy that, Sheriff. I'm contacting them now."

The Deputy drove into town to lock up PJ and then headed to Wabash Valley Hospital in Mount Carmel to find out what information he could get from Shawndrea.

"Dispatch to Sheriff."

"Sheriff here."

"The State boys should be there in about an hour and a half."

"Copy that."

§

When Deputy O'Grady walked into Shawndrea's hospital room, she was asleep. Her appearance took him aback. Her eyes were dark and sunken in, her hair was wild-looking, and she looked very frail. He was so busy staring at her that he bumped into a chair, and the sound caused her to wake up. She looked over at him and quickly sat up.

"Sorry, I did not mean to wake you," Deputy O'Grady apologized.

"It's okay," Shawndrea said, looking around the room. "Where is my baby and where is my mom?"

"I'm not sure. I just got here. I need to take your statement," the Deputy said. "We have been searching for you for months."

"Really?" Shawndrea said through teary eyes. She put her hands to her face. The Deputy felt awkward. He stepped forward to comfort her but took a step back. Before stepping forward again and placing his hand on her shoulder. "I thought everyone had forgotten about me and that no one was looking for me."

"No, we have been searching for you, but we did not have any clues as to what had happened to you. Where have you been?"

"I-I was locked up in a barn for what seemed like forever," Shawndrea explained through her tears. "This crazy woman kept me tied up and tortured me. She starved me, cut me, cut my hair, killed my baby, and then took off with the body before I even had a chance to hold it."

"Baby?" Deputy questioned, looking at her like she was crazy. "Who's baby?"

"My baby," Shawndrea said, bawling as she laid her head back onto her pillow and put her arm over her face."

"Do you know who this lady was or where you were being held captive?"

She was inconsolable, and the Deputy was unable to get another coherent word from her. A nurse ordered him to leave and told him he must return tomorrow because she needed rest.

§

Ninnie was about to take a hot bath when there was a knock on the door. She ran to get the door and almost fell over the boxes that had still not been unpacked since her mom moved into the apartment. It was like her mom was still in limbo. Letty had planned to move to California after the sale of their house, but with Shawndrea still missing, she decided to stay until she was found.

Ninnie had come home from school for the weekend. She was going to go through her belongings to decide what to discard or take with her. She was having a hard time letting go of some stuff. She would take a little bit with her on each trip home, but she was running out of room in the little apartment she and Tommy shared.

Ninnie had no clue who could be knocking on their door at this hour. She was hesitant to open the door since she was home alone, and her mom had forgotten to pay the rest of the phone bill before leaving for California, so there was no phone. Ninnie looked out the peephole to see Sheriff Bolden standing there. A bolt of fear shot through her body, and her stomach seized. Ninnie took a deep breath before she opened the door.

"Hi, is your mom home," Sheriff Bolden asked.

"No, she is out of town," Ninnie replied.

"May I come in?"

Ninnie opened the door, and the Sheriff took his hat off as he entered. She had never seen him without a hat, which made him seem normal.

"Your sister has been found," he said, wasting no time. Ninnie's knees began to buckle. She thought he meant her dead body. "She is fine, and at Wabash General, I didn't mean to startle you," He apologized, putting his hand on her shoulder after seeing her initial reaction.

She sat down on the couch with a lot of mixed emotions. Her initial emotion was damn, she is okay, but mixed with guilt, as the Sherriff explained, she had been kidnapped and tortured.

"You or your Mom can call me if you have any questions," he said as he started to head for the door and showed himself out. The Sheriff left Ninnie sitting on the couch. He paused as he took one last look at her before he closed the door.

§

When Sheldon got home from work, Mandy and Damian weren't home yet. He figured they must have gone somewhere to have dinner and drinks after they got off from work. He saw the answering machine flashing, so he pushed play.

"It's common courtesy to return someone's call, especially when it's your mother," Grammy's voice said. "I have not heard from you in days, so call me, and that is not a suggestion; that is an order."

Sheldon felt bad because Mandy always avoided her mother. There were times when he wished Mandy was more like Grammy.

He was tired from a rough week and had to work in the morning, so he decided to watch a little TV before bed.

On the other hand, he was excited to see Chase the next day and could not focus on what he was watching, so he shut the TV off and headed to bed.

He got into bed, and as he lay there, he thought about all stuff he wanted to share with Chase. Also, he thought about their last couple dates and how nice they had been. Thoughts kept racing through his head. They both had been swamped lately and hadn't gotten much time to catch up with one another. Chase had been busy with football, and Sheldon had been working overtime.

Sheldon had only gone to a couple of Chase's home games. Lately, though, he has been too tired from working so much overtime to go as often as he would have liked.

He was starting to drift off to sleep when he heard something banging. At first, he thought he was hearing things, but it came again. He sat up in bed listening. He thought he heard someone yelling, too. He threw back the covers. He was afraid to leave his bedroom.

He opened his bedroom door and went to see where the noise was coming from. He was tempted to get his mother's shotgun from upstairs, but he heard a familiar voice yelling.

He looked out the window and saw Ninnie pounding on the door. "Were you in bed?" Ninnie asked as he opened the door. "It's not even nine o'clock yet." She did not even give him time to answer. "I need to use your phone."

"Come on in," Sheldon gestured, opening the door further. "What is so urgent?"

"I need to call Mom in California and let her know they found Shawndrea," Ninnie said, walking over to the phone, "And our phone is not working. I think Mom forgot to pay the bill again." Sheldon stood there in shock, expecting to hear that she was found dead. "She is in the hospital. I will explain more in a bit. I need to call and let Mom know."

She quickly dialed, and the line began to ring. There was a click, "Mama…"

Chapter Twenty-Six

The Hammer Made Me Do It

It was Saturday morning at the factory, and Dani's shift was beginning. Before they had a chance to get settled into work, their foreman explained that since the holidays were coming, they would need to increase production. This news meant they would continue working Saturdays. Dani and her coworkers were already killing themselves to keep up with the line.

Dani was utterly exhausted at the end of her shift as they cleaned up to head home. She clocked out and headed for the exit.

Sheldon, who was in his department, had not seen Dani for a few days because he had just been having lunch at his workstation. He cleaned up his work area and clocked out at the end of his shift. He was walking towards the exit, headed home. Dani was walking out the front doors, but he was lost in thought. When he noticed her, he called after her twice, but she did not turn around. When he called her name a third time, she finally turned to greet him.

"You, okay?" Sheldon asked, looking at her with concern. He thought she was tired, but one look in her eyes, and he could tell she was far worse than him.

"Yeah, I'm just exhausted," Dani replied, "I'm just glad it's finally Saturday, but I could use two days to recover."

"I hear ya," Sheldon added as they walked to their vehicles. "They are talking about having us working Saturdays for another month. It will be good money to buy holiday gifts, but I'm already tired between working Saturdays and trying to find a school, so I can't imagine having kids too."

"You're telling me," Dani said, opening her car door. "They told us the same thing today. Plus, I have been having bad dreams."

"Still? Are they about work or Billy?" Sheldon asked.

"They have been about Billy and my children. I tell myself I'm overreacting," she replied. "But you know that gut feeling you get?" She continued before Sheldon could answer. "Anyway, I hope you have a nice weekend, and I will see YOU on Monday." She laughed awkwardly at herself.

"I will see you Monday," Sheldon replied with a smile as she waved goodbye and got in her car. He watched her drive away. He was concerned about her but did not know how to help her.

Usually, he would share his concerns with his mom on the ride home, but she does not work Saturdays at her new job, so he turned on the radio. Trisha Yearwood's song "She's in Love With the Boy" was on, and it made him think about Chase. He forgot all about his concerns regarding Dani and figured he would see her on Monday, and maybe after a day off, she would be feeling better.

Sheldon headed home to get cleaned up before meeting Chase, who wanted to talk to him about something. As he drove through town, it occurred to him that he should have brought a change of clothes and cleaned up at Chase's house to save himself time.

When Sheldon finally arrived at Chase's house, he hoped to chill because he was tired from the busy week. He let himself inside and made his way to Chase's bedroom. Chase was lying on his bed working on homework.

"Hey, it's good to see you. how are you doing?" Chase asked as Sheldon entered his bedroom.

"I'm doing well, but you looked completely wrecked," Sheldon remarked because Chase's hair looked messy.

"Thanks," Chase smirked.

"Sorry," Sheldon replied, kissing him.

"I'm literally pulling my hair out with these trigonometry problems," Chase explained.

"Awe, sorry to hear, and unfortunately, I cannot help you," Sheldon remarked. "I'm the worst at math. My brother was always good at math."

"I know I was going to see if he could help me, but he is so busy working at his after-school job that I did not want to bother him," Chase stated.

"Yeah, I never see him anymore," Sheldon remarked. "It's weird growing up with someone you are around every day, and then suddenly, they are no longer there, and you can't help but feel abandoned. I realize that is how life is, where people are in your life for a little while and then move on to other things."

"I know what you mean," Chase said thoughtfully. "I thought I would stay in touch with the friends I grew up with, but I never hear from them, and I don't write to them either."

They snuggled on the bed and stared into each other's eyes. Sheldon brushed a strand of hair out of Chase's eyes. "Your hair is getting long," Sheldon commented. "It's cute."

"I'm exhausted. Would you mind if we ordered a pizza and stayed in?" Chase asked.

"Not at all. I was just thinking the same thing," Sheldon replied.

"Perfect. We can walk to pick it up, which will get me out of this house even for a little bit," Chase said. They got up and got dressed and put on their coats and shoes.

As they were walking, they were talking about current events. "How is work going?" Chase asked.

"My life has been busy but pretty boring, actually. Though we have been doing a lot of overtime to make up for all the times we had shut down early because we were out of parts, I have not had much time to think about it," Sheldon explained. "However, the paychecks have been good, saving a little back for my future. Other than that, my life is pretty boring at the moment, and not a lot going on."

"Huh," Chase responded thoughtfully. He was lost in his thoughts, thinking about his life and the topic he wanted to share with Sheldon.

"How about you? How is school going?" Sheldon asked.

"My life has been kind of mellow, too," Chase responded. "Football season is over, so I'm mostly just focused on schoolwork; not much is happening now. I'm debating on whether to play baseball or basketball next season. I'm starting to feel like that part of my life is behind me, and I'm preparing for something completely new."

"Hmm," Sheldon remarked, thinking about how much his life had changed, too. "That is understandable because I can tell you your life will completely change after graduating."

"I don't think I'm going to buy another car because when I go to college, I will get a dorm near the college." Chase stated as they crossed the street.

"That makes sense to me, considering you can't store it here at your parents because they will be moving back to Santa Monica," Sheldon responded. "You could probably store it at my house, but if I eventually move away to college, that doesn't make sense either."

"Thank you. I wanted your input, considering this impacts us both," Chase said. "Because I won't be able to just drive out and see you like before."

"Don't worry about it. We will make it work," Sheldon said as they waited to cross the busy street to pick up the pizza they had ordered at the gas station. Sheldon looked around to make sure no one could see them and kissed him on the cheek.

"What was that for?" Chase asked with his dimpled smile.

"Just because I love you," Sheldon responded.

"I love you too," Chase said, kissing him back. They picked up their pizza and made their way back to Chase's house. Something about that pizza was so delicious that they enjoyed every bite of it, and then, with their stomachs full, they took a nap.

§

Something startled Dani out of her sound sleep. She was suddenly aware that a shadowy figure was standing over her. In her panic, she reached for Dennis. She felt something wet, sticky, and warm when her hand touched his body.

"Dennis!" she cried out, but no response came from his side of the bed, and he did not stir.

She did not even have time to investigate the wetness on her hands. She had to duck as the shadowy figure lunged at her. She swung her feet around to get out of the bed, and as she did, she knocked the shadowy figure into her nightstand.

The figure crashed into the nightstand, knocking her lamp onto the floor, and everything on it went flying. Dani ran for the door, and as she reached for the handle, she discovered it was locked.

She scrambled to unlock the door when there was a flash of light. She reached for the back of her head to feel where something had struck her, and it was still lodged in her head. She fell to the floor as she lost all sense of reality and consciousness.

Her body lay there on the floor, lifeless, with a hammer lodged into the back of her head. The attacker tried to pull the hammer from her head, but it was lodged in so deep it took a firm tug. Her head smacked the floor when the hammer finally pulled free. Blood trickled down the hammer and onto the floor.

The hammer hit the floor, and the attacker started to drag her body and placed her in bed next to her lover like they were dolls.

The attacker pulled the hood off, and it was Billy. He walked over to the bed to examine the bodies. He left the bedroom and walked into the living room, where the two children's bodies were posed on the couch like they were watching TV. He talked to them as if they were able to converse with him and that he had not just taken their life.

§

On Monday, Sheldon went over to see Dani at lunch and see how her weekend or one day off was. Her coworkers said she was a no-call no-show. He thought that it was not like Dani. She must be sick or one of her kids. Sheldon went over a few days later, and she was still not there. Their foreman said he would be firing her if she did come in. This news broke Sheldon's heart because he liked her a lot, and this did not sound like her at all.

Sheldon and Mandy were driving home from work. "Dani has not been at work all week, and today, I found out she has not been calling in either," Sheldon shared his concerns with his mom.

"That doesn't sound like her," Mandy remarked.

"That is what I thought, too. Dani's boss is going to fire her when she does come in," Sheldon shared.

"That prick! He is ridiculous because she is a hard worker, and something must be going on," Mandy said. They road in silence for a bit. "I thought I would call her, but I realize I don't even have her phone number. I don't even know exactly where she lives," Sheldon said.

"Me either," Mandy stated. "After all this time knowing her, I don't have her number or where she lives either."

§

Billy sat on the couch for a couple of days, laughing at the TV as he continued to talk to the children. He would do things to them so unimaginable that it went beyond someone who was crazy but sick and demented.

One day, he told the children's corpses he was going to the store for food since they had run out. He entered Dani's purse, got some money, and headed to the store like it was just another day. He even stopped by the video store and rented some movies before returning to the house. He went about his life like nothing had happened.

When Dani's mom came home from her trip, she called Dani's house to see how she was doing. After two days, she did not get her on the phone, so she went over to check on them. She was not prepared for what she saw when she walked into Dani's house and saw her grandchildren's corpses on the couch. She let out a wail and ran out of the house to the neighbors to call the police because she could not be in that house for one more minute. Doing so might have saved her life as well.

Billy was asleep between his brother and Dani in the bedroom when he heard the scream. When he got up and walked into the living room, no one was there, and the front door was left wide open. Billy walked over, looked out, and then closed the door. He went back to bed. When the cops found him, he was curled up with Dani's dead body.

When the cops questioned Billy at first, he acted as if everyone was still alive. Asking where was his brother and Dani. After several hours of interrogations, he finally confessed, stating, "The hammer made me do it." He sat there staring with a blank look on his face. "The hammer told me that I had to kill them all before they got rid of me," Billy confessed.

§

Mandy pulled up to the front of the video store. Sheldon jumped out and ran inside to return the movies they rented over the weekend. He climbed back inside the vehicle.

"Did you return Grammy's phone call?" He asked as he put on his seatbelt.

"No, I did not," Mandy said, seemingly annoyed by the question.

"Well, she has called a few times, and you have not spoken with her," Sheldon pointed out.

"Oh, yeah, and since when did you become the police of my phone calls to MY mother?" Mandy asked rhetorically, and there was a long silence.

"She drives me nuts constantly calling to check on me like I'm still a child," Mandy declared, breaking the silence. "I'm an adult now, living my own life."

There was silence. "Growing up, my mom was not there for me because she was always working, so I raised myself," Mandy confessed. "Now she has all this guilt and is always bugging me. Why do you think I moved away from her? I wanted a life of my own, but nooooo, she had to go and buy a place down the road from me. I swear she moved here just to keep an eye on me."

"I do not think she is trying to control your life," Sheldon asserted. "I think she just wants to be a part of it. What is so wrong with that?" She did not answer his question. "Also, you must realize she is not going to be around much longer, and we should spend as much time with her as we can before she dies," Sheldon added. "One day you will regret..."

"Enough!" Mandy snapped, interrupting Sheldon before he could finish his argument. "How dare you say that? She is not dying, so do not say that!"

"I'm sorry, but it is a fact of life. She will not be around much longer, and we need to spend as much time..."

"I said ENOUGH!" Mandy shouted, cutting him off again. He knew then to leave well enough alone, so he did not press the subject further. She did not speak to him for the rest of the ride to work or for the next few days. It was the longest she had ever gone without talking to him. But he was not about to apologize for stating the facts.

A few nights later, on her way home from work, Mandy started talking to Sheldon again, acting like their previous conversation never happened. "A friend told me tonight what happened to Dani," Mandy said. "From what little I have heard, it was pretty bad, and I'm not sure you want to know because I still can't believe it or get the images out of my head."

Sheldon was quiet because it sounded like she was no longer with them and that something terrible had happened to her. "What happened?" Sheldon reluctantly asked.

"I guess the little brother killed them and sat in the house with the bodies for a few days," Mandy explained. "And Dani's mother discovered them. I was told it was a pretty gruesome scene, and he did unspeakable things to the children."

"Oh my god," Sheldon gasped. "What is wrong with people?"

"I don't know," Mandy replied.

As they rode to work the following week and Dani's funeral loomed on the horizon, Mandy confessed that she was really torn up about what happened to Dani and had been taking it out on him and Damian. "I just feel like I should have done something," Mandy stated as she drove down the highway.

"I know what you mean," Sheldon responded. "I feel terrible because she kept saying something was off with Billy, but you don't think something like that will happen."

"No, you don't," Mandy agreed.

Sheldon's heart broke for her and her children. All the life they would never experience, or her dreams would never come to fruition. "I know exactly what you mean," Sheldon responded, staring out the window. He sighed a deep sigh.

"We can go to the funeral together," Mandy stated.

"I would like that," Sheldon responded.

Chapter Twenty-Seven

Falling into Daddy's Grave

Numerous rumors were circulating in the factory about what had happened to Dani. One rumor going around was that she was having an affair with Billy, another claimed she was in a cult, and yet another suggested she was running a sex ring out of her house. Sheldon was tired of correcting people. He still could not believe it when he heard what Billy had done to his brother, Dani, and her children. He could not imagine Dani's mom coming home and discovering the gruesome scene involving her daughter and grandchildren.

Sheldon still felt terrible that he had not taken Dani's concerns about Billy more seriously. He felt sad that she would never see her kids grow up, travel to all the places she had yet to see, attend school, and do amazing things with her life. She was way too young to die. It was like something was missing from his life; not having Dani in it and no longer seeing her at work was a sorrowful time.

Sheldon sat down to have lunch with his coworkers Lana and her sister Edith, who everyone called Eddie. They had started working at Pathmaster a few months back.

"Well, I be damn, look who finally decided to join us," Eddie teased Sheldon in her Kentucky accent. "We thought you were too fucking good to sit with us," she laughed at herself and then snorted.

"Edith Joan, what kind of language is that to use?" Lana scolded her sister. Lana's accent was not quite as thick as her sister's. "His friend just died. Show some respect like Momma and Daddy taught you..."

"What are you talking about? She has been dead for weeks; they just found the body," Eddie blundered on till she caught the looks on everyone's faces at the table. They were shocked by her frankness. "Damn, I'm sorry," Eddie apologized loudly. "There goes my mouth again."

Eddie tends to be blunt and talk loudly, especially during awkward situations. "So, what happened to her anyways?" Eddie asked.

"She was the girl that got hammered," Lana quietly explained on behalf of Sheldon.

"Hammered?" Eddie questioned with a screwed-up face. "She drank herself to death?"

"No need to talk so loud," Lana stated. "No, it was with an actual hammer. Her boyfriend's little brother killed her, her kids, and his brother."

"And you'll all think us Kentucky people are fucked up? That's some messed up shit right there," Eddie stated. "Damn, I'm sorry, Shel; let us know if there is anything we can do."

"Thank you," Sheldon replied. "The visitation is tomorrow, and the funeral is Friday. I don't want to go, but I need to go out of respect."

"I don't blame ya," Eddie remarked. "I hope her face isn't all messed up, you know, open casket and all," Eddie stated loudly.

"Ugh…I give up," Lana said, throwing her hands in the air. "I'm sorry, Sheldon, for my sister's lack of manners."

"What?!" Eddie questioned loudly as Sheldon and Lana got up from the table to head back to their workstations. "What did I do?"

"I don't have the patience or breath to explain it to you," Lana stated. "I'm actually going to the bathroom first."

At the end of their shift, they gathered around the time clock, talking, telling jokes, and laughing.

"I will go with you to the funeral if you like," Lana offered.

"Hey, I wanna come too," Eddie demanded.

"Eddie, we aren't going to a bar for drinks. We are going to a funeral," Lana remarked, looking plainly at Eddie.

"I know you're not going to a bar," Eddie retorted, kind of offended. "What kind of idiot do you think I am that I don't know that? Do you think I only go to bars?"

"Well, you said it, not me," Lana said with a chuckle. "It's going to be very emotional."

"What, you don't think I have feelings and emotions, or that I cannot be empatatic or emptetix," Eddie stumbled, trying to use the right word.

"The word is empathetic, and no, I do not," Lana replied

"Oh yeah, and why is that? Huh?" Eddie demanded, tapping her foot.

"Oh, I don't know; maybe, for starters, you showed up at Daddy's funeral drunk out of your mind and falling all over the place. To top it off, the preacher was saying the final words at the cemetery and lowering Daddy into the ground. You jump up in the middle, saying you'll be sick. Then proceeded to throw up in the grave, and then you fell in the hole."

Sheldon chuckled at the idea of Eddie falling into the grave, which made Lana laugh, too.

"You two are assholes for laughing at me for that," Eddie snapped. "It was a very emotional time. And you call me cold? Besides, who has a funeral at a cemetery and does not protect someone from falling in the hole? I say they need to protect the hole," she said louder than intended and caused everyone to look at her. Sheldon and Lana busted out laughing. "Well, isn't the casket supposed to cover it?" Eddie asked. "That was not my fault. That is on them."

"Whatever you say sis, but it was clear to everyone else they were lowering the body into the ground, and we were to throw some dirt into the hole, not ourselves," Lana explained.

"Shut up; I swear I can't stand you sometimes," Eddie growled at Lana.

"Then, at Mama's visitation, you show up at the funeral home with some stranger, drunk again. This time, during the viewing, you proceeded to have loud sex on the other side of a curtain behind Mama's casket. You thought that was a separate room when, in fact, it was the same room, and the curtain was the only thing separating the two spaces."

"I will never forget the look on the preacher's face when you called out Jesus's name during your orgasm and you pulled the curtain down," Lana shared. "There you were, with your titties bouncing up and down, and that guy's white as a ghost ass in the air. Daddy was probably rolling over in his grave that day."

"Nah, he was probably laughing his ass off," Eddie stated. "I will give you that one. That wasn't one of my finest moments. It wasn't funny at the time, but it sure is funny to hear you tell it now." They all chuckled.

"I promise, Sheldon, those days are far behind me now," Eddie said. "But I will understand if you don't want me there."

"I think the more the merrier," Sheldon responded.

"I would say it's your funeral," Lana said. "But I guess it's not. I will leave you with good luck with that."

§

Sheldon and Mandy were headed to attend Dani's funeral. Mandy decided she wanted to drive.

"I can't believe this is the second unexpected funeral we're attending this year," Mandy commented as they headed towards Olney where the funeral was taking place.

"It is, and it's hard to wrap my mind around that we are headed towards work, but we are not going to work; we are attending a funeral, and I won't see Dani again at work. Do you think it will be an open casket?" Sheldon asked.

"That is a good question, and due to how she died, I doubt it," Mandy responded. They were quiet for a moment.

"Also, do you think they will have her children's caskets there too?"

"Oh god, I didn't think about that, and I'm not sure if I can handle it," Mandy responded, taking her hand off the steering wheel to cover her mouth. "I was just thinking about how hard it will be seeing her mother dealing with all of this."

As they entered the funeral home, Mandy saw old coworkers she had not seen since she left Pathmasters. For some of the people, it was like a mini reunion. Sheldon and Mandy approached the front and shook the family's hand.

"Did you know any of those people?" Sheldon asked, waiting their turn to walk in front of the casket.

"No, I couldn't tell which one was her mother, and which one was the aunt because they were both crying so hard," Mandy whispered. "I think she was the one on the end."

"It's an open casket," Sheldon whispered.

"Oh, lord," Mandy groaned under her breath. "I don't think I can do this," she said, grabbing Sheldon's arm.

It was their turn to step up to Dani's casket. "How did they make her look okay despite what happened to her?" Mandy whispered to Sheldon and looked at the two smaller caskets beside hers. "Thank god the children's caskets are closed."

They made their way to their seats. "Okay, that wasn't as difficult as I thought it was going to be," Mandy said. However, she broke down when Dani's mother got up to speak about how a parent should not have to bury their child.

Sheldon put his arm around his mother, and she leaned over and cried a little on his shoulder. Sheldon felt a hand on his other shoulder and turned to see Lana's smiling face, and Eddie was seated next to her. He wanted to talk to them, but Mandy was ready to go home after the services. He hugged them and thanked them for coming. "See, I can be good when I want to," Eddie said.

Mandy hugged her old coworkers, too. They made promises to get together and do something soon.

Sheldon and Mandy were quiet on the ride home. "I don't know why I got so emotional at the services," Mandy said. They were both silent again.

"I guess when I think about it, it reminds me of my loss. I lost a child just before Susan," Mandy confessed. "I wonder every day what the child would be like today." This news was a complete surprise to Sheldon.

"How did you lose the baby," Sheldon asked cautiously.

"Your dad and I were on our way back from visiting Grammy in Mt. Carmel," Mandy explained. "We were stuck behind a line of slow-moving cars that were stuck behind a tractor on the highway when a truck rammed us from the rear, which hit us so hard it shoved us into the truck in front of us. I was knocked unconscious, and the next thing I remember, I woke up in the hospital, and the doctor told me the baby was gone. I could not believe it, and it felt like a bad dream. I have not talked about it to anyone, not even your dad or my mom."

"We went on like nothing ever happened, and before we had a chance to remove stuff from the nursery, we got pregnant with your sister, and life just continued like nothing ever happened," Mandy explained. "But today, sitting there listening to Dani's mom talk about her, it was like a wave of grief and suppressed emotions and memories swept over me."

There was a moment of silence as they drove. "Do you know what you were going to have?" Sheldon asked, breaking the silence.

The car was quiet, and Sheldon was unsure if Mandy heard him, and he was not about to ask again. "A boy," Mandy croaked out. "I don't want to talk about it anymore."

Sheldon looked out the window at the farmhouses and fields passing by and wondered what it would have been like to have had an older brother.

§

Chase and Sheldon visited Charlotte and Levin on Sunday afternoon to see the twins. Sheldon was amazed at how Charlotte was able to hold the two babies at once, rocking one while feeding the other.

"Here, take Kaylynn while I change Ashildr," Charlotte requested, looking at Sheldon. He got up and took Kaylynn in his arms. After Charlotte changed Ashildr, she gave her to Sheldon, too. It was awkward for Sheldon to hold two babies at the same time. "Let me take a picture," Levin said, grabbing the camera.

"I don't know how you do it," Sheldon said. "I'm so afraid I'm going to drop one of them,"

"You would be surprised what you're able to do when you have no choice," Charlotte replied, taking Kaylynn from Sheldon to change her. "Also, I'm just glad they have started sleeping at the same time. I'm very fortunate to have Mom close by, too."

"How do you not mix them up because they look identical," Sheldon said.

"It's easy for me because I'm with them every day, but it's hard for Levin," Charlotte explained. Ashildr's hair curls to the left, and Kaylynn's hair goes all over the place."

"They are adorable," Chase remarked.

"Do you want to hold her?" Charlotte asked, handing Kaylynn to Chase, who looked scared. "You two look adorable holding the babies. You two will make great parents one day."

Chase smiled at Sheldon and back at the baby, cooing up at him. "They look adorable now, but when they start crying at 2 a.m., you have a different outlook until you look into their eyes, and they are looking up at you so helplessly," Levin stated.

"So, what have you been up to besides work, school, and canoodling together," Charlotte asked, winking and smiling at Sheldon and Chase.

"I'm going to start college in January," Sheldon explained. "I go soon to pick up my books."

"Oh, nice," Charlotte said, taking Ashildr from Sheldon to feed her. "Once these two are a little older, I want to take accounting classes at the community college. I kind of miss it, which is hard to believe because I couldn't wait to graduate."

I know what you mean I could not wait to get out of there, and now I'm looking forward to going to college, Sheldon responded.

"I figure I can do my homework between feedings and changes somehow," Charlotte stated. "Plus, Mom has agreed to help, too. She is thinking of working part-time for a while."

"That is amazing," Sheldon responded. "Maybe we will end up having a class together at some point."

"That would be so cool," Charlotte said. "Chase, do you know where you're going to college?"

"Not yet, but I will have to decide soon," Chase explained. "None of the places I visited stood out to me."

"Levin, will you take classes after you graduate?" Sheldon asked.

"I want to take some classes at the community college so I can transfer to a university and take some marketing classes," Levin shared. "And down the road get a job doing marketing for a company or maybe become a realtor."

"Charlotte, what is your dream job?" Sheldon asked.

"You know I always wanted to work on a horse ranch with a lot of horses," Charlotte explained as she put Ashildr over her shoulder and patted her gently on the back, trying to get her to burp. "I would love to work with a ranch that takes in retired horses or the ones that are unable to work or ride. I want to protect them from being sent off to the slaughterhouse."

Levin gave her a peculiar look. "I did not know that was your dream job," Levin stated.

"Yeah, well, you never asked," Charlotte said.

"Well, I love it, and it sounds like a wonderful job," Sheldon commented.

"Thank you," Charlotte said as she got up to lay Ashildr down in her bassinet so she could sleep. "I think it's time they will probably fall asleep for a bit."

"We better get going," Sheldon said, getting up. "I almost forgot, why aren't you no longer working at the Dairy King in Albion?" Sheldon asked Levin.

"Oh, they needed a manager in the Fairfield location, so I agreed to go work there," Levin explained.

"Oh, so you got a promotion," Sheldon said.

"I guess so," Levin responded.

"Congratulations. I will see you all later," Sheldon said.

"Bye," Chase said, waving bye to them.

§

On Monday after the funeral, Sheldon was at work eating lunch with Lana when Eddie came over. "Hey guys, mind if I sit with you," Eddie asked, sitting down before waiting for them to answer. "What are you all talking about?" Eddie asked as she pulled out a peanut butter sandwich.

"I was just telling him what it was like growing up in Kentucky," Lana responded, taking a bite of her tuna salad sandwich. "We did not have running water back then and had to use the bathroom in the outhouse. Hell, we didn't have electricity till I was about twelve."

"Oh god, here we go, hearing about how rough you had it growing up," Eddie teased.

"You were lucky. By the time you came along, Daddy had moved the family into a house with indoor plumbing and electricity," Lana said. "Daddy and Mom were always having more babies, so they had to get a bigger place."

"You were done gone when I grew up, so you don't know how rough I had it," Eddie said, talking with her mouth full. "He used to work us from sunup to sundown."

"Why do you think I couldn't wait to get out of there," Lana said with a boisterous laugh. "There for a while, it seemed as soon as one of us moved out, Mama was having another to replace the one that left. That poor woman was a baby-making machine. I think she died just to escape the torture."

"How many of you are there?" Sheldon asked.

"There were fifteen of us that lived. There are ones that died prematurely," Lana explained.

"Holy cow, that is a lot," Sheldon said. "Daddy always told Mom he wanted to have enough kids to have his own baseball team."

"I told you guys I could be on my best behavior," Eddie proudly said as she threw her garbage away and opened a can of Mountain Dew. Sheldon and Lana looked at her, confused, trying to see how they related to the conversation. She saw their confused looks. "At the funeral dummies. I was good and did not cause a scene."

"I'm sure the family is grateful," Lana said rolling her eyes and getting up to throw her stuff away. "I'm gonna head to the bathroom before lunch is over."

After eating, Sheldon felt sleepy. He saw Eddie's Mountain Dew, so he decided to get one for himself from the vending machine. Marcus was standing at the other vending machine, with chips and snacks. Marcus was bent over, looking at something in the machine, and Sheldon could not get around him to get to the soda machine.

"What the fuck you are looking at faggot?" Marcus asked, snarling at Sheldon.

"I'm just trying to get a soda," Sheldon said.

"Good, because my ass is off limits," Marcus said, pushing the buttons to get some peanut M&Ms. He smirked at Sheldon and turned to walk away but turned around to see if Sheldon was watching his ass. He had on a tight pair of black jeans that hugged his bubble butt, and Sheldon could not help but watch him walk away. It was as if Marcus was flaunting it in his face. He quickly looked away when Marcus turned around. He did not want to give Marcus the satisfaction that he was looking at his ass.

Chapter Twenty-Eight

Ashes of Many

When Letty's Mom woke up, she started talking about her life before she had gotten married to Letty's dad. This turn of events took Letty back because her Mom had always been very private and would never talk about her youth.

The phone rang, and Letty assumed it was Ninnie looking for an update.

"Hello," she said into the phone receiver.

"Mama," Ninnie's voice came through, and immediately Letty could tell that something was not right.

"What's wrong?" Letty asked.

Ninnie explained that Shawndrea had been found and was currently in the hospital. After Letty hung up, she looked at her Mom, and they stared at each other for a moment with a slight smile. Letty had not left her Mother's bedside since she had woken up, and she did not want to leave it now because this was the closest, she had ever been to her Mother in some time.

"Go. Go, be with your daughter," her Mom insisted. "I promise I will still be here when you get back."

"Okay, Mama. I will call you as soon as I arrive to let you know how she is doing," Letty said as she kissed her Mother's forehead. She held onto her Mother's hand as she turned to leave, not wanting to let go. Bye, Mama."

Letty was conflicted about leaving her Mother the whole way back to Illinois. However, she was utterly elated that Shawndrea was found alive, but she loved this new side of her Mom. She only hoped she would be just as open when she returned.

§

When Letty walked into Shawndrea's hospital room, she was asleep. "Sweetie, Mama's here," Letty whispered as she leaned over and kissed her daughter's forehead like she had recently done with her Mom. Shawndrea started to stir awake.

"Mom, is that you?" Shawndrea said in a small voice. She started to act like she was in a lot of pain when, in fact, she was about to be released. She knew exactly how to pull at her Mom's heartstrings.

"Yes, baby, it's Mama," Letty said, running her hand down what was left of Shawndrea's hair as she examined how chopped up it was. "Baby, what happened to you? The Police said you refuse to talk about it."

Shawndrea looked away from her Mother and ignored her request. "Sweetie, tell Mama where you have been."

"I don't know," Shawndrea said in a low voice and started holding her stomach. "Where is my baby Mama? Did they find it?"

"Baby?" Letty questioned, giving Shawndrea a concerned look.

"Yes, Mother, she took my baby and said it was dead," Shawndrea replied as she looked at her Mom with sad eyes.

"You're talking crazy now," Letty scoffed, getting frustrated with her daughter's lack of seriousness about explaining where she had been. "Did you run off and get into trouble? Where have you been for the last six months?" Letty commanded.

"I told you I do not know. Some woman was holding me in some old barn," Shawndrea explained. It was like she had been mentally suppressing the last six months, and she was starting to remember.

"She? A woman was holding you captive all this time," Letty questioned in disbelief. She was starting to think Shawndrea was making this whole situation up when a nurse walked into the room to check on Shawndrea.

"How's my daughter doing?" Letty requested sternly, skipping the formalities and not wasting any time. The Nurse was caught off guard by her bluntness.

"Hi, she is doing much better than when she first arrived here," the Nurse replied. "She was extremely dehydrated, malnourished, and appeared to have just delivered a child."

"A child? You have to be mistaken. She wasn't pregnant," Letty retorted.

"Well, Mrs. Meyer..." the Nurse started to say but was interrupted by Shawndrea.

"That is what I was trying to tell you. I was pregnant before that bitch took me hostage," Shawndrea explained. "Then she ripped my baby out of me, claimed it was dead, and then left me for dead. I do not know who she was or where she was holding me."

"Can you at least describe what you saw or heard? How far did you have to walk?" Letty probed. The Police had told her what to ask since they were not having any luck getting answers from her. Finally, Shawndrea started to recount the events from the last several months.

When Letty left her daughter's room, she pulled the Doctor aside. "What else can you tell me about my daughter," Letty requested.

"It's a miracle that she was able to conceive a child, given the extensive damage and scar tissue I observed during my examination. Also, it would have been unbelievable if she was able to carry a baby to full term, given how malnourished and dehydrated she was when she arrived here. How old was she when she was raped?" The Doctor asked.

"Raped? But she was never raped. I would have known about it," Letty stated as she glanced through the window at Shawndrea, who was resituating herself in her bed. She was silent for a moment, thinking back to what Laynardia had shared with her, and she did not know that had happened. What else has happened to her children that she was not aware of?

"Based on my examination, she was, and it looked like it was pretty bad, too," the Doctor explained. "Also, whoever helped with the delivery had to be someone with some medical knowledge. You should think about getting her some additional help when she leaves here. I can recommend a good therapist."

"Therapist," Letty scoffed as she left the hospital.

Letty explained everything Shawndrea had told her to the Sheriff. Based on this information and the location of the house where she turned up, the Sheriff pieced together where Shawndrea had been held. He realized that his gut instinct had been correct and that something fishy was happening at PJ's place.

Also, he assumed the woman who held her captive had to be PJ's girlfriend, Kelli, who had some medical experience and whom PJ claimed took off with no idea where she would have gone. Kelli's mother supposedly had not heard from her in over a year, but it was later discovered she had stayed in contact with her adoptive father, Berry.

Since the State Police took over the case, Sheriff Bolden relayed the information. It was now up to them to piece together what happened to Kelli. It was hard for Sheriff Bolden to relinquish that responsibility to someone else because he liked controlling things. He knew that with this case, he was way over his head and that it was a more significant case than a simple abduction. This case would be beyond the resources he had at his disposal.

§

The State Police brought in forensic specialists from the FBI to investigate the possible remains found at PJ's place. After several weeks of sifting through the massive pile of ashes they found in the silo, they were able to determine that the remains belonged to over seven females.

The Chief Crime Scene Investigator interrogated PJ regarding the remains found on his property, the bloody scene found in his barn, and the damage to his truck.

PJ explained that it was his uncle Berry Price who had been burning what he thought to be garbage in his silo. He had no idea that it was bodies. He explained that his uncle had borrowed his truck last year, which was involved in an accident. He did not know that it was his truck that ran Chase off the road or that his uncle had shot Laramie. Also, he knew nothing about the bloody scene in his barn. After the Chief investigator spoke with Shawndrea, based on her accounts of the ordeal, she never saw PJ during the time she was being held captive.

However, the FBI investigator still had difficulty believing PJ had no knowledge or involvement, considering the crime happened on his property. He found it implausible that he had no idea where Kelli was or if she had the baby.

The BOLO they put out on Kelli's vehicle had finally come back. Her car was found abandoned at a truck stop in Tennessee. They suspected she left her car there and caught a ride with a truck driver.

The one working surveillance camera outside the truck stop only showed Kelli pulling into the truck stop. They could not see who she left with or if she had a baby. They were about to give up when they noticed something in the corner of the screen.

It appeared to be Berry's Semi truck pulling out of the parking lot shortly after Kelli had pulled into the truck stop, but they could not be sure. They did find empty bottles of baby formula and dirty diapers left inside Kelli's abandoned vehicle, which proved the baby had not died. Unfortunately, the leads went cold, but the case remained open.

§

Jerni had been listening to her police scanner when she heard that the Police found Kelli's car at the truck stop. Jerni decided to pay the owner of the truck stop a visit and discovered that the owner of the gas station, Fred, was a bit of a paranoid, suspicious person who did not trust any of his employees or customers, so he liked to watch back the tapes to spy on the employees and customers so kept all the recordings on VHS cassette tapes. He confessed to Jerni that he had a secret camera inside, too, so she convinced the owner to allow her to review the older tapes. She agreed to meet him at his storage unit, where he stored the tapes.

When she pulled up, she started to rethink meeting him there because it was very creepy, and she began to wonder if he brought her there to kill her, too. What if, somehow, he was in on it all? "Stop it, Jerni. You have been watching too much Law and Order." She said out loud in the empty car as another car approached.

The truck stop owner Fred exited his car and waved for her to follow him. She hesitated for a moment, thinking she should have brought backup. "But you have no backup because you chose not to tell Franny or Letty," she said again to the empty car as a light rain began to fall on the windshield. She took a deep breath and said, "Here goes nothing," as she stepped out of her vehicle and followed the owner.

"The unit is over here," the owner said as he waddled over to storage unit 113 and bent over to unlock the padlock. Jerni quickly looked away at the sight of his butt crack. "I'm not sure what you are hoping to find here." He said, turning and looking at her inquisitively.

"You would be surprised at what you find sometimes in the most unlikely places," she replied as the owner started moving stuff around. There was old furniture covered in plastic, along with a floor lamp and numerous tools. "This is my parents' stuff. When they passed, I did not have a heart to sell it."

"Some of these VHS tapes went back about ten years ago when I first purchased the truck stop. I bought the surveillance equipment because things always seemed to go missing," Fred said, pointing to several boxes stacked on top of each other with dates on each one. "Did you ever catch anyone?" Jerni asked.

"I sure did; it came in handy a few times. I found kids and employees stealing from me, and I dealt with it right then and there," he boasted. "I have thought about starting to record over some of the older ones but haven't done it yet, but these tapes are getting too expensive. I have heard they are coming out with a recording device that saves the recording on a computer, but that is too fancy for me to figure out."

Looking at all the stacks of boxes, it was a more significant undertaking than she realized. It also seemed weird that Fred kept them all and continued to buy new ones, but that was not for her to question. Her instincts told her she was on to something, but her common sense told her she was wasting her time.

She was unsure what she would find on these tapes as she started looking at the dates on the boxes. However, one jumped out at her: July 1986. Something about that date swirled through her memory. She moved a few boxes and pulled one out, looked inside, and started to carry it to her car.

"Wait a minute, where are you going with that box?" Fred asked her as he wiped the sweat from his brow.

"I need to take these home and review them on my VHS re-corder," Jerni said with a furrowed brow. How did he think she was going to view them in a storage unit?

"Well, I can't just let you take them with you," Fred protested. "How do I know you will bring them back?"

"Can I buy them from you for the price of new ones?" Jerni asked, thinking, what am I doing? Fred thought about it a moment.

"I think we could do that," Fred replied.

"Perfect. I will take those other three boxes as well," Jerni said as Fred's eyes lit up, thinking about making money on some dusty old tapes. She put the four boxes in her car and handed him forty dollars, hoping he would take it and not ask for more because these boxes were packed full of tapes.

"You have a deal," Fred said, stuffing the money into his wallet before waddling out to close the storage unit door. "If you want to buy more, just let me know," he said, locking the padlock on the door. "Also, if you know anyone who would like to buy old furni-ture, let me know. I will make them a good deal."

"I will do that," Jerni said as she got into her car. Fred had a lit-tle pep in his step as he walked back to his car.

Jerni had to get these boxes into the house without her husband seeing them because he would have all kinds of questions.

§

The next day, Jerni went to the library to look up the archived news for July 1986. She wanted to dive in watching the VHS tapes, but because she could not get that date out of her head, she had to find out what it meant first.

As she was scrolling through the microfilm of old local newspa-pers, starting with the first of July 1986, nothing was jumping out at her. Not much was going on except on the Fourth of July when there was some controversy over illegal fireworks and another about kids burning a barn. She kept scrolling until she got to a headline that stopped her in her tracks, and chills ran up her spine.

"That's it," she said out loud, and the librarian gave her a stern look. The headline read Edwards County Missing Girl reported that Sherri Lowery was last seen driving back to school after coming home for the 4th of July celebrations. She remembered it so well because Sherri went to school with her sister Mercedes. Their parents started lecturing Mercedes on how to be safe and what to watch out for because there could be a kidnapper on the loose. She was petrified to leave the house but had to go to work.

Jerni grabbed a tape dated around the time Sherri went missing. She popped the tape into the VCR and hit play. Jerni would fast-forward when there was no movement, but as soon as someone entered the frame, she would stop and watch. Jerni went through a few tapes and started to doze off when she saw someone who looked like Sherri walk into the frame and away from the gas pumps. She followed a dog into the dark but did not come out.

She fast-forwards it a little; maybe she walked the other way out of the camera shot, but that does not make sense when she suddenly saw headlights come on, and then a semi-truck pulled out of the same area Sherri had disappeared. She paused the video so she can try to make out the license plate, but it is too blurry. Jerni pulls out the tape and sets it aside to give to the FBI agent. She pulled out another tape and pops it into the machine.

Chapter Twenty-Nine

Weld Splatter

Christmas music drifted out of the car speakers with the fogged-up windows. Sheldon had driven Chase home and parked in front of Chase's house. It was a cold night, so Sheldon turned up the heater as Chase turned up the radio. "Isn't it kinda early for Christmas music," Sheldon remarked. "It's not even December."

"As soon as Thanksgiving is over, Christmas music starts, and the countdown begins," Chase responded with his cute dimple smile and sparkling eyes.

"You know, just cause you say it with a sexy dimple smile doesn't make it so," Sheldon said playfully, poking him. "Besides, it's still Thanksgiving, and the day isn't quite over. But it's okay 'cause I love Christmas music," Sheldon said as he snuggled up to Chase.

"I have decided I want to go into journalism," Chase stated.

The surprising news took Sheldon back. "I had no idea you wanted to be a journalist," Sheldon replied.

"I didn't either until now," Chase explained. Chase had a hard time telling him the next part. "I've had to come to terms with the fact that I'm not as quick on the field as I was before the accident."

There was a pause before he continued, "I will more than likely not get the scholarship to play football," Chase expounded. "This realization has gotten me thinking about my life, where I want to go to school, and what I want to do with my life." Sheldon was quiet. He was searching for something encouraging to say.

"I'm thinking of attending school in New York or Los Angeles," Chase added. "I could stay with my parents if I go to school in Los Angeles, but New York has a lot of opportunities." Sheldon was trying hard to be happy for him, but he felt he was looking at their relationship from the outside.

"Also, I have officially decided not to get another car. You are right, since I will be leaving for college in the fall and will not need one," Chase continued. There were a few beats of silence. "You're being really quiet. What do you think?"

"I'm happy for you," Sheldon said, still extremely conflicted by this news. "It's great to see that you're very excited about your chosen path." Sheldon felt like he had been left out of Chase's decisions.

Sheldon did not want to talk about him leaving or anything else, so every time Chase started to talk, he would kiss him. He wanted to just enjoy the Christmas music and their time together.

§

Sheldon had been doing his current job as a dyno filer for six months and had gotten pretty good at it. Cary was having a bad night and sending many bad welds down the line for them to clean up.

Sheldon and his coworker Ben had to return many bike frames to be repaired. They were telling each other jokes to help pass the time. Cary heard them laughing and stopped working to see what was going on. When he pulled back the curtain, one of the stacks of frames to be repaired fell over.

Cary became even more pissed when he saw how many bike frames needed to be repaired. He stormed up to Sheldon's table and got in his face. "What the fuck is all this," Cary demanded. Anytime Sheldon was in an awkward situation, he would smile unintentionally. "You think this is funny? You think you can do a better job?"

By this point, everyone was watching. Sheldon just stood there, unable to respond. He wanted the moment to be over.

"I said, Do you think you can do better? Huh?" Cary asked again. "Here, knock yourself out." Cary handed him his welding glove, jacket, and helmet.

Sheldon looked around in disbelief. Was this really happening? As he looked at everyone, they began to encourage him to go do it. Cary stormed off, pissed at everyone's encouragement of Sheldon.

"Fuck yeah," Ben cheered and applauded. "You got this, Sheldon."

"Hell at this point, it can't hurt," Old man Moe commented. "You sure as shit can't do worse than he has been doing all night. Go!"

Sheldon walked over to the entrance of Cary's welding station. Marcus was standing there and had been watching the whole scene play out. Sheldon was bracing himself for his snarky comments, but Marcus only held back the curtain." After you," Marcus gestured.

Sheldon did not have the first clue what to do. He put on Cary's equipment. The jacket was a little big on Sheldon, and the helmet felt heavy on his head. He tried to flip the helmet up and down. He flipped it a little too hard, and it went flying backward. Luckily, Marcus caught it before it fell to the ground.

Marcus put a frame in the welding jig and explained how to weld it to Sheldon. Sheldon was taken aback by how friendly Marcus was being towards him. It actually felt pleasant to be standing there, having Marcus show him what to do.

Sheldon got into position like Marcus and had instructed. When the helmet came down, he could not see anything, so he flipped the helmet back up. "I can't see where I'm supposed to be welding," Sheldon stated.

"That is why you have to get the welding gun into position, and as soon as you flip the helmet down, you pull the trigger," Marcus explained. "As soon as it sparks, you will see what you're welding. You have to move fast, or you will blow through the metal."

Sheldon felt like he was never going to be able to weld. He got the welding gun into position, flipped the helmet down, and hit the trigger, but nothing happened initially. Suddenly, sparks started to dance across the table next to him.

"What the Sam Hell are you doing," Moe yelled as he pulled back the curtain to see what was happening. Marcus laughed so hard he was doubled over.

When Sheldon flipped the helmet down, he had moved the gun slightly out of position. The welding wire came out of the gun and kept running until it hit the table next to him, sending sparks in Moe's direction.

"Make sure to hold the gun steady when you flip your helmet down," Marcus explained. "Moving your arms when you flip the helmet down is a natural reaction, so be sure to hold your arms steady."

Sheldon tried it again and was amazed by the fact he could see through the helmet lens once the spark started. He immediately stopped, flipped up his helmet to inspect the weld. He had only welded a small spot.

"Wow, that looks good," Marcus commented. "Now you only have to run the bead down the rest of the joint. If you can do that, you will have it down."

Sheldon was excited to get a spark. He went in to finish the rest of the weld. As the spark started, he did not move fast enough, blowing through the frame and creating a large hole.

"Damn, you blew that one out," Marcus chuckled as he held it up and examined it. "You have to move faster. You have to run the bead down the joint. If you hover too long, the metal weakens, and it will blow out. Try it again, and this time, you have to use a smooth, steady, and drag the bead of the weld in a sweeping motion. You got this," Marcus encouraged him as he patted Sheldon on the back.

Sheldon gave it another try. This time, he managed to run a bead without blowing out the frame, but suddenly, something started burning his foot. He immediately removed his helmet and then his shoe.

A spark had landed on his shoe and started to burn through his sock. "Here, let's duct tape your shoe, so you that won't get burnt," Marcus said. "Put your foot on this table."

Marcus started taping Sheldon's shoe. This situation gave Sheldon a good feeling of having Marcus touching him. However, these feelings made him feel guilty.

Strand pulled back the curtain. "Hey," he shouted. Sheldon thought he was in trouble, and Strand was about to lecture him about being in there. Instead, he handed Sheldon a brand-new welding glove, jacket, and helmet. This gesture made Sheldon smile and gave him a warm feeling. He handed Strand Cary's equipment in return.

With his shoes taped and new equipment, he gave it another try. He flipped down his helmet, and sparks flew. They both hovered over the bike frame and examined his weld.

"See all this splatter here," Marcus asked as he pointed to the metal splatter along the sides of the weld. "This is caused by being slightly too far from the frame, but again keep in mind that if you're too close, you will push through the frame. Also, being slightly too close can cause the tip of your welding gun to melt or become clogged from the weld splatter. You have to find the perfect distance and repeat that over and over."

Moe raised the curtain to see what was happening. Sheldon could see Cary had an armload of bike frames that needed to be repaired and was carrying them to another welding station to make the repairs. Sheldon still could not believe this was happening. It all seemed surreal. Plus, at this point, everyone was watching, waiting to see how he would do, so he felt a lot of pressure to do well.

"You can do this," Marcus said as he slapped Sheldon on the ass and then winked at him.

Sheldon proceeded to give it another try. This time, he was a little too close and burned right through the frame. He kept at it, and he slowly started to improve.

Before Sheldon knew it, Moe raised the curtain and shouted that it was lunchtime. Sheldon caught sight of Cary sitting on a stool doing Sheldon's job and skulking. It was extremely strange to see Cary Dyno filing bike frames.

After lunch, Cary resumed welding, and Sheldon returned to his job. Sheldon started to clean the bike frames he had welded and noticed quite a bit of weld splatter on them. He thought he had done a better job than what he was seeing.

"Hey, you didn't do half bad," Ben remarked. "Hell of a lot better than I probably would have done." Sheldon did not believe that, but it was nice for Ben to say.

Sheldon smiled and went about cleaning the welds, proud of what he accomplished and surprised by what he could do.

"You think you want to do that some more," Stella asked as she came over to help clean some weld splatter from a bike frame they had missed.

"Oh, I don't think so," Sheldon responded.

"You should. They get paid more money than the rest of us," Stella said, and Moe nodded in agreement, turning around from his job.

"Hhhmmm, I had no idea," Sheldon said thoughtfully.

§

The buzzer rang, and it was time for their last break of the day when Lana walked up to Sheldon. "I need you to do me a favor," she said in a low voice.

"Ooookaaay," Sheldon agreed hesitantly, unsure what she was about to ask him to do.

"I need to go over to that fucker's department and see if their line really did shut down for the day," Lana requested. "He came over forty-five minutes ago and yelled that his line shut down early, that he was heading home, and that I should catch a ride with someone else. It's my fucking car, and he holds onto the keys like it's his car. Will you look and see if his department did leave early? I will explain everything when you get back."

"You can tell me on the ride home unless you want to ride home with your sister, ha-ha," Sheldon teased because he knew she did not like riding with Eddie.

Lana's boyfriend, Stanley, worked on the trike line in a part of the factory that Sheldon rarely visited. Stanley was a quiet man and seemed to be much older than Lana. Sheldon found it hard to believe he was capable of doing the mean things Lana accused him of doing and saying to her.

That was until about a week ago when Sheldon gave Lana a ride home. She had invited Sheldon into her house for a bit. She wanted to show him some old photographs. Stanley was in the living room watching sports.

"I'm home!" Lana called from the kitchen as they walked in. "Fucker," she whispered when he did not respond back. Sheldon felt awkward for a moment, thinking maybe he should leave. He did not want to get in the middle of anything.

Sheldon and Lana were both seated at the table, looking at photographs and laughing. Lana was telling Sheldon some crazy stories about her childhood when Stanley came staggering into the room. "Why the fuck do you have to be so fucking loud," Stanley slurred as he walked to the fridge to get another beer.

"Don't you think you have had enough beer?" Lana asked Stanly. He completely ignored her and walked back into the living room. "Damn Drunk."

Sheldon looked at the pictures and did not see Stanley walking back into the kitchen. Suddenly, Lana screamed out as her head was pulled backward. Stanly had grabbed a handful of hair and jerked her head backward, staring her in the face.

"What did you say, you dirty, fat whore?" Stanley snarled at her. "I do not need a mother. If you do not shut the fuck up, you will be dead just like her." He grabbed a knife from the counter and put it to her throat. "And if you even think about leaving me, I will slit you from ear to ear, and then I will do the same to that whore you call a sister."

Sheldon's eyes were the size of quarters, and his heart was pounding in his chest. He was afraid to breathe or even move.

"Stanley, you better remove that knife from my throat, old man, or I will cut your balls off," Lana demanded through gritted teeth. Sheldon was shocked at how evil this seemingly nice old man turned into right before his eyes.

Stanley dropped the knife on the table. As he left the room, he muttered, "You're not worth it."

Sheldon walked into Stanley's department, which was dark and quiet except for air escaping from the hoses used for the power tools. A few machines were humming, but no one was working. He turned to head back to his department.

As they drove home, it started to snow. At first, it was only light snow, but then it started to come down heavier, making it harder to see the road ahead of them. Some of the snow started sticking to the windshield wipers as they moved back and forth across the windshield, making it even harder to see. Sheldon began to slow down as Lana cranked up the heat.

"Okay, so the reason I wanted you to check on Stanley was to see if he had really gone home early. A couple of weeks ago, I went to his department to get a couple of dollars to buy a soda when

I saw him flirting with this young blonde. She was probably young enough to be his granddaughter. I think he is buying her stuff so that she will sleep with him."

"What makes you think that?" Sheldon asked.

"I found a receipt in the car for jewelry, and I waited forever for him to give it to me, but he never did. Also, I have found women's panties left in our bed that were not mine," Lana replied. "It's like he wants me to know he is fucking someone else without really admitting it, if that makes sense. He wants to hurt me, but at the same turn, stay with him so he can use me for my money."

"Why don't you just leave him, or kick him out?" Sheldon inquired.

"Because everything is in both our names," Lana answered. "Plus, he controls the money. He makes me sign over my paycheck to him and he deposits it into the checking account. He gives me an allowance for the week. I'm not allowed to touch the checkbook or draw money out of the account. I do not even know how much is in the account because he keeps telling me we are broke. However, I know for a fact that I have an extra two thousand dollars deposited in that account on a monthly basis, and that does not even include our paychecks. Our entire bills combined do not come anywhere near that amount."

"Living with this man for the last fifteen years has seriously aged me, Sheldon. Things were pretty good in the beginning, but these last five years have been a living nightmare for me. Especially since moving here, things have gotten worse between us. The only positive thing to come out of this move has been seeing my family more and meeting you. Things were great when we lived in Vegas."

"Just look at me," Lana said. "I'm stuck working at a factory and living in a prison. There are mornings I get up, look in the mirror, and ask myself what the fuck I'm doing with my life."

"Would you believe the roof has holes in it and raccoons live in the attic? If you had asked me six years ago if I saw myself working in a factory, and living in this dump, I would have told you that there was no way in hell."

"He is right about one thing. I have let myself go, but I sure as hell will not let him have the satisfaction of knowing he is right. I think I have been depressed since we moved here. All I did for the first three years was cook, eat, and get fat."

They started to turn down the gravel road and headed to Lana's house. It was becoming hard to see where the road was because the snow had begun to drift across the road. "Damn, it must have been snowing here for quite some time now," Lana remarked. "Do not pull into my drive. You might get stuck. Just pull up out front, and I will jump out. I see the lights are still on, so he must still be up. Lord knows what or who I'm going to find in my house."

"Are you sure you and Chase will be able to pick up your schoolbooks tomorrow?" Lana asked, looking out at the snow coming down.

"I have to go get them because I have put it off too long, and my classes are starting in a couple of weeks.," Sheldon said. "Like you said, I must do things to help get me out of here."

"Okay, well, be safe. Have a good night, Sheldon, and thank you for driving me home."

"It was not a problem. You're on my way home anyway. Have a great night, and see you tomorrow." As Sheldon drove home, he could not help but worry if his friend was going to be murdered in her own home. He wanted to turn around and ensure she would be okay, but he kept driving because, realistically if he did go back, what could he do? Stay outside or sleepover?

The following day, the snow stopped long enough for Sheldon and Chase to go and pick up his schoolbooks. Sheldon had spent the night at Chase's in case their country roads were snowed in.

"This is kind of exciting," Sheldon said, carrying his books to the car. It feels so different from high school.

"I bet I can't wait to start college too, but I first have to get through the last few months of my senior year," Chase said.

"Also, I feel relieved; I was afraid I had waited too long to pick up my books because she had said sometimes, they run out," Sheldon said, putting the car in drive to head home. "Next time, I'm not waiting so long."

§

The factory gave everyone a coupon to pick up a free ham at the local grocery store. The factory was planning to be shut down for the weeks of Christmas and New Year's Day. They did not really get a break to exchange gifts, so some people either had to do it during lunch, before, or after work.

Sheldon gave Lana a tin of her favorite butter-flavored popcorn and she got him a bottle of his favorite cologne. Next, Sheldon surprised Teana with a stylish new scarf he had bought when he was in Rhode Island, and she gifted him a sleek new belt.

"Now we won't have to see you continually pulling up your pants and showing off your boxers," Teana teased.

"I like seeing your boxers," Marcus whispered in Sheldon's ear as he passed by. Teana gave him a strange look as he turned to lick his fingers and then gave her the middle finger. "I just don't know about him sometimes," she said to Sheldon, who only shook his head.

Teana left to go back to work, leaving Sheldon alone for a moment, thinking if he should put on his new belt now or later, when someone suddenly put their chin on his shoulder, causing him to jump slightly. "Do you need help putting that on," Marcus teased him. "I have your present right here," he whispered in Sheldon's ear and then licked his ear. "What the fuck," Sheldon said, half laughing as Marcus left to head back to his workstation.

§

Sheldon handed Chase his Christmas gift, and Chase's face lit up with a wide grin as he began to unwrap it. Inside, he found a thoughtful care package filled with his favorite soaps and colognes, a few journals for his writing, and a brand-new Speedo.

"Wow, these are all the things I'm either running out of or was planning on getting," Chase said as he kissed Sheldon. "Thank you, this is a very thoughtful gift."

"I threw in a couple of journals so you can perfect your writing skills or write down your thoughts or help prepare you for journalism."

Chase pulled out a small, nicely wrapped gift and handed it to Sheldon. Sheldon was excited as he started to tear at the wrapping paper. He felt bad destroying such beautiful paper, but he was excited to open it. He removed the paper and discovered it was a small black box. He pulled off the lid, and inside the box was a necklace with an infinity symbol in the middle.

"I hope you like it. I made the infinity symbol in shop class. I had it smoothed out and polished with silver," Chase proudly explained. "It's like our love. No matter what happens or where we end up, our love for each other is forever."

"It's amazing!" Sheldon expressed with glee as he kissed Chase. "I'm completely speechless. I was not expecting something this incredible."

"I'm glad you like it," Chase beamed as he kissed him back. "Merry Christmas."

"Merry Christmas," Sheldon replied as he admired his new gift. "It's wonderful, and I'm impressed that it looks like a professional made it."

"Thank you. That means a lot to me," Chase said. "Let me help you put it on."

"You just had to outdo me, huh?" Sheldon teased as Chase got the necklace clasped out Sheldon's neck.

"Of course, you know me," Chase laughed. They were kissing when Susan and John walked in with the baby.

"Don't you two get enough of each other," Susan joked. "You aren't going to give us another show, are you?"

"Wait an hour, and the show will start," Chase teased as Sheldon turned red.

"Where is Mom?" Susan asked as she and John sat down on the couch. The baby started fussing, and Susan got the baby out of the car seat.

"Mom and Damian went shopping together," Sheldon replied as Susan picked up the baby, took out her breast, and started feeding him. "Whoa, something things can't be unseen," Sheldon joked.

"Calm down," Susan demanded as she covered herself. "I'm sure you don't complain when Chase starts sucking on your tits." Chase busted out laughing as John just shook his head.

"Did you say shopping?" Susan asked, realizing what Sheldon had said.

"Nothing like last-minute shopping," John commented, looking around at their gift wrappings. "Guess you two couldn't wait till tomorrow?"

"Haha, I guess not," Sheldon responded.

"Well, show us what you got from each other," Susan requested.

§

The house was filled with the delicious smell of cooking food on Christmas morning, accompanied by laughter and conversation. A light frost covered the ground, and the crispness of the morning air added to the festive atmosphere. From the tree, the gentle melody of Christmas music played from the carousel, setting a warm, joyful tone for the day.

"You may want to get dressed before everyone starts arriving," Mandy told Sheldon. Susan was feeding the baby, and John had gone out hunting something. "Levin and Charlotte will be here soon with the twins. Mom just called. She is bringing the rolls that I forgot to pick up, and Bob is bringing the ham and some new lady friend of his."

"Uncle Bob is dating someone?" Sheldon questioned as he stretched and yawned.

"Yes, Grammy said she is kind of homely looking, so be nice," Mandy explained. "That goes for both of you," Mandy requested, bumping Susan's chair with her hip.

"Hey, I'm a complete angel," Susan said as she laid the baby over her shoulder and started to burp him.

"Shit, I better get my boots on," Mandy joked as Susan gave her a shocked look.

"Language," Susan joked as if the baby could understand.

"In this house, that child will hear a lot worse than that," Mandy declared as she took a pie out of the oven.

"Ain't that the truth," Susan said as she watched Mandy place the pie on the counter. "How many pies are you making?"

"Only the three," Mandy replied.

"At least Shawndrea is not here to eat all the pumpkin pie this year," Susan said, standing up.

"Oh, didn't I tell you? They should be here shortly," Mandy tried to say with a straight face.

"Not funny, mother," she growled as she handed the baby to Sheldon. "Will you hold him while I go to the bathroom?"

Sheldon raised the baby over his head and made funny faces, making the baby giggle.

"You better be careful. John did that last night, and he threw up all over his face. It was hilarious," Susan warned as she headed to the bathroom. Sheldon looked frightened as he slowly lowered the baby to a safer, puke-free zone. The baby burped and vomited down the front of him. "Eeew," Sheldon said as the baby giggled and hiccupped.

"Hold still, let me get something to clean that up," Mandy said with a chuckle.

"I told you," Susan said from the bathroom.

§

Ninnie, Tommy, and Chase were seated in Shelon's living room while Sheldon was getting them something to drink when Levin, Charlotte, and the twins arrived. "Trey is in town and wants to hang out with everyone and maybe go roller skating," Chase mentioned.

"Roller skating?" Ninnie questioned. "We haven't done that in a while."

"How is Trey doing?" Tommy asked. "I have lost touch with him since he started dating Tiffany."

"This is why he wants us all to get together to introduce us to his new girlfriend," Chase explained.

"I don't know how I feel about that," Charlotte stated as she placed one of the car seats with one of the twins inside onto the floor.

"Same here," Ninnie and Sheldon both said.

"You can't blame him," Levin said, digging through the diaper bag for the spare pacifier as Charlotte gave him a sharp look.

"He is right," Tommy said; this time, Ninnie gave a sharp look. "What? Didn't Sheldon say Ruby is dating a senior boy who drives a Porsche?"

"How is your sister doing?" Charlotte asked, changing the subject and quickly realizing that might not be the best subject change, but asked what everyone was thinking anyway.

"Are you sure you want to know?" Ninnie questioned as they all nodded yes.

"She's doing okay, but she still doesn't know who kidnapped her," Ninnie explained, her voice tense as everyone leaned forward, hanging on every word. "Apparently, it happened right after our graduation. Supposedly, she was walking to her car when someone covered her face with a rag that had some chemical on it, which caused her to pass out."

"Supposedly?" Sheldon questioned.

"Didn't the doctor confirm it?" Chase added.

"I say supposedly, but she says factually, but I don't believe her or the doctor, because she could have cooked this whole thing up and slept with the doctor," Ninnie explained as Tommy rolled his eyes. "Allegedly, she had a baby while being held hostage."

"A baby!" Charlotte said louder than anticipated.

"Yeah, supposedly she had been raped not long before our graduation, and then while being held captive, she had the baby, but it didn't make it." Their mouths were hanging open.

"Hey, you asked, and I warned you," Ninnie plainly said.

"Do they have anyone they suspect of kidnapping her?" Chase asked as he could not take the suspense anymore.

"They suspect some guy named Berry Price," Ninnie explained.

"Price," Sheldon remarked as the name sounded familiar.

"Yeah," Chase agreed. "I heard that name recently."

"Where is she now?" Levin asked.

"She was just released from the hospital and is now under Mom's care," Ninnie explained. "I think Mom plans to take her with her to California when she moves there in a few weeks."

"Where is the Berry Price now?" Charlotte asked, concerned that he was still on the loose.

"No one knows. The police are looking for Berry and someone named Kelli," Ninnie explained as they sat there wide-eyed, looking at her.

"This feels like something from a soap opera," Chase remarked.

"Well, get this: She was being held at PJ Ferguson's house, and he used to date Laynardia," Ninnie explained.

"That is crazy," Sheldon commented. "Small world. Was he in on it?"

"Apparently not, he says he did not know anything about it or about all the bodies that were burned in his silo either."

"Burned bodies!" Chase exclaimed. "This IS crazier than any soap opera and crazier than anything you hear about happening in Los Angeles. Well, expect the occasional serial killer, but that is what this sounds like."

"That's about the level of information I have, but I will keep you posted if I hear more," Ninnie explained as Mandy called them all to come and eat.

"I think we will all have to get together to go roller skating," Charlotte said, getting up and heading towards the kitchen. "Even if it's to hear more about what happened to Shawndrea."

"Oh, you know that is my favorite subject to talk about," Ninnie sarcastically responded.

"Though, I don't know if I can skate since having the girls, but it would be nice to get out of the house," Charlotte explained, turning around to check on one of the girls who had started crying.

Chapter Thirty

Sheldon's First Day of College

It was the first day back from holiday break, and the press department had run out of parts, so they offered to send people home early or stay to work on odd tasks or in another department.

"Hey, if you're leaving early, can I get a ride home?" Lana asked. Sheldon thought about it for a moment because he usually liked to stay and work so that his paycheck was not short, but being back from the holiday break, he did not feel like working.

"We can go get pizza," Lana said, tempting him.

"Sure, why not? That sounds good right now," Sheldon said.

When they arrived at Pizza Hut, it was about to close in thirty minutes. "We just put that last of the pizzas out on the buffet; once they are gone, that is it," the waitress explained before she turned to go get their glasses so they could fill up their drinks at the soda fountain.

"Between the salad bar and a couple of slices of pizza, that should be enough for me, " Lana said. "We better get going and grab ourselves a few slices before the family over there eats them."

"Sounds like a good idea to me," Sheldon said as they headed towards the buffet.

Sheldon put salad on a plate and grabbed a slice of deep-dish pizza, pepperoni, ham and cheese, and a little cup of extra pizza sauce. Lana got a plate full of salad and grabbed a second plate to get a slice of Hawaiian pizza and a slice of pepperoni.

"What is that brown stuff on your plate?" Sheldon asked as Lana sat down.

"It's chocolate pudding," Lana responded, getting herself situated. "I like to dip my pizza crust into it." Sheldon gave her a peculiar look and was not sure if she was joking.

"Seriously?" Sheldon questioned.

"It's actually good because you have salty and sweet," Lana said.

"This is heaven," Sheldon said, eating his pizza. "I love to dip the crust in the extra pizza sauce, and its crunchiness of the deep dish crust is just perfect."

"You are right; this is really good pizza, and it hits the spot," Lana said. After they enjoyed their dinner, they decided it was time to head home.

"This was such a good idea," Sheldon commented, taking a sip of his Mountain Dew.

"Yes, I'm so glad we did this. It's the perfect treat for us," Lana said.

As they headed home, they were both quiet on the ride home, stuffed with pizza and lost in thought. They pulled up in front of Lana's house.

"There are no lights on, so either he is passed out drunk in his chair or went out with his little hoe of a girlfriend," Lana said. "I wouldn't care if he never came home."

"Do you think he will move in with her?" Sheldon asked.

"Oh, no, he can't afford to live without my income," Lana said. "You won't believe what that asshole got me for Christmas."

"I don't think I could even guess," Sheldon responded as he shut the car off.

"That mother fucker got me a vacuum telling me he got it because he was tired of the place being so dirty. I could just strangle him sometimes," Lana seethed. "After, I spent what little money I had left on the items he wanted. He said it's a woman's job to keep the house clean."

Sheldon sat there with his mouth hanging open. "I can't believe he said that," Sheldon commented.

"That's okay. I went and opened my own bank account and I'm going to start putting money in it so I can leave his sorry ass," Lana said. "He won't even see it coming. I better get inside. See you tomorrow, Sheldon."

"See you tomorrow," Sheldon responded as he started his car.

§

The search for Berry Price and Kelli was stalled. The FBI agents found his semi-truck abandoned at a truck stop in Kansas, and there were no leads on where they took off.

They found a newspaper in the front seat of his truck. The front page mentioned the discovery of the remains, and his name was in bold print next to his picture. Also, in the truck's cab was a small box with several little trinkets that he had kept from his victims. The agents also found some of Kelli's clothing and empty baby formula bottles. It appeared that Berry and Keilli left in a hurry because he would not have left some of that stuff behind.

Tucked in a pocket in the back of the driver's seat was a bundle of letters, which were love letters written between Berry and Kelli. The letters from Kelli explained how the two of them had been secretly seeing one another. The letters from Berry had detailed accounts of what he did to the women he murdered, and some were pretty graphic. Kelli's letters seemed to fuel Berry's obsession with killing these young women, and she seemed to draw pleasure from reading his recount of the brutal murders.

The letters outlined how she helped him improve his luring women to his truck. She would instruct him on how he should torture them and how he should kill them. It was her idea to burn the bodies, which inevitably led the police to figure out the identity of some of his victims. Before Kelli, he would leave the dead bodies in rural areas where they had yet to be found for months or years, and some bodies might never be found.

The turning point for the agents was a letter in which Berry had confessed to rapping Shawndrea twice, once years ago, before he started killing his victims and again most recently. There was another letter talking about his first victim, a girl named Sherri. The day Shawndrea returned home, she was at the grocery store when Kelli saw Shawndrea buying a pregnancy test and thought she might be pregnant. They found another letter explaining how Kelli planned to kidnap Shawndrea to take the baby for themselves since Kelli could not have children of her own.

Since Berry rapped Shawndrea twice and did not kill her either time, Kelli got it into her head that she was her competition, and since she was pregnant with Berry's baby, she wanted the baby for herself. When it came time for her to kill Shawndrea, she could not do it, so she left her to die on her own.

The federal agents interviewed Berry's wife, but she did not know where Berry had run off to. She did not even know he was seeing Kelli or that he had been killing women. His kids were too young to know anything, either. His wife could not believe he was capable of hurting anyone, let alone killing them.

§

Sheldon parked in the college campus parking lot. He was excited to start taking college classes finally, but he immediately felt overwhelmed as he entered the building. He was completely lost and did not know where his class was or how to figure it out. A few other students did not seem to know where they were headed and heading in the wrong direction. Many of the experienced students knew where they needed to go.

In the distance, he saw a familiar face from high school talking to a group of people, but they were too far away to ask. They waved at him as they headed in the other direction. He was surprised they even waved at him because, in high school, they never even gave him a second look.

As panic set in, he started frantically scanning the right and left to see if he could find a map or anything to help him determine the direction of his classroom. Then he saw another familiar face approaching. It was Kent, and he smiled as he approached.

"Hey there, it's good to see another familiar face here," Kent said. "I'm just heading to my class before I'm late. What class are you in right now?"

"I have English class in room 148, but I'm not sure where that room is located," Sheldon explained.

"It has to be just past my class, which is in room 140," Kent said. "Follow me."

Sheldon followed him, but he did not want Kent to know that his English class was remedial English, and his next class was basic mathematics because he did very poorly in both subjects on the entrance exams. Sheldon would be completely mortified if anyone learned he was in these introductory classes.

"My dad thinks I'm wasting my time taking college classes because he intends for me to take over the farm, but I want to experience college life even if it is just at a community college," Kent explained as they walked down the hallway.

"Don't they have a good Agricultural (AG) program here?" Sheldon asked.

"Yes! But try telling him that. All he says is back in my day, we blah blah," Kent said, rolling his eyes. "There are things in the AG program here that I can learn about and help us with on the farm," Kent said enthusiastically. "Sorry, I get passionate about it. Here is my class. Yours should be down that way. It was good seeing you, and I'm sure I will see you around."

"See you later," Sheldon said as he continued down the hall.

When he entered his classroom, the teacher was already talking, and all the seats but one in the front row were open. Sheldon quickly rushed to his seat. Sheldon could tell immediately that this would be different from high school as they promptly went through chapter one of his English book. He felt behind and wondered if he should have read chapter one before the first day of class.

Halfway through the lecture, he quickly glanced to the back of the room at the clock and noticed everyone had a notebook out and had been taking notes while he just sat there listening, trying to follow along in the book. He suddenly felt embarrassed and even further behind than he thought as he tried to quietly pull his notebook from his bag and get a pen. He wanted to return to school, so he had to make it work.

Sheldon looked around the room and wondered if he should even be there. He began to wonder if he was wasting his time, but before he knew it, the class was over, and it was time for his next class. Luckily, the next class was just down the hall, and this time, he got a seat in the back.

Sheldon pulled out his notebook and was ready to take notes this time. He thought this was math and that probably no prework was required, but the teacher jumped in immediately and talked about chapter one. He followed along and took notes on things he thought were important or didn't understand so he could look them up later.

After math class, it was time to head home so he could have lunch and do a little homework before heading to work.

"How was your first day of college?" Mandy asked Sheldon as he entered the house. She was relaxing in her chair, watching her soap operas.

"We already have homework and a quiz on Friday," Sheldon responded.

"I just made a sandwich for lunch," Mandy said. "Everything is still on the counter if you want to eat something."

Sheldon quickly made a sandwich and grabbed some chips before heading to his bedroom to work on his homework. When his mom knocked on his door, he was working on his second-to-last math problem.

"It's almost time to head to work," Mandy said, sticking her head inside.

Sheldon had to rush to get ready for work, so he grabbed one of his books as they headed out the door.

§

During his dinner break at work, Sheldon read his English textbook and answered questions from that week's homework assignment.

"How are your classes going?" Lana asked, sitting down at the table. "How are you finding time to get it all done?"

"It's been tough, but if I could get some done here and there, it should not be as overwhelming," Sheldon explained. "I just don't know how they expected us to finish all these required readings."

"I think you're doing the right thing, doing it a piece at a time," Lana explained. "Boy, I don't envy you either. You couldn't pay me enough to go back to school. I went to beauty school, and that was enough for me."

"All Sheldon's talk about going back to school has got me thinking about returning and getting my GED," Eddie remarked. "But then I see all this extra work you have to do, and I just don't think I have it in me or the patience to listen to someone tell me what to do."

"You were never good at taking orders from anyone," Lana teased.

"Damn right," Eddie said as they, one by one, got up from the table.

"You think you're a big shot now that you're in school, huh." Marcus teased Sheldon. "Don't forget us, little people." He slapped Sheldon on the ass as he walked away.

"Damn, he can slap me anytime like that," Eddie teased as she walked up and stood next to Sheldon.

"Be careful what you ask for because you might not be able to handle it," Marcus said as he turned around and winked at Sheldon.

"Did he just wink at me or you?" Eddie asked, furrowing her brow. "I'm so confused," she said laughing.

"You think you're confused. I think he is the confused one," Teana said, walking by them as she headed to get some clean work gloves.

"Is it bad that I'm kind of turned on at the same time?" Eddie asked. "The idea of two guys making out makes my nipples hard and my pussy wet."

"Oh my god, Edith Jean, if Mama could hear you now," Lana said.

"What, I'm just telling the truth; what is so wrong with that," Eddie said, heading back to her workstation. "Sheesh, lady, you need to get laid more."

"I get laid plenty," Lana huffed as she headed towards her workstation.

"Oh yeah, who with?" Eddie asked, but Lana ignored her.

"Come on, Sheldon, or we will be late," Lana said.

When Sheldon returned to his workstation from lunch break, Moe asked him what he was doing that weekend.

"I'm hanging out with Chase, and we might go to the movies," Sheldon said.

"You are always hanging out with Chase," Stella remarked.

"Yeah, don't you have a girlfriend to hang out with?" Moe asked. Sheldon always tried to play it off because he'd heard them making disparaging comments towards gay people, so he chose to stay in the closet with them as Ben looked up, waiting for Sheldon to answer as well.

"No, not yet, " Sheldon responded as he continued to work on a bike frame and felt isolated and somewhat alone again. It's very isolating being the only possible gay person in the area surrounded by straight people.

Ben looked at him, acknowledging that he knew, so he changed the subject. "Moe, do you mind helping me straighten a bike frame?" Ben asked as he put a finished bike over for Stella to do her work.

"You shouldn't always talk about this Chase guy because some people might get the wrong idea," Stella whispered to Sheldon as she passed by him.

"Would that be bad if I was?" Sheldon responded, annoyed by the comment and not really thinking about the consequences.

"Well, it is a sin," Stella said. "But I guess it's not for me to judge." Sheldon noticed Stella kept staring at him after that and seemed to be stewing.

When Sheldon came back from their last break, he saw Stella whispering to Moe, who gave him a disgusted look and immediately acted differently toward him.

He started aggressively sliding the bike frames in Sheldon's direction, and Ben looked at Moe and then at Sheldon with a "what the hell is going on" look.

After about twenty minutes, Moe's reckless behavior and bike frame almost hit Sheldon. "Hey, watch it," Ben shouted at Moe. "You almost hit Sheldon."

Moe only snarled, started mumbling to himself, and aggressively straightened the bike frames. Stella began to notice what was going on and watched Moe. She started shaking her head as she was nervously chewing her gum. Sheldon could tell she was about to talk to Moe. She begun to walk towards his area when a bike frame flew towards Sheldon and almost hit him.

"Hey!" Stella shouted as she marched up towards him. She was at least a foot shorter than him but was not afraid to let him have it. "Enough! That is uncalled for and unnecessary."

Moe just glared at her as she walked away, returned to her workstation, and resumed working as if nothing had happened. Sheldon had never seen that side of her before, and by the look on Moe's face, he hadn't either. The next couple of weeks were awkward between Moe, Stella, and Sheldon. Moe acted as if Sheldon was not there and tried to keep his distance from Sheldon.

Chapter Thirty-One

Harriet's Date

I t was an unusually warm January morning as Harriet exited her truck and walked up to the back door of Mandy's house. They had finally decided to go through the stuff they had picked up in the alley a few months ago.

"If we do not go through this stuff now, we probably won't get to it until spring," Harriet commented as she walked into the kitchen and started to take off her coat. However, Mandy handed her a cup of coffee before she could get her coat off.

"Well, let's get to it then," Mandy said. With a cup of coffee in hand, they headed to the garage.

"My lands, Mandy, don't you dust out here?" Harriet teased as she blew dust off the box she was about to open. As she opened it, she noticed it was full of books. She could tell right away that a few of the books were very old.

Some of the books were about New York, others were about trees, or about historical figures. They started organizing the books by what they could sell and the ones that were too badly damaged.

Harriet picked out some books for herself. Some of the boxes were full of romance novels. They decided to let Letty go through those boxes the next time she visited because she was obsessed with romance novels.

"Most of this is just plain junk," Harriet grunted, lifting another box to go through. "Man, will I be sore tomorrow." She opened the box and looked inside. "This box looks like a mix of old clothes and broken knickknacks."

"You're telling me all I'm finding is old clothes," Mandy said, holding up an old, tattered nightgown. Why on earth did she keep some of this stuff?" She shoved it into a trash bag, reached in the box for something else, and came up with granny panties. "Seriously?" Mandy said, holding them up, trying not to laugh. The two chuckled.

"Lord, why would she save those? Was she planning on using them to clean the oven?" Harriet joked as she pulled something from the box wrapped in a very old cloth. "Well, I be darn, would you look at this? I think it's an old diary of sorts," Harriet said as she lit a cigarette and pointed to the object she had placed on top of the old dresser. "Shall we have a look at it?" She queried while raising her eyebrows and then chuckled. "Some of these old bitties led secret and interesting lives. Wanna see if she was one of them?"

Harriet did not wait for Mandy to respond, she cracked open the journal and started reading. "The first entry appears to be that of a very young girl named Clarabell, maybe eight or nine years old," Harriet explained as she continued to scan it. "It talks about how she used to get up early every day to milk the cows, gather the eggs, and dump the Chamber Pots for the entire family. Clarabell went to a one-room school with children of all ages. She wrote that she had to wade through the snow in the winter to get to school. Man sounds like *Little House on the Prairie* if you ask me, no thank you."

"Let's see, when she was twelve, she met a boy that stole her heart. He was five years older than her, and at thirteen, she married him. Here is a photo of them on the next page."

Mandy walked over to take a look. "You forget how young people were allowed to marry back then," Mandy commented.

"She goes on to write about having three boys, and their photos are here too, along with a family photo," Harriet explained.

"This is more than a diary. It's like a talking photo album," Mandy remarked. "I feel bad looking through it."

"Yeah, me too, but I cannot stop looking," Harriet confessed as she flipped quickly through the pages. She came to a photograph of an older couple. Below it was written, "Our last photo together before the love of my life left me."

"Oh my god," Harriet choked up a bit as she slammed it shut. She had a tear in her eye. "That is the saddest shit… What the hell… Damn it, I think something flew in my damn eye."

"What did you expect that her story was going to end with them living together forever," Mandy stated. "It's like watching the movie Titanic and expecting it to end differently. We already knew she was dead."

They both laughed. "Okay, smart ass, but you have to give this back to him," Harriet said as she picked the book up to put it in a bag just as something fell out.

"I have to give it back to him?" Mandy questioned. "Aren't you the one that has his nuuuumber?" Mandy teased. "Do you still have it?"

Harriet bent over to pick up the item that had fallen out. It was a key. "You. Have. Got. To. Be kidding me," Harriet remarked. "This just keeps getting weirder. How was this key in this book?"

Mandy picked up the book to examine it closer. She looked at the front cover and then the back. The back cover had a small pouch in it. "This is where," Mandy said, showing Harriet.

"Well, I be-damn. What do you think it goes to?" Harriet cooed excitedly.

"I saw a little wooden box in here somewhere," Mandy said as she dug through the boxes. After a few minutes of searching, she pulled out the small wooden box. "It feels empty, so I didn't think much of it when I first saw it," she said, handing it to Harriet.

Harriet tried opening it, but the key did not work. "Huh, wonder what it goes to then," Harriet commented as she held the key up to examine it closer."

"Maybe it goes to Ricardo's heart," Mandy cooed, then giggled at Harriet, who rolled her eyes.

"Don't be ridiculous," Harriet quipped. "Everyone knows the quickest way to a man's heart is straight through his chest," she stated as she made a thrusting gesture as if she were ripping out someone's heart. They both laughed.

"When you put it like that, there is no arguing with such sound logic now, is there?" Mandy sarcastically said, and they both chuckled. Mandy was glad to have Harriet back in her life. They finished going through the boxes, and both randomly chuckled here and there, though it was clear that Harriet was pondering something silently to herself.

§

Harriet was furiously digging through her glove box. She looked under the seat and between them. She was about to give up when she sat back in the seat and saw a reflection in the windshield. The piece of paper with Ricardo's number had slid between the dash and the windscreen, stuck in the crack.

After some effort, she was able to pull the piece of paper out. Harriet ran into the house and picked up the phone. She took a few deep breaths before dialing.

"Well, that took long enough," the voice on the other end of the phone said.

"Ricardo?"

"Yes, I thought you would have called much sooner," Ricardo replied, and Harriet laughed loudly.

She explained what they had found, and they agreed to meet on the condition that she would allow Ricardo to cook her dinner as a thank you.

§

Harriet was getting ready to go to Ricardo's place. "Why are you so nervous, old woman?" she said to her reflection in the mirror as she put on eyeliner. She kept messing with her salt-and-pepper grey hair and could not decide whether to wear it up or down. So, she put a headband in her hair, applied some lipstick, and headed out the door.

Just before she knocked on Ricardo's door, she took a deep breath and exhaled. As she was about to knock, the door opened. He greeted her with a smile and a hug.

"Well, aren't you very forward," She remarked as she patted him on the back.

"Come on in and let me take your jacket," Ricardo requested. "Would you like something to drink? " he offered as he hung her jacket in the hall closet.

"I believe this is yours," she said as she handed him the book. "And this key fell out of it."

"Peculiar," he remarked as he held up the key to examine it closer. "I wonder," he said as he left the room and returned with a medium-sized chest. He inserted the key, and it opened.

On top was an old blanket, and underneath it was an old photo album full of newspaper clippings. As Ricardo looked closer, he noticed they were all about him, which made him a little emotional. He never knew his mom paid close attention to the things he had done with his life.

"I think I'm going to have to continue looking at this later," Ricardo said, clearing his throat as he placed the album back in the chest and closed the lid. He walked into the kitchen without saying anything else, like he had forgotten entirely about her.

Harriet did not know what else to do but follow him. When she walked into the kitchen, he poured wine into a glass and handed it to her. He poured himself one and then took a big gulp. "Let's eat," Ricardo stated. "Have a seat, and I will serve you your salad."

He placed a plate of salad in front of her, and she looked at him with a peculiar expression. "Is everything okay?" he asked.

"Yes, it's just that I have never seen salad served on a plate before; it's usually in a bowl," she explained. Ricardo chuckled as he took his napkin and placed it on his lap.

"You must not get out much," he replied with a smile. "Oh, I forgot," he said, getting up and digging for something in one of the drawers. He pulled out a book of matches.

"What is this salad dressing? It is terrific," She asked after taking a bite.

"It's an old Italian recipe from my grandmother," he replied as he lit the candles on the table.

"Well, aren't we just Mr. Fancy Smancy," Harriet teased, then returned to her salad.

After they finished their salads, he cleared their plates. Then he plated seared baked chicken breast with roasted garlic potatoes and asparagus. "Would you like more wine," he offered.

"Sure, I would love some."

While eating dinner, they both talked about their families and failed relationships. "It must be the wine because I do not like to talk about myself this much," Harriet confessed.

"I believe it has affected me the same as you," he expressed.

They ended up sharing a nice dinner and a lot of laughs.

§

Sheldon was at his workstation and ready to work when Strand approached him. Sheldon panicked for a moment because he never came up to him.

"You wanna give welding another try?" Strand asked.

"Sure," Sheldon replied reluctantly.

"That's good because Cary called in sick, and we have no one else. I would rather not do it myself, if at all possible," Strand explained. "Grab your gear."

Sheldon returned from grabbing his gear and saw Ben waiting at their station.

"Let's do this," Ben cheered as he clapped his hands. "You got this, Sheldon!"

Sheldon smiled. The encouragement felt nice. However, Marcus saw Sheldon heading for his workstation with his gear. "Oh, fuck no! I have to work with this fag again," Marcus said.

Sheldon pulled back the curtain and started to get ready. When Marcus entered the station, Sheldon grabbed Marcus's duct tape and began taping his shoes.

"Hey, did I say you could use my tape faggot?" Marcus asked Sheldon as he got up close behind Sheldon and tried to grab the tape out of Sheldon's hand, and in doing so, he rubbed his crotch against Sheldon's ass. "Don't get any ideas queer. I like girls." He said into Sheldon's ear as he grounded his hips into Sheldon.

"I will be sure to keep that in mind," Sheldon replied, turning around to put on the helmet and winking at Marcus.

"Did you just fucking wink at me?" Marcus asked, getting in Sheldon's face. He thought Marcus was about to kiss him. He could feel the stubble from Marcus's face against his own.

"Let's get to work," Sheldon said firmly. "Are you going to put the frame in the jig or just stand here jacking each other off?"

Sheldon's assertiveness took Marcus aback. Sheldon was also surprised by his boldness but felt proud of himself.

"Yes, Sir!" Marcus stood at attention and saluted.

Sheldon messed up a couple of frames until he got the rhythm down. Welding while the line ran at full speed was a different experience; welding was slower when the line was already down. He started to fall behind, and his station was backed up, so the line had to shut down to let him catch up.

He did not like the pressure and started to make mistakes because he was rushing. It was finally time for a break, and when he walked out from behind the curtain, he saw Teana doing his job, which was very strange because she had seniority and always got assigned the best jobs.

Sheldon saw their table was piled high as he walked up. "God damn could you get any more weld splatter on these damn things," Teana joked and went back to grinding on a bike frame.

However, Sheldon did not know her well enough to know if she was kidding. "Hey, kid, I'm just joshing you," she said, noticing he did not realize she was kidding. "I sure as hell know I couldn't do that job."

"You want to have lunch with me today?" Teana asked.

"What about your husband?"

"He is home sick with the flu. I think it has become quite the epidemic around here."

After Dani's death, Sheldon started eating alone most of the time, occasionally with Lana and Eddie, or doing schoolwork. It was nice having lunch with Teana and not being focused on schoolwork. As they talked, he realized she was not as stuck up as he had thought. Also, he liked the way she laughed; it was very infectious.

"So many people are out sick that Torrie and I are filling in for other people," she explained.

"I heard they are going to start another line," Teana said, taking a bite of her sandwich. "Maybe they will ask you to be one of the welders. I hear it's a special kind of bike that requires a special kind of equipment. The Setup Men have been working on line one for the last couple of weeks."

"I wondered what was going on over there," Sheldon replied.

"That line has not run since I have been here," Teana remarked. "Plus, being a welder would mean more pay. It's definitely something to think about," she said, getting up to throw her trash away.

After lunch, Sheldon was not looking forward to going back to welding. It was a hot and smoky job, and more pay or not, he wasn't sure he even wanted to be a welder on the new line.

Ben was already working at his workstation when Sheldon returned to his work area. When Sheldon saw the stacks of bike frames on their table, he felt bad for making them work so hard. Ben spotted him and just gave him a thumbs-up, and Sheldon smiled.

Sheldon was focused on getting better and faster at welding, but he kept getting the nozzle slightly too close, and the welding gun kept getting clogged up. He would have to stop to clean the welding gun and apply some nozzle gel. He ended up putting an excessive amount of gel on the tip of the nozzle.

Marcus noticed this and stopped Sheldon. "Here, let me show you how to do it right," Marcus said, reaching his arms around Sheldon and taking Sheldon's hands as he gently dipped the tip into the gel. Marcus was so close to Sheldon that he could feel his crotch rubbing up against Sheldon's leg.

"Then the trick is to tap the excess off before screwing it back on." As he said screw, he rubbed his semi-hard-on up and down Sheldon's leg.

"If that thing gets any harder or comes near me again, I might bang it with something, and it won't be gentle," Sheldon said, staring Marcus straight in the eyes. Sheldon enjoyed it too much and had to stop it from going further.

"Hot damn, aren't you a fiery one today," Marcus said, seemingly even more excited. "Make sure to tap the nozzle regularly to knock off the splatter to help avoid build-up."

With Marcus's helpful tips, Sheldon improved his welds, and was slowly getting faster. He kept telling himself he would get even better with time.

§

"We have only been on a couple of dates, yet somehow it feels like he owns me," Harriet told Mandy as Harriet filled her cup with coffee.

"Has he started to get possessive?" Mandy asked.

"Not quite, but he asked if we could see only each other," Harriet replied as she sipped her coffee. "What happened to the good old days when you could date other people without questions?"

Mandy thought for a moment. "Was there ever a time that was a thing?" Mandy thoughtfully posed. "Besides, who else are you thinking of dating?"

"I don't know, but I'm not ready to close the door and want to keep my options open," Harriet replied. "I want to be carefree and sleep with as many men as I wish."

"You know what they call people who like to date around like that, don't you?" Mandy teased. "Some consider them WHORES!"

"Ha-Ha. Very funny, Mandy, but you know what I mean," Harriet said.

"I'm just saying…"

They both laughed. "Well then, just call me a whore!" Harriet whaled. "But seriously, why is it when we get with a man, we think we own them and vice versa? Where did this notion that a man should be with one woman, or women with one man for that matter? I will admit that I get very jealous when someone else tries to mess with my man, but why is that, and who made the rules anyway?"

"The bible," Mandy replied literally.

"Oh, Lord Jesus, I'm a sinner and a whore!" Harriet shouted. "Do you honestly think that is what God intended, or is that how "Man" interpreted it? Ooor is it just another way for men to control women?"

"Oh… I don't know. I have never really thought about it," Mandy replied. "I was taught never to question the bible."

"Exactly! Do you think men honor this rule? Hell no," Harriet continued before Mandy had a chance to respond. "They do whatever the hell they want and when they want. Well, I say to hell with that!" Harriet said, slamming her fist onto the table, causing Mandy to jump.

"No, my answer is no, Ricardo. No, we cannot be exclusive," Harriet demanded as Mandy's eyes were about to pop out of her head.

"Good for you!" Mandy cheered proudly on Harriet for proclaiming her independence. "But seriously, who else are you seeing?"

"No one, yet. BUT, if I wanted to, I wanted to be free to do so," Harriet replied, pleased with herself.

"You know you're crazy, right?" Mandy asked.

"That I may be," Harriet chuckled, lighting a cigarette.

"But you make some good points, but you are still a little crazy. However, I like my fairytale endings," Mandy confessed, stomping her feet, causing Harriet to chuckle again and shake her head.

§

In the following several weeks, Sheldon was so consumed by work and school that he did not have time to socialize at school and barely saw Chase. As soon as he finished his class, he had to head home while some other students would congregate and socialize. Sheldon did not see Kent again.

On weekends, Chase would come over, and they would both work on homework so they could spend as much time together as possible and rest from the busy week.

Sheldon met with his guidance counselor, Beth, to work on his fall schedule. She recommended that he take Western Civilization and an Intro to Algebra class, but Sheldon wanted to take something more interesting, like Choir or a keyboard class, which would help him type better.

Beth recommended, "If you're going to add a third class, it should be an introduction to literature."

"How about I take all of them?" Sheldon asked.

"You want to take a full course load and work full time?" She asked.

"Yes, that is what I want to do," Sheldon replied.

"I don't recommend taking five courses and working full time," she said, trying to dissuade him. "You should at least drop one of the classes."

"I think I can handle it," Sheldon responded, full of confidence.

"Well, if you find out you cannot do it all, please come to me," she pleaded as she hit print on his class schedule. "Your books will be available sometime in August for you to come and pick them up."

"No problem," Sheldon said as he took the class schedule and left her office, confident that he would handle it all. As he drove home, he was excited about the fall term and finally being back in school because it somehow gave his life meaning and purpose more than just working in the factory. Subconsciously, he wanted to keep himself busy because he knew Chase would not be around in the fall.

§

Chase and Sheldon were lying in bed, talking to one another about the future. They everything was all uncertain, and each felt their lives pulling them in different directions. They wondered what it all meant.

"One thing is for certain, I'm in this queer love with you," Chase said with his dimple smile.

"You are such a dork," Sheldon said, laughing and then snuggled him face to face before kissing him. "but I'm in this queer love with you, too."

"I cannot get the love story in that play you were in out of my head," Chase said. "People go their whole lives and never experience this kind of love, which makes it even more special and makes me feel very fortunate."

"Well, the one thing I know for certain is that our love for one another will never die, no matter how far apart we end up," Sheldon said, lying his head on Chase's chest, listening to him breathe in and out and his heart pound.

"That's how I felt when making the infinity necklace for you," Chase remarked. "Did you know I was a bit jealous seeing you kissing that other guy during the play?"

"No, I had no idea," Sheldon responded. "You hid it well."

"I was just thinking back to our first date and how afraid I was to hold your hand because mine was so sweaty because I was very nervous around you," Chase explained.

"I felt the same way," Sheldon said, kissing his chest. "I was afraid you would be disgusted by it, but as soon as our hands touched, I had forgotten all about being nervous or my sweaty palms."

"Me too," Chase acknowledged as he hugged Sheldon tighter.

They fell asleep in each other's arms, knowing that no matter what was to come or however far apart they were, they would still have this special connection and this indescribable love for one another.

To Be Continued....

Book Three Sneak Peak

Sheldon Majors and the Whispers of You

Mr. Thompson and his friend Ralph were seated at his kitchen table. They were having coffee and talking about old times. It was a typical Friday night until they saw a light go across the living room wall.

Mr. Thompson lived on a dead-end road and up a long lane. His neighbors were the Majors and the Reds, who lived a few miles away.

"You's specting company?" Ralph asked with a surprised look.

"Nah, I reckon we should check it out, though," Mr. Thompson replied, getting up from the table.

They could see headlights at the end of his lane as they looked out the front door. It appeared to be a car at the end of his driveway, and it was just sitting there.

"Let's go see if they need help or are just lost," Mr. Thompson said as he turned to get his keys.

"Sounds good to me," Ralph said, seemingly excited that something out of the ordinary was happening.

They climbed into Mr. Thompson's old truck and started down the lane. The car was still sitting there and not moving. As they pulled up, they could see it was a grey Chevy Lumina. Mr. Thompson and Ralph got out of the truck and started walking up to the car. Before they stepped a foot past the front of the truck, two guys jumped out of either side of the car and one of them had a gun in his hand and started shooting.

Before Ralph realized what was happening, he was shot in the abdominal area and the side of his face, and fell to the ground.

Mr. Thompson responded faster than Ralph when he saw the gun. Mr. Thompson turned to hide behind his truck as a bullet went into his right shoulder, and another went through the side of his neck. Immediately, Mr. Thompson was disoriented and heard a ringing sound as he hit the ground. He wanted to get away before they shot him again.

However, when Mr. Thompson looked back, he saw one of the two men walk over to Ralph, who was still moving. The young man put another four to five shots into Ralph till there was no more movement. When Mr. Thompson saw this, he realized he would not make it even if he tried to run because they would shoot him, too.

Mr. Thompson could feel his blood start to run as it covered his face from the hole in his neck, and he could smell something burnt. He thought maybe if he were to lie still enough, they would not shoot him again. He could hear them move closer to him. His heart rate sped up. He could feel his blood pounding, and with every pound, more blood poured out of the hole in his neck. He knew he needed to relax and think about something else to slow his heart rate.

One of the two men walked up and kicked him several times. Mr. Thompson laid entirely still, playing dead and trying not to let them see him breathing or cringe in pain. They checked his pockets for money and then gave him one last kick.

The two men got back into their car, and he could hear the tires turning in the gravel as they backed out of his driveway. When he could no longer hear the vehicle, he started to crawl across the driveway and down into the ditch so they could not see he was still alive. He made his way to the house, crawling in the ditch.

He was trying to apply pressure to the hole in his neck as he continued to crawl towards his house, but he could still feel the surge of blood with every heartbeat. Mr. Thompson was afraid he was going to pass out but knew he had to keep pushing because if he lay there, he would be dead for sure. His persistence was the difference between his living and dying. He kept low to the ground as he crawled back to his house. When he made it inside, he called 911 and asked them to hurry just before he passed out…

Acknowledgements

Kevin Morgan, thank you for being there for me every day and for helping keep me grounded.

Jana Davis, thank you for always lifting my spirits and helping me hold onto my sanity.

Denia Andersen, thank you for always making me laugh and reminding me that it's not that serious.

Pam Pile, thank you for believing in me and for being my cheerleader. I truly appreciate your support at my event, and I consider you the best Buffalo teammate anyone could ask for.

Paula, thank you for being there cheering me on, supporting me at my event, and helping me stay positive.

Alex Waters, thank you for pushing me to keep going and for helping make my dreams come true.

Dr. Glenn D. Pascual, thank you for your constant support, day in and day out. I appreciate you more than you'll ever know.

About the Author

 Jason George Waters, born to middle-class farmers, worked on the family farm until its sale. Despite enduring childhood bullying for his feminine traits, he found solace in books and was encouraged by his high school English teacher to write. After working at a bicycle factory, he earned a bachelor's in political science from Illinois State University in 2006. Moving to California in 2008, he secured various roles, including at Kaiser Permanente in 2015. He later graduated with an MBA in healthcare. Inspired by his mother's passing, he began writing the Sheldon Majors series in 2015. Now residing in Southern California, he balances writing with his job as a National Account Manager at Kaiser Permanente. Throughout, storytelling remains his passion, aiming to inspire and entertain.

ALSO, BY:

Sheldon Majors and the Chase